Kelegeen

By Eileen O'Finlan

Amazon Print ISBN 978-0-2286-0029-9

BWL Publishing Inc.

Books we love to write ...
Authors around the world.

http://bwlpublishing.ca

Dedication

To my mother, Barbara Charbonneau, in memory of my father, Robert Charbonneau, and to the entire Charbonneau, Finlan, Beecher clan.

Special dedication in memory of my undergraduate professor of Irish history, the late Alwyn Fraser, without whom the idea for this novel would never have been conceived.

Acknowledgements

There are more people who helped bring this book into being than I can possibly mention, though they all deserve my heartfelt thanks. Among them are, first and foremost, Eileen Charbonneau, author and editor extraordinaire. This book would have sat in a drawer forever if it weren't for you, Eileen. I can never thank you enough for your help, guidance, patience, and mentoring.

To everyone at BWL Publishing, Inc., especially Jude Pittman. Thank you for the chance to make my most cherished dream come true!

To my always supportive and enthusiastic family: My mom, Barbara Charbonneau (91 and still going strong – you are amazing), my dad, Robert Charbonneau (I miss you so much, Daddy), my sister Cindy Kazanovicz and her husband, David, my niece Jen and her husband, Michael Bragg, my niece Rachel and her husband Chris Bergman and my brother-in-law David Benoit.

To my dearest friend and favorite research historian, Tom Kelleher, as well as all my former colleagues at Old Sturbridge Village, all of whom taught me so much about historical research and some of whom were kind enough to read early drafts of chapters and offer feedback: Lynne Bassett, Shawn Parker, Frank White, Nan Wolverton, Ed Hood, David Lee Colglazier, Meg Hailey, Kathy Pratt,

Theresa Rini Percy, the late Jim Bump and the late Jack Larkin. I had the time of my life working with all of you.

To Cynthia Kennison, facilitator of the Worcester Writers Workshop, where most of the first draft of this novel was written and to all the WWW writers. I miss you all!

To the members of my current writing workshop who I sincerely believe will see their own work in print some day: Pam Reponen, J.D. Roy, James Pease, Cindy Shenette, Lee Baldarelli, and Rebecca Southwick.

And finally, to everyone who has inspired, supported, encouraged and rejoiced with me: LaVerne Bertin, Rev. Father Tim Brewer, Deacon Tim Cross and everyone at St. Mary's Parish in Jefferson (the Place to Be!), Alan Derry, Father Henry Donahue, Father Charles Dumphy, Father Ronald Falco, Stephanie Goodwin, Janice Hitzhusen, Katie Kelley, Tammie Kent, Kathy Leal, Father Michael Lavallee, Father Brice Leavins, Sister Mary Daniel Malloy, Sister Marie Therese Martin, Father Paul T. O'Connell, Heidi Pandey, Monsignor F. Stephen Pedone (best boss EVER!), Linette Provost, Sheila Rosenblatt, Myron Wehtje, Liz Woods, St. George's Book Discussion Group, the monks at St. Joseph's Abbey in Spencer, everyone at 49 Elm Street, the Adult Degree Program at Atlantic Union College and the Pastoral Ministry Program at Anna Maria College.

A special thank you to the folks at Computer Central, especially David, for keeping my laptop up and running so I could write this novel.

Undoubtedly, I've missed some – the omission is unintentional. I thank you all!

Chapter One

August 30, 1846

"Thank God the Bishop is gone," Father O'Malley whispered to himself as the first strains of music floated over the late summer night air.

"Pardon, Father?"

"What? Oh. Didn't realize anyone was near."

"Sorry, Father. I didn't mean to disturb you."

Though he could barely see the young woman in the diminishing light, he knew by the voice it was Meg O'Connor, the eldest daughter of the O'Connor clan.

"No bother, Meg," he said. "It happens to the old. We talk to ourselves. Lose a bit of our minds along with our eyesight."

Meg laughed. "You're not old, Father!"

Father O'Malley guessed that Meg was on her way to meet her intended, Rory Quinn, for a moondance held in a field by the edge of the sea. In the distance he could hear a fiddle and a concertina tuning up. He thought of what Bishop Kneeland would thunder out. "Night time dances are a sin. They must be abolished!"

But the ancient tradition was one of the few pleasures known to Kelegeen's cottiers. As much as Father O'Malley believed in obedience to his bishop, he also believed in keeping his people's culture intact, whatever harmless remnants were left of it. Their land was no longer their own, their language had been outlawed, their system of government dismantled, and their religion barely tolerated. A few endearing customs were nearly all that was left. The British had stripped away everything else. The young people of Kelegeen kept the moondance tradition alive. He had no desire to take it from them. His Excellency had not been able to find fault with the condition of Father O'Malley's vestments, chalices, altar cloths or any part of the church itself. All had passed grudging inspection, including the proper behavior of his parishioners during Mass, thank heaven. But Father O'Malley's attitude toward his people was not quite to the bishop's liking.

"You coddle them! Strict obedience to authority is what's necessary. How else will they respect the perfect authority of God?"

"Aye, Your Excellency, and does that include obedience to the British as well?" Father O'Malley hadn't been able to resist the question.

Bishop Kneeland's face purpled. "Indeed! They are in power, like it or not. Our clergy are tolerated now and are no longer deported nor executed. We will be grateful for that and acknowledge British authority if we wish to continue."

How can you defend them when the words be like to strangle you? The question remained unvoiced. Father O'Malley was tired of lectures.

"Now then, Father, I've yet to see a wake or any superstitious behavior, but sure as I'm sitting here, these people are still at them. It's obvious the way they go on about faery folk and such. These things are not to be tolerated anymore."

Father O'Malley tried to keep his face from showing his anger.

"If ever you've wind of such goings on, you are to put a stop to them immediately," Bishop Kneeland continued. "I'm tired now so I'll retire. We will speak more on this subject tomorrow."

Speak more on it he did. It was nearly all Father O'Malley heard for the rest of the bishop's visit. Each night he thanked God and all His saints that they'd heard no music starting up in the distance, come across no group of pilgrims circling a sacred well on their knees, and especially that no one had died, necessitating a wake filled with frivolity as the mourners sent their loved one off in fine fashion to an eternity so much better than their earthly life. No, his good people had behaved unwittingly British enough to keep them all out of trouble with the bishop for

6

the time being. They had pleasantly waited until tonight to have their moondance now that Bishop Kneeland had gone home. Father O'Malley was eternally grateful.

He continued to stand in the twilight, gazing off in the direction of the music. What would happen, he wondered, if he was forced to choose between obedience to the bishop and protecting the last remnants of his people's culture? He was a priest through and through. To him that meant serving his people, caring for their souls. And wasn't their identity part of their souls? It seemed so to him.

He was tremendously fond of his little flock in Kelegeen. Being their spiritual leader gave purpose to his life. He'd once lost his sense of purpose and nearly lost the will to live. The priesthood had given that back to him. He feared he might flounder if it was gone. Just as long as the bishop's visits remained few and far between, perhaps he would never have to make the choice.

"Such a cowardly thought, but I can muster no better at present," he grumbled to no one.

In the distance he could barely discern images of whirling couples. Laughter and music wafted gently through the air. Moonlight drenched the dancers and they became ethereal. The sight conjured memories of another moondance thirty-five years earlier when he'd been sixteen.

That night long ago he'd heard a sound so full of exuberance that he'd followed it to its source—a field where a group of merrymakers danced in the moonlight. A figure standing on a rock played the fiddle while long thick tangles of hair bounced with every energetic movement of her body.

"God be between me and harm. 'Tis a cavorting band of faeries," he'd muttered and crossed himself. He'd watched a moment longer, then his curiosity had propelled him down the hill into their midst.

"Welcome!" exclaimed one of the males of their tribe.

"Have a jig with us," called another. He gave up all inhibitions and danced their wild dance with them.

Once close enough, he determined the fiddle player was the oddest but most beautiful sight he'd yet seen in his

7

young life. The moonlight revealed a gypsy-like creature. She hopped from one foot to the other in time with the rhythm. Her arms jerked wildly as they carved the music from her instrument and sent it flying through the air. Her long curls bounced, performing their own frolicking dance. By the moonlight Brian could see that her hair was red, but with each movement it appeared a different shade. It would take the light of the sun to show him the real richness of its color. The sound of the fiddle was enhanced by her laughter.

When the tune ended she leaned forward. "Do you like my playing?"

"Indeed. Do you dance?"

"I am dancing."

"Without the fiddle, I mean. Or are you the only one who can play?

"My brother can play. He taught me."

"Ask him then, please, and have a dance with me." Brian smiled broadly, surprised at his own boldness.

"Quentin!" she called, and in a second a grinning giant took the fiddle from her hand. He was the only youth Brian had ever met who was taller and broader across the chest and shoulders than himself. Before he could offer his hand to the lass, she leapt into the air, her dress revealing a flash of sculpted muscle in her calves as she landed easily on the ground. Quentin, the dark-haired giant, took her place on the rock and played. Brian and the girl whirled and jigged. Two more dances before a woman's voice called name after name from the cottage door.

"That's all," said Quentin.

It was like being rudely awakened from a splendid dream. The music stopped and the enchanting revelers became youths again, responding to their mother's call. "Quentin O'Toole," the giant said, coming down off the rock to shake his hand.

"Brian O'Malley, from the neighboring farm." He'd pointed in the direction of his family's cottage. "You must be new here."

"We've only just arrived. This is my sister, Siobhan."
Quentin indicated the red-haired gypsy-like girl.

"I've not heard of a lass playing the fiddle before."

She'd laughed again, that lovely laugh that he would hear for the rest of his life.

"Siobhan O'Toole, you come home now!" her mother called louder from the cottage door.

"I'm not like most lasses," she whispered before breaking into a gallop for home.

* * *

"Not at all like most lasses," Father O'Malley whispered, coming out of his reverie. He turned his back on Meg O'Connor's moondance and headed for his cottage across from Saint Mary's Church. The music and revelry receded further into the distance. He fought the urge to turn around for one last glimpse. In his head he heard Siobhan's voice urging him to run down the hill and join the dancers.

"I've Mass to say and families to visit in the morning," he admonished, chuckling to himself. "So no more of your nonsense tonight, my dear."

* * *

"Come on Meg, you let me once before," Rory pleaded.

"But I won't again. Not until we're married," she told him, pulling away from his embrace.

"Why not?"

"Because I've decided that's the way it's to be. Let's go back and dance now. I've no wish to miss any more before it's time to go home."

"You aren't being fair, Meg. It isn't like we've never kissed before and none can see us here. There's no one will know of it."

The last time they had moondanced, Rory had guided her away from the other dancers to this same spot behind a high stone wall. She had let him take her in his arms and

9

press his lips against hers in a long, ardent kiss. She had enjoyed it immensely. That was the problem. Powerful sensations rippling through her body had taken her by surprise.

This time he had taken her away earlier. She knew what he wanted and she'd decided not to give it to him. After that first kiss, she knew their wedding night would be a night to be savored. Surely they deserved one night of pure, glorious physical joy. She would not have either of them deprived of it through lack of resolve. If she gave in now she would never forgive herself.

Almost as strong was the fear of being found out. Her mother thought she was taking an evening stroll. If ever it was known that she was dancing with a lad, her intended or not, that she had gone off alone with him, that she had allowed the unthinkable act of letting him kiss her, it would bring permanent shame upon her and ostracism would be her future. Her stubborn nature and need for adventure made her defy the rule. But loyalty to her family and respect for herself put limits on how far she would go.

Meg and Rory had known each other all their lives. A childhood friendship had grown up into a courtship. Everyone had expected it. They planned to be married the following year when Rory would be twenty-one and Meg nineteen. Once they were married they would be recognized as adults in their community. That was nearly as desirable as any other benefit of marriage.

"We might as well go back," Rory motioned towards the others and started to walk away.

"Wait," Meg called out.

He turned back. She watched, bemused, as a look of hope flickered across his face.

"My hair's coming undone. I want to do it up again before we go." Carefully she re-wrapped her hair which had started to come loose from its perfectly braided coil.

Rory leaned against the wall, watching.

"How long is your hair?"

"What are you about now?"

10

"When you were a wee lass your mother put it in braids. Now that you're grown it's on top of your head. Are you hiding it from me? Do you keep some secret wrapped up in those coils?"

"Aye, but you're daft. I put it up to keep it out of my way."

"Take it down for me, Meg."

"I will not. I'll only have to put it up again."

"You could do that in your sleep. Please take it down, Meg. You do love me enough to do one simple thing for me, don't you?"

"Oh, for Heaven's sake!" She unwrapped the coil she had just finished securing and ran her fingers through the braid until her hair hung loose and free.

"Glory be!"

A mild breeze lifted her long hair, making it billow around her. She watched, fascinated, as Rory stared at her. She relished his hunger for her, matched by her own for him. It would be harder than ever to go back now, but she knew they must.

"Are ye done gawking?" she asked, breaking the spell. Meg pulled a wooden comb from her pocket and quickly ran it through her hair.

Rory smiled broadly. "I'm glad to see that gets good use." He had carved the comb himself and presented it to her the day he'd proposed.

Meg returned it to her pocket, then began braiding and piling the thick mane on top of her head. "We've been gone long enough for people to wonder. I don't want anyone going on about us."

"What does it matter? Everyone knows we're going to marry."

"But we aren't married yet. I won't have my reputation ruined just because you wanted to kiss me. And here you be not even thinking of our wee ones yet to come. Is that the life you wish for any bairns we have—being shunned all for the sake of stealing a kiss from me now, Rory Quinn?"

"I suppose not."

They walked toward the field where the dancers were winding down their activities. Rory looked so dejected that Meg was suddenly overcome with the urge to tease him into a better humor.

"'Tis a task to put my hair up every day. Perhaps I'll shear it off."

Rory stopped walking and stared at her, horrified.

"It would be out of my way then and I wouldn't have to worry about it." Meg broke into laughter. "I'm teasing you."

His look of relief made her laugh all the more.

"Seems you've been doing that all night," he muttered.

She gave his shoulder a playful shove. "I'll run ahead. Give me a few minutes to get there before you come so no one can say they saw us returning together."

"No one here will care. Why don't we just race back?" he suggested.

"We already know who would win." She winked and ran off ahead of him.

* * *

The moon was high overhead when Meg approached the door to her family's cottage. Just before she reached it, it cracked open and the slight figure of her sister, Kathleen, emerged, her long wispy blond hair almost silver in the moonlight.

"Was Kevin there?" Kathleen whispered.

"Aye, he was."

"And?"

"And what?"

"Did he dance with anyone?" Kathleen's voice was desperate.

"Of course he did. What else would he do?"

Kathleen looked pained.

"If you're so interested in keeping the likes of Kevin Dooley from dancing with another lass you'd best come and dance with him yourself."

Kathleen frowned. "Did you speak of me to him?"

12

"I did."

"What did he say?"

"He asked why you never come. I told him 'twas because you've no suitor to dance with."

Kathleen drew a sharp intake of breath. "What did he say?"

"He said nothing."

"Nothing at all?"

"Aye." Then, leaning forward, she brushed Kathleen's shoulder with her own and whispered, "But he did grin from ear to ear."

Kathleen squealed just as the door was flung wide and their mother stood outlined in its frame.

"Margaret Mary O'Connor, do you think you could come home from a simple walk at a decent hour for once in your life?"

"Aye, Mam. Sorry."

The two girls scooted inside and took up their sleeping places on the floor by the fire. Just before they drifted off, Kathleen inched up to Meg and whispered in her ear, "I'll come with you next time."

Chapter Two

Deirdre O'Connor's hands moved rapidly as she braided her youngest daughter Brigid's hair.

"Morning, Deirdre," Father O'Malley called through the open cottage door.

"Good morning, Father. Come to see my Denis, have you? He's out back working the potato bed."

"I saw him and Brendan breaking their backs there as I came up, but I thought I'd stop inside first and have a bit of rest before your mister puts me to work." He took a seat on the only other chair in the cottage.

"You're not afraid of a might o' work, now are ye, Father?

"Not at all, but I must say I'm better at saving souls than potatoes."

Brigid darted away, squealing with delight as she chased the pig across the cottage floor.

"Outside with ya, now," Deirdre commanded. Brigid and the pig darted out the door and into the yard.

"How is Meg this morning?"

"Fine. She and Kathleen are over at the Quinns."

"Did she tell you I bumped into her last night?"

"She didn't mention it. Did you speak with her long? I wondered why she was so late getting home."

"Only a moment. She was eager to get to the dance."

"What dance?"

"The moondance in the field last night. You knew, of course?"

Deirdre looked him in the eye. "The lass will be seeing you shortly for confession, Father."

"Oh."

Deirdre took up the needlework that rested on her chair. "Meg and Rory are to marry in a year. I pray for them."

"You're not worried about the match, are you Deirdre?"

"They're both strong willed." She laughed. "Like mad bulls, sometimes. And they've both got tempers. But they've been together almost since birth so 'tis nothing new to them. They'll find a way to manage that part."

"What troubles you, then?"

Father O'Malley caught a wary look pass over Deirdre's face. "Just a feeling," she said.

"About the marriage?" He pressed.

"No, about life. The weather this year's not been good for growing. There's worry about the potato crop. I hate to see Meg and Rory start off with that against them."

"Last year's crop was a poor showing, but not the worst we've ever had."

"As I said, Father, 'tis a feeling." She leaned toward him, a strange look in her eye.

"What is it Deirdre? Please, tell me."

She hesitated. He nodded for her to go on.

"At certain times in my life, Father, I'm certain sure that something bad is coming."

"And you have that feeling about Meg and Rory marrying?"

"About them marrying within the coming year," she corrected.

In his head he heard Bishop Kneeland's voice. *Admonish her for superstitious nonsense.* This was immediately drowned out by the voice of Siobhan. *That woman's got a gift from God. Who are you to stand in its way?*

Father O'Malley couldn't contain a smile at the argument brewing in his head. Deirdre stiffened. "You're laughing at me, Father," she said. "I suppose you think I'm foolish."

Father O'Malley forced his face to behave. "Not at all. I believe some people have a stronger intuition than most. Perhaps you're one of them."

"I'm not saying I can predict the future or anything of the like."

"I understand, Deirdre. So would you have Meg and Rory put off their wedding?"

Deirdre shrugged. "There's no saying when a better time will come. I don't want Meg to wait forever."

"She's your eldest. Do you feel as though you're losing her?"

Deirdre shook her head. "She'll not go far. The marriage will only pull our families closer together." She sighed. "There's nothing for it, I suppose. They'll marry no matter what the crop is like and they'll get on as best they can like all the rest of us."

"Don't forget how much they love each other. Their love will give them strength." Father O'Malley stood. "Speaking of crops, I'll go see how Denis is faring. Good day to you, Deirdre. I'll keep Meg and Rory in my prayers. And you as well."

He left the cottage, skirting the manure pile outside. Before shutting the door behind him he heard Deirdre mutter, "Love don't grow potatoes."

* * *

"How's the work going?" asked Father O'Malley, coming upon Denis and his son, Brendan, standing over their potato bed, the family's main sustenance for the coming year.

"If you call hoping and wishing work, then it's going very well," said Denis.

"I've missed the physical labor, then? Good! I've come at the right moment." In truth, he loved to work with his hands in the earth.

"Do you know a prayer for potatoes, Father?" asked Brendan. "Da's been worrying over them since way back when we planted. Mam says if he don't leave them be, the potatoes are likely to die of being bothered to death."

"Better would be a prayer to keep the rain away." Denis looked up at the sky. "If it storms one more time I fear it will wash away all I've planted. As it is, I've got more of a mud pit than a potato bed."

16

"'Tis a wonder, the amount of thunderstorms we've had this summer," remarked Father O'Malley, following his skyward gaze. So far the weather was holding. "Are the storms keeping you awake? You look tired, Denis."

"Aye. They disturb Deirdre something awful. If she doesn't sleep, neither do I."

"Truly? I'd never have pegged her as one to fear thunder storms."

"It's a curious thing. They never bothered her until this summer. All of a sudden she's turned timid as a mouse at a crack of thunder. The wind picks up on a storm and she's about sent for. She says they give her a bad feeling."

"Indeed. I will be praying for you and your potatoes, Denis."

"Thank you, Father. You've got lots of families to visit so we'll not hold you up. Come back at suppertime. We'll be happy to share what wee bit we've got."

* * *

Father O'Malley made his rounds, visiting as many of his parish families as possible.

"Do not put yourself on their level," Bishop Kneeland had instructed him just two days ago. "You must make them respect you. How else do you expect to lead them?"

"But Your Excellency, I feel that as their friend—"

"Friend? They will walk all over you. Command their respect. Generals of armies are not friends with common soldiers."

"We are not in the army."

"We, Father O'Malley, are the leaders of God's army and you will behave accordingly."

He wondered what Siobhan would say to that. Well, Bishop Kneeland was not in Kelegeen today. Father O'Malley continued on, caring for his people in the manner of his mentor, Father Francis Coogan. Father Coogan had saved his life long ago by being his friend rather than just his priest at a time when he'd needed a friend more. There would always be some distance between Father O'Malley

17

and his parishioners, but he did the best he could and his people knew he cared.

At suppertime he returned to the O'Connors' cottage. Knowing he would be joining them, Deirdre had mashed up the potatoes, adding a dollop of buttermilk and a few slices of onion for extra flavor. The cottage was hot from the fire and so many bodies crowded into one small space. The family sat on the dirt floor to eat. By all rights it should have been an uncomfortable ordeal, but being included in the O'Connor clan—Denis, Deirdre, Meg, Brendan, Kathleen, and Brigid—made him feel welcome. Memories of his parents, long since dead, and his brothers and sisters, some living, others not, came flooding back to him, as comforting as wrapping himself in a warm coat on a winter day.

Denis gave his wife a kiss on the cheek. "Deirdre, that was wonderful as always."

"Exceptional," agreed Father O'Malley. "My thanks to you for such kind hospitality."

"You're quite welcome. Now, off with the two of you so we can get on with the cleaning up."

Denis and Father O'Malley went outside, walking around the cottage toward the potato bed.

"It's going to rain again," Denis said in disgust, holding his hands, palms up, as if he could feel the rain coming.

"I'd better get home before I'm drenched."

Despite the coming rain, Father O'Malley took time to inhale deeply as he walked. The smell of the earth just before a storm was sweet. He might get caught in a downpour, but it made no difference as long as he could feel the land under his feet, breathe the air and hear the sea lap in the distance.

Look at all the incredible beauty the good Lord has created and I am blessed to be a part of it.

He hurried his steps as he watched the puffy clouds tumble end over end down the hills, entering his cottage just before the first drops fell. No sooner had he closed the door behind him than the thunder let go with a mighty crack shaking the walls. Within seconds the rain became a pelting torrent.

Thunder boomed again. He looked up in time to see lightening flash through the only window. Once in bed, he stared into the darkness. Usually he enjoyed a good rip-roaring thunderstorm. He loved listening to the fury without while he was tucked safe inside. The sound of tonight's storm, truly no different from any other, unnerved him though he couldn't explain why. He wondered if Deirdre felt the same.

When he opened his door the next morning and stepped outside he was immediately engulfed in white fog. *'Tis uncommon thick*, he thought. *Like I've wandered into a sea of cream.*

As he walked to the church, he thought he detected a strange, unpleasant odor in the air. By the time Mass ended, the fog had begun to lift. Stepping outside, that same smell hit his nostrils. Only now it was so powerful it turned his stomach.

A voice called his name. Meg ran toward the church. It dawned on him then that Deirdre had not been at this morning's Mass.

Dear Lord, what has happened?

Together they headed back towards the O'Connors' cottage, Meg relaying her story as they walked.

"Da went out to check the potatoes early this morning just after the fog lifted. There was something white all over the stalks. He called us all out to help him. We dug up the stalks. They were covered with ugly sores. When Da cut into one it was black and the smell nearly made us all sick." Her words scrambled as fast as her hurried steps. The fog was now gone, replaced by an almost tangible sense of foreboding.

In the O'Connors' yard they found the family standing over their potato bed, the stalks all cankered and strewn about; a white frost-like substance clinging to them. All stood with heads bowed, as though paying final farewells at a newly-dug grave.

"Denis, might I help?"

Together they dug up what they could salvage. At such an early stage in their growth the potatoes were puny and didn't look as though they'd feed the family for very long. Father O'Malley helped carry them inside to the storage bin.

"I must tell you, Father, I'm not sure we've done the right thing. These few won't last long. I've got to save something for seed for next year. Once these are gone, what will we do? On the other hand, I'd rather have some than none. If I'd left them in the ground who knows if they'd continue to grow or just go to mush like the others?"

"Denis, there's no way to tell the future. You make the decision you think is best and forgive yourself if it was wrong."

"I'll be hard pressed to forgive myself if what I'm doing ends up starving my family."

Father O'Malley stayed the rest of the morning. Just before noon, Rory and his father, Thomas Quinn, arrived to see how the O'Connors were faring.

"You dug them up, Denis?" Thomas asked. A skeptical look covered his weather-beaten face.

"Aye, we did. And what did you do?"

"Ripped up the stalks, but we reburied the potatoes that weren't spoiled. For God's sake, Denis, the canker is in the stalks. If it hasn't hit the potatoes yet why not put them back in the ground? They may still grow."

"Aye, and they may not. I'd rather have the few I know I've got than take a chance on losing them all."

"They won't last long nor be of much good."

"It's the decision I've made."

Thomas argued no more, but the look on his face said he thought his friend had made a grave mistake. Father O'Malley had been speaking to Deirdre, trying to keep up her spirits at the same time the two other men were talking, but he heard their conversation. Though Denis would not show it, Father O'Malley knew he was tortured over his decision.

20

Meg and Rory stood together. Father O'Malley started towards them, but stopped when he realized they were deep in their own conversation.

"Don't worry, Meg. When our potatoes come up I'll save some for you, as many as I can. You won't go hungry if I can help it."

"And what makes you think your da's right and mine's wrong?"

"I didn't mean to insult your da, Meg. But do you really think you'll go long on those pebbles he's dug up? He should have left them in the ground. It was a stupid thing to take them now."

"No more stupid than leaving perfectly good potatoes in the ground to rot so you'll have nothing. I'm the one who'll have to save potatoes for you." Meg turned toward the cottage.

"Meg, wait!"

She went straight inside and slammed the door. Rory started after her, but Father O'Malley grabbed his arm. "Let her be for now, lad."

Father O'Malley spent a bit longer with the men then prepared to leave. He wanted to see as many other parish families as possible and offer whatever consolation and encouragement he could.

"Denis, Thomas, my prayers are with you and your families."

"Thank you, Father. I fear we'll be needing the power of Himself to make it through this one," said Thomas.

Denis said nothing, just stared at the ground. The sound of a door banging shut made them all look up. Meg emerged from the cottage.

"I was just leaving, Meg, but I will be praying for you all."

"Thank you, Father." Meg stood with her hands on her hips, feet firmly planted in the muddy ground. She looked Father O'Malley in the eye. "We've had difficult years before, but we made it through. We will again."

The O'Connors were the first family Father O'Malley had met in Kelegeen and they'd quickly become friends.

21

He remembered quite vividly the night of Meg's birth. He had only been in the village a few days. Stopping by the O'Connors' cottage one evening in early January, he had found Denis pacing outside the door.

"What are you doing outside?" Father O'Malley had to yell the question over the wind roaring across the countryside.

"Deirdre's time's come. The midwife's been with her all afternoon. They tossed me out to the manure pile," Denis had yelled back.

Together they'd stood, rubbing their hands, heads bowed and shoulders hunched. Without warning, the door cracked open and the midwife popped her head out. She spoke, but the wind ate her words and the two men only saw her mouth move. She closed the door as quickly as she'd opened it.

"I've had enough of this," Denis yelled and went in. He'd left the door open behind him, but Father O'Malley felt it was not his place to be in the cottage at such a time. He didn't want the new mother and baby to take a chill, so he'd leaned in to catch the door handle and pull it shut. In those few seconds he heard two things that set his mind forever on the character of Meg O'Connor.

The first came from the midwife.

"You've a girl child. And a wee banshee of a lass she is, too. Not only did she give her own mother a rough go of it, but I'll be deviled if she didn't wriggle so hard in my hands, I almost dropped the new sprout."

The second was the sound of the infant's cry. It was strong and lusty, and powerful enough to carry over the fury of the raging January wind.

As Father O'Malley walked back to his cottage he thought to himself what interesting characters the good Lord drops down upon this earth.

Now Father O'Malley had a strong feeling that if anyone could fight the awful battle of hunger that surely would come, Meg O'Connor was the one.

* * *

22

A few weeks later Meg was with Rory, his parents, and brother, Aiden, when they decided to dig up the potatoes they had left in the ground. Thomas was nervous. "I can't stand not knowing if we've got food out there or not."

Meg knelt in the dirt at Rory's side while Thomas and his wife, Anna, dug into the ground.

"Oh dear Lord!" Anna gasped, quickly crossing herself when she saw the piles of stinking black mush they unearthed.

Thomas looked at his wife and two eldest sons kneeling in the dirt beside him. "I'm sorry," he whispered.

Meg watched the notch in Rory's throat move up and down. She put her hand into his, entwining their fingers. Dirt from both their hands smeared from one to the other.

Anna rubbed her husband's arm. "Thomas, don't blame yourself."

Aiden said nothing, but stared at the ground in disbelief.

Rory looked at his father. "Nearly everyone did the same, Da." He glanced at Meg. "Almost everyone." She gave his hand a squeeze.

"Let's not tell the wee ones yet," Anna pleaded. "They'll know soon enough."

The family pig wound its way in and out among them, but even the pig would have nothing to do with the black gunk.

* * *

The weeks progressed and autumn arrived, bringing with it a drop in temperature which seemed to intensify everyone's now familiar hunger pangs. On an evening in mid-October, after Brigid was asleep for the night, the rest of the O'Connor family huddled together in a corner of the cottage.

"That was the last of it," Denis whispered, referring to the potatoes. That evening's supper had finished off the year's meager harvest.

"We've still a few eggs and a bit 'o cheese, though I wish we'd been stingier with the two chickens," Maeve said. "Other than that there's some oatmeal. I'll stretch it all as far as I can, but everyone's portions will be smaller."

"We've got those turnips that Brendan pulled from the field," Kathleen offered.

"Do you really think they're safe to eat?" asked Brendan.

"The gentry's cattle don't die from eating them. God knows they don't think of us as much better." Denis's whisper was harsh.

"Hush, you'll wake the lass," Deirdre admonished.

"Rory's mam says you can cook them just like potatoes," Meg explained. "He says they aren't too awful if you can forget you're eating cattle fodder."

Deirdre stared with disdain at the two turnips she held. "They'll have to do, I suppose."

The pig grunted in her sleep, nestling closer to her two piglets.

"At least that will keep a roof over our heads for a while," Denis said. The animal was to be sold the following month to pay the rent money due on Gale Day. "Thank God she birthed a couple more, may they stay healthy."

Chapter Three

"I suppose it will be a while before there's another dance," said Kathleen as she and Meg trudged up the hill toward their cottage, arms full of mending work picked up in town.

"No one feels like dancing. I certainly haven't the strength for it. Nor the time." Meg nodded toward the bundle of clothes in her arms.

"I know. I'd just like to see Kevin."

"He's friendly enough with Aiden." Meg said.

"Do you think Rory would help get us together?"

Meg shrugged. "Why are you so sweet on Kevin Dooley? Mam wouldn't approve. His family don't go to church."

"I like his smile. And he says I'm pretty."

"Is that all? Lots of lads have nice smiles and think you're pretty."

"Go on with you! They do not."

"Aiden thinks so. Rory told me."

"Rory's family is like brothers and sisters to me. Marrying Aiden would be like marrying my own brother."

"So it's marrying you're after?"

"What else?"

"Make sure you pick the right lad. Marrying is for a lifetime."

"I could look at Kevin's smile for a lifetime." Kathleen laughed.

"How do you know he'll always be smiling?"

"Every time I see him, he is."

"Might not be so if you saw him more often."

"What do you mean?"

"There's more to courting than him smiling at you and saying you're pretty. You need to know the way of each other. See if when one or the other of you is sad or angry or has gone and done something stupid and you still want to be together. If so, then you can start thinking about marrying."

"You've known Rory your whole life. I don't know why you don't feel the same about him as I do about Aiden."

"Well, I don't. I love Rory. It's too bad you don't feel so about Aiden because I think he's sweet on you. But if you don't feel right about him, then it wouldn't work. But that's what I'm saying. You've got to know how you really feel deep down inside. A smile and a compliment won't tell you that."

"I'll never know if I don't get to spend some time with Kevin."

Meg sighed. "I'll talk to Rory."

"Will you, Meg? Thank you!"

"Just heed what I said. Don't hurry."

Brigid opened the cottage door when Meg kicked at it.

"This should keep us going for a bit, Mam."

"The Lord has blessed us," Deirdre said looking over the clothes the girls placed on the table. She sorted them into piles according to the degree of expertise necessary to mend them.

"There's not much light left of the day so let's get the easiest done now while we can still see." Deirdre and her two eldest daughters huddled together near the cottage's one window, using up what was left of the daylight.

"Brigid, stir the pot for me," Deirdre instructed.

Brigid swirled the spoon in the kettle.

"Is it thickening?" asked her mother.

Brigid scooped up some of the contents then let it splash back down.

"More water than porridge," Deirdre muttered.

"Better than nothing, Mam," Meg answered.

"Nothing's what we'll be down to soon enough. I still wish we'd held onto those chickens a little longer."

"There were only two. It wouldn't have made much difference, would it?" asked Kathleen.

"Every bit matters."

"We've been hungry before," Meg said. "Besides, all this sewing will get us something."

"That it will," Deirdre agreed.

The cottage door banged open. Denis and Brendan returned from helping to repair a section of thatching that had come loose from the Quinns' roof.

"How did it go?" Deirdre asked.

"All fixed," Denis answered. "Anna sent you this." Denis offered a dish with a handful of chopped chicken meat.

Deirdre pushed the bowl away. "We can't take that. They've more mouths to feed than we do."

"I know. It was from the last of their chickens. I told Anna we couldn't accept it, but she said they'd no other way to pay for our help."

"They don't need to pay. We're neighbors."

"I said that, too, but she insisted. She said their roof would have come clear off with the next good wind if not for our help. She wanted to give us the whole chicken, but I talked her down to just this handful. If I hadn't taken it I think she'd have cried."

Deirdre threw the meat onto a pan to cook over the fire. "Poor woman. I'll thank her tomorrow."

"Couldn't Mr. Quinn, Rory and Aiden fix the roof themselves?" asked Kathleen.

"They could, but seems Rory's not at home."

Meg looked up. "Where is he?"

Brendan stood near the fireplace breathing in the scent of cooking meat. "Ah, but that smells good," he said.

"Went into town to sell something. I didn't get the all of it. Brendan, what did Aiden tell you?"

Brendan turned to them, sucking thin gruel off one finger.

"He carved a bunch of stuff and took it to sell in town."

"He didn't tell me he was going to do that," Meg said.

Brendan shrugged. "Aiden said he came up with the idea a few days ago. Been spending all his time carving

27

away like a madman. It figures he'd pick today to go to town, the day the roof nearly blows off."

"No one realized the roof was that bad until the wind picked up during the night," Denis said.

"Still, he could have stayed around today and helped."

"Didn't need to. We were able. Rain's coming in soon, you can feel it. If he's got a chance to bring in some money with his carvings then he was right to get to it as soon as he could before he'd be stuck at home waiting out the weather."

Rory possessed a genius for carving; a talent he discovered by accident. Meg remembered the story he'd told of when he was nine years old. He had stolen his mother's one sharp kitchen knife. He'd taken it out to the field behind his cottage and begun to whittle away at a chunk of wood. When his mother went into the house to cook supper, she realized that her knife was missing. After searching the cottage, she'd come back outdoors. It was then that she'd seen Rory sitting on a rock in the middle of the field.

"What the devil is that lad doing?" she had whispered as she'd watched his hands make small jerking movements. Sunlight struck the metal blade and with the flash of its reflection, his mother had known he had her knife.

With as much nonchalance as she could muster, she'd crept forward trying to be both quiet and obvious so as not make him slip with the knife. Only when she'd seen that she would not startle him did she allow her temper to flare.

"What do you think you're doing with me best knife, Rory Quinn? Will you be after chopping all your fingers off so's you won't have to help your da digging potatoes? And did none ever tell ye taking things without asking is stealing?

By the time she'd finished her tirade she was standing right over him. She grabbed the knife handle from his grasp with one hand and gave him a swipe on the head with the other.

"Sorry, Mam. I was making a pig."

Anna Quinn stared blankly at her son.

He held up the block of wood. Taking it, Anna nearly threw it into the trash heap when a carved swirl spiraling upward on the rounded end caught her eye.

"Well, I'll be if it don't look like the arse end of a pig!"

"Can I finish it?"

She looked at him uncertainly. "I suppose if the good Lord gave you the gift to make something with such life in it, I'm no one to stand in His way. But you'll be doing it after supper. I need the knife now."

* * *

"Is he back yet?" Meg asked her brother.

"Not when we left," Brendan answered.

"Supper's ready," Deirdre announced.

Though there was barely enough meat for each to have more than a few bites, it seemed like heaven to taste it. The last of the daylight had disappeared by the time the meal was over. They cleaned up by firelight.

As she was putting away her sewing box for the night, Meg overheard her mother's whisper. "I've got the feeling again, Denis."

Deirdre's hearing the wail of the banshee the night before her mother died was a well-known family story. But Deirdre also got what she called a feeling like something creeping in her bones. Whenever it came it meant trouble. Meg's stomach fluttered at her Mam's whispered words.

"About what?" Denis asked.

"I never know the details. I only know something's coming. We shouldn't have eaten that chicken. It wasn't right."

"That's just you feeling guilty. But what was I to do? If I'd refused, Anna would have been insulted. That little bit wouldn't have made much difference."

"Everything makes a difference now." Deirdre still whispered, but the conviction in her voice made Meg uneasy.

29

Rory knocked at the cottage door early the next morning.

"Meg, I've something to tell you," he said as she ushered him in.

"And I've something to ask you," she said. "Why didn't you tell me you were going to sell your carvings?"

"That's what I've come to say. I got the idea a few days ago. I didn't want to tell until I saw if anything would come of it."

"So, did you sell any?"

"I sold all! I got enough to buy bread and cheese. Mam sent me over to tell you all to come and have some with us."

"You sold them all? Rory, that's wonderful!" Meg wanted to throw her arms around him, but her parents were awake now so she didn't dare. Instead she grabbed her shawl.

"We can't, Rory," Deirdre's voice stopped Meg.

"Why not, Mam?"

"We've already taken some of your family's last chicken. We'll not be taking what you've worked to earn."

"But I'm going to make lots more and keep selling. The closer we get to Christmas, the more I'll sell, I'm sure. There will be bread and cheese and more than that, too, so don't worry."

"I hope you're right," Deirdre said, "but we can't count on anything being for certain these days so we'll not take from you what's not a sure thing."

Rory's voice changed to a plea. "But my mam and da want to celebrate. We think we've got a sure thing or at least the closest we can come to one. For a while, anyway."

Denis put a hand on Rory's shoulder. "Your family should celebrate, Rory. But we don't want to take from what you've been able to gain."

Rory straightened his back. "We've been neighbors and friends for years. Meg's to be my wife. That will officially make us all family." He looked at Denis. "If you don't come, my mam and da will take it hard."

"Mam, don't you think it would be all right if we don't eat much?" Meg asked.

Brigid held out a small jar. "There's still a little oatmeal left. We could bring it to share."

"What do you say, Deirdre?" Denis asked.

Deirdre sighed. "I say it won't do to offend Meg's future in-laws."

A smile spread across Rory's face.

"We can't stay long." Deirdre nodded toward the pile of mending. "The days are getting shorter. We need to work while we've got the light."

"Bring it," Rory said. "Mam will be happy to help."

Before anything more could be said, Meg and Kathleen scooped up the clothes. "Brigid, carry the sewing boxes, please," Meg directed.

"I'll take them," Deirdre said. "Brigid, you carry that jar of oatmeal and mind, don't drop it."

Chapter Four

The women sat in the corner of the Quinn cottage nearest the window, sewing. The O'Connors merely nibbled, though it took great restraint. They were held in check by Deirdre's steely-eyed gaze whenever a hand ventured toward an extra piece of cheese or bite of bread.

Thomas, Denis, Brendan, Rory and Aiden lounged on the other side of the cook fire conversing about the weather and speculating on the possible cause of the blight. Rory, sitting closest the fireplace for the light, had his carving tools out, working while they talked.

The tiny cottage was even more crowded than the O'Connors. Rory had six brothers and sisters. With the exception of Aiden they were all much younger, Anna having miscarried several times between Aiden and Aisling, the next oldest child.

Loreena was eight, the same age as Brigid. The two girls who shared a love for pigs could be heard outside the open door, cooing over the newest piglet. Unlike the O'Connors', their pig had only one surviving baby, but it was enough to get from the coming Gale Day to the next.

The other Quinn children, Darien, Lizzy and Seamus weren't much more than babes. They busied themselves playing with a few toys Rory had carved for them as they crawled or toddled about the cottage. Only ten-year-old Aisling showed any interest in what the women and older girls were doing.

"She wants to sew," Anna explained as Aisling sat with them eagerly watching the deft movements of their hands. "I've been teaching her on some old cloths. She'll be good at it one day."

"I wish I could help," Aisling said.

"I know you do, *a stór*," Anna said, giving Aisling a hug, "but this mending is for pay. It's got to be done just so. Why don't you get some cloths? You can practice while we work."

"I wish Brigid would take an interest," Deirdre complained. "I've tried to teach her, but she's more of a mind for animals than for sewing. I've started her on dishcloths and such, but she gives up halfway through."

"She's no patience," Meg observed. "She can't get the stitches straight, but instead of starting over she drops it to go off with the pig."

"She's young," Anna observed. "She'll likely grow into it."

"I hope," said Deirdre. "She'll need a skill to trade for food or money and I don't think there's much call for pig chasing."

Meg nudged Kathleen, then jutted her chin slightly in the direction of the men. Kathleen looked over and saw Aiden smiling at her.

The sun rose higher and late morning approached. "This is a bit better," Anna observed. "I can see more clearly. I thought for sure it would rain today."

"I think it will," said Deirdre, "but at least it's holding off for now."

Aiden topped a slice of bread with a hunk of cheese and brought it to Kathleen.

"Thank you, Aiden," Kathleen said, taking the food.

A shadow crossed the open doorway. Kathleen gasped. Kevin Dooley had just stepped into the cottage. Aiden's smile faded, but he moved to welcome his friend.

"What brings you by?" he asked.

"I'm going fishing. Wondered if you'd want to join me."

"Since when do you fish?" Aiden laughed.

"Since right now. We ran out of food."

"Completely?"

"Aye. There's nothing left. Da said to take the *curragh* out and see what I could catch."

"Is it even in shape?" asked Thomas. "That old *curragh* hasn't seen the water in years."

33

"Might need some work first. That's why I came. I was hoping maybe I could get some help from Aiden to make it seaworthy."

Aiden glanced at Kathleen. "Of course, I'll help. Not sure I know much about *curraghs*, though."

"Can't your da fix it?" Deirdre asked, her voice sharp.

Kevin looked at the women as if he'd just noticed them.

"My da's a bit under the weather this morning."

"I see." Deirdre and Anna exchanged glances.

Meg looked at Kathleen who couldn't take her eyes off Kevin. Kevin must have noticed, too, for once she'd caught his eye his mouth widened and his eyes lit up. *She's right about his smile. 'Tis a grand one*, Meg thought.

"So Aiden, shall we go?"

"Da?"

"What do you say, Denis? I've a feeling those two lads would be more likely to drown themselves than fix the boat if we leave them on their own."

Kevin's face reddened. He turned his back to the group of women.

"Why not? We've nothing else to do. Brendan, why don't you come, too. You could stand to learn something about fixing a *curragh*. Maybe someday you'll even learn to handle one on the water."

"Aye, the three of us could go into the fishing business. What do you say to that, Kevin?" Aiden clapped his friend on the shoulder.

"Suits me fine. You coming, too, Rory?"

"No. Seems you've got enough help and I'm busy."

"Making toys?" Kevin laughed.

"Making money."

"Rory carved a bunch of wooden animals, boxes and such and sold them in town yesterday," Aiden explained. "Made enough money to buy some bread and cheese. He's carving more since he did so well."

Kevin picked up a trinket box Rory had just finished. Flowers tied with a flowing ribbon were carved in relief on the lid. "Fancy," said Kevin. "I guess we'll leave you to your lady's work then."

Rory glared at Kevin, but said nothing.

"Seems to me providing food for a family is the work of a man," Meg said.

Kathleen jabbed her with her elbow, but Meg took no notice.

Kevin whirled in her direction. "That's why I'm fixing up the *curragh*."

"Not by yourself, I notice." Meg's face felt lit by fire.

"We all need a little help at times. Let's be on our way," said Thomas as he steered them toward the door.

"Wait," said Anna. She grabbed the end of a loaf of bread. "Take this to your mam," she said, handing it to Kevin. "Tell her I'll be looking in on her soon."

"Thank you." Kevin said, stuffing the bread in his pocket.

After the men left the cottage, Deirdre asked, "Why'd you give the last of that bread to him?"

"You heard him say all their food is gone."

"I'm not surprised. That family's lazy. His da does nothing but drink himself into oblivion. They don't plan nor save. It's no wonder they've no reserves. 'Tis their own fault. And that Kevin's so full of himself. As if he's anything to be so proud of."

Meg and Kathleen glanced at each other.

"Still, I hate to see anyone in need. His father's drinking is not Kevin's fault. He's got no brothers. His Mam ain't got much in the way of brains nor skills, but that's just how she was born. I don't see their hurt as her fault nor certainly that of his two sisters, poor lasses."

"You're a good woman, Anna Quinn," Deirdre said. "God love you, you put me to shame sometimes."

"Mam?"

Deirdre glanced at Kathleen, "What child?"

"Don't you think it's good that Kevin is going to fix up the *curragh* and take it out fishing?" Kathleen asked. Doesn't that show he's trying?"

35

"I suppose. But I'll reserve judgment until I see how far he gets. If he's anything like his father, he'll start, but won't finish. That's the way of it. Children learn from their parents, be it good or bad."

"But Mam—"

Meg nudged Kathleen. She shook her head to warn her off further discussion of Kevin or his family.

"Meg, can you take a break for a moment?" Rory asked. "I want to show you what I've done."

Meg crossed the room, picking up baby Dairen on the way, settling him on her lap as she sat next to Rory.

"What do you think?" he asked.

Meg looked over the assortment of carved pigs, sheep, and dogs. Darien's hand reached for one.

"Sorry, lad, that one's for sale," Rory said leaning over to retrieve an old wooden horse from the floor to hand to the baby.

Darien grasped it in his chubby fist, the head disappearing into his mouth. Drool slid onto Meg's hands. She laughed. "He'll be getting teeth soon."

"The animals are fine for the wee ones, but I can set a higher price for a piece like this, don't you think?" Rory held up the trinket box with the beribboned flowers Kevin had mocked.

"Rory, that's beautiful. How much will you ask for it?"

"I've no idea of a fair price. I suppose I'll have to dicker though I fear I'll be cheated. Still, whatever I can get will help."

"To be sure." Meg bounced Darrien gently on her knee. "But you've put so much work into it. Something like this takes more time and effort than the little animals. I hope you'll not be cheated too badly. Do you have more of these?"

"I'm working on one now." He showed her a half-carved piece of wood.

"What's it to be?"

"Another box. But this one will have the moon and a few stars on the lid."

Meg watched Rory's hands as he worked. She was amazed to see the crescent shape of a moon emerge.

"It's like seeing magic to watch you work," she remarked. "When I look at my comb I wonder how you made those hearts and roses stand out from the wood. I could look at it forever and never figure it out."

"You like that comb very much, then?"

Meg smiled at him. "It's the most treasured thing I own. Sometimes I can't believe I possess something so beautiful."

"I'll never make another one, Meg. That will be forever one of a kind meant only for you."

"Oh, Rory," she sighed.

They gazed intently into each other's eyes, everyone else in the tiny room forgotten. Darien squealed, raising the wooden horse in his fist between them. They laughed at the baby's gesture, realizing they had moved very close and now pulled back.

"Chaperone," Rory whispered to Darien, chucking him under his chin.

Meg kissed the top of Darien's head, then cradled him in her arms. Taking the wooden horse she marched it up and down his little body making him squeal.

"Just wait till we have bairns of our own, Meg. You'll make a great mother."

Meg smiled. She held the baby tightly against her, wishing that day was here and that this was her and Rory's child. "Soon," she whispered.

When Meg looked up, she caught sight of Kathleen gazing at her.

"Rory, what do you think of Kevin Dooley?" she whispered.

Rory shrugged. "Not much. He's friendly enough with Aiden, though. Why do you ask?"

"Kathleen likes him. She asked me if you could find a way to get them together."

Rory stopped carving. He looked at Meg. "You know Aiden's hoping to court her."

"I've spoken to her about that, but she says Aiden's too much like a brother to her. She can't think of courting him. She's set on Kevin and no mistake."

Rory shook his head. "It would be a mistake to set her sights on the likes of him."

"Why do you say that?"

"His da's a drunkard. I know that's not Kevin's fault, but he takes after his da in other ways. Both are terrible lazy. Kevin's da used to be a good fisherman, but he ain't fished since the drink took him over. Why do you think they have to fix the *curragh* before they can take it out? Nobody's kept it up. Kevin could have taken care of it, could have been fishing right along, but he's as lazy as his da. He waits until there's nothing left and looks to it as a last resort. I'm not wishing it on him, mind you, but I'll be surprised if he don't end up as much a drunkard as his da. Tell Kathleen to find another."

Meg sighed. "I wish she would, but she's determined. He's gotten into her heart."

"I'm sorry for her, then, as I fear he'll break it."

Meg looked at her sister again. Aisling was showing Kathleen her practice work on the dishcloth. Kathleen leaned in close to examine the stitches. "You're doing well, Aisling. Your stitching is nice and straight. Looks like it will hold well, too," Meg heard her say. Aisling beamed at Kathleen's praise.

"She'll make a good mother, too," Meg whispered to Rory.

He nodded his agreement. "Too bad she won't think of Aiden for the father of her bairns. Though she'd not believe it now, I'm certain she'd be a sight happier with him than she would ever be with Kevin Dooley."

Chapter Five

It was late in the day when Father O'Malley wound his way down the side of a hill. He came up behind a small girl peeling the inner, fleshy bark from an old oak tree. Her scrawny arms, draped in a tattered black shawl, moved in quick spidery motions.

"What are you doing, child?"

Startled, she jumped and turned, flattening her back against the tree. She relaxed when she recognized her priest.

He forced himself to smile but it was difficult in the face of a ten-year-old girl whose ragged shawl appeared too heavy a weight. "I'm sorry, Biddy. I didn't mean to frighten you."

"I'm getting supper, Father." She looked at the ground.

He noticed a small pile of tree bark at her feet.

"Is this your family's supper?"

"Aye, but I only ate a little, Father. I was so hungry."

He noticed the crumbs of bark around her mouth. Biddy came from one of the poorest families in his parish. They and a few others like them felt the suffering most keenly.

"Please tell your mam I'll be by to see her in the morning. I think I can bring a bit of something to make a better meal than this."

"Thank you, Father. We'd be most grateful." A shy smile exposed gaps where two teeth were missing.

Father O'Malley continued down the hillside. Waves of green spread before him, dipping and rising with the shifting of the land. Tips of rocks jutted from the earth, scattered across the field as though a giant hand had sprinkled the ground as a confectioner liberally tops his cake with powdered sugar. Bushes sprouted up making knobs of darker green against the lighter shade of the grass.

Below him a band of boys combed the field. He saw only empty hands and sullen, sunken faces

Heaven help them, poor lads, he thought.

* * *

Upon entering his cottage Father O'Malley built up a fire then dropped into a chair. He had a bit of food but he was too tired to bother cooking so instead placed it into a small sack to take to Biddy's family in the morning. His head ached. He rested it in his hands. The heat from the fire warmed his face making his eyelids grow heavy. He thought back to a day long ago.

Siobhan stood before him again—alive, vibrant, and radiant. It was a warm summer afternoon and she had come to visit him while he worked the small patch of land behind his family's cottage.

Intent on his work, he hadn't heard her approach until she spoke.

"Would you care to walk with me, Brian?"

With the sun at her back, her red hair blazed. She was barefoot, her dress tattered, torn and patched, but her glittering emerald eyes overshadowed her clothing, adorning her better than the finest jewels.

Hand in hand they walked across the field and up the side of a sun drenched hill. There Brian lay back, reclining on his elbows. Siobhan sat looking out over the water.

"What?" Brian asked, wondering at her dreamy smile.

"The water."

He glanced at the sea. "So?"

"It's dancing with the sun. Doesn't it look happy?"

Sparkles of sunlight played off the gently rolling billows, making the bay a patchwork quilt of varying hues, in some spots so bright it hurt to look.

"None other than yourself would think of it that way."

"Go on with you now," she said, giving his shoulder a playful shove.

"Siobhan, you told me the first time we met that you weren't like other lasses." He pulled himself up and faced her. "Unless, of course, the lass be a faery."

"A faery!" She'd laughed. That musical sound that he loved so much.

"You have enchanted me now, haven't you? Admit it." He moved his face closer to hers until they nearly touched.

"I shall never tell." Her whole face smiled. He leaned in the fraction it took for his lips to touch hers. Her eyes now burned with passion. His heart beat hard in his chest. He gently stroked her cheek and traced her jaw with his finger.

"I love you," he said, his voice a deep husky whisper.

"I love you, too, Brian."

In his mind he'd practiced what he wanted to say next over and over again. Now the words froze in his throat. He closed his eyes in concentration.

"Are you praying?" she asked.

"No, but perhaps I should be."

"Why is that?"

"Because I've something important to ask you."

"And what might that be?"

He opened his eyes to find her glistening green ones fixed on his own. What if she refused? It would be over and those eyes would someday belong to another man's gaze.

"I was wondering, Siobhan, if you would be at all agreeable to…" He was making a terrible mess of it.

She laughed. "Brian O'Malley. What bewitches your tongue?"

"You, lass."

"Me?"

"Indeed. 'Tis not easy to be asking so lovely a creature as yourself to be my wife. Do you wonder at my befuddlement?" What was wrong with him? He could speak anything he wished to anyone but he could not say plain and simple 'will you marry me?' to her.

"Your wife?" She'd put a soft hand against his face. "Truly, do you want me for your wife?"

"More than anything on earth."

41

"Then, aye, Brian O'Malley. I will be your wife and gladly." She threw her arms around his neck, pushing all her tiny weight upon him.

Brian wrapped his massive arms around her waist and stood up, swinging her round. Her legs flared out, making her half supine. He'd slowed his spinning, bringing her gently in, feeling her legs toss lightly against his. Then set her down.

"You said 'aye'!" How had he, Brian O'Malley, claimed the love and devotion of this faery creature?

"Why wouldn't I? I could nay possibly love another more than you."

They tumbled together on the lush green hillside, laughing, hugging and kissing until they were spent. Then Siobhan had leaned her head against Brian's shoulder as they watched the afternoon sun dance with the water.

* * *

"Ah, Siobhan," he whispered to the fire. "Those were fine days. But now? What are we to do?"

Thoughts of Siobhan faded, replaced by Biddy and the boys in the field. There were some, like them, the most vulnerable who would not make it through. It always happened during times of famine. The weakest were culled. A heaviness settled in his heart at the thought. Another feeling followed, one that had been growing since they day at the O'Connors when he'd seen the rotten potatoes. Sure enough there'd been famines in the land before, but something about this one felt different. He couldn't explain it. He only knew that a feeling of dread unlike anything he'd ever felt washed over him. He believed the culling would go deeper this time. The idea of watching the deterioration of those who would normally scrape by depressed him more than he could bear.

Chapter Six

"You look fine, Denis," Deirdre said, smoothing the front of his one good shirt.

"I don't know why I let you dress me up like a doll. What I look like won't matter to Blackburn."

"Maybe not, but it can't hurt. 'Tis an important conversation you're to have."

Smiling, Denis kissed Deirdre on the cheek. "I'd best be off. Thomas'll be waiting."

"Is it a very long walk, Da?" Brigid asked.

"A few miles, lass. The landlord don't care to live too close to us."

Deirdre huffed. "The landlord lives a mite further than a few miles. I can count the times I've seen him cast a shadow on the soil of Ireland."

"Aye, but his agent is here. Blackburn takes care of business for Stokes so he's the one to see. Wish me luck."

"Da, do you truly think he'll change us and the Quinns to indenture?" Brendan asked.

"Won't know until we ask."

"What's indenture?" Brigid asked.

"Just a different way of being in relationship to the landlord," Denis answered.

"Different how?" Brigid persisted.

Denis sighed. "You see lass, right now we are what's called tenants at will. It means Stokes can decide he no longer wants us on our land at any time, rent paid up or not, and make us leave. With indenture we sign a contract in which we agree to work the land for him and he, in turn can't simply remove us if the whim takes him. Provided we keep up with the rent, of course."

"The very idea of indenture makes my blood boil," said Deirdre. "This land is ours. A king there was in your own family, Denis. He owned and ruled this land." She pointed at all her children. "You remember that. Remember where you came from." She turned back to Denis. "To ask for indenture and serve a Prod like a slave. Shameful, it is."

Red splotches crept up Denis's neck. "'Tis true, *a ghrá*. But right now, with no contract, we can be evicted any time Stokes takes a fancy to do it. With indenture there's a bit of security."

Deirdre couldn't meet her husband's eyes. "I know," she whispered. "You're doing what's best. It's the damned land thieving Prods got me in a fury." Deirdre took a deep breath to calm herself. "*Dia dul in éineacht leat.*"

With that blessing from his wife, Denis left the cottage.

Deirdre stared into the fire.

"Mam, you don't look well. Are you alright?" Meg asked, squatting next to her mother.

"'Tis the feeling, Meg. It grew strong in the wee hours of the morning. Woke me out of a sound sleep. I can't seem to shake it."

"Is it that you don't think Da will be able to get us changed to indenture or just that you don't like the idea of it?"

"Neither. I don't need the feeling to know Blackburn won't bother to ask it of Stokes and Stokes wouldn't change a thing if he did, but your da needs to ask to know he's tried every way he can to take care of us."

"Then what is it?"

"I don't know. I only know that something is going to happen. The feeling gets stronger every day."

Deirdre wiped her hands across her face as if using them to change her expression. "Let's not talk about it. There's no sense in getting everyone into a fright."

"Shall we get on with the sewing, then?" Meg asked speaking in a tone meant for all the cottage's inhabitants.

"Aye. Sun's up enough to see by." Deirdre looked at Brigid. "And you, lass, are going to help. No pig-chasing today. 'Tis time you got serious about learning to stitch a straight line."

Brigid sighed, but joined the others near the window.

44

"What'll you be doing today, Brendan?" Kathleen asked.

"Don't know. Aiden's going fishing with Kevin. I suppose I could join them, if Kevin will let me."

"Why wouldn't he let you?" asked Kathleen.

"Kevin doesn't like having me around. Just because I'm a year and a half younger he treats me like I'm a wee lad. I don't like it, but I could put up with it if it would get us a fish or two."

"I'm sure he's only teasing," Kathleen said.

"It's a teasing I don't like. He knows it, but he keeps right on anyway."

"Does Aiden tease like that, too?" Deirdre asked.

"No. Aiden and I always get on well."

Deirdre smiled. "Aiden's a nice lad. Don't you think so, Kathleen?"

"Aye, Mam," Kathleen studied her sewing to keep the annoyance from showing in her face. "All the Quinns are nice."

"He's especially so, though, isn't he?"

Kathleen shrugged. "I don't see much difference between him and the others."

"Perhaps you should look a little harder."

Brendan got up. "I think I will see if they'll take me with them today. It would be nice to have a fish for supper."

"How well do they do with that *curragh*?" Meg asked. "Those take a lot of skill to handle. Kevin's da was an expert fisherman, but Kevin was too young to have learned much from him before he quit and Aiden's got no experience at all."

"Not to mention, from what your da said that boat was in poor shape." Deirdre added. "It took them days to fix. A hole right through the bottom and all."

"It's patched well enough to stay afloat," Brendan answered. "Though 'twas Da, and Mr. Quinn who did most of the work. None of the rest of us knew how to fix it. We watched and helped out as we were told."

"And where was Kevin's da, the great fisherman, all that time?" Deirdre asked.

"In the cottage, I suppose. We never saw him. Kevin said he wasn't feeling well."

"Sure it is he felt well enough the night before," Deirdre muttered. "Right up until he felt nothing at all."

"What does that mean, Mam?" Brigid asked.

"Nothing, lass. Just you watch your stitches. You're beginning to lose your straight line."

"I hate sewing!" Brigid said, ripping out the stitches that had begun to stagger.

"Does Mr. Dooley ever fish anymore?" Kathleen asked.

"Not that I've seen," Brendan answered. "'Course Kevin won't let me come with them much, so I don't know for sure."

"You've still not answered my question," Meg said. How well do they handle the *curragh*?"

"Well enough. They keep to the cove rather than taking it out in the open water. It's not so rough there. It's hard enough to keep it upright and fish at the same time."

"They're smart to stay where it's fairly smooth until they're more experienced," Kathleen noted.

"The cove's filled with jagged rocks," Deirdre said, almost to herself.

Meg noticed a far-away look pass over her mother's face.

"They've caught some fish so they must be doing well enough," Kathleen stated. "I think it shows that Kevin's not just like his da. He's willing to do what it takes to help feed his family." She sat up straighter, a satisfied look on her face.

"He should take over the fishing since his da's apparently no longer capable," Deirdre stated. "He should have started before this, rather than waiting until there's a famine upon us and he's got to learn the hard way. If he was really a worker he'd have learned the handling of a *curragh* and the ways of fishing by now. His da's not the only fisherman around. There's others would have taught him if he'd a mind to ask."

Kathleen put down her sewing. "Mam, why can't you see anything good in Kevin? He's got to be the man of his family now. He's doing what he can."

Deirdre eyed her daughter. "Don't think I'm a blind fool, Kathleen. I know you've feelings for that lad. I can see why. He's good looking and a sweet talker when he wants to be. I don't blame Kevin for his da's ways, mind you, but as they say, one beetle knows another. I'll see no lass of mine wedded to a lad who's like as not to follow in the footsteps of his da. It would be a miserable life, you'd have. Just look at Noreen Dooley if you don't believe me. Does she seem like a happy wife to you?"

"But Mam, just because Kevin's da is one way doesn't mean Kevin has to turn out the same. Isn't it possible he sees the wrong in his da and wants to do better?"

"Possible, aye. Likely, no. Bairns take after their parents most of the time. They learn what's set before them. Why don't you give Aiden a chance?"

Kathleen threw her head back in frustration. "Why does everyone think I should marry Aiden just because Meg's marrying Rory?"

"It's not just because of that," Deirdre answered. "You'd make a good match."

"No we wouldn't."

"Why don't you like Aiden?"

Kathleen appeared close to tears. "I do like Aiden. I love Aiden, but I love him like a brother, not like a husband."

"Is that all?" Deirdre chuckled. "You'd grow into it in time."

"I don't want to grow into it. I want to be in love."

Brendan headed for the door. "I've got to do something with myself. If they won't let me fish I'll see if Rory's taking his carvings into town today. Maybe he'll take me with him."

"I'm so proud of Rory doing well at selling his carvings," Meg beamed. "He can turn out those little

47

animals quick as a wink now. It takes longer for the fancier ones, but they earn him a bit more."

"I wonder if he gets what they're really worth," Deirdre said.

"He worries about that," Meg confided. "But he takes what he can get. It's keeping them in bread and cheese and sometimes eggs."

"What will we get for this sewing?" asked Brigid.

"Not a thing if you don't keep your stitches straight," Deirdre answered.

"*Is fuath liom fuála!*" Brigid exclaimed.

"So you've said," Deirdre answered. "But hate it or not, it's a necessary skill you'll be glad you learned one day."

"*Is mian liom riamh go raibh mé a sew.*" Brigid stabbed her needle through the cloth.

"Mind your temper, lass, and your tongue," her mother scolded. "Life is full of things we wish we didn't have to do."

"Does that include marrying someone you don't love?" asked Kathleen.

Meg watched her mother's face, saw her mouth open then quickly snap shut, biting back the words that wanted to fly out.

"No one ever said you have to marry Aiden."

"Good." A furtive smile spread across Kathleen's downturned face, her eyes intent on her sewing.

"But you can forget about Kevin Dooley and that is for certain," Deirdre said in a tone that allowed no room for argument. Kathleen's smile faded.

"Who should I marry, Mam?" Brigid asked. "Rory hasn't any brothers my age."

"Lass, you're too young to even think of it yet," her mother answered.

"We don't all have to marry Rory's brothers," Kathleen interjected, never lifting her gaze from her sewing.

Deirdre sighed. "If you don't want Aiden, it's too bad, but I suppose there's nothing for it. There are plenty of

48

other lads in Kelegeen. And most any come from families a sight better than the Dooleys. Doesn't anyone but Kevin interest you?"

"Not particularly."

"Well, look around then. There's as many good fish in the sea as ever came out of it."

"Ouch!" Brigid jumped. "Now look." She squeezed her pinpricked finger forming a large droplet of blood.

"Don't!" Meg pushed away the injured hand Brigid held out to her.

"Stick it in your mouth, quick lass!" Deirdre ordered. "Don't get any on the mending."

"Too late," said Meg. "There's a drop on mine already. It would be on white, too."

"I'm sorry," Brigid called after Meg who was attempting to remove the blood from the shirt she'd been mending by rubbing it with a clean, wet cloth.

"Is it coming out, Meg?" Deirdre asked.

"Some. This water's not cold enough, though. I can't get it all."

"Brigid, that was careless," her mother scolded.

"I said I was sorry. I told you I hate sewing." The words bubbled out amongst tears. "I'm no good at it and I never will be."

"Don't take on, lass," Meg said, resuming her seat. "It's not a very big stain and I got most of it."

Meg held the shirtsleeve towards her sister. A round red spot stained the inside of the cuff.

"It's not gone, though," Brigid observed.

"I don't think it went all the way through," Meg answered. "Being on the underside, maybe they won't notice." Her voice shook a bit as she spoke.

"Whose is it?" Deirdre asked.

"The Hoffreys," Meg said.

"I thought it was the Bricks." Kathleen sounded alarmed.

"That is," said Meg, pointing to the mending work in Kathleen's lap. "I grabbed one of Hoffreys' because we were falling behind and I wanted to get started on them."

49

"Dear God, not Hoffrey." Deirdre's words came out in hoarse whisper.

Brigid's eyes darted from one to another. "Why does it matter?" She asked.

"When we take the finished work back most folks, like the Bricks, look it over, see that it's fine and give us our pay," Meg explained. "But the Hoffreys search over every inch, looking for something to be wrong so they can find fault."

"They seem angry when they can't find anything," Kathleen added. "It's as though they want something to be wrong so they can complain and not have to pay."

"Why would they do that?" Brigid asked.

Kathleen shrugged. "Some folks are pickier than others."

"It's more than being picky," Deirdre said. "They may be rich, but they're cheap. Besides, it gives them pleasure to find fault with the work of poor Irish Catholics. Prods!"

"I'm sorry, Mam," Brigid said, wiping tears away with the side of her palms.

Deirdre patted Brigid's knee. "What's done is done. Only do be more careful. If a customer thinks we've ruined their property we'll be charged for it rather than paid. We could even lose them as a customer. We can't afford that. Now let me see."

Brigid held out her finger. Deirdre placed a small wad of clean cloth from her sewing box over the pinprick. "Hold it tight until you're sure it's stopped completely. No sense getting blood on your piece of mending as well."

Brigid sighed deeply as she held the cloth on her finger.

Meg playfully nudged her sister's shoulder. "We'll keep you on the other side of the cottage from now on when we work on the Hoffreys' mending."

"Or out with the pig," added Kathleen.

* * *

As the sun set, the light from the cottage's one window was no longer sufficient. They set aside their unfinished work and packed up their sewing kits.

"I'll see to supper. What there is of it," Deirdre said going towards the cook fire. "It'll be nothing more than mashed turnips tonight, I'm afraid. We'd better get this set of mending done and back to town soon."

The door opened just as the peeled and chopped turnips slid into the boiling water.

"Denis! How did it go?" Deirdre rose to meet her husband.

Denis threw his hat into the corner of the cottage in disgust and dropped down in front of the fire. "No better than expected, I suppose."

"He said 'no' then?"

"Aye. We asked him…begged him, I'm ashamed to say, to at least ask Stokes, but he refused. He said he makes the decisions when Stokes is away. He couldn't allow such a change as us going over to indenture. Claimed it was something beyond the scope of his authority."

"If that's the case, Da, isn't it only right that he bring the matter to Mr. Stokes?" Meg asked.

"One would think so, lass, but what he claims is in his authority is deciding what matters to bring to the great master's attention and which are not worth his time. Apparently, our request falls into the latter category."

"Is there nothing to be done, Denis?" Deirdre asked.

"We can wait until the next time Stokes is in residence and ask him directly. That is if we even know he's here. And if he'll see us. We'll still have to get past Blackburn to get to him."

"So there's no hope." Deirdre stirred the contents of the pot.

"Thomas and I discussed it on the way home. We're thinking of asking Father O'Malley to write a letter to Stokes for us. Stokes may well say no, but at least we will have asked him directly. In any case, we're no worse off than we were when I left this morning. I count it a good day when there's no setback."

51

The door opened again. The smell of freshly caught fish permeated the cottage, making everyone look up. Brendan and Aiden entered. "Look what we've got," Brendan announced.

"You went fishing, after all?" Kathleen asked.

"Not me. When I got to the Quinns Aidan had already left, so I went into town with Rory. On the way back we passed the cove. Aiden and Kevin were just pulling the *curragh* out of the water and divvying up their catch."

"Is that your catch, then, Aiden?" Deirdre asked.

"Partly. I took the other two fish home," he answered. Then looking at Kathleen, he said, "This one I brought for you."

"That's very kind, but we can't take it," Kathleen told him.

Aiden looked crestfallen. "Why not?"

"Mam says we shouldn't take what others have earned."

"It's alright," Brendan explained. "I helped Rory in town today. He was going to give me some bread and cheese, but when we came across Aiden and Kevin we agreed on me taking one of Aiden's fish instead. They still have two plus the bread and cheese Rory got. It all comes out the same in the end, don't it?"

"It does," Deirdre agreed, taking the fish. "And you're a dear lad for bringing it to us, Aiden. Don't you think so, Kathleen?"

"Aye. Thank you, Aiden." Her tone was flat.

Deirdre handed Kathleen a fry pan. "Why don't you cook this up for us?"

"Rory did well in town again?" Meg asked.

"Well enough for a bit of bread and cheese."

"Isn't he getting a good price for his fancy work?"

"He didn't have much of that to sell. It was mostly the animals and a few baby rattles. The fancy work takes longer to make and he can only get one or two done before it's time to go into town again to sell."

Meg sighed. "It's too bad. He'd do much better if he could only make them faster."

"That's why we've made a deal. I'm to take his easy pieces into town on a regular basis and sell them for him. I'll get a cut for doing my part. That'll free Rory up to spend more time at home working on the fancy stuff. When he's got a good set of it he'll take it in himself to sell. He's hoping to have a good lot come Gale Day and then some more as it gets nearer to Christmas."

"I like that plan," Denis said. "That lad's smart. He'll make a fine husband for you Meg."

Meg beamed.

"Sure you must be as good a catch, yourself," Deirdre said to Aiden.

The lad blushed. He looked at Kathleen whose back was turned to the others as she gutted and prepared the fish.

"Will you stay and have some with us?" Deirdre asked.

"No, thank you. They're waiting for me at home."

Meg followed Aiden out of the cottage. "Tell Rory I'm so proud of him, would you? Tell him we'll bring our finished mending work into town in a day or two. If he's got a few samples of his fancy work ready, we could show them to our customers. It might help that we've already got connections where he doesn't."

"I'll tell him. He'll be pleased you take such an interest in what he does."

"Why wouldn't I?" Meg was all smiles, full of hopes for the future.

"I wish Kathleen would feel the same about me. I thought she'd be happy to have fish for supper."

"She is. We all are."

"She didn't show it."

"She's got a bit of a headache, is all. We spent the day sewing and the light wasn't good. It strained her eyes." A complete lie, but the defeated look on Aiden's face made Meg's heart ache.

He nodded. "I'll bet she'd have forgotten her headache if Kevin had brought in that fish instead of me." He swallowed hard. "I'll be sure and tell Rory what you said," he assured her, then left for home.

* * *

As the family prepared to sleep, Brigid scooted up close to Meg. She whispered to her, "Do you really think the Hoffreys will charge us for that bloodstain? We've no money. How can we pay?"

"We won't pay. They'll just take it out of the amount they would have given us."

"Would they really do that?"

"Only if they notice it."

"But you said they check every piece carefully, looking for any mistake."

"Aye, they do. But it's a wee spot and on the back of a cuff. Don't worry so. They probably won't even see it. Now go to sleep."

Meg thought about it, though. It was a small spot and she'd gotten most of it out. Not one of her other customers would notice it. But the Hoffreys had eyes like hawks when looking for a mistake. What Meg feared most wasn't that they'd notice it and reduce the pay, but that they'd talk. They'd say the O'Connors' work was slipping. Would their other customers begin to lose trust in them? Might it even affect her newly hatched plan to help Rory sell his fancy work? It seemed unfair that such a small thing could cause profound problems for her family, yet that's the way life turned sometimes. It was no use worrying until she returned the work, so best not to lose sleep over it. In the corner of the cottage she could hear her mother constantly shifting position. Was the feeling upon her? If so, did it have anything to do with the same thoughts that worried Meg?

Chapter Seven

As Father O'Malley feared, the famine began to take its toll on the most vulnerable. In the past week he'd buried two infants, a pregnant mother, and an old man all from the poorest of his parish families. He worried over Biddy Rooneys' family. They'd been living on tree bark, foraged vegetation and whatever scraps he was able to bring them. As he walked home from visiting them, he reflected on the feeling that Biddy seemed to be disappearing before his eyes. So lost in this thought was he that he didn't notice the two men waiting outside his cottage door until he was nearly home.

"Denis! Thomas! To what do I owe this visit?" he asked, shepherding them inside.

"We've a favor to ask of you, Father," Thomas said.

Denis and Thomas described their unsuccessful visit with Blackburn and their plan to write directly to the landlord himself.

"We need you to write the letter for us, Father, as we don't have the English," Denis explained. "Will you do it?"

"I'd be happy to write for you. I'm just not sure it will do much good."

"So you don't believe Stokes will change us to indenture?" Thomas asked.

"I've no idea. You know him better than I—"

"We hardly know him ourselves," Denis interrupted. "He's rarely in Ireland. I can count on one hand the times I've laid eyes on him."

"That's my point," said Father O'Malley. "Do you know where in England he resides? If not, the letter will have to be given to Blackburn to pass on to him. I doubt he'll do it. Even if we could send it directly to him, the answer would undoubtedly come back through Blackburn. Some landlords prefer to communicate with their tenants solely through their agents. If he's one of those, he might not take kindly to your bypassing Blackburn."

"We already know Blackburn's answer," said Denis. "So Stokes can't say anything worse. If that's the case we're at no less of a disadvantage than we are now."

"It seems worth the risk," Thomas added. "But you're right about not knowing how to get the letter to him. All I know is that he lives in England."

"Well that covers a bit of territory, doesn't it?" said Father O'Malley.

"Is there any way you can find out for us, Father?"

"I can ask around. What's his first name?"

"Alfred, I believe," said Denis.

"Alfred Stokes." Father O'Malley scribbled the name on a piece of paper. "I'll see what I can do. Meanwhile, let's get the letter written so it's ready to go if we do get an address." He pulled out a clean sheet of paper. "Tell me what you want to say."

"You know our situation and the change we're hoping for. Could you put it in your own words?" Denis asked.

"Then read it back to us in Irish," said Thomas. "We'll let you know if there's anything we want changed."

"You know, of course, that I'll have to explain I'm writing for you. He knows you can't write in English. Have you any idea how he feels about Catholic priests?"

"No idea at all," Denis stated.

"We'll just have to take a chance on it, then," said Father O'Malley.

He thought for a moment, then began to write. The other two sat quietly as Father O'Malley's pen scratched across the paper.

When he settled his pen in the inkwell the two leaned forward, eager to hear what he'd written.

"'Tis a good letter, Father," Denis said when he finished. "It says just what we want."

"Do you agree, Thomas?"

"Aye, Father. I'd not change a word."

"Now all we have to do is find a way to send it to him without going through Blackburn." Father O'Malley held up a finger as a thought occurred to him. "Gale Day is only weeks away. Sometimes the landlords attend. Do you think he might be there?"

"'Tis possible," Denis said. "I believe that one time I spoke with him it was at Gale Day. It was years ago, though. I can't remember seeing him there since. It's usually just Blackburn."

"Well, there's always a chance. Why don't we wait for it? Even if he's not there, it will be a good place to ask around for his residence. Someone there's bound to know of his whereabouts."

"We knew we could count on you, Father." A broad smile spread across Thomas's face.

"Don't praise me too much yet, Thomas. At the moment the letter still sits on my table. Wait until we get it into his hands or at least on its way to him," Father O'Malley laughed.

"Still, Father, we'll gladly take what shreds of hope we can get," said Denis.

* * *

"I hear them, Meg." Kathleen hurried ahead. The two were coming home after returning the finished mending. Kathleen had insisted they take the route past the cove. Rounding the bend, they came upon Kevin and Aiden pulling the *curragh* out of the water.

"Did you catch anything?" Kathleen called from atop the small rise in the land.

The boys glanced up while dragging the wooden boat ashore.

"A bit," Aiden called.

"How much is a bit?" Meg asked as she and Kathleen half-walked, half-slid down the embankment.

"Five total," said Aiden.

"Two are Aiden's," said Kevin. "Three are mine."

"You caught three?" Kathleen said, giving Kevin a warm smile. He smiled back, but said nothing.

"Not exactly," Aiden explained. "But the boat's his so he gets the extra."

"Why?" Meg asked. "Seems to me you should be able to keep what you catch."

Aiden shrugged and looked away.

"You lasses don't understand the ways of business," Kevin informed her.

"I understand the ways of fairness," Meg retorted.

"It's fine, Meg," Aiden said. "We made an agreement when we began and I mean to keep my word."

"At least you're honest, Aiden," Meg said.

Kevin ignored her remark. "What have you got there?" he asked Kathleen, pointing to the sack she held.

"Food," she told him. "We returned our mending work and got our pay." Kathleen opened the sack. "Two loaves of bread, cheese, a dozen eggs, and some oatmeal."

"You did well," Aiden complimented her. "Better than a couple of fish, for certain."

"We'll be bringing some 'round to your family this evening," Meg told him. "Your mam helped with the mending and is entitled to a fair share." Meg glanced sideways at Kevin, "Despite they be our customers, a person should get paid what they've earned for their work."

Kevin didn't look at her, but continued to gaze at Kathleen as if the others didn't exist.

"And is that more work to do?" Aiden pointed to the garment bag Meg carried.

"Aye," Kathleen answered. "Not nearly as much as the last time. But perhaps there'll be more work for us by the time we return these. It tends to go like that."

Aiden looked down at the two fish by his feet. "I wish I'd caught more so I could give some to you." He looked at Kathleen who hadn't taken her eyes off Kevin since they'd arrived. "Did you enjoy the last fish I brought over, Kathleen?"

"Aye."

"I think I'm improving with practice. Soon perhaps, I'll be able to bring more."

Kathleen glanced at him. "It's kind of you to think of us."

"I think of you all the time." Aiden blushed at his own barely audible words.

Kathleen turned her attention back to Kevin. "Your family must be proud of you, fixing up the *curragh* and shouldering the responsibility for them all."

Kevin straightened up to his full height. "I'm doing my best by them. I am the man of the family, after all."

"Does your da know that?" Meg asked, her head cocked a bit sideways.

"My da's not well these days." His eyes narrowed to slits as he spoke. "I've no choice but to be the one in charge now."

As Kevin turned his attention back to Kathleen, his eyes softened. He plastered his most handsome smile across his face. "It's hard to live on just fish, though," he said, glancing at her food sack. "It would be refreshing to have a wee bit of something else to go along with it. Kathleen, do you remember the day I went to Aiden's to ask if he could help fix up the *curragh*? You were all there."

"Aye. I do," she nodded.

"His mam gave me the last of their bread. I'll never forget that kindness." He looked down at her from under his long lashes, his smile warm as the sun.

Kathleen drew in a breath. She looked at the sack sitting open at her feet. "I'm sure we could—"

"'Twas meant for your mam and sisters," Meg interjected. "Did they get any?"

Kevin threw an icy glare at Meg, but said nothing.

Kathleen crouched down.

"Put it back!" Meg commanded as Kathleen pulled a loaf of bread from the sack.

"Couldn't we spare half?" Kathleen asked, looking up at Meg and squinting against the sunlight.

"No. We've to give some to Aiden's family for the work his mam did to earn it." Her focus returned to Kevin on the word earn. "We've got to get on now."

Meg started off.

"Thanks, Kathleen," Kevin called once she and Meg were back to the top of the embankment. "You're a kind and generous lass."

Meg looked back at Kevin. Seeing a hunk of bread in his hands she realized Kathleen had defied her. "I'm sure Aiden's Mam will be very happy to know her kindness is repaid by you cheating her son," she called over her shoulder.

Grabbing Kathleen's wrist, she practically dragged her to the path. Once they were out of earshot of the boys Meg rounded on Kathleen. "Why did you give that bread to Kevin?" She leaned toward her sister, her feet firmly planted, one hand on her hip while the other clutched the garment bag to her chest.

Kathleen backed up a step. Then jutting out her chin she retorted, "I don't take orders from you."

"Fine. You can explain to Mam why we've come up short on the bread, then."

Kathleen swallowed. Her eyes darted one way then the other. "It would have been rude not to give him some. It was obvious he needed it."

Meg straightened up. "It was obvious he knew he could manipulate you!"

"He didn't!" Kathleen protested.

"He can tell as well as anyone you're moon-eyed over him. He used it to get what he wanted from you. If I wasn't there, you'd have given him the whole bag." Meg turned her back and resumed walking towards home.

"I would not."

"You would. And what's more, it was cruel to Aiden to go on the way you did."

"How so?" Kathleen asked, catching up alongside Meg.

"You know how he feels about you. Yet you carry on with Kevin right in front of him."

"How many times need I say I won't have Aiden as a suitor?"

"You could at least be kind to him."

"I was never unkind. Giving him false hope would be cruel."

"You don't have to marry or even court Aiden if you don't want him, but you could at least take his feelings into account. How do you think he felt about you handing over food to Kevin after he'd brought that fish for you?"

"That fish was for all of us, not just for me."

"Aye, for all of us, but the gesture was for you. And what of his talk of improving his skill so he can bring you more fish? He wants to get better at it for you, Kathleen."

"I can't help it, Meg. I've only sisterly feelings for Aiden, but whenever I see Kevin I just, just…"

"Doesn't it bother you that he's cheating Aiden out of his rightful share of the fish? And then how he used you to get some of our own food?"

"Aiden himself said they had an agreement about the fish. He didn't seem bothered by it so why should I be? And Kevin never asked me for food."

"He didn't have to, did he?"

"Stop it, Meg! You're being hateful." Kathleen's eyes filled with tears.

Meg came to a halt. She put her arm around Kathleen's shoulder. Purposely softening her tone, she said, "Kathleen, I know you think you're in love with Kevin—"

"I am and I think he might love me. Didn't you see how he looked at me? How sweetly he spoke to me?"

Meg sighed. "Kathleen, he did that to get what he wanted from you, that's all."

Kathleen looked up at Meg through tears. "That can't be true."

"I wish it weren't."

"I don't believe it."

Meg let go of her. "You are as stubborn as the day is long. And for a smart lass, you're an idiot when it comes to men."

"Meg!"

"'Tis the truth. But we've more important matters to deal with now."

Kathleen dried her eyes. "You mean the Hoffreys?"

61

Meg nodded. "I worried they'd notice that blood stain, wee as it was."

"They took more out of our pay than was necessary, don't you think?"

"Aye. But what concerns me more is whether they'll talk. There's more competition for mending work than ever now. I hope we don't lose customers."

"But we've an excellent reputation."

"I hope it's enough to save us. If the Hoffreys say our work is slipping our customers might look to others."

"It was only one small mistake. A child's accident."

"Did they seem to care?"

Kathleen shook her head.

"We'll have to tell Mam how they took on about it and docked our pay. It cost us in provisions," Meg said, pointing to the food sack. "We still have to share some of that with the Quinns. And this," she flipped the garment bag, "won't bring in much."

"Let's say nothing in front of Brigid. She'll feel so bad knowing she caused us to lose pay," Kathleen urged.

"I've been thinking of that. We'll tell Mam privately and let her decide how to talk to Brigid. I don't want her to feel guilty, yet she needs to learn not to be careless. We can't afford another mistake."

As they neared their cottage, Meg noticed Brigid heading behind it, the sow in the lead and the piglet in her arms. She was glad the lass would be outside when they explained the situation to their mother.

Meg placed the garment bag on the table. "That's all we could get."

"Not surprising," Deirdre answered. "They're should be more next time. How did it go with the Hoffreys?"

"As expected," Meg said.

"Tell me." Deirdre sat at the table, unloading the paltry mending work from the garment bag.

"As usual, Mrs. Hoffrey and her two daughters went over every inch of mending work as if it was going to be handed to the queen herself," Meg explained.

"We hoped their maid would handle the stained shirt," Kathleen interjected. "I get the feeling she's a bit more lenient."

"Probably knows what it's like to be on the receiving end of their wrath," Deirdre stated. "Go on."

"Unfortunately, it was Mrs. Hoffrey herself who examined the shirt. She found nothing until she turned it inside out. When she came to the stain on the cuff, she actually smiled."

"First time I've ever seen that," Kathleen mused. "Not a nice smile, either, though she was happy in a way."

"Happy to have finally found a flaw," Meg continued. "'Ah-hah! What's this?' Meg mimicked her. "And she shoved the shirt so close to my face I thought she would punch me with it in her hand."

"'Tis true, Mam. She came so close to Meg's face, she had to step back and nearly knocked me over."

"Then the daughters started in," Kathleen continued. "'What is it? What did you find? Let me see.' They were all so excited, as if they'd won some grand prize."

Deirdre snorted.

"Why are they like that, Mam?" Kathleen asked.

"Lass, there are some people in this world who are simply not happy until they can find fault with another. It makes them feel superior."

"Seems a shameful way to live."

"It is, Kathleen. Be grateful you're not one of them. So what did you tell them?"

"The truth, Mam," Meg said. "I simply explained what happened. I said I did my best to remove the spot. That I got out all I could." Meg sighed. "Apparently, I should have stopped there."

"What do you mean?" asked Deirdre.

"I went on to say that the stain was so small and I got to it with the water so quickly that it never had time to penetrate the fabric. It's only on the underside, which no one sees."

"That's when Mrs. Hoffrey said the worst thing I could imagine." Kathleen blinked hard to staunch the tears.

"And what might that have been?" Deirdre's own eyes narrowed.

"She said, 'No one may see it, but we'll know it's there,'" Meg returned to mimicking the tone of her arrogant customer. "There's blood on the inside of this shirt. It's almost worse than a stain on the outside. This is my husband's shirt and Mr. Hoffrey shall not go about with blood, tainted Irish blood, touching his own person. Not ever! This shirt is ruined beyond repair. The cost of it will come out of your wages."

Deirdre's face looked as though a thundercloud had settled upon it, but she pressed her lips together and said nothing.

"She also told us we'd better be more careful in the future if we don't want to lose business," Kathleen finished.

"I see," said Deirdre. "How much food were you able to get all told?" She held out her hand for the food sack. Kathleen reluctantly handed it over.

Deirdre emptied the contents on the table. "Why is there a handful ripped from this bread?" she asked, picking up the loaf in question.

Meg looked at Kathleen whose gaze had dropped to the floor. "I did that, Mam. I'm sorry." Kathleen's words came out in a hoarse whisper. Meg held her breath wondering how much Kathleen would tell and what their mother's reaction would be. "I was overcome with—"

"Don't worry, lass," Deirdre said, reaching out to pat Kathleen's hand. "I understand how hungry you must have been."

Kathleen looked up. She and Meg exchanged glances, surprise registering on both their faces.

"Just know, Kathleen," Deirdre went on, "we have to ration carefully now. Since you've already eaten some, you'll be allotted a smaller portion for supper." She squeezed her daughter's hand.

Meg looked at Kathleen, but saw only relief on her face. *You'll be hungrier than ever tonight*, she thought. *I hope you're smart enough to blame Kevin Dooley for it.*

The cottage door opened and Brigid entered still carrying the piglet in her arms, the sow following behind her. "Mam, can I go to the Quinns when Meg takes their share of the food over? Loreena and I want to play babies with the piglets."

"Come here, lass," Deirdre said. "And put the pig down. I've something serious to tell you."

Deirdre put one hand on either of Brigid's shoulders. "Look at me, now. I want your full attention."

Meg watched as the child went rigid.

"Do you remember when you pricked your finger and got blood on the shirt Meg was mending?"

Brigid nodded.

"The people who owned the shirt saw the stain. They were very angry. They felt the shirt was ruined so they docked our pay for the price of the shirt."

Brigid swallowed hard. "But the whole shirt wasn't ruined. Meg said so herself." She glanced at Meg. "She got most of it out and said it wouldn't even show, that they probably wouldn't even notice it." Her face scrunched up as she finished talking.

"But they did notice," Deirdre continued. "And they were very displeased."

"But it's not fair," Brigid's words spilled out along with her tears.

"No, it's not. But there's nothing we can do about that. We work for them, which means we have to meet their standards, fair or not. Else we'll lose customers. When that happens we lose pay, which means we haven't money to buy much food. This year more than ever we have to rely on paying customers as we've no potato crop."

Brigid sobbed so hard, she collapsed into her mother's arms. Deirdre held her close, cradling the girl on her lap. "I know it was an accident. But you're old enough now to help with the mending work. I'm sorry you don't like it, but life is full of things we don't like. It's time you got serious about learning to sew properly, with no carelessness."

Deirdre tilted Brigid's chin so that she looked directly into her face. She wiped away her child's tears. "This is no game we're playing, lass. This is our survival."

Chapter Eight

Father O'Malley wiped the dirt from his hands. The graveside service concluded, he walked, heavyhearted, behind Nan and Owen Rooney as they returned to their cottage.

"Biddy was such a good lass. What'll we do without her?" Nan asked as they entered a cottage so small it could barely contain them. Father O'Malley had to stoop to prevent scraping his head along the ceiling. Nan collapsed by the cold fireplace, the child she'd been carrying settling into her lap.

"Life will go on," said Owen. Father O'Malley watched as Owen went through the motions of tossing peat into the neglected fireplace. In moments it sparked. Owen stared at the flames.

"There's not much one can say at a time like this," Father O'Malley acknowledged. "Except that for Biddy all suffering is over. She is with God now."

"Aye, Father. I believe it's so," Nan agreed. "But there's an ache in my heart that hurts more than I can say." Tears streamed from her eyes. "Am I sinning for wishing she was still here rather than with God?" Her voice was a raspy whisper.

"No, Nan," Father O'Malley, squatting behind her, patted her shoulder. "It makes you a loving mother who misses her dear child. God does not expect you not to mourn."

Nan's tears continued to flow as her body heaved with sorrow. She held James tightly to her chest, resting her head upon his. The usually active four-year-old remained oddly quiet as if sensing something profoundly amiss with his parents.

"She gathered bark from the trees for supper," Owen said, never looking away from the fire. "She had but ten years. What child should be doing that?" Owen threw another clod of peat into the fire making sparks fly. "Didn't even eat her full share just so she could give a little extra to her brother."

Father O'Malley remembered the guilty expression upon the lass's face when he'd surprised her as though she thought he might be angry that she had eaten some of the bark. His felt a stab in his heart at the memory.

"The child has earned a glorious place in heaven, to be certain," Father O'Malley assured them.

Nan nodded through her tears, rocking James in her arms.

The boy's face, pressed against his mother's chest, was turned towards Father O'Malley. His large eyes seemed to silently question the priest. "You've got another dear one here," he said.

"May God allow us to keep him," Owen whispered.

Nan's face crumpled. She held the child tighter. At first her mouth was a craggy oval emitting no sound until a deep intake of breath was followed by an air rending howl. Father O'Malley traced the Sign of the Cross on James's head, praying a blessing over him.

Father O'Malley stayed the afternoon with the Rooneys. He prayed for them, aloud at times, but mostly silently as he, too stared into the fire. He wondered what God's plan could be that included the starvation of a ten-year-old child and the agony of the family who'd lost her.

It is beyond my human understanding, he prayed, *but I know that Your thoughts are above our thoughts and Your ways above our ways. We are but journeyers trying to find our way.* "Give us unending trust in you, Lord."

Father O'Malley was startled when Owen and Nan responded, "Amen." He hadn't realized he'd spoken the last words aloud.

As he prepared to leave, Owen accompanied him to the door. Stepping outside with the priest, he said, "Father, pray for us, please."

"Of course, Owen. All three of you are surely in my prayers."

"Four," Owen corrected.

Father O'Malley placed a hand on Owen's shoulder. "Of course, I will pray for Biddy's soul. But you needn't worry. A child so young and innocent. Besides, she'd been to confession just a few days ago. You can be sure the Lord has brought her straight to Him."

"Father, I believe she's watching over us from Heaven this very minute. 'Tis the new one I mean."

"New one?"

"Nan's to have another. She's due in March, though I fear she'll lose it. She hasn't enough to feed herself. How can she nourish a new life as well?"

Father O'Malley's hand tightened on Owen's shoulder. The announcement of a new baby on the way should be a moment of joy, but today it brought only anguish.

"I will pray for you. All four," he stated. "If it is God's will that this new one enter His world, then somehow it will be. It is in God's hands. Pray, Owen. Pray and trust."

* * *

Once back in his cottage for the evening, Father O'Malley found himself staring into his own fireplace, still wondering at the ineffable mystery of God's plan.

Well, Siobhan, you are on the other side. What do you know of why things unfold as they do?

All was silent but the crackling of the flames.

Not talking tonight?

He heard her familiar voice in his head. *"'Twould be easier to make a squirrel understand how a bow pulled across a fiddle's strings creates music than to make a living human understand the tapestry of life being woven by God."*

"So you've seen the whole tapestry? You're privy to it all from your vantage point? I envy you."

"There are still things God alone knows. It unfolds over eternity."

"In the meantime, what am I to say to a family like the Rooney's?"

69

"Just what you did. Pray and trust."

* * *

Father O'Malley knocked at the door of the Kilpatrick cottage the next morning.

Father, a pleasure to see you," Rose Kilpatrick welcomed him. "What brings you to us?"

"Making my rounds of the parish. I meant to stop by yesterday, but was unable. I spent most of the day with the Rooneys. When I left them, I hadn't the heart to do other than go home. I thought it would be better to come today."

"Poor little lass," Rose said, shaking her head. She kissed the cheek of her own toddler, riding her hip.

"You're looking well, all things considered," said Father O'Malley. "I'm glad to see it. So many are suffering."

"We are in want, as well, but not so badly as most."

"Edwin still has a bit of bloom in his cheeks," Father O'Malley noted, lightly chucking the toddler's chin.

"That he does. We've been blessed with healthy children, praise the Lord. Please, Father, have a seat."

Before Father O'Malley could sit, the door opened. Rose's husband Dacey entered with their son, Nathan and daughter, Kate. The two children, arms piled with peat, greeted their priest then set their burdens down by the fireplace. "To what do we owe the honor?" asked Dacey.

"Just making my rounds. I like to know how my parishioners are faring. You all seem well, I'm happy to note."

"Well as can be, given the current circumstances. But then luck has always been with me." Dacey grinned as though he held a secret.

"Luck?" asked Father O'Malley.

"Aye, Father. Last year's crop was terrible for others, but mine held well. Not as well as in some years, but much better than most. Even now I've still got potatoes left from last year as well as the few from this year that I took before the blight destroyed them."

70

"Still? Everyone else has run out."

"That's what I'm saying. Everyone I know has gone through whatever they had left. We're rationing, mind you, but we're making do, faring better than others hereabouts. There's cheese and oatmeal enough as well. Did ye notice there's still a few chickens strutting about the yard? Katie, lass," he turned to his daughter, "bring that bin and show it to Father."

Kate carried a small container to the priest. Inside were nearly a dozen eggs.

"You see," Dacey's eyes twinkled. "You needn't worry about us. This year's crop's a lost cause, but we'll make it."

"Let's put that back now," Rose murmured to Kate. She busied herself with the three children around the fireplace.

"How do you manage when others can't?" asked Father O'Malley.

"Partly, I'm just devilish lucky. My crop comes up good every year even when others fail." He shrugged. "Except this year, of course. No one escaped this year's blight. But I'll wager this time next year, even if the others are still going to mush, mine will be back to right. It's happened before. I can't explain it except to say I seem to have a magic touch." His eyes twinkled.

"That's the luck part," Dacey continued. He leaned closer to Father O'Malley as if imparting information of great importance. "The other part is in the knowing how." He tapped his forefinger against his temple.

"And what is that?" asked Father O'Malley.

"Being smart about what you have." He announced, straightening up to his full height. "Everyone is forever giving away to someone in need what they ought to keep for themselves. If they weren't so stupid they'd have plenty more than they do. Instead they hand over to their neighbors any extra food they get and look where it leaves them. You won't catch me making that mistake."

Dacey's stinginess was well-known throughout the parish, but this was the first time Father O'Malley had

71

heard him speak so. The self-congratulatory tone irritated him.

"Dacey, did you ever think that others give, not out of stupidity, but out of love? The love that Christ wishes us to share with one another."

"And what's it getting them, Father? A ticket to heaven, perhaps, but a miserable existence on earth." He snorted and crossed his arms over his chest.

"It may not be as miserable as you think."

"Truly? Didn't I hear that just yesterday you buried a young lass who starved to death? You tell me she hadn't a miserable existence, nor do her parents?"

From behind Dacey, Father O'Malley saw Rose look up. Her eyes met his, then darted away.

The muscles in Father O'Malley's jaws clenched. "And you tell me you would willingly turn your back on a starving child when there is something you could do to help?"

"Look over there, Father." Dacey pointed to his wife and three children. "I've mouths of my own to feed. I'd never let my own wife or children starve if I could help it. But I place them first. I'm sorry the lass died, but I've got to take care of my own. If I was to give away to every family in need I'd soon find my own in the same straights. Then what kind of husband or father would I be?" Dacey threw his head back, jutting out his chin.

"One who set an example of good Christian charity."

"Bah!" Waving a hand, Dacey turned away.

Father O'Malley felt fiery indignation rise in his cheeks. Dacey had joined his family at the chimney, leaving him standing to stare at the other man's back. Rose came towards him, a look of distress on her face.

"Father, before you go, would you be so kind as to hear my confession?" she asked.

"Of course," he said, trying to keep the residual anger from his voice. "Shall we step outside?"

In the chill air, Rose made the Sign of the Cross. "I've been disobedient as a wife," she began.

"How so?"

"Dacey doesn't know it, but I've given food away."
She stared at the ground. "Not a lot. I can't give much or
he'd know. And I daren't let the children know either for
fear they'll slip and tell him. Besides I don't want to teach
them to lie to their father nor to keep secrets from him."

"Go on."

"It is as you said, Father. Our Lord commanded us to
feed the hungry, clothe the naked, give drink to those who
thirst. I cannot disobey the command of our Lord so I give
what I can get away with. Yet I keep it secret from Dacey
because I know he'd never allow it. I know I'm going
against him, but how do I choose between obeying my
husband and obeying God?"

"Which do you believe it is more important to obey?"
he asked.

"I know it is God." Then she shook her head. "But I
also know that a wife is supposed to be obedient to her
husband."

"You are a good woman, Rose. Yet you find yourself
in a conflict not of your own making."

"Father, there is so much I don't understand. I don't
know why our crops always seem to fare better than others.
I don't know why God has blessed us in so many ways. It
makes me feel guilty."

"There's no need to feel guilty about God's blessings,
Rose."

"There is if they are not shared."

"But you are sharing them as best you can. And even if
your husband does not, you can pray for him. Perhaps it
will be your prayers that bring him 'round."

"Do you think God is testing me, Father?"

"In what way?"

"To see if I will obey. If I'll choose the right form of
obedience. To see if I am worthy of His blessings." She
shook her head. "I don't know which test it is, let alone
how to pass it."

"Rose, I don't believe God puts us to tests."

She looked askance. "You don't?"

"No. I believe we find ourselves in situations. Sometimes they arise from the choices we make. Sometimes they are not of our own making at all. But whatever brings them about, I believe God walks with us through them. God is there to love us through it all, not to test or to punish."

Rose's brow furrowed. "That is a very different way of thinking than I've heard before."

"It comes from my own prayer and experience."

"It gives me much to ponder."

"Ponder it in prayer, Rose. Talk to Jesus about your thoughts and conflicts. Let Him lead you."

"I will, Father. Thank you."

"And don't forget to pray for Dacey. He needs your prayers more than he can imagine."

"Will you pray for him, too? I know you are angry with him right now, but he's a good man. Really he is, though it may not seem so. He loves me and the children. He'd give his very life for us if he had to. 'Tis why I feel so guilty for going against his wishes."

"I understand, Rose," Father O'Malley told her. "I will pray for him to be sure and for you. Dacey simply needs something to soften his heart. Keep praying and it will come."

* * *

After leaving the Kilpatrick cottage, Father O'Malley fell victim, as he often did, to ruminating as he walked. Lost in thought, he had little notion where his feet were taking him. He was nearly to the outskirts of his parish's territory when laughter broke through his reverie. He knocked upon the Hoolihans' door.

"*Fáilte, a Athair O'Malley!*" Adam Hoolihan said, swinging the door wide. "Rejoice with us!"

"What's the occasion?" Father O'Malley asked, entering the small, nearly barren room.

"We've eggs for supper and a loaf of bread and oatmeal!" Corrine Hoolihan danced a few steps of a jig.

"Mam's funny!" laughed one of the many children crowding the cottage.

Father O'Malley's smile disappeared as Corrine swayed. She grabbed the back of a chair with one hand, as the other went to her forehead. The two men rushed to her. Each of them taking an arm, they lowered her into the chair.

"Corrine?" Adam asked, squatting, his worried face close to hers. "Are you alright?"

"Aye," she said, her voice breathless. "That was foolish of me."

She lifted her hand slightly to look at her priest from beneath it. *"Ní mór duit smaoineamh dÚsachtach dom."*

"No, I don't think you're mad," he chuckled realizing the woman was more embarrassed than endangered. "Except, perhaps, mad with joy."

She let her hand drop to her lap. "I couldn't help myself. It's been three days since I've eaten. I'm a bit lightheaded, is all."

"A sudden bounty is enough to make anyone dance," Father O'Malley said.

"I was good at it once, Father." She smiled at the recollection.

"Aye, she was," Adam agreed. "Mixed her legs the best of anyone at a moondance." Caressing her hair, he added, "But she'd only dance with me."

Corrine took his hand and laid it against her cheek. "There's no one else I wished to dance with. Then or ever."

Father O'Malley beamed at them. Adam and Corrine held a special place in his heart. They'd been the first couple he wed upon arriving in Kelegeen. He rejoiced in witnessing love still strong these many years and five children later.

"It was silly of me," Corrine said. Her easy smile back in place. "I should remember my age. I'm not a lass at a moondance anymore. Those days are long past," she laughed.

"You could dance again and best 'em all, I say." Adam held out a chair for Father O'Malley and drew up the stool next to his wife for himself.

"Go on with ye, now." She playfully shoved his shoulder.

"What brings you to us, Father?" Adam asked.

"Just doing my rounds. Checking to see how my parish families are faring."

"Not well for many, I'll wager," Adam said, his tone serious.

Father O'Malley shook his head. "I buried a child yesterday."

"Biddy Rooney," Corrine said, as a little girl climbed into her lap. "Poor lass. My heart aches for Nan and Owen. I'll go see them soon. Tomorrow, perhaps."

"It's a long walk from here," Father O'Malley observed. The Hoolihan cottage nearly bordered the neighboring parish, St. Timothy's, of Clonmalloy. "Are you sure you have the strength for it?"

"I'll manage," she asserted. "I'll set aside some of the bread and eggs to take with me."

Father O'Malley looked at the roomful of children. "Will you have enough?"

"Sheer luck's what got it for us today," Adam explained. "So why not share our windfall?"

"How did you come about it?"

"I was checking on my cousin, Rodney, in Clonmalloy early this morning. Three families nearby to them had been wiped out with sickness. There was still some food left in their cottages so Rodney helped himself. He supposed it couldn't be thievery seeing as how no one was left alive in the cottages to eat it. It would have been a bigger sin to let it go to waste. He gave some to me." Father O'Malley took Adam's earnest tone as hope that he wouldn't see it as ill-gotten gain.

"I'm sure those families would have wanted others to have it," he assured him.

"Not luck, Adam." Corrine corrected him. "We can't think of the death of anyone as lucky. I see it as a blessing from God. A blessing that they suffer no more, but have gone to God and a blessing that the food has gone to feed us who are hungry." She looked at the children playing on the cottage floor. Rocking the little one in her lap, she added, "That's why it's only right we share with the Rooneys. We've been blessed and so we pass on the blessing to someone else in need. It's what God wants, isn't it, Father?"

"Indeed it is. But I worry about you making such a long walk. If you like, I can bring the food to them for you."

Corrine smiled. "Thank you Father, but I'll go myself. That mother has just buried a child. She'll want another woman to cry with." She leaned toward the priest. "That may be as important as the food."

"Father, will you stay with us for supper?" Adam asked.

"Very kind of you, but I've a long walk home and I'd like to get a few more visits in on my way."

"Aye, then, take some food with you." Corrine set down the child. She scooped some oatmeal into a small pottery vessel, added two eggs atop it and set the lid.

Overwhelmed by their generosity, Father O'Malley, hardly knew what to say. "I couldn't possibly—" he began.

"Nonsense. You'll need a meal after the long walk you've had today."

"I have some provisions at home. I couldn't possibly take this from you. You've so many mouths to feed."

"So we'll give more to them and take less for ourselves," Adam explained.

Father O'Malley, held out his hands in protest.

"If not for yourself, then give it to someone you meet along the way. Surely, there are plenty of souls who need it even more than we." Corrine thrust the lidded vessel into his hands.

"Are you sure?" he asked, looking at the wide-eyed children.

"Father, they have to learn to share their blessings, too."

77

Father O'Malley could only imagine what Dacey Kilpatrick would make of the Hoolihans. "I will take it for someone in need, then," he said. "And I thank you on their behalf."

* * *

Dusk was descending when Father O'Malley heard a scraping sound. He was nearly two-thirds of the way home in an area with few cottages, mostly rugged hillside. In the gloaming he could just make out a bent figure.

"What are you doing?" he asked.

Startled, the man dropped the broken side of a cart he'd been dragging. "Just getting this debris out of the way 'tis all...Oh, it be you, Father," Larry Donnelly breathed a heavy sigh once he made out the form of Father O'Malley in the diminishing light.

"Where are you going with that, Larry?" he asked.

Larry looked in each direction before answering. "You'll not breathe a word?"

"Of course not."

Larry's gaze continued to dart in various directions. He leaned in close. "I'm building a *scalpeen*."

"Whatever for? You've got a cottage."

"For now. But I can't pay the rent. Come Gale Day I fear it'll be gone."

"What happened to your pig?"

"Died. Starved like the rest of us are doing. We ate what was left of it, not that there was much. Now there's nothing to sell for rent money. We'll be evicted for certain."

"Is there no way your landlord will give you an extension?"

"What would be the use? I'll never come up with the money."

"You could appeal to his mercy long enough to let you stay through the winter. Perhaps by May Gale Day you'll have enough."

"And then I'd owe two times the rent when I can't even make one."

"You are in a bind," Father O'Malley acknowledged wishing he had the money to pay Larry's rent.

"I am. And I'm not waiting to have my cottage set alight to find other shelter. I figure if I work on it a bit each evening, no one will see and it'll be ready when we need to move in."

"Where are you building?"

"Come. I'll show you."

Father O'Malley helped Larry haul the broken side of the cart further around the hill until they came to the abandoned and burned out cottage. Not much more than a hole in the hillside was left, but Larry had been using odds and ends to extend what still existed of three walls.

"If you could give me a hand, Father, I'd be grateful. I'd like to get this cart side up top. I need to build up the roof a bit."

Father O'Malley set down the small pot of oatmeal and eggs. Together they hoisted the large piece of wood, laying it so that it rested flat against the edges of the walls.

"I'll need more than that for a roof, but it'll do for now. I don't know what they'll do when they evict us. Knock down the cottage or burn it. I'm hoping for a knocking down. It's more likely I can return to salvage some of the parts once the constable's men have gone."

"It'll be a tight squeeze for five in here," Father O'Malley observed.

"Could have been seven. The Lord does dole out His blessing in an odd fashion."

Larry's wife had died in childbirth along with the baby last winter. The poor man was raising four children on his own.

"Not that I mind helping you, Larry, but may I ask where your sons are? Your two oldest should be big enough to help."

"I've sent them all into town to beg in the wild hope we can scrape together enough money for the rent. It means saving any money they get rather than buying food with it.

I remind them we'll need a roof over our heads come winter. I'm doubtful they'll get enough for the rent, though. That's why I'm preparing a shelter for when the cottage is gone. There's no way to build a fire inside so the tight quarters will keep us warm."

"If you're saving all your money for rent, what are you eating now?"

"Whatever we can scrounge. We're close to out of all we saved from last year. Neighbors share what they can from time to time."

"Do you have more to bring here tonight?" Father O'Malley asked.

"It's too dark now. Can't see what I'm doing."

Indeed as they'd talked dusk had shifted to dark. They made their way to Larry's cottage. Inside the four boys sat near the peat fire.

"Home safe and sound, I see," said Larry, his grimy hand tousling the blond hair of one child's head. "Any luck?"

The oldest held out his hand in which lay a few coins.

Larry sighed. "Put it with the others."

The boy deposited the coins into a clay jar. Judging from the paltry amount, Father O'Malley guessed the jar's contents might buy a meal for the family. By Gale Day they could have enough for two meals if they were lucky. They certainly would not pay the rent.

"Have you anything for supper tonight?" he asked them.

The boys stared into the fire. "No, Father," said the oldest in a voice just above a whisper.

"We ate a bit yesterday. So we can't again tonight," another said.

"If we don't make rent, we'll use the money to buy food once we've moved into the *scalpeen*," Larry explained. He glanced at the coins in the jar. "I'm glad we're nearing Gale Day. By then we'll know what we're about. It's the waiting it out that's the hardest part. I look in that jar and wonder why we're even trying. But if there's any chance we can keep a decent roof over us, at least

80

through the winter, I don't want to lose it. I wish I knew if I was doing the right thing. What do you think, Father?"

Father O'Malley remembered Denis O'Connor's words when he decided to dig up what few good potatoes he had rather than return them to the ground. He glanced at the jar. "You'll need much more than that to pay the rent. With Gale Day only a few weeks away, I don't think you'll make it."

Larry looked at the ceiling, around at the four walls, then to his boys seated by the fire. He squeezed his chin with his hand, started to say something, then stopped, letting out a long hiss of breath.

Father O'Malley put a hand on his shoulder. "It's a tough decision, Larry. I understand your desire to do all you can to save your home. Yet you can survive in a *scalpeen* if need be. You cannot survive without food. On the other hand, Gale Day is only a few weeks away. I suppose if you want to wait it out and see if you can scrape together the money…"

Larry threw his hands in the air. "I don't know what to do."

"Perhaps if you gave the landlord however much money you have by Gale Day and promised to keep working at getting the rest?"

Larry's eyes narrowed. "You don't know Ernest Chambers well, do ye, Father?"

Father O'Malley shook his head.

"*Mac soith*, he is!"

Father O'Malley cleared his throat. "In that case, I suggest you eat and make the best *scalpeen* possible. I'm glad I'll know where to find you."

He handed Larry the clay pot Corinne had given him. "Meanwhile, eat this tonight."

After blessing the family, Father O'Malley left the cottage, making his way home by the light of the moon.

Chapter Nine

November's Gale Day dawned sunny and cold. Father O'Malley roamed the fairgrounds. He had no need to pay rent as his cottage was supplied by the Church, but he always kept a careful watch over his parishioners. In his pocket he carried the letter he'd written for Denis and Thomas. Walking among the gathering crowds, he felt a tap on his shoulder.

"Glad we found you, Father."

"Ah, Denis. Thomas. I was looking for you. Any idea if your landlord is here?"

"We took care of selling our pigs and paying the rent first off," Denis answered. "'Twas only Blackburn we saw."

"I asked him if Stokes was around," Thomas continued. "He said, 'no' and asked why we wanted to know. I told him 'just curious' but he looked at me odd."

"'He made sure to remind us that we do all our business through him before we left," Denis added. "I don't think he's going to take kindly to us going directly to Stokes about the indenture."

"If Stokes isn't here, the only other option is to see if we can find out his address and post the letter. Do you still want to do it?" Father O'Malley asked.

"We've been discussing that matter," Denis said. "It seems we're at an impasse. I feel that we've aroused Blackburn's suspicions. If we go directly to Stokes now, assuming the letter even gets to him, Blackburn will find out. Even if Stokes has a mind to give us indenture, Blackburn will influence him against us. Either way, he'd make our lives miserable."

Thomas shook his head, sighing heavily.

"You feel differently, Thomas?" Father O'Malley asked.

"I don't disagree about how Blackburn will react, but if we don't send the letter, we'll have no chance for indenture. I say it's worth the risk. If Stokes says 'no' we're in no worse position than we are now. If he says 'yes' Blackburn might not like it, but there's nothing he can do about it. Stokes is his boss."

Denis turned towards his friend. He ran the palm of his hand up the center of his own forehead. "But Blackburn is here, all the time. Stokes never is. Even if we get indenture, Blackburn will be after us. Right now he leaves us alone for the most part. I'd just as soon that didn't change. If I thought the chance of Stokes agreeing to indenture was a good one, I might consider it worth the risk, but I don't."

"But Denis, it's our only hope. It's a risk I'm willing to take to help my family. Don't you see that?"

Denis shook his head and stared at the sky. "You see what I mean, Father? An impasse."

"I do see."

"Father, what is your opinion?" asked Thomas.

"There's sense in what you both say. However, I think it imprudent to arouse Mr. Blackburn's ire. Denis is probably right about the poor likelihood of Stokes agreeing to change your terms to indenture. Given what Blackburn said about doing all your business through him, if you send that letter now and he finds out, well…"

"I believe we've a right to speak our grievances or make requests directly to our landlord," said Thomas, his hands balled into fists. "We've done as we're supposed to by asking Blackburn first. Not being satisfied with the answer, it should be our right to make our request directly to Stokes himself."

"I'm not disagreeing with that, Thomas." Father O'Malley looked at both men. Their brows were furrowed, jaws clenched. Denis stood with one hand across his body, holding his elbow as he rubbed his chin with the other hand. Thomas's fists were on his hips. He swayed slightly back and forth. It was like the potato digging all over again.

"I'll tell you what," said, Father O'Malley. "I'll ask around and see if I can find out where to send this letter. Someone must know."

"Blackburn knows," Thomas muttered.

"Well, we damn well can't ask him!" Denis exploded. Then with a quick glance at his priest, "Sorry, Father."

Father O'Malley waved off the apology. "My proposal is this. I'll try to find out Stokes's address without arousing suspicion. Neither of you had better ask anyone. If that got back to Blackburn it would be all over. Meanwhile, both of you think very carefully about how you want to proceed. If I manage to get an address, we'll talk again about what to do. If I don't, it's a moot point anyway. Are we agreed?"

Both men nodded.

"Good. I'll let you know what I find out."

* * *

While Denis and Thomas were busy making the rent payment, their wives and children strolled the fairgrounds on their own. Meg walked beside her mother. She noticed Deirdre rubbing her fingers, then fidgeting with her shawl as if she didn't know what to do with her own hands.

"Mam, you seem worried. What's wrong?" Meg asked.

Deirdre glanced at her. "Nothing, lass," she said then looked away.

"Mam, that pig ate better than the rest of us put together. She'll sell. We'll make the rent."

"Aye. That's not what I'm worried about."

"So you are worried. What is it?"

Deirdre looked Meg in the eye. "I wouldn't burden my children with such cares, but since you're to be married soon, maybe it's best you hear it. You'll be involved in these matters soon enough."

Pride and trepidation created an odd mix in Meg. She inclined her head towards her mother as she walked, giving Deirdre her full attention.

"Your da and Thomas had Father O'Malley write a letter to Mr. Stokes about changing us over to indenture.

84

Since Blackburn has already denied the request, they can't give the letter to him to pass on. Father O'Malley hoped Stokes might be here today so they can hand deliver it, maybe even speak to him privately."

Kathleen and Brigid walked a few steps behind. Meg kept her voice low so that the conversation remained between her mother and herself. "What will they do if he's not here?" she asked.

"Then they'll have to decide whether or not to send the letter. And that depends upon finding out where exactly Stokes lives."

Meg nodded. Despite the gravity of the situation, she felt a pleasant sensation at being included in the details of adult life.

"Brendan! *Táimid thar anseo!*" Brigid's voice called to her brother.

Meg and Deirdre looked up.

"English only, child!" Deirdre admonished. "Remember where we are."

Brendan had gone with his father to sell the pig and pay the rent. "He'll know if Stokes is here," Deirdre whispered to Meg.

"The rent's paid." Brendan said once he caught up to them. "We're set until May."

"That's a relief," said Deirdre. "Where's your da now?"

"He and Mr. Quinn went to find Father O'Malley."

"Who took the rent money?" Deirdre asked.

Brendan looked puzzled. "Mr. Blackburn, of course."

"Was no one else with him?"

"No. But Aiden's da asked him if Mr. Stokes was here."

"What did he say?" Meg felt her mother's hand grip her own.

"He said 'no'. Then he told them to remember they do all their business through him. He seemed angry. What do you suppose that was all about, Mam?"

Deirdre's grip slackened, her hand sliding off Meg's. "It only means he's annoyed at having to be here."

85

"I'm sorry," Meg whispered.

"No more than expected." Deirdre's shoulders sagged.

Kathleen tugged on Meg's arm. Meg fell back into step with her at the same time Kathleen prodded Brigid forward to walk with their mother and Brendan.

"Have you seen him?" Kathleen asked, bobbing up and down on her toes, looking this way and that.

"I suppose you mean Kevin Dooley. No, I haven't seen him and I'm not looking."

"He must be here. I'm sure he must have come with his da to pay the rent. He's got to be around somewhere."

Deirdre turned back. "Don't forget to look for possible customers…Kathleen, what are you doing?"

Kathleen's attention snapped to her mother. "Looking for customers."

Deirdre eyed her daughter, cocking an eyebrow before turning back.

"I wonder how Rory's faring," Meg said. "He told me he was going to bring his tools and some wood so he can demonstrate his work as well as set out his finished pieces."

"That seems a likely one," Deirdre said, indicating a well-dressed young couple crossing the field. "Kathleen, give me the sample."

Kathleen handed the finely mended skirt she'd been holding to her mother who hurried off toward the couple, Brigid tagging along behind.

"I'm going to go find Da," Brendan announced.

"Kathleen, why can't you give up on Kevin? Even if he does ask to court you, Mam and Da will never allow it."

"Don't you think they'll come around? Da helped repair the *curragh* so he knows Kevin is doing his best."

"Da would help anyone who asked. He didn't do it because he thinks highly of the Dooleys."

Kathleen stamped her foot. "It's all because of Kevin's da's drinking and that's not fair! It isn't Kevin's fault his da's a drunkard and it doesn't mean he'll be one. Why won't anyone give him a chance?"

"It's more than just his da. Kevin's rude. He cheats Aiden, his best friend, from his rightful amount of fish. He rarely lets Brendan fish with them and when he does he's mean to him."

"He's just teasing. He doesn't mean anything by it."

"He makes fun of Rory's carvings," Meg continued.

"That's the real reason you don't like him. That and the fact that everyone is so set on my marrying Aiden, which I promise you will never happen."

"Truthfully, I never cared for Kevin since long before Rory started selling his carvings, but his jealousy over Rory's success is one more flaw to count against him."

"Lasses," Deirdre said, returning a bit breathless. "I think we've got ourselves a new customer. That lady I spoke with is a Mrs. Hammond. She's new in town and looking for someone to do mending work. She asked for references. I gave her the names of our best customers."

"Not the Hoffreys, I hope," Meg said.

Deirdre put her hands on her hips. "Do I look like a blithering fool to you, Megeen?" she asked.

"No, Mam." Meg laughed.

"She lives on Fownes street, two doors down from the Altons. You're to go to her house three days from now. That gives her time to check our references. She'll give you mending work to bring home."

"What's going on over there?" Brigid asked pointing to a small crowd gathered across the field.

As they approached, Meg heard Rory's voice coming from within the knot of people. "Does that suit?" he asked someone in the crowd.

"It's lovely," she heard the voice of a young lady proclaim.

"How much for it?" This voice, a young man's.

Meg was on her tiptoes trying to see over the crowd, but it was impossible. A moment later the small throng parted and a young couple emerged, the woman carrying a trinket box with a butterfly carved in relief on its lid. She slid one finger along the delicate wings as she walked. The gentleman whose arm was linked with hers wore a self-satisfied smile. Meg hoped he was pleased at making his lady happy rather than for cheating Rory out of a fair price.

Before the hole in the crowd closed completely, Meg squirmed her way in. Rory sat at a small table. He'd set out his few carving tools and wood blocks of all sizes. Meg saw no finished products, so assumed he'd sold them all. Instead the table was covered with square and round box bottoms. The wood blocks were waiting to become lids.

"What next?" Rory called out. He'd been spending every free moment practicing and could now carve even the fancy pieces much more quickly. The better he got at it the more people seemed to enjoy watching him work. Once he'd realized that, he'd decided on not only selling, but demonstrating at Gale Day, taking orders on the spot.

"Can you make a heart?" asked a young lady.

"Hearts are easy. Do you want a round or square box?" He pointed to the different shapes on the table.

She picked up a medium sized round receptacle and handed it to him.

Meg maneuvered her way to the front of his table. He looked up, smiled and winked. Picking up a wood block, Rory quickly measured the size, carved it to fit the box then went to work. Meg's eyes never left his hands as she watched the graceful curves of a heart emerge. She followed the trail of his knife as he coaxed the rounded shoulders and pointed tip from the wood. She thought of the two hearts mingled with the roses on her comb and imagined his hands carving them. Finished, he set the top on the box and handed it to the young woman.

She smiled her appreciation. "Is it the same price as the butterfly?"

"Better not be," said the gruff looking man next to her before Rory could answer.

"Oh, Papa, please. It's so lovely. I do so want it."

The man scowled at Rory. "You said yourself, hearts are easy. If that's the case it should cost less than the butterfly. Didn't even take you half the time to make. Here's what I'll give you. Take it or leave it." The man held out a coin.

The crowd was silent. Meg knew Rory had little notion of the worth of coins. She herself had only a rudimentary

88

understanding from payment for her mending work. This was Rory's first foray into the world of commerce. Neither of them knew what a truly fair price would be for the box, but looking at the coin, she believed it was far too small a sum. Hold out for more she wanted to tell him. The girl wants it, she'll beg her papa. She willed Rory to look up at her so she could shake her head 'no' ever so slightly, but his eyes were fixed on the coin, his hands starting and stopping in its direction.

"Come on boy. Take it or leave it," the man said.

Rory bit his lower lip. He shook his head.

"That's it, Annabelle, put it back on the table. If the rabble thinks he's too good for what I give him, that's his problem."

"No, no, Papa, please. It's so pretty and was made just for me. I want it, Papa. Please!"

"I said, 'no'." The man took the box from her hands and slammed it on the table. Turning her by the shoulder he ushered the crying girl away from the crowd.

Rory looked at Meg. She gave him a resolute nod. A look of relief washed over his face. "There's a box for sale for a fair price," he said pointing to the box the man had left on the table. "Does anyone want to buy it?"

"I do," said a young man. He passed two coins to Rory. Meg looked at them. It was more than the first man had offered. "It's yours then, fine sir. Now then, what else can I make? Can anyone give me a real challenge?"

People came and went from his table. "I'll be in town with more stock near Christmas," he reminded customers and onlookers. "Lots of animal toys for the wee ones and pretty boxes for your favorite lasses. Look for me in town.

Meg stayed the rest of the afternoon at his table. Rory carved until he ran out of wood. "I'm so proud of you!" Meg beamed as Rory packed up his tools. "You're going to be a great success."

"Look, Meg." Rory held open a pouch filled with coins. "How much do you think I've got here?"

"I'm not sure. I can try to count it when we get home, but I might not get it perfectly right." Meg glanced around.

"Close up that bag now and hold tight to it. There be thieves aplenty around here."

"Here comes one now." Rory nodded his head towards Kevin and Aiden who were making their way towards them.

"Why do you say that?" Meg asked. "Is it because he cheats Aiden out of some of his fish?"

"Some of them? The last time they went fishing, Aiden caught twice as many fish as Kevin, but came home with less than half what he caught."

"And what was Kevin's excuse for that?"

"He said Aiden caused him to lose his own. That he'd tipped the boat or some such nonsense. He keeps coming up with ways to take more fish from Aiden than he catches himself. Lazy bloke. He just wants Aiden to do the work while he takes all the fish."

"Why does Aiden let him get away with it?"

Rory shrugged. "Kevin's bossed him around since they were born. Aiden's too easy going for his own good. He also thinks that if he doesn't agree with Kevin he won't get to fish with him at all and then he'll have no food to bring home. I keep telling him Kevin won't get rid of him because he's not about to do all the work himself, but Aiden keeps on with him. Friendship, I guess."

"Some friend." Meg grimaced as Kevin strode up, Aiden following a step or two behind.

Kevin threw his arm over Rory's neck. "How did the selling go? Ladies all swoon over your fancy work?" Meg wanted to scratch the smirk off Kevin's face. What, she wondered, does Kathleen see in him?

Rory removed Kevin's arm. "It went quite nicely, thank you," he said. "Aiden, where's Da?"

"He and Meg's da went off to find Father O'Malley after we paid the rent. I haven't seen him since."

"And you, Kevin?" Meg couldn't resist. "Did your da get the rent paid?"

Kevin bowed slightly in her direction. "I took care of that myself."

"Oh?" she asked. "Your da still feeling poorly?"

90

"As a matter of fact, he is," anger began to creep into Kevin's tone.

"Come Aiden, let's go find Da. It's about time we got home," Rory said. "Meg where are your Mam and sisters?"

Meg looked around. Once she'd realized it was Rory the crowd was watching she'd forgotten about the others. Now she wondered what had become of them.

"We saw Kathleen just a wee bit ago, didn't we, Aiden?" The smile that returned to Kevin's face made Meg's stomach knot.

"Where?" she asked.

"Oh, around," he gestured to the fairgrounds in no particular direction.

"She was alone?"

"Aye. And we had a lovely conversation."

"About what?" Meg asked, eying him closely.

"Oh, this and that."

Meg looked at Aiden.

"It was nothing," Aiden told her. "Just barely said good day, when your Mam came up and hurried her off."

Meg relaxed.

The smirk returned to Kevin's face. "Too bad for you," he said, giving Aiden's shoulder a shove. "I'm sure you wished she'd stuck around."

Aiden blushed, but said nothing.

"Sorry, lad," said Kevin with a laugh. "But I seem to be the one that lass has eyes for."

"A pity for her," Rory muttered.

The smile slid from Kevin's face. His eyes narrowed as he looked from Rory to Meg. "At least one lass in your family has good taste," he said.

"Indeed she does," said Rory, grinning. "And I thank you for complimenting the good taste of my darlin' Megeen." With that he turned his back on Kevin. "I'm going to find Da, Aiden. You'd best come along," he said as he and Meg walked away.

Shortly, they noticed Thomas, Denis, Deirdre and Father O'Malley knotted together in earnest conversation.

Kathleen, Brendan, and Brigid were seated on the ground nearby.

"What's that all about?" Aiden asked motioning towards the group.

"I think I know," Rory stated. "Aiden, go keep Kathleen company."

"Don't mind if I do," he said, hurrying over to join the trio.

"I do wish Kathleen would love Aiden," Meg said.

"If only we could keep Kevin away, Aiden might have a chance," Rory suggested.

"How do we do that? Aiden and Kevin are always together."

"Not in the evening. This will keep us in food for a bit." Rory shook his money pouch. "You'll all come to share with us. And Kevin Dooley will be nowhere in sight." Rory tossed the money pouch in the air.

"Be careful!"

"Don't worry, Meg. I'll not let a single coin get away from me."

They neared the group of adults.

"I suppose they're trying to decide whether to send the letter to Mr. Stokes," Meg said.

Rory looked surprised. "You know?"

"Aye. Mam explained it all to me this morning." Meg hoped her tone sounded matter-of-fact. It was difficult to keep the pride from her voice.

Rory smiled at her. "Let's find out."

"Are you absolutely certain you want to do this, Thomas?" Father O'Malley asked.

"Aye, Father. I know you don't agree, but you'll send it along just the same?"

"What's going on?" Rory asked as he and Meg joined the group.

"Father O'Malley has found where to send the letter," Thomas explained. "Denis wants his name removed from it, but I'm of a mind to send it."

"Blackburn is already suspicious," Denis interjected. "He'll be furious if he finds we've gone to Stokes after he's already denied our request."

"And I say we've a right to do so," Thomas stated.

"A right, aye. But what we don't have is influence. Blackburn does. He'll poison Stokes against us easy enough. To him we're nothing more than names on a paper. Blackburn can tell him anything. I'm set to leave well enough alone."

Meg looked from her Da to her Mam. For the first time she noticed the lines around their eyes and mouths created by years of struggle and worry. Those lines seemed to deepen before her eyes.

"And I say we've nothing to lose," Thomas retorted. "No letter means no indenture. Perhaps Stokes won't like that Blackburn made that important a decision without consulting him. Perhaps he'll even remove him from his post."

"Oh, now you're dreaming, my friend. I'll tell you what will happen. Stokes will deny indenture. He'll ask Blackburn why he didn't take care of this matter. Blackburn will be pissed as all hell at us and the rest of our lives will be more miserable than they already are. I'm having no part of it."

Thomas slammed his folded arms across his chest. "You're a stubborn man, Denis O'Connor."

"I'm stubborn? You're the one who insists on following a foolish course because you can't bear to change your mind."

Thomas opened his mouth for a retort, but Father O'Malley held up his hand between them. "Now, now. Let's not have two good friends getting in a row. Here's my suggestion, for what it's worth. Denis if you're certain you want out of asking for indenture I will rewrite the letter so that it comes only from Thomas."

"Aye, Father. I have made up my mind to that."

"Fine." Father O'Malley turned to Thomas. "I will rewrite the letter from you only. But I want you to do me one favor."

"And what would that be, Father?"

"Talk it over with Anna," he glanced at Rory and Meg. "And Rory as well. Think over all the possible outcomes, good and bad. And sleep on it. In fact, give yourself a few days to mull it over. After that, if you're still determined on this course of action, I will post the letter for you. Can you agree to that, Thomas?"

Thomas let out a huge sigh. "I suppose."

"Good then. It's settled."

After bidding farewell to Father O'Malley, the two families headed off. Father O'Malley's inclusion of Rory in the coming discussion had not been lost on Meg. Despite hunger pangs and aching legs a swell of pride rose like a balloon inflating inside her, rising from her belly to her heart, then her head. A new, adult life seemed to be dawning on them. Troubles, worries, difficult decisions that lay ahead felt more like challenges to be met and conquered than hardships to be endured. She thought again of how she'd noticed the lines in the faces of her parents but quickly replaced the thought with one of herself and Rory heading a cottage of their own with wee ones around them.

"What are you thinking, Meg?" Rory asked. He and Meg hung back a little from the rest of the group as they walked home.

"Our future."

"I'm glad it makes you smile so."

Meg looked at Rory expecting to see her own feelings reflected in his face. Instead she saw that same tightening she had seen on the faces of the adults moments ago.

"What's wrong?" she asked.

"I think your da may be right about the letter, but I know my da won't back down once he's made up his mind about a thing."

"Won't he do as Father O'Malley asked?"

"Oh, aye. They'll be discussion aplenty. But it will be quite one-sided. That letter will be sent, no doubt about that."

"Will you try to talk him out of it?"

"I'll try, but I doubt it will do any good."

"Can it really cause much harm if it's sent?"

"I don't know for sure, but Father O'Malley certainly seemed to be against sending it. I trust his judgment."

"Don't your da trust it, too?"

"Normally. But when he's got hold of something it's like trying to take a bone from a snarling dog."

"Then we'll just have to pray that the letter does no harm. Perhaps Stokes won't even get it. Or if he does, he may just ignore it and Blackburn will never be the wiser."

"Perhaps."

Rory still looked worried. Meg wondered what, as a wife, she would do to ease his concern. Maybe changing the subject would help.

"You did well today, Rory. I knew your work would sell. Will you make other things besides toy animals and boxes?"

"I'd like to, but I'm not sure what to make. I don't know what the fancy ladies in town would like. You must see what they have when you go for mending work. What do you suggest?"

Meg reached into her pocket. "You could make more like this," she said holding the comb Rory carved for her.

"You have it with you?"

She smiled at him. "I'm never without it." She gazed at the comb in her hands, running her fingers lovingly over the hearts and roses. "Every time I look at it I remember the day you asked me to marry you." She returned the comb to her pocket. Looking up at him, her vision blurred with unshed tears, she said, "It's the most cherished thing I own."

Rory stopped walking and took her hands. "Meg," he spoke in a low voice, filled with emotion. "That comb is one of a kind, made only for you. It's the nicest thing I'll ever be able to give you. I'll not cheapen it by making copies for any other lass in the world."

As Meg gazed into his eyes, she felt cocooned in a tiny world of love that surrounded only her and Rory. It was only when Thomas's voice pierced the invisible bubble that she remembered they were not alone.

"Rory, are you listening? I said how did you do with your carvings?"

Meg and Rory turned toward the voice, realizing that the others had walked on ahead of them. They hurried to catch up.

"Extremely well, Da! I sold everything I brought and made more to order right there at the table."

"It was a good idea to demonstrate your talent," his father said.

"It would seem so. We should get food enough to hold us for a bit with this," he said, handing the money bag to his father.

"Appears a goodly amount. Well, done, lad." He clapped Rory on the shoulder.

Rory turned back to Meg. "If you need to, you and your sisters could sell the trinket boxes I made for you."

"You wouldn't mind?" Meg thought of the boxes Rory had made for each of the girls years ago. They weren't as intricate as the ones he made now, but they were nice enough to fetch a little money.

"Of course not. You need to eat. I can make new ones for you all sometime. Better than the ones you've got now."

An idea popped into Meg's mind. "You could make the small combs ladies wear in their hair."

Rory looked perplexed.

"Oh, of course you wouldn't have seen them," Meg laughed at her mistake. Rory had never been inside any of the fine homes in town. Any lady he saw would be out and, therefore, wearing a bonnet. "They're like regular combs, but much smaller. They're used to hold stray hair in place."

"You don't wear them."

"I'm not a fine lady."

"Finer than any other," he said, giving her a quick peck on the cheek.

"I'll ask to borrow one from a customer so you can see what they're like."

Rory smiled at her. "We do make a fine team!"

Chapter Ten

Resting his pen on the table, Father O'Malley looked up at Thomas Quinn sitting across from him.

"You're certain about this, Thomas?"

"Aye, Father."

"You know I strongly advise against it."

"I do." Thomas's hands fidgeted. "I appreciate your concern."

Father O'Malley drew a long breath, leaned back in his chair, taking the measure of the man who seemed to vacillate between indignant determination and misgiving.

"Denis changed his mind after Gale Day, understanding that if Blackburn gets wind of this, which he is bound to, he will make your lives miserable. Does that not worry you?"

Thomas's fingertips drummed the tabletop. "It does."

"Anna and Rory have grave reservations about this course of action."

"I know."

"Yet you are still determined?"

Thomas inhaled loudly, his lips folded tightly. "I am."

Father O'Malley rubbed a hand across his forehead. "Why, Thomas? When everyone else sees the danger in it, why do you persist?"

"Father, I can't...I don't..." Closing his eyes, he pressed his fingertips over his eyelids. "It is difficult to explain," he said, dropping his hands to his lap. "I was wrong about the potatoes."

"What has that to do with it? No one was sure what to do. Besides, it made little difference in the end."

"True enough, but that's not the point. I am the head of my family and I failed them. Now my lads are the ones keeping us going, Rory with his carving and Aiden with whatever fish he can bring home."

"So your pride is hurt?"

Thomas looked away. "I suppose you may see it that way."

"Thomas, everyone is doing what they can to get by. The O'Connor women are doing the most for that family at the moment. There's no shame in your lads helping the family. It shows you've raised them to be industrious."

Thomas turned back to the priest. "Don't misunderstand, Father. I'm proud of my lads. I could not ask for better. But I need to take the lead. I can't sit idly by while my children carry the burden. I've got to do something. This is the one thing I can do that might bring us a measure of security. I know it's a straw I'm grasping at, but I can't rest unless I've done everything possible. With indenture we can't be so easily thrown off the land. I've got to keep a roof over our heads somehow. Far from ideal it may be, but it's the best way I know of right now."

"In the end it may lead to greater misery," Father O'Malley said, keeping his voice gentle.

Thomas lowered his head. "All I'm doing, Father, is respectfully asking the landlord for a slight change in our situation. Granted, he'll probably say no. But if he says 'yes' it will give us just a slight edge that could make the difference in the end."

The look of desperate hope in Thomas's face, a hope so unfounded, so unlikely to be realized, but so deeply desired was painful to observe.

"Yet if Blackburn hears of it, and surely he will—"

"I've heard enough of Blackburn!" Thomas's fist slammed the table. "He hears or he doesn't. He gets angry or he doesn't. What can he do about it in the end? If Stokes says 'yes', he's no choice but to go along. And if he says 'no' he can say to me 'I told you so' and that should be an end to it."

Should be, but probably won't, thought Father O'Malley, though he knew voicing any more objections was useless.

"I will ask one last time. Are you absolutely certain you want me to post this letter?"

Thomas straightened in his chair. "I am."

"And you won't take even a day or two more to think it over?"

"I've thought it over till my head aches. There's nothing going to change my mind."

Father O'Malley sighed. "I will post it for you then, but I must tell you I don't feel right about it. I'm afraid it will come back to haunt you."

"Father, you're doing only what I, of my own free will, have asked. I will not hold you responsible for any bad outcome, but I will thank you heartily for any good."

"I thank you for that, Thomas," said Father O'Malley, who did not feel in the least alleviated of responsibility. "And I will pray mightily for a positive outcome."

Father O'Malley saw Thomas out, then returned to the table, the letter before him. He had worded it carefully, making sure to commend Blackburn on his fairness as an agent. He hoped that would mollify the man if the letter fell into his hands. Father O'Malley sighed heavily. He believed no good would come of it, yet what could he do? Thomas was a grown man with a right to decide for himself about what he thought best. Still, Father O'Malley knew that if anything bad happened he would feel partly responsible. Yet there was nothing to do now, but post the letter. He might as well get it over with.

* * *

After returning from town, Father O'Malley headed for the *scalpeen* where Larry Donnelly and his four boys were holed up. Larry had been right. He had not made rent, had been evicted and his home torn down. He had, as he'd hoped, been able to salvage a few pieces of the cottage, but only a few as the constable's men had done a thorough job. The *scalpeen* was barely big enough to house the five of them. Once all were inside, there was little room to move.

"Larry! It's me!" Father O'Malley called as he neared the *scalpeen*. Larry, he knew, lived in fear of being found by the authorities and forced to move on as he was occupying land he neither owned nor rented.

A head poked out from around the corner. Larry had deftly covered the sides with rock and vegetation. Unless standing directly in front of the open end, the *scalpeen* appeared nothing more than a natural outgrowth in the hillside.

"Father, it's good you've come. I was thinking of sending one of the lads for you."

"Is something wrong?"

"Aye. Sean is sick," Larry caught Father O'Malley's arm as he came around the corner.

He stood in front of the *scalpeen* with Larry looking at the four boys huddled close to ward off the early December chill. One boy, the youngest, did not appear cold. His cheeks flamed red.

"He's the look of fever," Father O'Malley observed.

"He's burning up, Father. I don't know what to do."

"How long has he been like that?"

"Three days now."

"Three days! It's a wonder the others don't have it, too."

Larry walked Father O'Malley away from the *scalpeen*.

"I fear we'll all have it if we don't get Sean away from the others. But what to do with him? If we still had our cottage we'd put him at one end and the rest of us keep to the other, but here," he jerked his thumb at the scalpeen, "there is no one end and another." Larry wrung his red, chapped hands. "Can you get him some medicine, Father?"

Father O'Malley wondered how he might do that. "I'll ask for a doctor in town," he said.

"Don't bring a doctor out here!"

Father O'Malley placed his hand on the despairing man's arm. "I'll say I need it for a sick parishioner and hope he'll give it to me without insisting on making a visit. In any case, I'll bring no one here."

Larry breathed a sigh of relief.

"I will bless your family before I go." He started forward, but Larry caught his arm.

"I'm wondering, Father. I mean just thinking…"

"What is it, Larry?"

"Perhaps you should give Sean the Last Rites." He kicked at a stone, his eyes unable to meet Father O'Malley's. "You know," he whispered, "just in case."

"Of course," he said. "I don't have my holy oils with me. I will return with them tomorrow."

"Thank you, Father." His voice broke as he tried to hold back tears.

* * *

When Father O'Malley returned the next day, he found that two of the other boys were also in fever.

"They took ill during the night," Larry explained. "Perhaps you should give them the sacrament as well."

"Aye." Father O'Malley sighed. He could see what was coming for this family. It would be only a matter of time before the last boy and Larry himself were sick with fever. He felt helpless. When he left yesterday, he'd gone straight into town for a doctor. The only one he could find would give him nothing without seeing the patient first. Then he'd tried the apothecary, but found he hadn't enough money to pay. The apothecary, an Englishman, refused credit to a Catholic priest.

As there was nothing he could do for them physically, he did the only thing he could. He knelt beside the sick boys with his prayer book and holy oils. Closing his eyes, he prayed, silently, deeply, feeling a current of energy run through him. As he anointed each of them, he felt the heat burn his skin. He knew it would not be long before God took them all home.

* * *

Immediately following morning Mass, Father O'Malley made his way to the *scalpeen*. As he approached he called out, "Larry! It's me, Father O'Malley." No voice responded. No head poked out from around the side wall. Father O'Malley felt his heart sink. He braced himself for what he would find. Reaching the front of the *scalpeen* he stopped and stared, unable to move or speak. The five family members lay lined up side-by-side. Sean and his two brothers who had taken sick only yesterday were dead. On either end lay Larry and his oldest son, Daniel. They were alive, but barely. Daniel was so still Father O'Malley thought he was dead, too, until he noticed the barely perceptible rise and fall of his chest. Larry was twitching and mumbling delirium-filled nonsense.

"Oh, dear Lord in Heaven," Father O'Malley said when he finally found his voice. This time he had brought his Holy Oils with him, having decided he should no longer be without them. He gave the Last Rights to Larry and Daniel. He wanted to find the nearest neighbors to ask for help in burying the dead children, but he didn't dare risk exposing anyone else to the fever. So, one by one, he carried them out himself. It was a long, exhausting day as he dug the graves in the cemetery, the ground close to frozen, laid the bodies in and covered them. He offered the prayers for the dead and blessed the graves before he left for home just as evening began to descend.

Once back in the cottage, he collapsed on his bed, sound asleep almost instantly. The next morning dawned so quickly he felt he'd only slept minutes before he had to be up and ready for Mass. He wished he did not have to return to the *scalpeen*, but he knew he must. As he trudged through the hillside, he wondered how long it would be before the father and his only surviving son would be gone as well. He did not have to wait long. When he arrived, he found both Larry and Daniel had succumbed during the night. He made the lonely trek to the cemetery twice more. Every muscle was screaming from the previous day's exertion.

He had planned to see other parishioners today. It had been a few days since he'd made his rounds, but once he'd finished his lonely graveside service, exhaustion claimed him. He barely made it back to the cottage before collapsing again, not waking until the following dawn.

Chapter Eleven

The winter progressed dreary and cold. Many had run out of their meager provisions. The town became more crowded with beggars. It was a wonder they did not freeze to death so wretched was their attire, for many, little more than tattered rags. Bare or nearly bare feet were an agonizing mix of chilblains and frostbite. Funerals increased as many succumbed to the combination of starvation and hypothermia. Still, many others hung on, their hope for a good spring planting giving them the shred of strength to endure.

Rory had done well enough selling his carvings in the weeks just before Christmas. He was able to add the hair combs Meg had suggested. She had begged the help of her favorite and most loyal customer, Amanda Brick. She showed Mrs. Brick a few of Rory's carved boxes, one of which the lady promptly purchased as a gift for her niece. Then Meg explained about Rory's desire to make carved hair combs, but had no original to go on. She wondered if Mrs. Brick could spare one just long enough for Rory to use as a guide. "He's a quick learner. He won't need it long," she'd told her.

Meg sensed Mrs. Brick's hesitation. Hoping Rory would forgive her, she added, "If you'd be so kind as to loan it to him, he'll give you a hand carved one for free."

"I suppose that would be very nice of him," said Mrs. Brick. "But he's never made them before. Do you think he'll do a proper job?"

Meg pulled her own comb from her pocket. "He made this for me," she said, beaming with pride.

Mrs. Brick looked at the intricate carving on Meg's comb. "Oh, my. That's exquisite! Well, if he can do that, I suppose he can make a nice hair comb. Wait a moment and I'll get one for you."

"Thank you, Lord," Meg whispered as Mrs. Brick left her in the kitchen. She returned a moment later with a simple hair comb, obviously not one of her best, but good enough to give Rory the right idea.

Grateful for the prototype, Rory readily agreed to Meg's promise of a free hair comb for Mrs. Brick. By the time he was ready to take his wares into town for the holiday sales, he had several wooden hair combs, all with various carvings, along with his collection of trinket boxes and wooden animals.

By the time Christmas came, Rory had sold enough to keep the two families in sufficient food. No one's belly was ever full, but neither was it quite empty. Brendan continued to assist Rory with his sales in town. His allotted portion of the income enabled him to occasionally enter the O'Connor cottage with a small bag of food and a smile so big one would think he'd carried in a feast.

Meg and Kathleen had not been so fortunate with their mending. The Hoffreys did indeed talk about the blood stain on the shirt, no doubt exaggerating far beyond its real proportions. When Meg and Kathleen appeared on Mrs. Hammond's doorstep on the day she'd agreed upon with Deirdre, they were promptly told their services would not be needed. Fortunately, most of their customers knew the Hoffreys well enough to know they were magnifying the mistake. Still, they were given less mending work and the fine work that would have brought them more money suddenly disappeared.

Aiden continued to fish with Kevin, but as the weather grew colder, the waters became rough and the *curragh* more difficult to handle. Unlike men who'd had years of experience, the two lads found it nearly impossible to fish while keeping the *curragh* from capsizing. It was a constant battle that resulted in less fish each day. Aiden suggested giving up for the winter, but Kevin insisted they continue as it was the only food source for his family.

"I could throttle Aiden," Rory told Meg one day as they sat together in the Quinn cottage, Meg doing her mending work while Rory carved. "He knows that *curragh* is impossible to handle in the winter. He spends days out on the water and if he catches anything at all, most goes to Kevin because of Aiden's own foolishness in allowing himself to be cheated."

"Why doesn't he stop, then and wait until spring?"

"It's the only food the Dooleys can get so they want to keep going. It's foolhardy. They're not experienced enough to handle the *curragh* in this weather."

"Can't Aiden refuse to continue until better weather?"

"That's what he should have done, but he says he wants to learn the trade and become a real fisherman."

"How's he to do that without an experienced one to learn from?"

"If not for the drink, Kevin would have learned it well from his da by now. It's said he was quite good at it once."

"'Tis a shame," Meg said.

From the other side of the fireplace, Anna yawned loudly.

"Your Mam looks awfully tired," Meg observed.

"She's not sleeping well most nights."

"Why not?"

"Worry over that letter Da had Father O'Malley sent to the landlord. It was a mistake to send it, but it's been done, so I try not to dwell on it. For all we know it may never reach Stokes. Unless we learn otherwise, I see no need to borrow trouble."

"That seems wise." Meg smiled at him.

Rory smiled back. He glanced at his Mam sitting with Deirdre by the window, the two struggling to sew by the waning light.

"Your mam looks tired, too."

"She's not sleeping, either."

"What's keeping her up?"

"'Tis her feelings. She's having them more than ever lately." Meg had told Rory about her mam's feelings years ago.

"It must be a dreadful burden to live with," he said.

"Aye. She gets such a strong feeling come over her of something bad about to happen, yet she doesn't know what or when. But when they come on strong and often like they're doing now, whatever it is can't be far away."

"Does it frighten you?"

Meg shrugged. "I'm used to it after all these years, but it is uncommon disturbing to see her twitch in her sleep, then suddenly bolt upright, shaking and drenched in sweat. It pains me to see her so afflicted."

After a moment's pause, Rory asked, "Do you ever get those types of feelings?"

A smile played around her lips. "Rory Quinn, do you fear a wife with the gift of the sight?"

He chortled. "Perhaps a bit. You don't make it sound very pleasant."

"You needn't worry. I don't possess such a gift."

"Are you sure? Isn't that sort of thing passed down in families?"

"If I had the sight I would know it by now." Meg grew serious. "I'm glad I don't have it. 'Tis a heavy burden. I wonder about Brigid, though."

"Truly? You think she has it?"

"I'm not sure. I notice a difference about her sometimes, but it's hard to put into words."

"It may have skipped you, Megeen, but it could pop up in one of our bairns. Then what will you do?" Rory was smiling at her again, his tone teasing.

Meg smiled at the thought of the children she and Rory would have. "I'll love the little changeling no matter what."

"Changeling? Who said anything about changelings? We'd best not have one of those!" In his glee, Rory's voice had risen above hushed tones prompting their mothers to look up.

"What's this talk of changelings?" Deirdre asked.

"Nothing, Mam. We were just joking."

"'Tis nothing to joke of, Meg. Be careful what you say of your future wee ones. You'll not want to borrow trouble by speaking careless words."

"Aye, Mam." Meg knew her mother's nerves were on edge. She gave Rory a warning look. He nodded, returning his focus to his carvings.

107

The door opened with a rush of cold air. Aiden entered shivering, his clothes wet.

"What happened to you?" Rory asked.

Anna rose, quickly ushering her son towards the fire. "Warm yourself. You've taken a chill. How did you get so wet?"

"The *curragh* tipped over. We were doing well enough at first, even caught a fish apiece, but then the waters got rough and spilled us and the fish right out of the boat. We gave up then, dragged the *curragh* ashore and came home."

"Why didn't you go in and warm up by the Dooley's fire before walking all the way back soaked to the skin?" Anna asked.

"I did for a bit. But Kevin was in a bad mood after the boat tipped over and his Da was angry we returned empty-handed. He was roaring about Kevin being too stupid to know how to handle a *curragh*, saying by his age he could fish with the best of 'em and would never have let the boat tip over. Kevin was yelling back, his mam and sisters crying. I decided to get out and head for home."

"Sounds like a loving, peaceful home," Deirdre observed, pursing her lips and giving Kathleen a pointed look. Kathleen bristled, but said nothing.

"We'll try again tomorrow," Aiden stated.

"You will not," Anna admonished. "Didn't today teach you anything?"

"Aye, Mam. It taught us we need to keep practicing until we can manage the *curragh* in any weather."

Aiden looked directly at Kathleen. "I mean to become an expert fisherman, whatever it takes. Potato crops may fail, but there are always fish in the sea. If I can learn the fishing trade, I'll be able to support a family well enough someday."

Kathleen glanced at Aiden, then back at her sewing. "I'm sure whatever lass marries you will be very lucky," she said, her tone flat. Then she looked directly at Aiden, her voice warming. "As will the lass who marries Kevin, seeing as how he's doing the same. Especially since he's the one who owns the *curragh* and, apparently, has the ability to be in charge."

Aiden hung his head and leaned toward the fire.

Meg's heart broke for Aiden, who looked as though he was fighting to hold back tears.

"It's getting too dark to see anymore," Deirdre announced. "It's time we headed home."

Gathering up their mending work, the O'Connor women took their leave of the Quinn cottage. Deirdre laid into Kathleen within a few steps outside the door. "Whatever possessed you to be so rude? I'm ashamed of your behavior."

"I'm sorry, Mam, but I feel 'tis better for Aiden to rid himself of the idea of courting me. It is never going to happen and the sooner he accepts it, the better. If he wants to find a lass to marry, he should start looking elsewhere."

"You needn't have been so hurtful about it. He does have feelings."

"So do I. Does no one ever remember that?"

"You are being selfish, Kathleen."

"How is it selfish to refuse to force myself to love someone I simply don't? Isn't it better to be honest about it rather than lead him on?"

"There are kinder ways. You'll regret your cruel words one day."

"I'm glad I said what I did. I hope it puts an end to any thought Aiden has of me ever being his wife."

Meg had been quiet, listening to the discussion between her mother and sister. Finally she asked, "Kathleen, what makes you dislike Aiden so?"

Kathleen stopped and turned on Meg. "How many times do I have to say it? I don't dislike Aiden. I'm quite fond of him, but as a brother, not a lover." White puffs of breath accompanied her words as they poured forth in the winter evening. "Why is that so hard for everyone to understand?"

"You say that, but your treatment of him is hardly sisterly. You act more as if you don't like him and actually want to hurt him."

"That's not true!" Kathleen stamped her foot. She turned towards home. Picking up her pace, she reached the cottage several steps ahead of Meg and Deirdre.

"How did you manage?" Deirdre asked Brigid as they entered. Since Brigid's sewing skills showed little sign of improvement, Deirdre had set her to cooking instead. It was now Brigid's job to prepare the meager meals while the others sewed.

"I think it's done right," Brigid answered.

"Well, there's not much to it," Deirdre said, leaning over her shoulder to peer into the cooking pot where chopped turnips simmered. Half a loaf of bread and a chunk of cheese were cut into pieces and set on the table.

"They seem soft enough to mash," Brigid said, taking the pot from the fire.

"Be careful draining them, lass. Don't lose any turnip along with the water."

* * *

Kathleen said nothing the rest of the night. She ate in silence, then went to sleep. No mention was made of the incident in the Quinn cottage, but Meg could tell that her mother was deeply disturbed. Late in the night Meg awoke to the sound of her mother thrashing about. She looked across the room in time to see Deirdre sit bolt upright, her form outlined in the dimming peat fire.

"No! It can't be! It can't be!" Deirdre yelled.

Everyone was awake now. Denis sat up and put his arms around his wife. "It's all right," he crooned. "It's just a bad dream."

"No. No. No." Deirdre put her face in her hands. Her body shook as she sobbed.

Meg crawled across the floor to her mother. This was the worst she'd ever seen her. The others sat up, too, but stayed in their spots, held there by fear.

110

"Mam, what is it?" Meg asked. She and Denis held Deirdre on either side as she rocked back and forth, crying hysterically.

"Mam, what is it?" Meg repeated. "Did you have a dream?"

Deirdre held her hands out to each of them. "It's bad, Meg, very bad."

"What is?" asked Denis.

"I don't know what exactly. That's the worst part of the feeling. Not knowing why I'm so afraid. I just know it's coming. Coming soon."

"What's coming?"

"Something bad." Deirdre turned her head to look at one face then the other.

"Mam, do you remember what you dreamed?"

"I felt a violent rocking, like being thrown about in a whirlwind. Then I couldn't breathe. There was pain, too. Pain in my hands, in my head. Cold. Icy cold. And so much darkness. I was sunk in darkness where there was no air and no way out."

"Is this what you've been dreaming every night?" Denis asked.

"Some nights I've felt the pain. Some nights the suffocation. Some nights the darkness. Each time they've awoken me with a terrible feeling of something bad to come. But this was the first time all those feelings have come at once and so strong. Oh, Denis, something is coming and it's going to be bad." Deirdre had her back to Meg as she gripped her husband's shoulders, whispering her fearful words close to his face. Meg could barely make out her father's face in the dim glow of the firelight. His shadowy features appeared distorted with fear making Meg's heart lurch in her chest. *'Tis only a trick of the firelight*, Meg told herself. They got her mother settled down again. Meg crawled back to her own spot, but it was a long while before sleep reclaimed her. Meg believed in her mother's feelings. She had never known them to be wrong. She had also never known them to be as overpowering as what she had witnessed this night. Though

111

her da had thrown more peat on the fire to warm the cold cottage before settling back down, Meg felt chilled by something no fire could thaw. Something bad was indeed coming. She was as sure of it as was her mother. It was not knowing what that chilled her to the bone.

Chapter Twelve

"Feel that wind. It's picking up something terrible." Meg wrapped her shawl tightly around herself. She and Kathleen had returned the mending work, received their meager wages and purchased a small amount of food. On the way home they'd encountered Rory and Brendan returning from an unproductive day in which they failed to sell any carvings. "Too soon after the holidays," Rory surmised.

"Do you suppose Kevin and Aiden are having any luck?" Kathleen asked as the group walked in a huddle against the cold.

"Can't be worse than ours," Rory said. "Might as well go by the cove and see how they fare."

As they approached the rise beyond which lay the cove, the wind again whipped so hard their clothing flapped. They stood still, eyes shut against it. The water roared just beyond the rise.

"I hope they've pulled the *curragh* in," said Rory once the wind died down.

Cresting the hill they watched in horror as the roiling water tossed the light weight boat like a toy.

Kathleen gasped.

"Saints preserve us!" Meg crossed herself.

Two heads bobbed about in the icy waves as frozen hands attempted to right the flipped *curragh*. The water appeared to play a game with the boys, trying to keep the boat from them. Each time they got a grip on it, a wave would wrest it from their hands.

"Stay here," Rory commanded. He raced down the incline, dashing into the water.

"I'm coming, too." Brendan started after him, but Meg grabbed his arm.

"Let me go, Meg."

"You can't swim. You'll only be one more person to rescue.

"We should get help," Kathleen suggested. "The Dooleys are closest. Brendan, run and get Kevin's da."

Rain began to fall, quickly gathering intensity.

"Let's go to the water's edge," said Meg. "We might be able to help them when they get closer to shore."

The wind forced a halting descent down the incline. As they neared the shoreline, Kathleen noted, "They're not that far out. Surely, they'll make it back safely."

Meg wanted to agree, but the many jagged rocks in the cove, the rain, like spikes of ice now seeping into her shoes, and the wind lifting the *curragh* clear out of the water and slamming it back down discouraged any optimism. Suddenly, Meg's thoughts turned to her mother's fit of the previous night. She'd spoken of being tossed by a violent whirlwind, icy cold, darkness, inability to breathe. Oh God, Meg thought, this is it. This is what Mam was feeling.

"Leave the curragh! Save yourselves!" Meg called, her voice cut off by the wind and waves.

"Look!" Kathleen pointed. "Kevin's made it up onto a rock. Thanks be to God!"

"What's he doing?" Meg asked as she anxiously watched Kevin slip haphazardly from one rock to the next. Rory, immersed all but his head, shouted at Kevin.

"I don't know," Kathleen answered. "I can't hear what they're saying."

Kevin, moving as quickly as the treacherous waves and slippery rocks would allow headed away from the others, towards the shore.

Meg scanned the scene. "Where is Aiden? I don't see him."

Rory dove under the water, resurfacing with his brother in a tenuous grip.

"Rory's got him," Kathleen said. "If they just get up on the rocks, too, they can get back to shore." They watched as Rory tried to drag Aiden towards the nearest rock.

Another blast of wind arose. The *curragh* erupted from the water. Meg and Kathleen screamed as it slammed

114

heavily down upon Aiden, knocking him from Rory's grasp. Rory and the boat were pushed hard by the waves toward the nearest rock.

"What's happening? Where are they?" Kathleen gasped.

"Rory's by the rock. The *curragh's* in the way, but I can see part of him. I don't see Aiden, though.

"I wish Brendan would hurry back with Kevin's da. They need help." Kathleen's voice quavered.

Rory finally managed to push the *curragh* away. He stared downwards in an obvious search for his submerged brother. By now Kevin was nearly at the shoreline. Meg and Kathleen ran to meet him.

"Why did you leave them?" Meg demanded.

"I nearly drowned just now," he choked out. "I've a right to save my own skin."

"And leave Aiden to drown?" Meg was indignant.

"Oh, God help us, no!" Kathleen cried and crumpled to the ground.

Kevin and Meg turned to see Rory kneeling on a rock, dragging the lifeless form of his brother up after him.

Meg crossed herself. "Please, Lord, may he not be gone from us," she pleaded.

"What's wrong with Rory's arm?" Kathleen asked.

Rory struggled to drag Aiden along the rocks as the waves splashed over them. Both arms wrapped his brother's torso, but there was something unnatural in the way Rory maneuvered his right arm.

Meg turned to Kevin who stood dripping wet and shivering, staring out at them. A feeling as furious as the wind rose up inside her. "How dare you stand here and watch. Get back out there and help them this instant!"

"Are you mad? It's suicide to go back out there. I nearly drowned once. I'll not do it again. I'll catch my death of cold if I don't get home to the fireside and dry out as it is."

Meg felt her eyes narrow and her hands clench into fists. Despite the spray of icy water, her face felt on fire. "Well, it doesn't surprise me." Her voice was low, but intense. "You've cheated Aiden out of his rightful share of fish all along and now you're going to leave him, your best friend," she sneered these words, "and Rory to fend for themselves. You're nothing but a shiftless coward, Kevin Dooley, and not worth the space you take up on the earth." She spit in his face and shoved him. Exhausted and half frozen, he staggered back.

"You're crazy," he yelled, regaining his balance. "I told him we shouldn't go today, but he's the one who insisted we learn to handle the *curragh* in all kinds of weather."

Meg's shock must have registered on her face because Kevin continued, "That's right, it was his idea, not mine. He wanted to become an expert fisherman to win the hand of his dear, sweet Kathleen."

Meg's eyes met Kathleen's, who was still huddled on the ground.

"That's right," Kevin repeated. "It was all for her that this happened." He kicked some gravel in Kathleen's direction. "And I'll be damned if I'll go back out there and risk my neck again after he nearly got us both killed." Kevin pointed at the two figures. Rory lost his footing and slipped into the water. Aiden lay motionless on the rock.

Kevin turned away, bumping into Brendan who slid down the incline. Breathless, Brendan gasped that Kevin's da was passed out cold and he couldn't rouse him. Looking out at Rory struggling to regain the rock, he ran into the water shouting, "I'm going to help and you can't stop me, Meg."

This time she had no heart to try. Instead, Meg crouched next to her sister who rocked back and forth, her head in her hands, crying. She wrapped her arms around Kathleen, holding her tight while she watched Rory and Brendan painstakingly drag Aiden to shore.

Once they'd heaved Aiden's body far enough from the water so as not to be reclaimed by the waves, Rory collapsed face down on the ground. Brendan dropped in a heap on the other side of Aiden. Meg and Kathleen crawled the short distance to them.

"He's not dead, is he? Tell me he's not!" Kathleen's tortured pleadings were addressed to no one in particular. She shook Aiden's shoulders. "Wake up! Wake up, Aiden, please wake up." Kathleen dissolved in sobs, her head on Aiden's still chest.

"Rory, you're hurt." Meg hardly knew where to turn her attention. Kathleen was distraught, Brendan shivering as much from shock as cold, and Aiden, beyond anyone's help. It was the blood seeping from beneath Rory's body that grabbed her attention. She remembered the odd way he'd held his arm while dragging Aiden.

"Rory, turn over. Let me see your arm."

"I can't." Rory's back heaved as he drew in great gulps of air.

Meg started to roll him onto his left side.

"God! Careful," Rory grimaced as Meg pulled him onto his back.

"Sorry." Meg looked at Rory's right arm and gasped, unprepared for the sight of his hand. It was smashed to a bloody pulp. The cold water had prevented massive bleeding, but now the blood was beginning to flow.

"It happened when the *curragh* slammed down on Aiden," Rory said, grimacing as he inched himself up to sit. "It knocked Aiden out of my hands and smashed my hand against the rock."

Rory's face, drained of all color, frightened Meg. She glanced at Brendan and saw that he, too, was pale. He stared at the scene before him as though entranced. Kathleen continued to sob on Aiden's chest, oblivious to anything else.

"Brendan. Brendan!" Meg shook his arm. "I need your help."

Comprehension dawned in his eyes. "What am I to do?" he asked.

"Give me your coat, quick!"

As soon as he had the sodden garment removed, Meg wrapped the frigid bundle around Rory's hand, hoping it would staunch the flow of blood and keep the swelling at bay.

"Kathleen, up!" She commanded, gripping her sister by her shoulders. Kathleen stood, still crying while Meg pulled the shawl from her and wrapped it around Brendan.

"Help me get Rory's coat off him," she told Brendan. "Be careful of his hand."

With Rory's help, the two worked to ease off Rory's soaked coat. Removing her own shawl, Meg wrapped it around Rory's shoulders. "We've got to get you both home and dry before you freeze to death."

"What about Aiden?" Brendan asked.

Meg looked down at the body. "Trying to carry him will slow us down. We need to get home fast. Rory's hand must be attended to as soon as possible."

"But we can't leave him here." Brendan looked aghast at Meg.

"We've no choice. Help me drag him further from the water."

They moved the body to a sheltered spot just below the rise of the incline. Meg lay Rory's coat over Aiden's body. "We'll have to send Da and Mr. Quinn here to fetch him. Now let's go."

Brendan and Meg helped Rory to his feet. He swayed at first. It took both of them to hold him upright. Once he was reasonably steady, they began their ascent up the incline. Meg looked back to see Kathleen standing where she'd left her, staring at the ground where moments before Aiden's body had lain.

"Kathleen!" she called.

No response.

Meg scudded down the incline, grabbed Kathleen's face between her hands, forcing the girl to lock eyes with her. "We haven't time for this, Kathleen."

"Aiden's dead." The words fell flat from her mouth.

"I know," Meg said, her voice low. "If we don't get Rory and Brendan home, they will be, too."

Kathleen's gaze shifted beyond Meg to where the two lads waited.

"Let's go," Meg whispered. She tugged Kathleen's hands, pulling her along until they reached the others.

* * *

Exhausted and frozen, they fell in a knot before the O'Connor's fire.

"What's happened?" Deirdre asked. "Brendan, you're soaked. Where's your coat? And yours, Rory?"

Rory held up his hand with Brendan's coat wrapped around it.

"How did you get so wet?" asked Brigid, wide-eyed.

"There's been...an...an...accident," Meg stammered through chattering teeth.

"Brigid, get all the blankets. Quick!" Deirdre commanded. "Tell me, Meg, what happened?"

"Mam, where's Da?" Meg asked.

"At the Quinns." Deirdre worked quickly, replacing the shawls Meg had draped over the lads with the thin blankets. "Get closer to the fire, all of you. As close as you can get without catching. Rory, what's wrong with your hand?"

"Careful, Mam," Meg said as Deirdre began to unwind the frozen coat. "His hand is smashed. I did that to stop the bleeding."

"Holy Mother of God, help us!" Deirdre exclaimed. The worst of the bleeding had stopped, but his hand was swollen and badly misshapen. "How did this happen?"

"We stopped at the cove to see how Aiden and Kevin were faring," Brendan started.

"The cove? Those lads thought to fish on a day like this?"

Meg saw the recognition dawn in her mother's eyes at the same moment she fell to her knees. "'Tis the meaning of the feeling," Deirdre whispered. She looked at each face in turn. When she came to Rory, she wrapped one arm around his shoulders. "Rory, where is your brother?" she asked quietly. "Where is Aiden?"

Rory looked down at his hand. "On the shore," he whispered.

119

"Aiden drowned, Mam," Brendan told her. "Rory and I pulled him ashore, but we couldn't bring him home."

"I tried," Rory said. "The waves were so high. The wind blew the *curragh*. It hit him. Knocked him out of my hands. I couldn't hold onto him. I found him, but it was too late." The words tumbled out of Rory.

"Aiden is dead?" Brigid asked.

"Brigid, run to the Quinns immediately," Deirdre instructed. "Find your da and tell him privately what has happened. Then come right back. Don't tell another soul. Let your da take care of that. You mind me on that, understand?"

"Aye, Mam." Brigid ran from the cottage.

"We'll need to do something about this hand," Deirdre said. "I've never seen anything like it. The rest of your arm seems fine, though." She felt his arm, bending it, making sure it moved normally.

"Only my hand is damaged, but I think it's beyond repair."

"It's your right hand," Brendan observed. "How will you carve?"

"I think my carving days are over."

Tears stung Meg's eyes. As the fire began to thaw her frozen body, so it seemed to thaw her emotions as well. Suddenly, all that had happened crashed in on her. She put her head in her hands and cried great, heaving sobs.

"Meg, darlin', don't take on so." Meg felt her mother stroking her rounded back. "There's nothing can be done for it now. We'll take care of Rory's hand as best we can. Perhaps it's not as bad as it looks. And we'll pray poor Aiden's soul to heaven."

A wail filled the cottage. Its high pitch descended like demented music down the scale until it became a jumble of blubbering, unintelligible words.

"Kathleen, child!" Meg felt the rustle as her mother leaned towards Kathleen, keeping one hand on Meg's back.

"My fault...my fault." These were the only words Kathleen could utter.

"How could any of this be your fault?" Deirdre asked.

"Kevin said so."

"Kevin! And what of him?" Deirdre's voice turned from soothing to indignant. "Where was he in all this?"

"They were both in the water trying to right the *curragh* when we got there," Rory explained. "I went in to help."

Meg sat up. "Kevin climbed onto the rocks and made his way to shore. Left Rory to rescue Aiden all on his own."

"Fine job I did of it, too."

"Rory, it was not your fault," Meg said. "There was no more you could do. The wind. The waves. It was too much for anyone alone."

"And Brendan? You went in as well?" Deirdre asked.

"Aye. But first Meg sent me for Kevin's da. I couldn't rouse him so I came back. I ran in when I saw Rory trying to drag Aiden to shore, but by the time I got there, it was too late."

"And where is Kevin Dooley now?"

"He went home," said Kathleen. "Like a coward."

Meg glanced at her sister's tortured face. Before she could speak, the cottage door burst open.

"Where?" was all Thomas Quinn asked.

"The cove. Near the edge of the incline," Rory answered.

Thomas and Denis raced from the cottage. Anna joined the group at the fire. She wrapped Rory's hand in the bandages she'd brought while her tears fell to the floor, unable to speak for weeping. Brigid slipped silently into the group by the fire.

"Shouldn't someone go for Father O'Malley?" Meg asked.

"I'll go," Brendan offered.

"You'll do no such thing. You're frozen to the bone," Deirdre stated. "I'll go."

"Mam, it's cold and the wind is strong," Meg remonstrated.

"I've felt cold before, Megeen, and will again." She wrapped her shawl about her. "Anna, do your bairns know?"

Anna nodded. "The ones old enough to understand," she murmured.

"Shall I bring them here before I see Father?"

Anna looked at her friend. She shook her head, then said to Rory, "Come. We should be in our home when they bring...when they bring Aiden back." She waited a moment, eyes scrunched tight. Taking a deep breath, she rose and helped Rory to his feet.

"I'll walk back with you before I go for Father," Deirdre said, putting Rory between them, helping to hold him up.

"May we come, too?" Meg asked.

Deirdre looked to Anna who nodded her consent.

* * *

Both families crowded into the Quinn's cottage when Deirdre arrived with Father O'Malley. All but Anna were gathered near the fire.

"I'm so sorry, Anna. So very sorry." Father O'Malley enfolded her in his arms, feeling her body crumple against him.

"How am I to bear it, Father?" she whispered, her face scrunched in agony. He glanced from Anna to the body laid out on the table that had been pushed to the farthest end of the small cottage. Deirdre was already busying herself with preparing the body for burial.

He looked back to Anna. "It will be terrible hard to bear. I can't pretend otherwise. You and Thomas must lean on each. Your children will need to lean on you. And you all must lean on our Lord. Remember, Aiden is in the Lord's care now. There's no more suffering for him. Only perfect peace."

"Aye." Anna said. She forced herself to stand upright and turn to the table. "My son. My lad," she whispered, stroking the beloved face.

"Why don't you join the others at the fire, Father," Deirdre suggested. "We'll let you know when we're ready."

Father O'Malley sat near Meg and Rory. "How is your hand, Rory?"

"Useless."

"For now. Surely it will mend."

"If you looked under these bandages, you would not be so sure, Father. I'm afraid it's ruined forever."

The full impact of this hit Father O'Malley all at once. "But your carving," he stammered.

"Finished."

"Are you certain? Is it really as bad as that?"

With his good hand, Rory unwrapped the bandage. Father O'Malley felt the color drain from his face. "Dear God! You need more than a mere bandage. It should be properly set."

"And who is there to do it?"

"I'm no doctor, but I have a bit of knowledge. If you'll let me, I will do my best."

Meg leapt to her feet. "Tell me what to do, Father. I'll help."

Father O'Malley thought a moment. He felt the absence of all but the most rudimentary medical training he'd learned in the seminary. "I'll need something to hold the bones in place," he said. "It's important to keep them immobile as they heal."

"There's plenty of wood from my carving supplies," Rory offered.

"Look for flat pieces," the priest instructed Meg.

Father O'Malley picked through the wood pieces of various shapes and sizes Meg brought him, choosing the ones he hoped would work best. A groan escaped through Rory's gritted teeth as Father O'Malley straightened the lad's hand. Glancing up, the priest saw Rory's face had gone white. He used the wood to set the hand and had Meg hold it in place as he rewound the bandage.

"I can't promise anything, Rory. My medical training is next to nothing. 'Tis the best I can do, other than to pray for a miraculous healing."

"Thank you, Father. You've done a better job than anyone else here knew to do." The words were barely out when Rory began to sway. Father O'Malley and Meg jumped at the same time, catching him before he could hit the floor. The jolt of being grabbed revived him enough to take a cup of water from Meg's shaking hand.

Father O'Malley was not at all assured that his ministrations would help, but he hoped and prayed that he'd done some good.

"Father, we're ready." Deirdre's solemn voice called them all to attention. The group at the fire began to rise, ready to gather round Aiden's body. Meg and Kathleen picked up the sleeping babes, Brigid took Loreena's hand, and Rory, with his good hand, patted Aisling, who had been sitting at his feet crying silently. "Come on, lass," he said. Brendan helped her to her feet. As the group was rising, the cottage door opened, with much bumping and banging. Thomas and Denis entered carrying a plain pine coffin. Placing it on the floor, they laid Aiden's body in it, then lifted it onto the table. Father O'Malley realized Thomas must have used the money he was saving towards the next rent payment to purchase it. A little knot of worry formed in his stomach as he thought of the letter he still regretted sending to Thomas' landlord.

Father O'Malley closed his eyes, bringing his focus to the immediate spiritual needs of these families and to the sacred prayers they were about to commence. He began, "In the name of the Father, and of the Son, and of the Holy Ghost." He blessed the gathering as they crossed themselves. Opening his book, he began the prayers for the dead in quiet, solemn tones. Whimpers and the hiccups of barely suppressed weeping punctuated his words. Finishing, he closed his book. "Let us now pray together the words Our Lord taught us."

They got no further than "Our Father who art in heaven," when the door swung open, sending cold air blasting through the room. Blackburn was standing in their midst as if blown in on the riotous wind. He waved a letter high above his head.

"So, you thought to go behind my back, did you?" he bellowed. "Did you think I wouldn't find out? All correspondence comes through me before it goes to Stokes and if I don't like what I see, you can be sure he'll never see it!"

At first no one seemed to know what to do. Shocked faces simply stared at him. Father O'Malley recovered first. "My good man, please. This family has just lost a son. We're praying for his soul now. Can this not wait until a more appropriate time?"

Blackburn's eyes narrowed. "I suppose you're the one who wrote the letter? God knows this ignoramus can't write," he tossed his head in Thomas' direction.

"I did. If you wish to take that up with me I will be willing to speak with you on it, but not now. Please, sir, show some mercy. Can't you see what is going on here?" he gestured toward the coffin.

Blackburn staggered a few steps towards the group. The smell of whiskey permeated the small cottage. "Well, I'd say the Lord punishes those who do wrong and has seen fit to do so today." A satisfied smile played about his lips.

Thomas stepped between Blackburn and Aiden's coffin. His shaking voice remained low as he forced himself to remain steady. "I've to bury my boy in the morning, so I'll thank you to leave my home."

"Your home? Hah! It's no more your home than it is the Pope's."

Father O'Malley watched as Thomas' hands balled into fists. He moved to intervene. "Please. I understand you are upset," he indicated the letter Blackburn held crushed in his hand. "In a few days, perhaps, we can all sit down together and work this out. But for now, I ask you again, as a man of honor, to let this family grieve in peace."

Blackburn appeared about to say something, thought better of it and turned on his heel. Father O'Malley breathed a sigh of relief as he watched the angry man grab hold of the door latch. But his solace was short-lived.

Turning back, door latch still in hand, Blackburn sneered, "They'd better get used to it. They've more grief to come. More than they can imagine." With a scathing look at the group gathered round the coffin, Blackburn slammed the door behind him.

Chapter Thirteen

It did not escape Father O'Malley that Kevin had not attended Aiden's funeral. Nothing had been heard from the Dooley family since the accident. The priest could not help feeling a twinge of regret at not working harder to bring the Dooleys into the fold. He knew the family rarely attended Mass, that Colin Dooley was a drunkard, Noreen kind but simple-minded, the daughters much like their mother, and Kevin headed for trouble. He had meant to visit them more often, take an interest in their needs, try to shepherd them as best he could. But the few times he'd presented himself at the Dooley cottage, he had been treated disdainfully by Colin. Though Noreen was as hospitable as she knew how, she and her lasses were easily cowed. Colin made it clear that he'd no intention of returning to church, he much preferred his *poteen*, thank you, and his family was to remain at home seeing to his needs, not spending all of a Sunday coming and going to Mass.

Though Father O'Malley firmly believed that no one was beyond God's grace, he felt it would take a miracle to reach Colin, but Kevin might be another matter. As yet, he was not a drinker. Still, Father O'Malley feared that even if Kevin never took up the drink, he would go down some other path that would lead to his destruction. His whole personality seemed designed for it. Yet he was a bright enough lad. He didn't have to follow the wrong path. Now, after the accident that had taken the life of Kevin's best friend, his failure to so much as acknowledge the incident, nagged at Father O'Malley. He'd been told the whole story of Aiden's death including Kevin's failure to help save anyone but himself. He could only imagine what turmoil Kevin's conscience must be in.

He thought of what he might say as he walked toward the Dooleys. He'd waited two weeks after the funeral before coming to give Kevin some breathing room. He did not want to appear accusatory. As he neared the cottage, loud voices assaulted his ears.

"You're a stupid lout, ye are! There'd be fish to eat if you hadn't destroyed my *curragh*." Colin's voice rang out as Father O'Malley approached the cottage.

"I didn't destroy it. The storm did." Kevin's voice was almost as loud as his father's.

"The storm. Oh, the storm did it, eh?" Colin's tone became a mocking sing-song. "And who took the damn thing out in a storm? A stupid lout, that's who."

"'Twasn't me who wanted to go. I'd have stayed to shore. It was him who insisted."

"So besides stupid, you're spineless as well? Couldn't say 'no'?"

"I did, but he really wanted to learn to handle it even in bad weather. Besides, when we first went out it wasn't that bad." Kevin's voice turned plaintive, almost wheedling. "The wind came up of a sudden. By the time we realized we'd have to turn back we were too far out. Then the wave knocked us out of the boat and it all…all the rest just happened."

"So, then it's two stupid louts what took my *curragh* out and broke it. 'Tis a good thing the other is dead and gone, leaving one less stupid lout on the face of the earth."

"Colin!" Noreen gasped. "'Tis not right to speak ill of the dead."

"Who asked your opinion?" Colin roared.

"Da, don't touch her!"

Father O'Malley's fist banged hard on the door, knocking it open. "Pardon me," he said, striding into the tiny cottage, pretending surprise at the manner of his entrance. "I surely didn't mean to pound your door open."

Everyone in the cottage froze in mid-motion as they stared at the priest. Colin, unshaven, dirty and disheveled was obviously drunk. Noreen was rail thin, her eyes sunk into dark hollows. The two lasses huddled together in a corner. Kevin's lower lip was swollen, his eyes black and cheeks bruised. Some looked fresh while others appeared to be waning.

Noreen recovered first. "Welcome, Father. What brings you?"

"I came to see Kevin."

"Me? Why?"

"What's he done now?" Colin growled.

"He's done nothing except lose his best friend. It's a horrible thing to endure, a young lad's best mate dying so tragically. Wouldn't you agree, Colin?" He turned toward Kevin, not waiting for an answer. "It must be terrible hard on you, lad. I came to offer what comfort I can."

"He don't need no comforting. He needs to get busy finding another way to feed this family before we all starve to death now that he's gone and ruined my *curragh*."

"Oh?" Father O'Malley lifted a brow. "It seems to me that burden rests on the head of the family. Would that not be you, Colin? Or have you handed that title over to a lad not even wed yet?"

"I be the head of this family and no mistake!" Colin thumped a stubby finger against his chest. Then his voice lowered. "But I've been a bit under the weather of late. So I've charged my son with the duty of providing. Just until I'm feeling better, mind you, Father." His voice rose again as he glared at Kevin. "And since he takes his orders from me, that's what he'll do."

"I'm sorry to hear you're not well," Father O'Malley fought to keep his tone conciliatory. "What ails you?"

Blinking, Colin rocked on his feet. "My head," he said holding his hand atop his matted bushy hair. "It feels like a blacksmith's hammering away inside it."

"Sounds awful," said Father O'Malley.

"And my stomach. Feels like it's on fire, it does."

"I'm sorry to hear it."

"Then there's my back," Colin was warming to Father O'Malley's feigned sympathy. "It aches from morning to night. It's all up with me, Father. I don't know when I'll be my old self again."

"What did happen to your 'old self' Colin?" Father O'Malley asked. "If memory serves you were once one of the ablest fishermen in Kelegeen."

"'Tis right, I was." The specter of a smile played around Colin's mouth. "Why, the haul I could take in one day couldn't be matched by any."

"So I've heard."

"'Tis true!" Colin's eyes took on a dreamy look. "My da taught me. He was the best of his day, but I surpassed him. And that *curragh*. It was my pride and joy. Built it myself, I did. Handled it amazingly, if I do say so, no matter what weather was dished up." Coming back to the present, Colin glared at Kevin. "It's gone now, though. Destroyed by two useless lads, who couldn't handle a little sea breeze."

"A sad thing," Father O'Malley stated, shaking his head. "Poor lads. And this one," he put his hand on Kevin's shoulder, "trying so hard to learn the trade, wanting to be just like his da." He turned back to Colin. "But you having been ill for so long, you've had no chance to teach him so he had to try to learn as best he could on his own. It must be terrible for you to think of your da teaching you so well and wanting to do the same for your own lad as any good father would, but your sickness not allowing it. Why, you must ache for the plight of your one lad."

Colin looked down at his fidgeting hands. There was silence for some seconds. Then he mumbled, "I'd prefer not to think on it," as he swiped the *poteen* bottle from the table.

"Perhaps if you're so ill, you might not want to drink that. I've heard it can make a sickness worse." Father O'Malley kept his expression pleasant and his tone even.

"'Tis the best medicine I know," Colin growled. He took a swig from the bottle then turned his back on the priest, collapsing in a heap at one end of the cottage. "Don't anyone bother me," he ordered.

Father O'Malley turned toward Noreen, speaking just above a whisper. "How are you faring?"

Noreen shrugged. "We're hungry."

Father O'Malley gestured towards the two girls huddled in the corner. They hadn't spoken nor hardly moved, other than to look up in surprise at his abrupt entrance. "Are the lasses ill?"

Noreen shook her head. "They sit like that all the time."

"I should have brought something with me to offer you."

"You have food, Father?" Noreen's eyes widened.

"Not much, but there's a little I can spare." He looked at Kevin. "If this young lad would care to walk me back to my cottage, I could give him some to bring home."

"Aye. Go, Kevin." Noreen nearly pushed them out the door.

Once out in the daylight, Father O'Malley had a better view of Kevin's face. His earlier assessment had been correct. Some bruises, probably incurred during the boating accident, were fading but several were new, including the swollen lower lip and black eye.

"My boy, what's happened to you? You look as though you've taken up boxing."

Kevin put a hand to his face. "From the accident," he muttered.

"Some. But it's been over a fortnight since then. What of these new ones?"

Kevin turned his head away. They walked on in silence.

"What will you do now?" Father O'Malley asked as they rounded a bend.

"What do you mean?"

"Apparently, your da is counting on you to feed the family." Father O'Malley was unsuccessful at keeping a tone of disgust from slipping into his voice. Kevin glanced at him. He cleared his throat and continued, "So I wondered if you have a plan."

"Go into town, I suppose."

"And do what?"

"Beg."

131

Something in the way Kevin said the word, turning his head away, unable to meet Father O'Malley's eyes, jolted the priest. It was one word, but there was another behind it, unspoken. He wanted to stop walking, seize the lad by the shoulders and drill into him that a life of crime would destroy him completely, but he knew such a tactic was likely to have the opposite effect. Instead, he continued at the same pace, brisk enough to keep warm, slow enough to converse in reasonable comfort.

"There's many having to do the same these days. It's humbling, but it's not dishonest. Certainly, there's no sin in it."

Kevin rubbed his arms from the cold, but said nothing.

"We're almost there," Father O'Malley nodded toward his cottage. Once inside, he stoked the fire, offering Kevin a chance to warm up.

"Here, have a bite," said Father O'Malley, holding out a hunk of bread and cheese. Once he'd packed a small sack with the few bits of food he had, he sat next to Kevin.

"It must have been an awful thing for you, that accident."

Kevin stopped chewing, a string of spittle hanging from his swollen lip. He wiped it, winced and stared into the fire. "Aye."

"It wasn't your fault, you know."

"Tell that to my da." Kevin shoved a piece of cheese into his mouth. Tears sprang to his eyes, though whether from the pain of his lip or a deeper pain, Father O'Malley didn't know.

"Your da has a sickness, you know."

"So he says."

"I don't mean the physical ailments he claims. I mean the drink. He's chained himself to that bottle and lost the key. It becomes a sickness when it takes over a body like that."

Kevin's eyes narrowed as he stared into the fire. "I should feel sorry for him, then?"

"Would you want to live that way?"

"He chose it."

"No one chooses it. When a person lets drink replace their pain, it takes over little by little until he's become a slave to it." He leaned forward, clasping Kevin's shoulder. "It's a sad thing, but it doesn't mean you need to let his illness ruin your life."

For the first time, Kevin's eyes met Father O'Malley's. "How? He did this." Kevin pointed to his face.

"I know. I'm sorry."

"He blames me for the accident. For letting his *curragh*, which he hasn't used in years, get destroyed. He doesn't care that Aiden died. He wishes I'd died, too." The tears flowed freely now.

Father O'Malley hugged him. "No. That's not true."

"It is. He said so."

"If he said so, it was the drink talking, not him. Not the real him."

Kevin sat up, wiped the tears from his face. He looked more like a youth than a lad on the verge of manhood. "I wish we could have the real him back."

"Do you remember? Before he took to drink?"

Kevin nodded. "A bit. He'd take me fishing sometimes. He started to teach me. He'd tell me stories about the great catches he'd made. He was teaching me to wrestle, too." Kevin got a faraway look. "He was kind to Mam then. He was tough with me, but never mean. I loved him. I wanted to be just like him."

"And now?"

Kevin swallowed hard. "Now I hate him."

Father O'Malley shook his head. "Don't, Kevin. Love him. Pray for him. But don't be like him, at least not like he is now. Never take to the drink. You see what it does, how it changes a person."

Kevin nodded slightly.

"Is he violent often?"

"He used to just drink until he passed out. He'd bellow if someone annoyed him, but he didn't hit anyone. It wasn't until the day Mam hid his bottle."

"She was brave to do that."

133

"She was sick of him always being drunk. She'd asked him to stop, but he just screamed at her. So one day, she took all the *poteen* bottles out and dumped them. When Da found out, he was so pissed he smacked Mam in the face. Then he started hitting all of us, convinced we were all in on it. Mam begged him to stop, saying we knew nothing about it. He hit her again till she bled. Then he threw her out. Wouldn't let her back in the cottage all night. Not until she replaced his *poteen*. She came back the next morning with three bottles. I don't know where she got them."

"Love of God!" Father O'Malley remembered Kevin telling his da not to touch his Mam just as he arrived at the Dooley cottage and thanked God he got there when he did. "Does he hit her often?"

"No. Mam don't touch his *poteen* now. But my sisters barely speak or move anymore. They're terrified to attract any attention from him."

"What about you?"

"He yells at me a lot. Calls me all sorts of names. But he didn't beat me much until the accident. That pushed him over the edge."

"And your sisters?"

He shrugged, looked away. "They're terrified of him."

"Do you think he's likely to become violent again?"

"Probably. He's angry most of the time now."

"Are you afraid?"

Kevin bristled. "Not for myself. Only that he might take his anger out on the others."

"You must find a way to protect them."

"How?"

"Let me think on it a moment," said Father O'Malley, as an idea began to form in his mind.

Kevin brushed the crumbs of the last bit of bread from his mouth, silently waiting.

"Kevin I didn't see a pig today. How is your family planning to pay the rent at May Gale Day?"

"Don't know. We had a piglet, but she died. Da wanted me to catch lots of fish and sell them in town for the rent money. Won't happen now. That's probably what's got him looking crossways at everyone."

Father O'Malley doubted it would have happened anyway. The two lads together couldn't have caught and sold enough to pay the rent, especially when the Dooleys seemed to be relying on fish as their main food source as well.

"If I don't find some way to get food, it won't matter anyway. We'll have starved long before May."

"What have you been eating the past few weeks?"

"Some days, nothing. Once a woman came bringing a few bits to Mam. Said her name was Rose Kilpatrick. She'd heard about the accident, that we'd been living on fish and now had none else so she brought us something. 'Twasn't much, but it was welcome."

"I imagine." Father O'Malley wondered how Dacey would react if he knew his wife was bringing food to the likes of the Dooleys.

"Da didn't like it," Kevin went on. "He said we didn't need handouts. Took the food, though. But told her not to come back. Mam nearly cried."

"Your da's pride won't help his family."

Kevin snorted. "Pride! How proud he looks when he's passed out in a pool of his own puke." He threw a piece of turf into the fire, making the flames hiss. "She came again, though," he added. "Just left a bit of food at the door. Mam said when she opened the door she saw a woman disappearing over the hill. She's sure it was her. Mam thinks she's an angel. She fears Da's soul will be damned for being rude to an angel."

"You can tell your Mam that I know Rose Kilpatrick. I assure you she's quite human."

They were quiet for a moment.

"I'm so sorry about the accident," Father O'Malley said, his tone gentle. "I know the loss of the *curragh* meant more to your family than just losing a boat."

Kevin nodded, swallowing hard.

"But the loss of your friend must be even worse. You will miss him something terrible, I'm sure."

135

Kevin stared up at the ceiling.

"You can speak of it, Kevin. The pain is great, I know, but it helps to talk about it."

Kevin looked across the room, into the fire, everywhere, but at the priest. "It's not a thing I care to remember," he said, his voice a harsh whisper.

"Aye, but it is not a thing you can ever forget. Trying to push it away won't make it easier. Can you tell me what happened?"

"You know what happened." Father O'Malley saw suspicion and accusation in Kevin's eyes as they darted in his direction for the briefest moment. "Haven't the Quinns and O'Connors, told you everything?" The fury in Kevin's voice surprised him.

"I was told things by some who were there," he began slowly. "But I would like to hear what you have to say."

Kevin looked at him sideways, his eyes narrowed. "Why? You want me to make a good confession, do you, Father? Is that the real reason you brought me here?"

"No, it is not. Why such anger? Do you think others have spoken of you untruthfully?"

"I'm certain they told you what they think is true."

"Why don't you tell me what you think is true."

"Why bother? Will you believe me over them?"

Father O'Malley sighed. "Kevin, there is always more than one side to a story. Two people may see the same facts in very different ways. I would like to understand how you see it. Your truth is as valid as anyone's."

He waited while Kevin decided whether or not to trust him. Finally, in a low voice, Kevin admitted. "They've told the truth."

"Do you even know what's been said?"

"I suppose they told you I didn't help. I saved my own skin and wouldn't go back in to help Aiden."

"And what do you say?"

Kevin took a deep breath. "When the first big wave hit, it lifted the *curragh* into the air. We were both thrown into the water. We worked together trying to right it. Both of us!" He pounded his fist on the floor. "We had it righted once. I started to help Aiden get back in. He was only about halfway when another wave broke and we had to start over. The water was freezing. The wind kept getting stronger. The waves tugged us under. We had to fight just to keep our heads above water. I thought sure we were both done for."

Father O'Malley pictured the scene. He rubbed his hands over his face. "It must have been terrifying," he said.

"The *curragh* had been thrown just beyond our reach. When the water settled enough we made our way toward it, trying again to right it. We were both frozen to the bone. Our hands could scarcely grip the boat.

"It was then that Rory came. I never heard him over the wind. He just appeared from nowhere. I had the strangest feeling, Father." Kevin stared at his hands, curling and uncurling his fingers as if trying again to revive them from numbness.

"What feeling?"

"I can't explain exactly. It was as if Rory was sent by magic to save us."

"Magic?"

Kevin blinked, shook his head. "God, I suppose. I didn't bother to suss that out at the time. But a feeling came over me that because he was there we were saved. He was closer to Aiden, trying to help him. It was only right he should help his own brother first, but I couldn't wait around for him to get to me. I gave the *curragh* up for lost and made my way to a rock. I'd never felt so relieved as I did once I was up on it. All I had to do was make my way along the rocks to the shore. I felt sure Rory had Aiden. It would all be fine. Maybe he'd even save the *curragh*."

"I can't even imagine what you must have endured, Kevin. But as you tell me this, I do understand why you felt as you did."

Kevin hung his head. "But I was wrong." He put his head in his hands and sobbed.

Father O'Malley rubbed his back. "It's all right, Kevin. You tried. You would never have left Aiden if Rory hadn't come. You thought he was going to be saved so you saved yourself. You had a right to. No one can blame you for that."

"Tell that to Meg O'Connor!" He yelled the words into his hands.

"Does Meg's opinion matter so much to you?"

He straightened a little, staring into the fire. "She wanted me to go back in. Thought me a coward. She's got the most murderous tongue in her head of anyone in Kelegeen."

"That's not the Meg I know," he said softly.

"She'd not speak like that to you. You've never been on the receiving end of her attack, I'll wager."

Father O'Malley could not help but smile at the thought of Meg in a temper. He would not at all like to be in that position.

"Kevin, you've only to worry about what you think of yourself. My advice is to find a quiet time alone and take stock of your character. We all have things to be proud of and things that challenge us. Find yours. Be proud of what you can and work on what you need to change. Honesty and integrity. Strive for those qualities."

Kevin was silent, brooding.

Father O'Malley stood. "You should be getting this food back to your family." He handed the sack to Kevin.

"Are you going to walk back with me?" Kevin asked as the priest exited the cottage with him.

"Not to your cottage. I want to take you a bit out of your way. There's something I'd like to show you."

At the bend in the road, they veered off the path into the woods.

"Where are we going?" Kevin asked.

"I've had an idea in case your da becomes violent again."

They walked through the woods until they came to the *scalpeen* that once housed Larry and his boys.

"I've been by here before and never even noticed this." Kevin was astonished as they rounded to the opening in the front.

"I've never seen a better one. The last occupant was determined the landlord would not find them once they'd lost their cottage. He did a fine job of concealment. I would suggest covering over the entrance as well so it's not noticeable from the front either."

Kevin nodded. "That would be easy enough to do."

Father O'Malley turned Kevin to face him. "Kevin, it is extremely important that you tell no one about this, especially your da. You need a place to bring your Mam and sisters where he won't find you if you begin to fear for their safety. And yours."

"It would prove well for us should we lose the cottage after Gale Day. I could even tell Da I constructed it. He would have to be proud of me once he sees it."

"Kevin!" Father O'Malley roared, startling the lad. "Did you not hear me? He is not to know about it. Should you lose the cottage, build a different *scalpeen* elsewhere. Then at least you could tell him the truth about your having built it. But keep this one a secret."

"But Father—"

"No!" Father O'Malley hated to say the words that followed, but they were necessary. "Your da is not likely to be proud of you. In the state he's in, he's far more likely to blame you for losing the house and forcing you all into a *scalpeen* no matter how well built it be."

Kevin's face reddened, but Father O'Malley did not regret his words if they'd keep the family safe. "Promise me, Kevin. Promise you will keep this a secret only to be used in an emergency."

Kevin looked longingly at the entrance to the *scalpeen*. "Aye, Father," he said reluctantly. "I promise."

Chapter Fourteen

Spring 1847

Father O'Malley couldn't shake the sense of foreboding that accompanied his walk home at the end of May Gale Day. The winter had been difficult. Rory's hand healed as well as could be expected, but he had little use of it. By late winter the remainder of his inventory had sold. Unable to carve, he brooded. Meg tried to cheer him, but it was little use. With greatly reduced income due to Rory's inability to carve and the dwindling of mending work, both families had to conserve what little food they could get. Their one salvation was that each still had a pig to sell.

At Gale Day Meg, Kathleen, and Brigid sold the trinket boxes Rory had made for them, receiving, Father O'Malley noted, far less than they were worth. He'd been unable to find any member of the Dooley family at the fairgrounds. They would undoubtedly be evicted. He hoped Kevin would take his advice to build his own *scalpeen*, leaving Larry's abandoned one for an emergency. The Dooleys would not be the only ones to lose their homes. Many had been unable to keep a pig alive when they couldn't even feed themselves.

"What's to become of us, Siobhan?" he asked, rounding the bend that led towards his cottage. "Everyone's growing so thin. My people appear to be melting before my eyes. What advice can you offer from you heavenly vantage point?" He stopped at the door of his cottage, picturing his lovely Siobhan, long red hair and sparkling green eyes floating behind his closed lids. "You're right, of course," he said. "I cannot save us, so I must look for strength and guidance from the One who can." Turning his back on his own door, he headed across the lane to his church where he passed the evening in prayer before the Blessed Sacrament.

* * *

It didn't take long for the evictions to begin. All over Kelegeen, families were turned out of the tiny hovels they called home. They'd come back in the night to find what they could salvage from the torn down cottages to build their *scalpeens*. Father O'Malley had to search the countryside to find them—no easy task as they kept themselves well hidden from the authorities. He learned the whereabouts of some through the few who straggled in to Mass. Others he all but tripped over in his treks across Kelegeen, coming upon them quite by accident, never knowing who would be where. He found the Dooleys' cottage a battered pile of plaster and thatch, just as he knew it would be. He wished Kevin would tell him where he had built, but he'd seen nothing of him. He held off from checking Larry's *scalpeen* for fear he would find them there.

The Rooneys were among the evicted. Nan had miscarried during the winter. Listless, cold and hungry, Owen worried Nan might slip away as well. Father O'Malley visited the Rooneys as often as he could, bringing a bite to eat when he had some to spare.

"Father, you've come just in time," Owen said, as Father O'Malley popped his head into the opening of the *scalpeen*. "Nan's in fever. She rambled on in her sleep all night, talking to Biddy. 'Tis a sign, I fear. Perhaps Biddy's come for her."

Nan lay on the ground, perfectly still, eyes closed. Father O'Malley would have believed her dead except for the shallow rise and fall of her chest.

"Will you do for her, Father? Before she's gone."

Father O'Malley nodded, pulling the vial of holy oil from his pocket. Hardly a winter's day had gone by that he wasn't giving the Last Rites to someone. He'd hoped the deaths would lessen with the spring, but as he anointed Nan, he realized that conditions caused by the evictions would carry off even more.

141

Owen knelt next to his wife, little James cradled in his arms. The baby slept quietly, but his red cheeks and parched lips testified that Nan was not the only one soon to depart this world. Father O'Malley lifted his gaze from the baby's face to Owen's whose nod was barely perceptible. Father O'Malley anointed and prayed over the child as well. Nan's maternal instincts must have been roused in that moment of grace for her eyes opened and she held out her arms. Owen gently placed James next to Nan. Her arm curved around his small body. Within moments of each other, the two stopped breathing, first the mother, then the son. A look of peace rested on each face.

Owen crumpled into a weeping ball. Father O'Malley bent close to him. "They are in God's hands now," he whispered.

Owen's head nodded. "That's where I wish to be as well." He prostrated himself over the bodies of his wife and child. Father O'Malley said nothing, but knelt in silent prayer, knowing that Owen would likely not have long to wait for his wish to be granted.

* * *

As spring blossomed across the countryside, a bit of hope budded within the hearts of many. There was no telling if the blight would return. There was always the chance this year's crop would come in strong and healthy. Even a small yield would be welcomed so long as no sign of the ugly cankers accompanied it. Though weak from the winter's hunger, those who had managed to pay their rent sewed their crop, daring to hope. Father O'Malley was often obliged to pray a blessing over a newly planted field.

"Go ahead, if you want, Father, but I'll wager they'll do just fine either way," Dacey Kilpatrick said to him after Rose requested a blessing.

"Dacey!" Rose exclaimed. "Don't tempt the Lord's ire!"

"Bah!"

"Father, tell him. He'll bring a curse down upon us with all his bragging."

Father O'Malley turned to Dacey. "Your wife is right. Mind you, I'm not saying that God curses anyone, but you'd do well to remember that all our blessings come from our Lord. You might want to give Him some thanks seeing as how he's blessed you so well."

Dacey shoved his hands in his pockets. Kicking at the dirt, he said, "Aye, Father. I do thank the Lord and I'll thank you as well if you'd bless our field."

Before leaving, Rose took Father aside. "Do you know anything of the Dooley family, Father?" She glanced over her shoulder as she spoke, making sure Dacey was out of earshot.

"They were evicted. I assume they've built a *scalpeen*, but I've yet to locate them."

"I went to their cottage not long after Gale Day. What was left of it," Rose told him. "I found no one."

"I heard you'd been leaving them food. You're a brave woman to cross the path of Colin Dooley."

Rose rolled her eyes. "Him! He's ashamed to show his face, as well he should be. That's why he didn't want me there. But I've no fear of the likes of him, except for how he might take it out on the others. That's why I started leaving food at the door." She glanced again at Dacey who was busy looking over the new potato bed.

"Not afraid of Colin, but you are afraid of Dacey?"

"Not afraid, Father. But I have to live with that one." She jerked her head in Dacey's direction. "And he'd be in a perfect fit if he knew I'd given away any of our food, especially to the likes of the Dooleys."

"Why did you do it?" Father O'Malley asked. "You barely knew the family."

"It was a terrible thing, that accident. Anna told me how her Aiden had been such close friends with the Dooley lad. I prayed on it, Father, and I felt the Lord was telling me to do it."

"You are a very good woman, Rose."

She shrugged. "I thought about what you told me. Dacey is my husband, but I have to serve God first. I'm wondering, Father, if my sharing might make up for Dacey's stinginess in the eyes of the Lord?" There was pleading in Rose's eyes.

"Are you worried about Dacey's soul, Rose?"

She nodded. "He's not a bad man, Father. He believes in taking care of his own. He just can't see his way to loving his neighbor as he ought." She sighed. "I don't want my bairns to grow up thinking hoarding things for oneself, sharing nothing with others, is right. It goes against the Lord's commands."

"Then you must be the one to teach them."

"How can I, Father, when I have to hide what I do from my own husband? I'm still in the same quandary of how to teach them generosity without teaching them to sneak behind their father's back."

"Have you ever spoken with Dacey about how you feel?"

"Aye, but it does no good. He doesn't want to hear it."

"Then perhaps you can speak to your children."

"But I'd be speaking against their da."

"Not if you present it as the Lord's teachings. You don't have to mention their da at all. Just tell them what Jesus taught and let them draw their own conclusions."

Rose considered this. "Thank you, Father. I'll think on how I can manage."

"Pray on it, too, Rose. God will show you the way."

* * *

As Father O'Malley continued his trek across the countryside, he wondered what conversations in the Kilpatrick cottage would be like in the coming weeks. He hoped he hadn't set into motion any marital discord. Still, something needed to move Dacey's heart.

Why is Dacey so stingy? He wondered. By his own admission he's been blessed more than most. He does do his job as provider, as well as anyone in his situation is

144

able. That's to his credit. On the other hand, he simply won't part with a scrap for anyone outside his family, even when it wouldn't be much of a deprivation. Why?"

Father O'Malley walked on, heading towards Larry's abandoned *scalpeen*, knowing he couldn't put it off any longer. His heart sank as he got close. The voice coming from its direction was distinctly Kevin's. *I told him not to do that!* Then another thought struck him. *Perhaps, Colin had become violent again. Perhaps Kevin was using Larry's* scalpeen *as intended.*

"Kevin?" Father O'Malley called, approaching the entrance.

"Father," said Noreen. "How did you know it was us?"

"I heard Kevin's voice." A quick scan of the occupants showed the Dooley family minus Colin. "Where is your Mister?"

Noreen shrugged. "Don't know."

Father O'Malley gave Kevin a questioning look.

"We haven't seen him since the eviction," Kevin explained. "We was all standing around watching them pull the cottage down. Next thing we know he's gone."

"Gone?"

"Aye," said Noreen. "Slipped away with none of us noticing. We'd have stayed to see if he came back, but the Sheriff's men chased us off. Said we was now trespassing. We've not seen Colin since."

"Why didn't you tell me, Kevin?"

"I went to see you once, but you weren't at home. I didn't know how to find you."

"Oh?" *Surely, that wasn't true. Kevin may have come when he was away, but he was easy enough to find.* "You'd have found me soon enough if you'd come to Mass."

Kevin looked away.

"Ah, well. I know where you are now." He returned his attention to Noreen. "How are you faring?"

"Well enough. At least we're under cover when it rains. Though I'd like to know where Colin is. How is he going to find us?"

"Who cares?" Kevin muttered.

145

Father O'Malley glanced at him. Kevin sat with his knees drawn up under his chin, jaws clenched and eyes narrowed.

"Are you managing to eat?"

"We beg in town. We get a bit, but it's hard. Town's full of beggars," Noreen said.

As Father O'Malley's vision adjusted to the dim interior of the *scalpeen*, he noticed that Noreen's eyes appeared sunken into their sockets. Her cheekbones were more pronounced than the last time he'd seen her. In fact, all the occupants of the tiny three-sided structure appeared more emaciated than at his last visit. This was becoming more common amongst his parishioners. But their weight loss wasn't all that bothered him. It was the haunted look so many now had, as if they were becoming ghosts while still alive.

"I've no food with me at present. I'll set something aside for you and bring it by soon. At least you have one of the best *scalpeens* I've ever seen. It should hold up well."

Noreen's face brightened a bit. "Isn't it, though, Father? It was smart of Kevin to build it ahead of time knowing that we would lose our home."

"Built it himself, did he?" Father O'Malley asked, raising his eyebrows at Kevin whose expression never changed.

"He's a good lad. He'll take care of us."

Father O'Malley couldn't help but smile as Noreen beamed at her son. Let her think it. Noreen had little enough to smile about.

* * *

The sun was low in the sky by the time Father O'Malley reached the Quinn's cottage. He found the Quinn and O'Connor families planting together.

"Father, you've come at the right time. We've just finished putting in both crops. Did ours this morning and Thomas' this afternoon," Denis explained.

146

"We'd be obliged if you'd pray a blessing over our field," Thomas said.

"And if you wouldn't mind, praying one over ours on your way home," Denis added.

After blessing the newly turned earth, Father O'Malley entered the crowded cottage. As he sat before the fire, little Seamus crawled into his lap. He bounced the child gently on his knee while addressing his father. "What is your sense of how this year's crop will fare?" he asked.

Thomas sighed. "There's no telling, Father. It could just as easily go one way as the other."

Aisling opened her mother's sewing box. "Can we work now?" she asked.

A few flakes of dirt fell from the creases near Anna's mouth as she smiled at her daughter. "Aisling, love, aren't you exhausted?"

"Aye, Mam. But sewing makes me feel better."

"It doesn't feel the same to them." Anna nodded towards Loreena and Brigid who stared at Anna as if she might tell them they had to dig a new potato bed this instant. "Tomorrow is soon enough." The two girls sighed in relief as Aisling closed the lid.

"You've mending work?" asked Father O'Malley, somewhat confused.

"Not at present," Anna said. "Aisling has taken it upon herself to teach these two to sew. No easy task, that!" Anna laughed. "It's just scraps they're practicing on."

"She's better at teaching than we are," Deirdre explained. "She has more patience than any of us."

"I see," said Father O'Malley. "Do you lasses like having Aisling for a sewing teacher?"

Both girls grinned and bobbed their heads. "She's good at showing us the stitches and doesn't try to make us work too fast," Loreena said.

"And she doesn't scold us when we make mistakes," Brigid added, looking pointedly at Meg.

"A good teacher, she is then," the priest agreed.

Aisling's cheeks colored. She lowered her eyes and smiled, pleased and a bit embarrassed by her pastor's praise.

"Were you able to help with the planting, Rory?" Father O'Malley asked, noticing him rubbing his injured hand.

"Aye. It's a bit awkward, but I made do."

"Well, that's something then, isn't it?"

"He'll get accustomed to using his hand in a new way," Anna said. "My uncle lost a foot, I keep reminding him, and he eventually learned to get around. No complaint was ever heard from him, either."

"I've made no complaints." Rory's tone was petulant.

"Didn't say you did. I'm just telling of my uncle, is all."

Rory stared into the fire.

"He's got better use of it than we expected," Meg said. "We'll be able to plant our own potato beds with no problem once we're married."

"If we get that far," Rory stated flatly.

"What do you mean by that?" asked Father O'Malley.

Rory looked him in the eye. Father O'Malley tried to read the emotion on Rory's face. Defiance? Anger? Bitterness? Fear?

"I mean that without being able to carve, I can't keep us in food. If the crop fails this year we'll not be getting married."

Meg's eyes widened. "We won't?"

"How could we think of starting a family when we can't even feed ourselves?"

"We were planning to marry before you ever thought of selling your carvings. Why should that change now?"

"It's not the carving, Meg! It's the famine. We're as likely to starve to death as not and I've no way to prevent it." Rory stood. Stepping over his brothers and sisters he flung open the cottage door and stormed out.

"Mam, are we really going to starve to death?" Loreena asked.

"Don't you worry, lass. We'll manage," she said squeezing the child's shoulders.

It was then that Father O'Malley noticed how thin they had all become. The faces around him looked drawn and pinched. Not as bad as some he had seen that day, but there was a notable change indeed.

Denis cleared his throat. "Perhaps it's time we headed home. Father, you won't forget to bless our field?"

As they left the Quinn cottage, Meg lagged behind, looking out for Rory, but he was nowhere in sight.

"Come along, Meg," Deirdre said, tugging her daughter's arm.

Though daylight waned, Father O'Malley could still see the tension in Meg's face. "Don't worry too much, Meg," he told her. "Rory will come around. He simply needs time to adjust."

"I can't help it, Father. He's been so moody since the accident. Not like himself at all."

"He's lost a brother and sustained a terrible injury. It's only natural. Just give him time."

"He's worried about Mr. Blackburn, too," Meg added.

Father O'Malley knew that Blackburn's threats the night of the accident had kept the Quinns on edge for some time, but as the months passed nothing seemed to come of it. He'd hoped Blackburn had gotten over his injured pride and forgotten the whole sorry mess.

"Have they heard from him?" Father O'Malley asked.

"Blackburn has a funny way about him, Father," Denis answered. "He kept quiet, not coming 'round. You'd think nothing had ever happened. Then at Gale Day when we paid our rent, he spoke oddly to Thomas."

"What did he say?"

"He said, 'You sold your pig, I see. You can pay your rent. Get to keep your cottage.' Then he leaned in close to Thomas like he was imparting some big secret and said, 'I hope you'll make the rent come November. What a pity it would be to lose your home with winter coming on.' Then he grinned in such a way, I tell you, Father, it made shivers run down my spine."

149

"You heard all this?"

"I was standing right next to Thomas. Rory was there, too. Heard it all."

"What did Thomas say?"

"Nothing. What could he say? He just paid his rent and left. He was shaken, though, I can tell you."

"Perhaps that's all Blackburn's doing, trying to shake him up." Father O'Malley tried to sound convincing, but wasn't sure he believed his own words.

"May it be so, Father."

When they reached the O'Connor's newly sown field, Deirdre sent Brigid inside to fetch Kathleen.

"She still won't go to the Quinns?" Father O'Malley asked.

"Not unless she's practically dragged," Deirdre said.

Father O'Malley shook his head in sorrow. Kathleen had gone to the Quinns cottage for Aiden's wake and after the funeral, but beyond that she refused to go. She'd come to him for confession, telling him that she'd been awful to Aiden. She confessed how she'd deliberately tried to dissuade him, even purposely favoring Kevin in front of him. "I only wanted to keep from leading him on so he'd not have a horrible let down. I thought I wanted to marry Kevin and everyone was pushing me to marry Aiden." Her words tore at Father O'Malley's heart. "Kevin told me that they only took the *curragh* out in the storm because Aiden was determined to learn to handle it in any weather. He wanted to become an expert fisherman so that I'd see he could take care of me." The lass had cried so hard she'd barely been able to speak. He was shocked by the words that finally poured out. "It's my fault Aiden died, Father." She'd lifted her tear streaked face. "Will God ever forgive me?"

He had tried to convince her that she'd every right not to let herself be forced into an unwanted marriage, that she was not to blame if the lad continued to pursue her despite her clear indications that she did not return his feelings and that taking the *curragh* out in a storm had been his decision. If she'd committed any sins they were simply

150

perhaps being a bit too hurtful towards Aiden in her anger at those who were pushing the relationship, but she was not responsible for his death. She'd nodded in agreement, but it was half-hearted at best. He feared the wound in Kathleen's heart would be more difficult to heal than Rory's hand.

Meg interrupted his thoughts. "She thinks she's to blame for Aiden's death and that the Quinns must hate her for it. None of it's a bit true, but it's a fancy she's got in her head that she won't let go. And it's all because of that fool, Kevin Dooley. He told her it was her fault. I'd like to drown him myself!"

"Meg!"

"I'm sorry, Father, but it's true. He's a *duine Uafásach*!

"There is much about his life you don't know, Meg. As the Lord told us, "Judge not lest ye be judged.""

"Aye, Father." Meg kicked at a stone. "But it's hard not to judge when all the evidence points in only one direction."

* * *

That evening, as Father O'Malley sat by his fire roasting a lone turnip, he ruminated on all that had unfolded that day. "Ah, Siobhan," he sighed. "Keep me company tonight, would you? This day has been a difficult one."

I'm here. Her voice, like sweet music in his head, seemed almost real.

"I wish I could get through to them. Kathleen. Rory. Kevin. I fear for them."

You were once like them. Believing a thing was your fault when it wasn't. Believing a tragedy in your life meant the end of everything. Turning the wrong direction for a time. But look at you now. God is with you in all things. God is with them, too.

"Aye, indeed. But God sent me Father Coogan. Without him it's certain I would have been lost. Now it's my turn to serve our Lord as Father Coogan did by rescuing me. What if I fail?" He lifted the roasted turnip from the fireplace with a pair of tongs. There was no answer from Siobhan, though he knew she had not abandoned him. He could feel her presence still.

"Have you no words of wisdom for me?" he asked, cutting into his turnip.

Think you must do it all yourself, do you? Her melodic laughter floated through his ears. *Your help will come. And from a place you least expect. God sends gifts in many forms. Have the grace to accept the one you will be given.*

Chapter Fifteen

"No!"

Deirdre's shout roused Meg from sleep. "What's wrong, Mam?" she asked, propping herself up on one elbow, fighting to keep her eyes open. Though Deirdre's cry woke Meg, it was no longer enough to startle her into alertness. The feeling had been coming over Deirdre again of late. At first they'd all assumed, though no one spoke of it until after the fact, that it was a sign the potato crop would fail. By mid-summer the crop's failure was painfully clear. After they'd dug up stinking, cancerous mush, Denis' only comment had been, "Well, at least your Mam's feeling can stop now. We know what it meant."

But it hadn't stopped.

"Nothing, lass. Go back to sleep." Though her mother's voice was shaky, Meg was too weak to argue. She dropped down, immediately plunging into a deep sleep.

The next evening Meg came across her da sitting outside their cottage with his head in his hands.

"What's wrong, Da?" she asked, sinking down next to him.

"Your Mam," he answered. "She's afraid to go to sleep. Afraid she'll have more nightmares. As if another year of hunger isn't enough, she's got to keep having these feelings. What more are we to expect?"

His accusatory tone surprised Meg. "She can't help it, Da. It's not like she's making bad things happen."

He patted her knee. "I know, Megeen. I didn't mean it to sound that way." He let out a long sigh.

"Mam's feelings are hard for you, aren't they Da?"

He glanced a Meg. "I shouldn't burden you with this."

"It's alright. I like that you can talk to me." Meg had always enjoyed a special bond with her father. Now that she was old enough to marry, the two seemed to grow even

153

closer. He spoke with her more as an adult. Not quite an equal, he was still her da, but he'd begun to confide in her, little pieces of his inner feelings.

"Ah, well, 'tis just that your Mam's feelings are never without reason. But once the thing that's brought them on has come to pass, they go away until the next time. I would have thought the day we found the crop had failed again, that would be the end of it for a while. But apparently there's more to come since her feelings haven't stopped. If anything, they're worse. And the nightmares. She wakes in terror, but can't remember what she'd just been dreaming."

"Nothing at all?" asked Meg.

"She says just blackness and a feeling of being crushed under a heavy weight."

"That's like her dreams of not being able to breathe before Aiden drowned."

"I can't pretend it doesn't worry me."

Meg was silent a moment, thinking. Then she said, "Da, there's nothing we can do to change what's to come. But at least we've warning that something will. That's more than most people get."

"True enough, Meg. But I wonder if they aren't the luckier ones. It's hard knowing something bad is coming, but not knowing what, when or to whom."

Meg leaned her head back against the cottage. "I'm glad I didn't get the gift."

"Not sure I'd call it that," said Denis. "Seems more a curse to me. Your mam never calls it a gift, though others do. Believe me, she'd rather not have it, but it's not a choice."

"Poor Mam. It hurts to see her like this." A new thought occurred to Meg. "Da, does it seem to you this latest feeling has been lasting longer than usual?"

"Aye, it does."

"Maybe it's not truly the feeling, then. Maybe worrying about what's going to happen because of another failed crop has her fretting to the point of it seeming like the feeling and she can't tell the difference."

Denis shrugged. "I suppose that could be," he said, but Meg could tell he wasn't convinced.

"Enough talk about Mam and her feelings. What about you, Megeen? Now that this year's crop is a guaranteed failure is Rory still keen on putting off the wedding?"

Meg's gaze dropped to her lap. Unable to speak for fear of crying, she merely nodded.

"I thought so. It's hard for you to hear this Meg, but I think the lad is right."

Meg's head jerked up. "What? You don't want us to marry?"

"I do want you to marry. Just not in the middle of this mess. It's not a good time to be starting a new life, not to mention bringing bairns into the world that you can't feed."

Meg looked down again. She said nothing, knowing her da was right, but not wanting to admit it. She pulled her comb from her pocket. Holding it in her lap, she stroked the delicately carved hearts and roses with the tip of her finger.

"A lovely job he did on that," Denis said.

Meg nodded.

"He was doing so well selling his carvings. Now that was a true gift. Not like what folks call your mam's gift."

"But now it's gone," Meg said, her voice barely above a whisper.

"So it is. And your mam, who would love to lose hers, can't get rid of it. Strange the way life goes sometimes."

Meg continued to stroke the delicate lines of the comb.

"It's not forever, Meg," Denis said. She looked up at him. "You will marry. Just not as soon as you thought. There's no need to hurry, lass." He smiled at her, but there was a sadness in his eyes.

"Is something wrong, Da?"

He leaned back against the cottage wall. "No, lass. 'Tis only right you should want to marry and have a family of your own." He made a noise that sounded a bit like a laugh, but wasn't really. "When your own bairns are grown and ready to go off to a married life of their own, you'll know."

"Know what?"

"How fast the time went. How hard it is to let go."

155

"Do you not want me to go?"

Denis looked her in the eye. "I want you to be happy, Meg." He sighed. "At least as happy as this life allows. I'll dance at your wedding with joy in my heart because I'll know you're marrying a good man who loves you well."

She cocked an eyebrow.

"But," he continued, "my joy will be mixed with an ache in my heart."

"Why?"

"Because my little Megeen is no longer a wee lass, but a grown woman. I'll miss the child."

"There's no way to stop it," Meg whispered. "We all grow up. You did. Mam did."

He laughed, a real laugh now. "I know, Megeen. It's all as it should be. Someday you'll know what I mean."

"Da, do you know why I want so much to marry Rory?"

"Because you love him, I would hope."

"Of course I love him. I'd not marry a man I didn't love. Nor one who didn't love me."

A broad grin stretched across Denis' face. "I'd expect nothing less."

Meg smiled, too, then becoming serious she said, "I want to marry Rory because of you and Mam."

Denis' brows furrowed in a puzzled expression.

"I know raising a cottage full of bairns on next to nothing is near impossible. I know life is full of heartache and backache."

"And?"

"And I've watched you and Mam lean on each other through it all. Awful things have happened, but you've always supported each other. When something good happens, even though it be just a little thing, you rejoice together like it's the Second Coming. What's missing in one of you is made up for in the other. Where Mam is weak, you are strong. Where you need an extra push, she's there to give it. You have a bond that it seems nothing can break. It's as though God made you to be together. I see the same in Rory's Da and Mam." Meg's voice caught. "It

156

overcomes me when I think on it. Especially when I think I could live like that with Rory, that we could have that bond. It's something special, something of God."

Denis made no effort to stop or hide the tears that rolled down his cheeks. Pride showed in his eyes. "Well," he said. "Seems my little lass really is grown up. I suppose I can let you go without worry, after all. Just remember that it doesn't happen out of thin air. A husband and wife have to work at it. They have to learn how to grow together, work together, live together. It takes some getting used to, but it's well worth the effort."

The cottage door opened and Deirdre stuck her head out. "So there you are. I wondered where the two of you had gone off to."

Denis got up and helped Meg to her feet. As they entered the cottage, he gave his wife a kiss. "We've done a good job *mo stór*, even when we weren't looking."

* * *

That night they went to sleep with no food in their bellies. There was simply none to be had. Meg's stomach growled and spasmed, making sleep difficult. She would return the finished mending work in the morning, collecting such meager pay the miniscule amount of food it would buy seemed almost not worth the effort. She and Kathleen were getting less and less work. There was more competition now with so many pouring into the town. Beyond that, the Hoffreys had done more damage than she had expected. "Mind you, be careful," Mrs. Airdale had said to her when handing her some older, inexpensive garments to mend. "I heard how Mr. Hoffreys shirt was completely ruined with a stain down the entire sleeve."

Meg was aghast. "Not the whole sleeve, Ma'am. It was just a tiny drop of blood on the inside of the cuff. My little sister accidentally pricked her finger and—"

"That is not what I was told. Are you telling me that Mrs. Hoffrey is lying?" Mrs. Airdale's eyebrows shot up, daring Meg to argue. Though burning with indignation, Meg knew she couldn't show it. Mrs. Airdale was one of her best customers. Already she was cutting back. Meg couldn't afford to lose her altogether.

"No, Ma'am." She said, keeping her eyes lowered so the woman wouldn't see the rage boiling beneath the surface.

"It's a shame you girls have become slatternly," Mrs. Airdale continued. "You used to do such good work. And now I see that you are ready to lie to cover your carelessness." The woman let out a heavy sigh. "I hope you'll manage to return to your previous form."

"Aye, Ma'am," Meg said, through gritted teeth. "It was an accident. It will never happen again. We'll be especially careful with these," she said, holding out the garments she'd been given.

* * *

"Did you get anything, Meg?" Rory asked. He'd been waiting for her to return from town. The garments had been returned to Mrs. Airdale that morning in perfect condition, but they didn't bring nearly enough to fill the family's bellies, which were now empty more often than not. Too tired to answer, Meg held out one small loaf of bread. Wisps of stray hair fell around her face. She had even lost the energy for her hair. It hung down her back on a braid made days ago.

"Come over after it gets dark," Rory said.

"Why?"

"You'll see."

"Rory, don't play games with me. I'm too tired."

"'Tis no game. I'm not supposed to be telling anyone. Even you."

"Tell what?"

He hesitated a moment. "Promise me you'll come."

Meg looked intently at Rory. His cheekbones jutted out under his skin. His tailcoat was frayed and trousers torn. His shoes had gaping holes showing raw, red skin.

"I'll come."

"Late. After everyone's asleep," he called as she headed for home.

Chapter Sixteen

That night Meg lay on the floor trying to stay awake so she could slip out of the cottage unnoticed. When the room was quiet, Meg rolled onto her side, drew up her legs and pushed herself onto her hands and knees. There she stopped, letting her head hang down between her arms, eyes closed, breathing deeply to gain the strength to continue. Slowly, she lifted her head and drew up her right leg so that her foot was flat on the floor. Leaning forward she put all her weight on her hands, brought up the other foot and slowly pushed herself to a standing position.

Dizzy, she waited in the darkness until her equilibrium returned. A line of pain ran from her head to her stomach, throbbed at both ends and flashed out in all directions. Slowly, she crossed to the door, opening it as silently as possible. Stifling a groan, she forced her legs to take her in the direction of Rory's cottage.

About halfway between the O'Connor and the Quinn cottages where the land sloped down to form a miniature valley, a figure suddenly loomed in front of her. She gasped.

"Hush. It's me, Rory."

In the moonlight she could make out his scarecrow silhouette though his face remained shadowed.

Meg's heart hammered in her chest sending the blood pulsing into her brain. "You've about scared me out of my skin!"

"Sorry. I didn't want anyone to see you. I want to share something, but you must promise you'll never tell a living soul of it."

"I promise."

"I've got meat."

"What?"

"Come." Taking her hand Rory led her behind his family's cottage. Meg caught the rich smell of roasted pork.

"Here," Rory whispered.

Meg collapsed on the ground, grabbed the bits he uncovered and shoved them into her mouth, barely waiting to have one piece chewed and swallowed before the next replaced it.

"I ate half of my portion and saved the rest for you. Da decided we should have one decent meal before we all starved. So we feasted tonight. We had to wait until after dark to begin cooking so no one would come to steal it. Or kill us for it. I hid some. Then I went to wait for you. Don't go too fast, Meg. It won't hold with you."

Rory talked while Meg devoured the small meal. When the last piece was gone she licked every finger then wiped her hands across the waist of her dress.

"Rory, where did you…" she began, but her stomach wrenched from the unaccustomed onslaught. She doubled over clasping her hands over her mouth. Gritting her teeth, Meg focused solely on keeping the food from coming back up.

"Keep fighting, Meg. It will stay down if you force it."

Meg lay curled on the ground. The battle between gasping for air and clenching her mouth shut consumed her. She was only vaguely aware that Rory was sitting next to her, stroking her head.

At last the struggle ended. She won. With Rory's help she rose to a sitting position, worn out from her ordeal.

"Rory," she said, her voice a hoarse whisper. "Where did you get it?"

He didn't answer.

She tilted her head to look into his face, barely visible in the moonlight.

"By the saints, Rory, you didn't?"

He turned away.

"That was your pig?"

"Aye," he replied, still looking away.

"What will you do come Gale Day?"

161

"We've still got the piglet. He'll be big enough to sell by then."

"But you've no female to breed. You'll pay the rent for November, but what will you do come next May?"

"We'll worry about that later. We were so hungry and the wee ones looking so close to death Mam was nearly driven crazy."

"'Tis the same with us."

Meg stared out across the land that was half in shadow, half in moonlight.

"What does it matter?" Rory asked. "If we can't pay the rent in May we'll build a *scalpeen*. Besides next year's crop will have to come in. I can't believe this can continue another year beyond this one. If it does, I think we're all done for anyway."

"We can't just give up. I won't. Promise me you won't either."

"And what am I supposed to do? I'm useless now." He shook his injured hand in her face.

"Eat the damn grass if you have to! But don't give up. Promise me."

"Aye, then, Meg." Rory's voice was weak.

They sat, not speaking, leaning against each other. Rory broke the silence. "Meg, there's a promise you must make to me."

"What?"

"If it gets to the point where you've nothing left, sell the comb."

Meg sat up straight. "Rory! I could never do that."

"Why not? It's just a comb."

"It's not just a comb. You made it for me, gave it to me when you proposed. There'll never be another like it."

Rory gave a derisive laugh. "Aye, that's for certain."

"I didn't mean it that way," Meg explained. "Even if you could make a million more I'd not part with that one. It's special to me."

"More special than your life?"

Meg was silent.

"Meg, this is no time for useless sentiment. This famine is getting worse. There's no telling when it will end. You just told me to eat grass if I have to. But you can't sell a comb to buy real food? I'd like to know what sense that makes."

Meg reached for the comb in her pocket, ran her hands over its smooth, intricately carved lines. She felt tears prick her eyes. "Rory," Meg took a deep breath. "Do you still want to marry me?"

Meg felt more than saw Rory turn towards her. "You need to ask me that?"

"I do. You've said we won't marry this year because of the famine. Now you tell me to sell the comb. What am I to think?"

"You're to think I'm trying my best to keep us alive." Meg heard the exasperation in his voice. "My God, Meg! We can't think of starting a married life, having wee ones when everything's in the state it's in. And if the comb would buy you something so you don't starve to death it will prove my love more than it would buried with you in your grave!"

"How much will it buy me? Enough for a few days? Then what?"

"Then you find another way. Eat grass." He pulled up a handful and tossed it at her.

"We'll still marry when this is over?"

"Of course we will." Rory's arm went around her shoulder, pulling her close. "Meg, I love you. Please, don't question that. I don't want us to start off at a time like this. Tell me you understand."

"I do, Rory. But I needed to hear it."

"Seems strange," he said.

"What does?"

"This conversation. You're usually the practical one. What happened?"

"Nothing. I'm still the practical one."

"Then prove it. Make the promise."

Meg sighed. "If it comes to it. If I absolutely have to…"

"Go on," Rory urged when she hesitated.

"If, and only if, it is absolutely necessary, I promise I will sell the comb."

* * *

From that night, Meg's determination fed strength into her body when the meager portions of what passed for food failed to. No longer the robust physical strength she had known before, it was now a strength of nerve.

The summer wore on. They took to scavenging the fields for whatever could be found. On a good day Deirdre made a watery soup of nettles, grass, dandelions, and the occasional leaf or two of cabbage. By taking small bites and letting them linger in her mouth, Meg tried to fool herself into believing she was receiving a feast. She concentrated on every swallow, picturing the soup sliding down her throat and landing in her belly. With each spoonful she imagined a whole layer of food was filling her up. At the last mouthful, she pictured it reaching the top of her stomach, convincing herself she was stuffed to the brim. Whenever hunger pangs doubled her over she told herself she had eaten too much and that her stomach was near to bursting.

When the strength of her body failed and her legs gave out beneath her, she stayed right where she fell, breathing slowly and deeply. Allowing herself to get lost in a daydream, she'd see herself walking down a long, thickly carpeted hallway, wearing a blue silk dress. At the end of the hallway were great double doors which a servant opened for her. Inside was a large dining room of red and gold. In the center was a long heavy table that went on forever. Her family sat around it. Upon the table was every kind of food she could imagine.

* * *

As summer inched into fall, mending work grew scarcer. Meg and Kathleen practically begged for the little work they were given. The Hoffreys were only partly to blame. Shaking hands slowed their mending work and made for less than flawless stitching, which only reinforced the belief of their customers that their work was becoming sloppy. Long time customers began to distrust their abilities with the more intricate sewing, giving them only easy work, and with it, lower wages. Some turned them away altogether.

"We've got to keep going as long as we can. A little work is better than no work. A little money, a little food is better than none at all," Deirdre would tell them as they dragged themselves out the door or sat together by the window's fading light, disheartened by only being entrusted with work they'd mastered years ago.

The ever present specter of Deirdre's feelings kept them all on edge, though she rarely spoke of it.

"Mam, it's been going on for a long time without anything happening. Do you think it's just worry about what's going to happen and not a true feeling this time?" Meg asked her mother one night when neither of them could sleep.

"Why do you ask, Meg? I've said little of it." Deirdre's voice shook.

"You're still having nightmares. I can tell you're anxious, though you're trying not to let on."

"I feared I was making everyone afraid so I've tried to hide it. Apparently, not very well."

Meg leaned against her mother's arm. "You wring your hands and pace the floor when any of us are gone until we're all home. You jump at the slightest noise. You're afraid, Mam. It's a hard thing to hide."

Deirdre wrapped her arm around Meg's shoulder. "I wish it were just ordinary worry, Meg, but I've been cursed with this so-called gift all my life. I know when it's upon me."

"Da thought that when the potatoes were bad again this year that was it, but it didn't stop."

"It did, though, Meg."

165

Meg looked up at her mother. "It did? It didn't seem so."

"There was such a short break between the bad crop and the feeling ending and starting up again that none but me could tell the difference."

"So this is something separate from the potato failure?"

"Connected, no doubt, but different."

A question nagged at Meg. She feared to ask it, but it pushed passed her tongue anyway. "Mam, does the longer the feeling go on for mean the worse the event will be?"

Deirdre leaned her head against Meg's. "'Tis my burden, Meg, not yours. Try not to think about it."

* * *

Fall arrived with no let-up in misery. Hunger pains, dizzy spells, fainting from fatigue—they had become a way of life. November Gale Day loomed. Just the thought of the walk to the fairgrounds exhausted Meg. They had their pig ready for sale. Only one piglet survived. Their hopes for the spring rent rested on that one baby, but they would take it one Gale Day at a time. Meg fretted for the Quinns, who now had no piglet in reserve.

Deirdre's nightmares had increased in intensity. The worst came at the beginning of November. Just as dawn broke, the entire O'Connor cottage was awakened by a scream so shrill it pulled Meg from a dead sleep, her heart slamming away at her ribcage. Though Deirdre sat bolt upright, it was impossible to tell if she were awake or still dreaming as she stared straight ahead, seeing something terrifying, something no one else could see. Denis wrapped his arms around her, gently rocking her, trying to stop the ear-splitting scream. "It's alright *mo grá*. 'Tis only a dream," he cooed.

Finally, Deirdre drew a deep, gasping breath. She fell against Denis, crying out "There's no pig! There's no pig! There's no pig!"

166

Chapter Seventeen

The evening before November Gale Day, Meg took all the clothing she owned except for her heavy shawl, the dress she was wearing, and her one pair of tattered shoes, and put them together in a small bundle on the table. The rest of the family slowly added their own clothing to the pile leaving each with one set of their warmest clothing to see them through the coming winter. Brigid cried as she laid one lightweight dress on top of the pile.

Deirdre caressed her youngest daughter's shoulders saying, "'Tis only a frock, lass. Just think of the food we'll be able to trade for it tomorrow."

"I'm scared to have only one dress," Brigid sobbed. "What if it gets worn out and I have to go naked? I'll freeze to death."

"If it wears out you will mend it," Meg told her.

"I don't sew good!" she yelled, turning to her mother's arms for comfort.

Kathleen crossed the room to where Brigid stood with her arms wrapped around their mother, her face buried in the waist of Deirdre's gown. Kathleen put a hand on either of Brigid's shoulders and leaned against her as much to support herself as to comfort her sister. Her long golden hair, now matted and dirty, fell across Brigid's face.

"I will mend it for you," Kathleen whispered.

Deirdre, Brigid and Kathleen were an intertwined cluster at one end of the rickety kitchen table. Meg, Brendan and their father stood well-spaced at the other. Deirdre looked as though she might fall as the two girls pressed against her. Denis gently unbound the three knotted up bodies.

"There will be plenty to do in the morning. We should try to sleep now," was all he said.

Meg was up early the next morning, hunger pains having kept her awake most of the night. She reached for her comb, absently studying the pair of intertwined hearts with a rose atop each one nestling close together. Rory had picked up the strongly scented wood while strolling the beach. From what faraway place had it drifted? Whenever she combed her hair she breathed deeply of its scent and pretended she was sitting in a dressing room like the ones in the large estate houses in town.

Meg undid the mangled mess of her braid. She was a long time getting all the mats out. The stench of long unwashed hair mingled with the rich sweetness of the comb's wood.

As Meg braided her hair, she glanced at the pathetic pile of clothing neatly stacked on the table. Trying to sell those was a useless effort, she knew, but her family was desperate and it was all they had with which to bargain. The pig would pay the rent, but they still had to eat.

She looked at the comb again. It was worth more than all their clothes put together. She'd made a promise to Rory, but continued to hold off. Not yet, she told herself. She kissed the hearts and roses then tucked the comb into her pocket.

Deirdre moved about the cottage in a flurry of nervous activity. Her sleep had been fitful, filled with nightmares and garbled talk of missing pigs.

"Deirdre, please sit", Denis begged. "We've a long walk to the fairgrounds. It won't do for you to wear yourself out before we've even left the cottage."

Deirdre was about to retort when a fist pounded on the door. Denis opened it to find Loreena breathless and stricken.

"Is our pig here?" she gasped.

"No. Why should it be?" Denis asked.

"It's gone. We hoped it had wandered over here."

Brigid ran to her friend, "What do you mean, gone? Wasn't he in the cottage with you last night?"

"Aye, but I let him out this morning. Just to have one last roam over the land before he goes to…well you know. I do it every Gale Day. Nothing's ever happened before."

"He can't have gone far," said Denis. "Brigid, go with Loreena to look for him. If anyone can get that pig back it'll be the two of you. Mind you, don't take too long. We need to be on our way soon."

Brigid and Loreena sped from the cottage calling for the pig before they were even out the door.

"Holy Mother, help us!" Deirdre dropped into a chair. All heads turned in her direction.

"Mam?" Brendan asked. "What is it?"

"The dreams. The pig. Oh, the feeling! It's strong as ever now."

The others exchanged glances. So this was it, thought Meg. The Quinn's would lose their one remaining pig on Gale Day. Suddenly, the taste of the roasted pig flesh resurfaced in her mouth, making her sick to her stomach. Though irrational, she couldn't help the feeling of guilt creeping over her. Watching her Mam rock back and forth in her chair, head in her hands, Meg knew the missing pig would not be found.

"Let's pack up. We need to be on our way," Denis announced. "Brendan, give me a hand with the pig."

"Aren't we to wait for Brigid to come back?" Kathleen asked.

"She knows where we're going. If she's not back when we're ready to leave she can walk with the Quinns."

"Do you think they'll bother to go, if they can't find the pig?" Brendan asked.

Denis shrugged. "If they don't, she can stay with them, but we need to be on our way. We've a long day ahead of us. I've no desire to extend it beyond the necessary. You lasses, see to your Mam."

Meg and Kathleen helped their mother from her chair. "Mam, you must get hold of yourself," Meg said.

"Let's get her outside," said Kathleen. "The fresh air might help."

169

Once the brisk November air hit them, they all braced against it, wrapping themselves in their shawls and coats as tightly as they could. Deirdre stood on her own, pulling herself up to her full height. "I'm fine, now," she said, walking away from the girls. But Meg could see that she still shook. It was not simply the cold air. Her face remained ashen.

Kathleen had noticed, too. "It's not over," she whispered to Meg.

"What do you mean?"

"Look at Mam. She wants us to think she's fine, but she's not. The feeling has not left her. There's more to come."

A sensation that her stomach had just plummeted to the ground overtook Meg. "She's just shaken up is all. It will take a bit to get over it."

Kathleen looked at her, shook her head. At a loss for words, Meg was glad to be interrupted by their da's call. Their pig was in the cart, the clothing in a bundle in Deirdre's arms. "We're ready, let's go!"

* * *

It was a long walk to the field where Gale Day festivities were held. The road soon became crowded with families and pigs, but it was strangely quiet. The flapping of rotting shoes and the squealing of pigs occupied the void usually filled by chattering voices.

Meg noticed others carrying clothes and household items to sell. When they reached the crowded fairgrounds Denis untied the pig and went off, taking Brendan with him.

"We had better sell these clothes as soon as we can," Deirdre said, looking around at all the ragged cottiers attempting to sell their own goods. "Why'd I think it was such a grand idea, us selling these useless rags? God knows the blasted Brits ain't going to be merciful, what with all of us begging after 'em."

170

"Don't blame yourself, Mam," said Meg. "It was a fine idea. It's just that we're all in the same way."

Deirdre began pushing her way through the crowd, searching for a compassionate face. "We've brought some clothing to sell," Deirdre called out to a nattily dressed gentleman. "It's all well made. My daughters and I are expert seamstresses. They will last you well."

He made no comment and looked past Deirdre as though he had not heard her.

"Please, sir! You can look them over all you like."

He threw the quickest glance at Deirdre then turned, making his way through the crowd.

"May the devil take you, then!" Deirdre shouted at his back.

Deirdre and the girls moved on, but no one was interested. Most would not even respond when she addressed them. As the day wore on irritation, worry and fatigue combined, slowing their progress.

"Mam!" they turned at the familiar voice. Brigid made her way through the crowd towards them.

"Did you find the pig?" Meg asked.

"No. We looked everywhere. I can't believe he just disappeared."

"Did you come alone, then? Where are the Quinns?" Deirdre asked.

"Over there." Brigid pointed in the direction from which she'd come. "Except for Mr. Quinn and Rory. They went to see the landlord."

"For what?" asked Meg. "If there's no pig to sell, they can't pay the rent."

"Mr. Quinn said something about asking for extra time to find the pig."

Deirdre snorted. "Fat lot of good that will do him."

"Father O'Malley said he'd go with them. Maybe he can talk Mr. Blackburn into it," Brigid offered.

"What's going to happen to them, Mam?" asked Kathleen.

A shiver ran through Deirdre.

171

"Mam, are you alright?" Meg asked, reaching out for her mother.

"Aye. I was just thinking of something."

"What?" asked Brigid.

"Never you mind, lass. Let's get on with trying to sell these clothes.

As Deirdre turned to move forward, Meg and Kathleen exchanged glances. They knew the answer to Brigid's question. Meg patted the comb in her pocket wondering if it could possibly bring enough money to pay the Quinn's rent.

Deirdre grabbed the sleeve of a passing middle-aged gentleman.

"Please, sir," she begged. "I have these clothes…"

"Get your filthy hands off me and take those disgusting rags away!" He gave her a shove, knocking her to the ground. Kathleen and Meg hurried to her side.

Deirdre tried to stand, but her legs gave way beneath her.

"Can't you get up?" Meg asked.

"No. My ankle's twisted." Deirdre's face contorted in pain. "I'm not moving from this spot. That's apparent," she said.

People continued to swarm about, cursing as they nearly fell over the group knotted around Deirdre.

"Get up, you lazy hag!" yelled a well dressed young man, his purposeful gait interrupted.

"I'll not be moving for the likes of you!" she spat back.

He pulled back one sharp-toed boot. Kathleen saw his kick coming and quickly stepped in the way, taking the blow a few inches above her ankle. She clenched her jaw when his boot struck, but not a sound escaped through her gritted teeth as she stared him in the eye.

"You're all useless hags," he muttered, but could not return her look and hurried away.

"Kathleen, why did you do that?" Deirdre's voice softened as she reached out for her daughter.

"No filthy Brit'll be kicking my Mam," she said through her pain.

"Let me see it," Meg insisted.

She winced as she held out her leg and made little flexing motions with her foot to be sure she could move it.

"You're a darlin' to be sure," said Deirdre, "but I'd as soon taken his kick than have it fall on one of my lasses."

Meg released her sister, but stayed by her side. Kathleen gingerly tried putting weight on it. "'Tis fine, I think. It hurts, though."

"Kathleen, can you help me get Mam to that bench?" Meg asked, indicating a seat at the edge of the fairgrounds.

Kathleen nodded, but when she took a step forward she winced and almost fell.

"I can help," Brigid offered.

"Take her under her arm," Meg directed.

Meg and Brigid got on either side of Deirdre. Kathleen hobbled around behind and put her arms around her mother's waist. Together they half-dragged, half-carried Deirdre across the field.

"Has there been an accident?" The question was posed by a white-haired, round-faced gentleman.

"We're fine, thank you," said Meg as they continued to drag Deirdre.

"Meg," Kathleen whispered.

"We don't need help from a Brit."

"Has your mother taken a fall?" asked the gentleman.

Brigid and Kathleen stopped, forcing Meg to stop as well.

"No, sir. She was pushed by one of your high and mighty gentlemen." Meg exploded.

"And another man kicked Kathleen," Brigid added.

"We're trying to help her to that bench," Kathleen explained.

"It would please me to lend you a hand."

He scooped up Deirdre. To Meg's surprise, her mother offered no resistance.

He sat her sideways on the bench. "Rest here as long as you like, Madam. It is best to keep that foot elevated."

Deirdre reached for his hand. "May Saint Patrick watch over you and yours."

173

"Thank you so much," said Kathleen, taking a seat at the end of the bench.

"My dear, I think your own leg needs treatment. You seem to be having trouble walking."

"Are you a doctor?" Brigid asked.

"I am indeed. My apologies to you ladies. I should have introduced myself from the start. My name is Doctor Martin Parker, late of East Anglia. I've only arrived in Ireland a short time ago." He turned his attention back to Kathleen. "Now, about your leg."

"'Tis only bruised."

"May I have a look?" he asked.

Deirdre nodded and Kathleen lifted her leg to show the swollen purple knot.

"How in the world—?"

"I told you," said Brigid. "A man kicked her. He was trying to kick my mam, but Kathleen got in his way, so he kicked her instead."

"You are a very brave girl." He looked admiringly at Kathleen. "That will take some time to heal. I will give you some camphor to put on it every day until it's better. You should stay off that leg as much as possible."

Meg smirked. "I suppose you will have to fly home, Kathleen."

"Meg, don't." Kathleen glared at her. "Thank you, sir."

Deirdre's eyes widened in wonder. "May Saint Brigid be looking after you, as well."

"Thank you kindly. I suppose someone does."

"None of this would have happened if someone would have just bought our clothes." Brigid pouted.

"Don't you have a pig to sell?"

Meg flashed indignant. "Of course we have a pig to sell. My da and brother are taking care of that right now. But that will only pay the rent. We still need to eat."

"Indeed you do."

"Would you like to buy our clothes?" asked Brigid.

"Well now, let me see what you've got."

Brigid handed him the pile. He inspected each garment thoughtfully, exclaiming over the workmanship.

"My mam and my sisters sewed them," Brigid beamed.

"They are fine seamstresses indeed. I am surprised you haven't been able to make a fine profit on them," he told her.

"Most people don't seem to share your opinion," Kathleen explained.

"Perhaps they are only worried that you need them and don't want to take them from you."

"They would not be taking them," Meg snapped. "They would by buying them. And it certainly never bothered the Brits to take anything from us before!"

"I see. Well, I have enough food to share. I could give you some, as much or more than you would make on these clothes. Then you could keep them."

"You would?" Brigid's eyes widened. "Mam, I won't have to go naked, after all!" Brigid clapped her hands.

Meg felt the gall rising within her.

"We will sell the clothes. If not today, then some other day," she said evenly.

"You are a determined young lady, aren't you?" His smile irritated Meg. "But you won't mind then if I buy this one article from you?" he asked, holding up an old, very worn apron.

"If you pay for it you may have it, though I don't see what use it could be to you."

"Meg, hush!" Kathleen hissed at her.

"Please excuse my daughter," Deirdre said. "She is stubborn, but she is not in charge. If you would like to buy the apron, we will be most grateful for whatever you would like to offer for it."

Suddenly horrified that she might be ruining her family's best chance at survival, Meg clamped her mouth shut.

"I hope this is sufficient." He held a glittering coin.

"May the saints be forever praying for you!" Deirdre answered, reaching for the coin. None of them had any idea of its worth.

He cleared his throat and nodded. To Brigid, he said, "I assure you I do have a very good use for it."

175

"What?" she asked.

He looked into Brigid's big dark eyes. "Watch."

He ripped the linen apron into long strips. Then he took the strips of cloth and bound up Deirdre's swollen ankle.

"You see, it will help to make your mother's ankle well soon. Now, might I ask your names?"

"I am Deirdre O'Connor."

"A pleasure, ma'am," he said gently taking Deirdre's hand in his own.

"Thank you, sir," she whispered. "May Saint—"

"Yes, ma'am," he interrupted. "All the saints may indeed pray for me if they like, but perhaps they'd do better to pray for you and yours."

Kathleen gestured towards the others. "This is my elder sister, Meg, and my younger sister Brigid, and I'm Kathleen."

"Now that we have made our acquaintances, please allow me to offer you a ride home in my phaeton."

"We don't need—" Meg began, but he cut her off.

"Your mother and sister really should not walk."

"We will ride with you, thank you," Deirdre answered, throwing Meg a stern look.

"But what about Da and Brendan?" asked Brigid.

"We'll wait for them. I am in no hurry," said Dr. Parker.

They sat together, resting and awaiting the return of Denis and Brendan.

Meg's hand gripped the comb in her pocket. The thought that Rory's family might be evicted sickened her. Getting up, she declared, "I have something to do," and ran off.

"Your da will be back soon, Meg," her mother yelled.

"I'll hurry," Meg called over her should and rushed into the crowd.

She pushed her way through the throngs of people as rapidly as she could, alert for anyone who looked like a good prospect. Her legs felt shaky and her heart pounded, but the importance of her mission carried her on. She caught sight of a handsome, well-dressed young man, barely older than herself standing with two other fellows near the woods. Perhaps if he had a sweetheart she could talk him into buying the comb for her.

Meg hurried to him, but when she got close, realized she'd made a mistake. He reeked of whiskey. Meg turned, but she had come too close. He caught her arm roughly pulling her into the center of his group which closed around her. Trapped, her heart raced.

"Looking for someone, wench?" he asked, staggering so that he nearly fell over her.

Meg turned her head away in disgust.

"I don't think she likes you, Frederick," said one of his companions.

"Oh, she likes me all right, don't you, wench?" Pulling her against him, he covered her mouth with his own. The taste of whiskey and foul breath made her gag. Though he had her arms pinned she struggled, trying to free herself. Realizing it was no use, she picked up one foot and kicked him in the shin as hard as she could.

"Bitch!" He shoved her to the ground.

Frederick caught her as she tried to regain her feet. Taking her by both arms he yelled in her face, "You stupid, popish bitch! You stink, do you know that?"

Meg returned his glare. "Aye, but at least I have an excuse!"

Frederick's companions laughed.

"She's too feisty for you," one of them teased.

Frederick slapped her hard in the face, knocking her to the ground. The comb fell into the dirt. Its retrieval became more important than her pain. She scrambled for it, covering it with her body. Barely did she have it in her hand than she felt herself being hauled up by the back of her dress. Strong arms closed around her, squeezing the breath from her body.

"What have you got there?" asked one of the young men.

"Looks far too fancy for the likes of you," said another.

Meg's hands tightened on the comb, its tines pressing into her palm.

"Not something you could afford. Must have stolen it, I'd say."

"Looks like something that papist bloke what used to do the carvings might have made," said the first man. "Hey, didn't he make that very comb for your Sally? And now it's gone missing, hasn't it?"

Meg's blood pounded through her body.

"Naw. His work weren't that good," answered the youth, either too drunk or too stupid to pick up on his friend's attempted ruse. "Besides, he don't sell no more. Heard he cut his hand off."

"Stupid clod," laughed his companion. "Forgot he was supposed to cut the wood and cut his hand instead."

Throughout this exchange, Frederick was still holding Meg in a tight grip. "Shut up!" he yelled at his friends. "Who gives a damn about a comb?"

Then he turned his attention to Meg. "You must learn to show more respect for your betters," Frederick's whiskey-drenched voice slurred in her ear. "Perhaps you would like to accompany us on a little walk in the woods."

The others laughed again, the sound of danger in it. As Frederick turned around, dragging her with him, they suddenly found themselves face to face with the massive form of Father O'Malley.

"Or perhaps she would prefer to go home with her family," said the priest.

"Father," Meg whispered. Relief flooded her.

Frederick let go and she fell gratefully into Father O'Malley's arms.

"Fancy her for yourself, do you, Father?" Frederick sneered.

Father O'Malley still had one arm around Meg's shoulder, sheltering her. She felt his body stiffen. His free hand clenched into a fist. For a moment she believed he would hit the young man.

"I want to go home," Meg pleaded.

Father O'Malley looked blankly at her for a moment.

"Please, Father," she begged.

Still keeping one arm protectively around her, he turned his back on the small group of obnoxious youths and walked Meg away from them. Stones flew after them as he ushered Meg in front of him, using his own body as a shield. Meg heard the thunk as a rock hit his back.

"Where is the rest of your family?" he asked once they were out of range and swallowed up by the crowd

"That way." Meg pointed.

When they got to the bench they found that Denis and Brendan had arrived.

"Father, you look tired," said Deirdre. "Sit down with us for a minute or two. Kathleen, give Father some room."

Seeing the bruise on Kathleen's leg, Father O'Malley would not allow her to budge. He sat on the ground and insisted on hearing what had happened to them.

"What in the world were you up to, Meg?" Deirdre asked after she finished telling of their ordeal.

Before Meg could answer, Dr. Parker, who had gone to fetch his horse and phaeton, returned.

He glanced at the bedraggled family, "I see you are all back together and you've brought a friend along, as well."

He walked toward Father O'Malley who stood at his approach.

"Dr. Martin Parker, at your service, Father." He smiled broadly and extended his hand.

"Father Brian O'Malley," the priest said, barely returning the handshake and not at all the smile.

Dr. Parker' genial countenance faded. "Well, shall we all be going?" He asked, turning to Denis.

As the family rose, Father O'Malley looked at them in bewilderment. "Going?"

"Dr. Parker has kindly offered us a ride home," Deirdre explained.

"I think we've had enough of Gale Day festivities," Denis added.

"He's a nice man, Father," Brigid told him.

"A Godsend, he is," Deirdre agreed.

"It would appear so," said Father O'Malley as he helped Deirdre into the phaeton while Denis tied his cart behind it.

Meg had been silent since returning to her family. She knew what would have happened to her if Father O'Malley had not appeared when he did. Her mind would not let go of the picture of herself in the woods at the mercy of a trio of drunken youths who hated her for her race and religion. As Father O'Malley held out his hand to assist her into the vehicle, she suddenly threw herself into his arms, sobbing. He hugged her close for a moment, then gently pushed her away, holding her at arm's length.

Dr. Parker, sitting in the driver's box, busied himself with the reins. Deirdre stared, incredulous. Denis came around the side of the phaeton to take his daughter in hand.

As Denis pulled her away, Father O'Malley put a hand on his shoulder and whispered, "Meg was trapped by a group of drunken British lads who were treating her roughly and had plans for much worse. By the grace of God I caught sight of what was happening. I was able to get her away before they could do much damage, but she has taken a terrible fright."

Denis looked into his daughter's dirt-smeared face. Her da wrapped his arms around Meg, hugging her tightly. "Tis a miracle you are standing here with me."

Denis turned back to Father O'Malley. "I owe you a great debt, Father."

"May I give you a ride somewhere, Father?" Dr. Parker called from atop the driver's box.

"I am much obliged, but I prefer to walk."

"Very well, then. It was a pleasure to make your acquaintance," Dr. Parker said with a wave of his hand and a flick of the reins.

The horse stepped smoothly forward, pulling the phaeton and its passengers away. From inside the vehicle Meg could hear the voices of Dr. Parker and her da who sat upon the box. Dr. Parker did most of the talking, mainly about his horse.

"She's a beauty, isn't she?" he asked Denis who merely nodded his assent.

"Lily's the best horse I've ever owned. Just watch how she moves. See that fine rippling muscle? She is so powerful and yet her pure white hair and her inborn sense of grace and majesty, well..." The doctor broke off in a sigh. He was silent for a moment, then suddenly burst out, "A goddess! Yes, a goddess of horse, that's what she is, my Lily."

"Aye," said Denis.

Behind them the rest of the family sat exhausted. Brigid nuzzled close to her mother and was soon lulled to sleep by vehicle's rhythmic movement.

None of the family had ever ridden in any sort of conveyance before. Under normal circumstances it would have been cause for great excitement. They would have absorbed the feel of the road as it passed under them, the rumbling of the wheels, the clopping of the horse's feet, and the sight of the countryside rolling past. Pain, starvation and exhaustion blotted out their pleasure.

Meg held the comb in her lap. Tiny indents remained in the palm of her hand where the tines had dug into her. She had no idea how much the rent cost nor the worth of the comb, but she understood from the drunken conversation of the youths that it must have value greater than Rory's other carvings. She determined that she would tell Rory of her plan to sell it to help pay the rent. She must do it fast, though, before the Quinn's were turned out of their house.

Chapter Eighteen

It was late the next day when Father O'Malley arrived at the O'Connors' cottage. The November sunlight barely penetrated the cottage's only window. Most of the light and all of the warmth came from the cook fire. The long, thin shadows of the cottage's inhabitants quivered eerily against the bare walls. Denis paced the cottage floor, looking over its sparse furnishings and muttering to himself. Father O'Malley peeked into the cauldron Deirdre was stirring. A handful of leaves and nettles along with a few chunks of a vegetable floated in the bubbling water. He placed a consoling hand on Deirdre's shoulder.

They were all there except Brendan. Kathleen and Brigid were seated on the floor, on either side of the fireplace. Meg sat at the table near the window, gazing out at a cold, lifeless world.

Denis continued to walk slowly about the room, puzzling over some unfathomable dilemma. His footsteps and the soft snapping of the peat fire were the only sounds. Though they had greeted him cordially, all were unnaturally quiet.

"What are you about?" Father O'Malley asked him, breaking the silence.

Denis stopped pacing, put his hands on his hips and said with resignation, "I'm trying to figure what we can best do without."

The rustle of clothing as all uncomfortably shifted position pinpricked the hush of the room.

"I'm going to pawn whatever we don't absolutely need. I'll barter for food if I can, or if not, I'll sell for cash. I prefer to barter if possible. It's few times in my life I've held money in my hands. I'd rather be holding something we can eat."

"Wasn't the coin that doctor gave you worth anything?" He had not seen the money Dr. Parker had given Deirdre for her old apron, but he had been told about it. Suspicious, he now wished he had insisted upon seeing it.

"Aye, it was and when he left us here at home he gave us food as well, just as I prefer. Some bread, it was and eggs and a few vegetables."

Puzzled, Father O'Malley turned back toward Deirdre, still stirring the cauldron of water and leaves.

"Then why...?"

Denis put a hand on the priest's arm and nudged him back to face him.

"I know what you're thinking, Father, but the food he gave us, we can't eat it all at once. It'll run out too soon. But if we eat only a small bit at a time, say each of us having a bite or two once or twice a week, well maybe we can make it last a while. Besides, if we eat it all now, then once it's gone we'd be starting our starving all over again and, believe me, one time is enough. So, I'm thinking now that if I can sell some of our things, and Brendan doing his part and all, well, we might just get through this winter."

A table and two chairs, a few cooking utensils, a wooden stool by the fireside, all of it crudely though sturdily made was of little value. Father O'Malley couldn't imagine that anyone with money to spare would be willing to buy it, but he didn't voice his opinion.

Instead he asked Denis, "Where is Brendan?"

"In town."

"Begging," Meg added.

Both men turned to her.

"He's been going into town nearly every day to beg for food. On the way home he searches the fields and woods for anything growing wild and usually has better luck with that."

"What of your sewing? Aren't you getting enough mending work?"

"We get little to none now."

"I'm sorry!" Brigid wailed from her corner.

"Hush, child," Deirdre admonished. "No one's blaming you."

Confused by this exchange, Father O'Malley wasn't sure what to say.

"Brigid got the tiniest blood stain on a shirt I was mending. It wouldn't come out and the Hoffreys whose shirt it was have spread it around that it was a huge stain, that we ruined their shirt and that we've gotten slatternly in our work. Now we get nothing," Meg explained.

"Surely, your regular customers know better than that."

"They'd rather believe their Brit neighbors over their own eyes and our word." Meg stomped off to a darkened corner of the room near the door and became only a huddled shadow.

"I think the table and chairs can go," Denis muttered, turning his attention back to Father O'Malley. "That stool by the fire, maybe, too, if we have to, but I'd just as soon Deirdre have something to sit on besides the floor."

Denis glanced toward the fire where Deirdre and the two other girls sat. "I think I'll ask Dr. Parker if he knows anyone who might buy the table and chairs."

"Is he coming back, then?"

"Aye. He said he'd come back to check on Deirdre and Kathleen."

Deirdre turned to look at them. "He's a good man." A smile spread across her face.

Denis dropped his tone to a whisper. "She does perk up whenever he's mentioned."

Father O'Malley went to the corner where Kathleen sat.

"How is your leg, Kathleen?"

"I still have trouble walking, but I think it's getting better." She grimaced as she patted the swollen bruised spot. "'Tis only a bad bruise. It will heal." She smiled, but there was something false in it, as though she didn't believe her own words.

Kathleen was an enigma to Father O'Malley. She'd always been a quiet child and now, at sixteen, was not much different. There was something in what she left unspoken and the stony way she had of setting her face that worried him. To be sure, she had an intelligence and a determination to match Meg's, but where Meg was impetuous and often explosive, Kathleen was silent. He could understand Meg because she never held back, but Kathleen remained hidden. Though she spoke little of it, he feared that she continued to blame herself for Aiden's death. He knew how detrimental turning blame inward upon oneself could be.

The door creaked open. Father O'Malley felt the cold air on his back as Brendan entered.

"Did you get anything?" Deirdre's hands were folded as if in prayer.

Brendan reached into his pockets as the family congregated around him. One hand pulled out a withered turnip and the other brought forth a fistful of acorns. "Only these."

Deirdre swallowed hard. "Good," she whispered. She gave Brendan a kiss on the cheek, took the food from him and walked to the cauldron.

"I almost had some bread," Father O'Malley heard Brendan whisper to Denis. "But another lad got the last piece before I could. I'm sorry, Da."

Denis patted his son's shoulder. "You did your best."

"You'll be staying to supper, Father?" Deirdre invited.

Father O'Malley was touched by her generosity. "I must go, but thank you," he said, and saw himself out.

He stood outside in the cold air staring at the tiny cottage, trying not to wonder if he would soon be called upon to bury any of its inhabitants as he had been doing for so many of his parishioners in recent weeks. Even Dacey Kilpatrick could not boast a successful crop this year. In fact, like everyone else, he had none at all. At Father O'Malley's last visit the Kilpatrick children appeared thin, hungry and bedraggled, a sight he never thought to see. Dacey, beside himself, could not seem to fathom how his grand good fortune had run out.

Now that the sun had set, the air was cold. He sped his gait to warm up as he headed home. The evening was silent

185

except for the sound of stiff, frosted grass crunching under his feet. Behind him a door banged shut. The sound of a young feminine voice calling his name sliced through the air. He stopped abruptly. Turning, he saw a waif-like figure running toward him. When caught by the moonlight, the flailing rags of its dress appeared as winding sheets. He forced that thought from his mind and hurried forward.

"Meg, get back inside before you freeze," he admonished.

Though her teeth chattered, she refused to yield. She held something out to him and asked, "Will you take this, please, Father?"

It was too dark to see what she offered. "What is it?"

"My comb. I tried to sell it at Gale Day." She paused for a moment, then went on. "Rory made it. He gave it to me when he asked me to wed. It's the only nice thing we've got. I doubt anyone will take our table and chairs. Even if they do we won't get much for them. But for this we might. I believe it's worth more than anything else Rory ever made. Will you sell it for me? Only do it quickly. I want to give the money to the Quinns to help pay their rent."

"Meg, this comb, no matter how fine it be, would not pay the rent. Keep it. I'm sure Rory wants you to have it."

"No, Father. He made me promise that if things got bad enough I'd sell it for food. He meant for me, I know, but he and I are as one. Well, almost. We will be after the famine, anyway. So I want to use it to help him."

"Have you spoken with Rory about what Blackburn said to his Da at Gale Day?"

"No. We've been too busy tending to Mam and Kathleen. I haven't had a chance to speak to him, but I know from Brigid that Mr. Quinn was going to ask Mr. Blackburn for some extra time to find the pig that ran off. She said you were going to speak on his behalf. Father, didn't Mr. Blackburn give them the extension?" Before he could respond, she rattled on, "I know that pig's gone for good. Mam's been having her feelings and dreaming about missing pigs for weeks so there's no use looking for it. But

186

if they got some extra time, maybe they can scrape some money together, sell their furniture like my da's doing, and that along with whatever you can get for this comb—"

"Meg, stop." He hated to tell her, but she had to know. "Blackburn refused to grant the extension. He all but admitted he set up the stealing of that pig. It's his way of getting back at Rory's da over the letter. They'll be evicted in a matter of days." Father O'Malley was glad for the dark. He did not want to see the pain in Meg's face. "Please, Meg. Go inside before you take a chill."

Meg was silent for a moment. When she spoke, her voice was resolute. "Then it's more important than ever. We must move quickly. I'll tell Rory to sell everything they've got as fast as they can and that you'll be selling the comb. We'll get the rent money together before they can serve the eviction notice."

"Meg, you know that's impossible."

"I know no such thing until it's done." Her voice turned plaintive. "Please, Father. It's the only chance we've got."

Father O'Malley knew that once Meg had set her mind on something it wasn't to be changed, so he chose another path.

"Maybe that doctor would do a better job of selling it than I." Father O'Malley hated to admit it, but the doctor undoubtedly had wealthy British contacts. "When he comes back you should—" Father O'Malley began.

"If he comes back. I know he's been kind to us, but he's a Brit and I don't trust him. I trust you."

Father O'Malley felt the hard, cold wood of the comb being pressed into his hands as her words pressed into his heart.

"You'll do it for me, Father?"

There was no sense in arguing. "I'll try, Meg. Now get back inside."

"Thank you, Father."

In the moonlight he could just barely see the quaking of her emaciated body. "In, Meg. Now!" he commanded.

187

She squeezed his hand, then turned to run home. A flash of firelight appeared as the door opened and, just as quickly, disappeared as it closed behind her.

Entering his cottage, he built a fire of his own. A sparse meal of roasted turnips left him even hungrier. He tried to forget the gnawing in his stomach by thinking about where he could sell Meg's comb. He pulled it from his pocket and held it close to the firelight. It was large and heavy. He ran his hands over the dark wood. He smiled at the intertwined hearts each topped with a single rose meshed so closely together that the petals of one became those of the other and it was impossible to tell where one rose ended and the other began.

My boy, if only you'd been born into different circumstances, oh, what you could have done with your life, he thought. Why had such talent had been given to one who was powerless to use it? He thought of the work Rory must have put into it and the pride he surely felt upon presenting it to Meg. He pictured the comb lying on the dressing table of a wealthy British girl, dwarfed among all her expensive baubles, uncared for, unimportant.

It does not belong there, he thought. *But where, then? Where else could it possibly go?*

"It should float on a star in the night sky." The words jumped into his mind from nowhere. Siobhan's voice.

"Oh, is this one of hers, then?" he asked Siobhan aloud.

He leaned back in his chair, allowing his mind to wander. He hadn't thought of that day in years, but now it felt comforting. And he desperately needed comforting.

They were walking up a hillside hand-in-hand on a glorious summer day. Early morning mist had given way to a burst of sunshine that seemed to light up the whole world. A million dew drop diamonds sparkled over the grass. Shimmering emerald leaves fluttered in the soft breeze. Creation was wide awake and laughing.

"Quentin has told me your secret," he'd teased Siobhan.

"And which secret is that?"

"He said that your great, great grandmother was one of the good people," he'd answered, using the self-protecting euphemism for a faery.

"'Tis no secret. Many people have heard that rumor."

"Aye, but he also told me that you are one yourself. Are you?"

"My brother has a wild imagination." She'd laughed, but there was a mischievous twinkle in her eyes. Oh, those eyes! They were a shade of green he had seen in no other human being before or since. The grass, the leaves, the mountainside, the greenness of the earth were in her eyes and he'd wondered if it felt different to possess eyes the color of nature.

"You haven't answered my question. Are you a changeling faery?" Only a small part of him really wondered.

"Do you think so?"

"Perhaps," he'd teased. "You are like no one else I've ever known. And I did see you skimming dew one morning from your landlord's pasture. Did his crops fail as you planned?"

"Who said I planned such a thing? I was only out for an early morning stroll. I like to go out when the sun is just rising."

She'd been walking backwards, pulling his hand, leading him farther up the hillside. He'd stopped her. "Don't you love me enough to share your secrets with me?"

"Brian, I love you enough to share my whole life with you."

It was what he wanted most to hear. He was about to take her in his arms to satisfy the overwhelming flood of emotion that filled his being. But before he could she'd scampered up the hill, always just out of reach.

"If I say, 'no, I am not a faery', then all the fun is lost, and if I say 'aye', you will never know whether or not to believe me. Now, you tell me, what am I to say?"

He'd thought a moment, then answered, "Tell me something only a faery would know."

189

She'd laughed, a flute-like sound, tugged his hand as they raced to the top of the hill. When they reached the summit, she dropped down. He landed in a heap beside her.

"I will tell you about someone I know."

"Who?"

"The West Wind."

"Please, do tell me all about him."

"Oh, no, no, no." She shook her head, her long, unruly copper curls like sparks glinting in the sunlight. "The West Wind is a woman."

"And what is she like?"

"She's beautiful. She has long black hair that goes on forever. It flies in waves all across the sky. At night she sprinkles stardust through it so it sparkles."

Oh, the fantastic quality of her imagination! Carefully, she watched his face as she wove her story.

"Her gown is as blue as the sky itself and her eyes are the deepest shade of blue, the color of Heaven's windows."

As she spoke, she stopped looking at him, shifting her gaze to the sky. Her fancy was delightful, but he wanted her attention for himself. Gently, he'd reached into her thick mane, letting fiery red strands twine themselves around his fingers.

"Does she manage to tame that mass of long hair any better than you do?"

"Aye, she keeps it very well. And well she might...she has a better comb than I."

He'd kissed the ends of her curls. "So where does she keep this comb of hers?"

"'Tis a magical comb. It comes whenever she calls for it. When she isn't using it, it floats on a star in the night sky."

* * *

Father O'Malley looked down at Meg's comb resting in his hands. Should he go outside and throw it into the air for the West Wind to catch?

"Foolish old man," he laughed at himself.

190

I trust you. This time it was Meg's voice he heard in his head. His heart sank at the knowledge that he could not possibly accomplish the task with which she'd entrusted him.

"Ah, Meg," he said, holding the comb reverently in his hands. "Paying the rent with this comb is as much a fantasy as Siobhan's West Wind."

Chapter Nineteen

"They're knocking it down!"

Brendan's yell from the doorway awakened Meg with a start. It was barely dawn. Meg heard banging coming from the direction of the Quinn cottage. Clutching her ragged shawl, she stumbled out the door and across the field. The constable and several of his men swarmed in and out of the Quinn cottage. Armed with clubs and crowbars, they pulled the timbers down. A small battering ram stood off to one side near a caved-in section of the cottage.

Meg searched for Rory. His back was to her. His arms flailed, the tatters of his black tailcoat flapping like a deranged crow. He yelled at one of the constable's men. The man held his bar horizontally, at ease, in front of him. Meg gasped when, without warning, the metal bar flashed upward, smashing Rory in the face and knocking him to the ground. The man turned away, disappearing into the cottage.

Meg ran the rest of the way down the incline, falling on her knees at Rory's side. His mouth was filled with blood but he was conscious and trying to get up.

"Ram it again," a voice called out.

"Wait! My wife is still in there!" Thomas Quinn shouted from somewhere in the din.

"I pulled her out once already. If she went back in it's her own fault. I'm not going to keep pulling you Paddies out all day. Ram it, again, damn it!"

Meg watched Rory's da lurch toward the doorway. Before he reached it the battering ram slammed into the cottage, shaking its entire frame. Smashing sounds resounded from inside. Rory choked on the blood in his mouth as he called out for his mother.

"Anna! Anna!" Thomas yelled. He stumbled through the doorway. Meg helped Rory to his feet, never taking her eyes off the cottage door.

"Oh, dear God in Heaven!" It was her mother's voice. Meg turned to see her parents and Brendan stumbling down the incline towards them.

"Rory, don't go in there," Meg called as he staggered toward the cottage. "Da, help me stop him."

She started after him, calling over her shoulder, "They've rammed it with Rory's mam inside and his da's gone in after her."

"May the Lord have mercy." Deirdre crossed herself.

Denis and Brendan hurried to catch up with Rory. They grabbed him and though he struggled to free himself, he was too weak and collapsed on the ground.

Deirdre ripped a large piece of cloth from the hem of her skirt and mopped at the blood. All four bent over him. A loud banging rent the air. Everyone's attention snapped back to the Quinn's cottage.

"May God damn their black souls to hell!" Denis thundered. "They've rammed it again with both of them inside."

Denis started toward the cottage, but Deirdre grabbed Brendan's arm and held him back. "I need you to help me with Rory," she told him. "Meg, go round up all the bairns."

"But I can't leave him."

"We'll take care of him. Off with ya, now."

Meg surveyed the scene. Rory's young brothers and sisters were everywhere. She staggered in among the swarm of people. Intent on pulling the house down, the Constable's men took little notice of her. One by one, she gathered them up, clutching little Seamus in her arms, snatching Lizzy away from the splintered, teetering wreck that was once a doorway, calling to Loreena to follow her. She found Aisling, sitting on the ground staring at the cottage. The baby, Darien, was in her lap, crying. Aisling wouldn't speak nor get up. She seemed not to even notice Darien's presence. Meg handed Seamus to Loreena so she could pull Aisling to her feet. Once Meg had all of the children gathered, she herded them back to where her mother sat with Rory and Brendan. Rory had regained consciousness and was struggling to sit.

Deirdre squeezed Meg's shoulder. "I think he's going to be all right."

The knot of children hovered about while the others helped Rory. Deirdre continued to hold the blood-soaked cloth to his lips.

Brendan peered closely at Rory's mouth. "The bleeding's nearly stopped."

"Mam! Mam!" The high-pitched screech of the child's voice caught their attention. Aisling, was hopping from one foot to the other, pointing with spastic motions to what was once her home.

"God in heaven!" Deirdre cried.

Denis and Thomas were crawling out of the shattered doorway, dragging with them a crushed and blood-smeared form. Even from a distance it was obvious that the body was too badly mangled to have any life in it.

"Meg, help me," Deirdre ordered. "We must get these wee ones home. They should not be seeing this. Brendan, help us lift Rory."

The three of them pulled Rory to his feet.

Rory leaned heavily upon Meg. She turned to ask Brendan's help only to find him racing into the Quinn's yard.

"Mam, Brendan's—"

"There's nothing we can do about it now. We have to get them home."

Meg and her mother hurried the children on as quickly as possible, occasionally stopping to nudge any who turned to look back. The weight of Rory's body eased up on Meg now and then, but he would fall again and their steps would slow. When they reached the O'Connor home they were greeted at the door by the anxious faces of Kathleen and Brigid.

"They've been evicted and the cottage wrecked," her mother told them. "Help me with these bairns. Get them settled 'round the fire."

Kathleen took over with the children, getting the shivering bodies warm. Before long, her aching leg forced her to sit with Darien in her lap.

Meg and Deirdre propped Rory against the wall. Meg took off her ragged black shawl and covered his chest with it.

Brigid stood in the middle of the room, looking about in wonder. "Where are Da and Brendan?"

"They've stayed behind to help," Deirdre answered.

"Help do what?"

"Go and sit with the others by the fire."

Brigid obeyed, but continued to ask questions. "Will Rory's mam and da be coming here, too?"

"My mam is dead!" Aisling cried. "They've knocked our house down on top of her."

Kathleen and Brigid gasped. All the Quinn children began to wail.

"Is it true, Mam?" Kathleen asked.

"Aye, 'tis. Damned Brits."

Deirdre left Rory's side to help Kathleen comfort the children.

Meg watched the scene in front of the fireplace, but she would not leave Rory. Ignoring propriety, she sat nestled against his side, one arm locked protectively across him. Placing her head on his chest she felt his body make slight jerking motions. He squeezed his eyes shut while drawing in deep breaths.

"There's no need to hold back, Rory," she whispered.

The last of his willpower melted. He cried as unashamedly as his younger siblings. Meg put her arms around him and laid her face against his cheek, mingling her tears with his. It seemed hours that they sat there before the door opened to admit Denis and Mr. Quinn.

Deirdre left her place by the fire to join them. Meg heard them whispering, caught a word or two. She heard her mother's surprised question, "No wake?" The men

195

hushed her, then more whispering. Deirdre, Denis and Thomas crouched next to Rory and Meg.

"Rory…" Thomas got only that far when the words choked up in his throat.

"It's all right, Da. I know Mam is dead."

"Where's Brendan?" Meg asked.

"We've sent him for Father O'Malley," Denis told her.

"Where is Mam?" Rory asked.

"Round back, out of sight.

Rory leaned forward. "You left her out there?"

"We couldn't bring her in, Rory. The wee ones. She's so…" Thomas broke off.

"But you can't leave her there."

"The wee ones, don't you understand?"

Meg stroked his cheek. "Rory, it's all right. Everything will be taken care of."

Rory gently removed her hands and set her away, never taking his eyes off his da.

Denis spoke to Rory in a low voice. "Listen lad, we did only what we thought best. She was no more of a sight for the gloating eyes of those bastards than she was for the innocent eyes of these wee ones." Denis nodded towards the group huddled around Kathleen in front of the fireplace.

Rory swallowed hard, blinked back tears and nodded.

"But I will see her." He started to rise.

"Lad, you don't want to." Denis tried to hold him back.

"No, I don't want to, but I have to."

"Why, Rory?" Meg clung to him, but he firmly set her aside and headed towards the door.

"I have to know what they did to her."

"Da, stop him."

"It may be best to let him go."

"Why?"

"He's not a child, Meg. He might as well see first-hand what's for us in this world."

"Aye, but not alone." Meg found Rory kneeling on the ground behind the cottage.

She caught a glimpse of the body placed on a plaster slab that had once been part of the wall of the Quinn

196

cottage. The shape only somewhat resembled a human form. Parts were crushed, others twisted. Brown, drying blood covered the remains.

Meg screamed.

Rory took her in his arms. "Why did you come out here, Meg?"

"To be with you."

"I wish you had not seen her."

"Why did you insist on it for yourself?"

Rory stared off towards where his family's cottage used to stand. "I had to know exactly what to hate them for."

Meg had never seen such a fierce look in his face.

Deirdre appeared in the yard carrying rags and a bucket. "I will need your help," she told Meg.

Gently pushing Rory toward the cottage she told him, "Go back inside, lad. This is for the women."

He obeyed without objection so she turned her attention to Meg. "Brendan will be here with Father O'Malley soon. We must work quickly. I've set Kathleen to sewing a shroud. You and I will have to wash and make her as decent as possible."

Meg pulled back in horror. She remembered Aiden's body, remembered thinking how awful it must be to prepare it for burial. This was worse. Aiden was not smashed and crushed like his mother.

"I cannot." Meg's stomach squeezed.

"Meg, you will have to be strong." In a softer tone, she added, "Think of it as a gift to Rory."

I already know what she looks like, Meg told herself. *It will not frighten me.* A shock rippled through her when the mangled body again came into view, but it was less intense than her first sight of the corpse. Meg could barely breathe, could not force herself forward. She watched her mother set the bucket down and place the handful of rags on the plaster slab next to the body. Deirdre called to her, but she still couldn't move.

"'Tis a terrible thing that your first time at this must be such a horrible one." Deirdre returned to Meg taking her

197

hands in her own. "The first time I helped was for my old aunt Sarah, may God rest her soul. She died a natural death, but even that was bad enough. I could not sleep for many nights afterwards. Meg, I can't do it alone and I've no one else to help me. Father will be here soon."

She tugged Meg's hands, succeeding only in inching her slightly forward.

"You will do this many times and it will never be easy, but perhaps after this one it will never seem quite so bad."

When Meg didn't move Deirdre dropped her daughter's hands and placed her own hands on her hips. She stuck out her jaw and demanded, "Are you going to tell Rory that you could not help prepare his sainted mother's body for a decent Christian burial because you were scared? Well, off with ye, then. Go sit with the wee ones 'round the fire, but don't be standing out here wasting my time."

Deirdre strode off.

Meg squared her shoulders. She would not go back inside. She would do this no matter what it took. Willing herself forward, Meg followed her mother.

Deirdre said nothing about Meg's new-found courage. Instead she dipped a rag into the bucket of warm water, handed it to her daughter and told her to begin washing. The blood pounded so hard in Meg's ears that she was barely able to hear her mother's instructions.

She swallowed hard, squeezed the rag with one hand and gripped the edge of the plaster slab with the other. Looking down she saw little that she could recognize as Rory's mother. Half the head was caved in, the torso crushed, arms and legs broken. Blood was everywhere. Worst of all were the eyes; wide open with a look of horrified surprise.

Meg kept one hand on the slab to steady herself.

"We shall do the face first," Deirdre instructed.

The face. With those horrible, staring eyes. Pressing the cloth gingerly against the cheek, she felt the softness of the skin as it moved gently over rough bone. Slowly, as she became accustomed to it, she scrubbed harder. Meg worked, thankfully, on the side that was not caved in while her mother did her best to clean up that most terrible part. It was slow work, but finally Deirdre said to stop.

"There now. Her face is finished. Stand back a moment, Meg and take a look at what a good job you've done."

Meg heard pride in her mother's voice. Looking at the corpse, she did see the difference. The face was clean. Her mother had done a remarkable job of removing the gore and, though still an awful sight, Meg was now able to look upon it with less revulsion.

She watched as her mother leaned over the body, looking directly into those staring, vacant eyes. "Don't you worry none now, Anna. We're going to do you up just right. My lass has got the way of it now and you'll be sent off to glory in fine fashion."

With the help of a large stone, Deirdre chipped two small pieces off the plaster. Gently, she closed her neighbor's eyes and placed the pieces over them.

This twisted, mangled mass had indeed been a woman. A wife. A mother. A friend and neighbor. Meg began to understand her mother's pride.

"We'd best remove her clothes next," Deirdre said.

It wasn't hard to do. What little clothing she'd had was torn to pieces. When the body was stripped they began to wash away the blood.

"It's like your sewing, Meg," her mother explained, as together they worked their way down the body. "Do it with care. 'Tis done for a practical reason, but done for love as much."

Meg managed a fleeting smile. As she scrubbed the length of Mrs. Quinn's arm, watching the drying blood vanish under her rag, she did feel a certain pride. Like her impending marriage, this chore, horrible as it was, was another initiation into adulthood. As her rag swept over Anna's throat and chest, a deeper feeling emerged in Meg. It was love. Love for Mrs. Quinn who had treated her like her own daughter. Love for her own mother, whose skilled hands had done this task more times than Meg cared to know. Most of all, love for Rory who had lost his brother and now his own dear Mam. The thought of the anguish he must be enduring edged out her revulsion. In its place was determination to do her very best by his mother.

"Here we be! We've come to help."

Meg and Deirdre looked up to see a small band of women approaching; all carrying buckets and rags.

"Your lass, Brigid, came 'round and told us what happened," one of them explained. "The men are all out getting the grave dug."

Suddenly, many hands joined in the task. Their years of experience made the work go quickly. Constant chatter filled the air with white puffs of breath.

"I sent all her bairns over to our place," Mrs. Devlin told Deirdre. "'Course they'll come back for the wake."

"Denis says we aren't to wake her. Just bury her and get it over with quickly."

"No wake!" exclaimed Mrs. Kilroy. "'Tis bad luck, I'd say. Very bad luck."

"Thomas wishes it so."

"If we don't wake her, might not her soul stay roaming until we do?" Mrs. Welch's voice held a note of fear.

"I told him. Said it wasn't right. But it's because of the bairns. Thomas doesn't want them to see her like this and who could blame him for that, I'm thinking."

Meg caught the sound of hammering.

"Thomas and your da are taking apart your table and chairs along with whatever scraps they could find from the Quinn's cottage to make a coffin for her." Mrs. Welch explained.

"Might just as well," Deirdre said. "We'd never be able to sell them."

"'Tis understandable about Thomas not wanting his bairns to see her, but I don't see why we can't wake her if we keep the coffin lid closed," Mrs. Kilroy suggested.

A smile spread across Deirdre's face. "We'll do that, Katie."

"What if Da and Mr. Quinn don't think that's a good idea?" Meg asked.

"It's been decided," Deirdre answered. "Meg, wash your hands off in that bucket of clean water, then go inside and see how Kathleen's coming with the shroud."

"Does she be needing a shroud if she's to have a coffin?" asked Mrs. Welch.

"We had to rip her clothes off and there's nothing else to dress her in. I suppose the shroud's not necessary, but I feel better her being covered decent in some way," Deirdre responded.

Meg found Kathleen sitting on their mother's stool in front of the fire. Brigid sat on the floor, solemnly placing the needle and thread back into the sewing box. The table and chairs were gone. Only the stool was left making the tiny room appear cavernous.

Kathleen looked up. "'Tis ready." She handed Meg a perfectly worked length of pristine white cloth.

"Is it one of ours?" Meg questioned. Yards of white cloth was kept carefully on a shelf against the days of the burials for their own family members.

"Mam said to make her a shroud. Did you suppose I'd be after hunting through the rubble to find one of their own?"

"Don't know what I supposed." Meg, still feeling dazed, took it and left the cottage. Outside, she noticed her brother and Father O'Malley approaching.

"Meg, I am so sorry. How is Rory faring?" Father O'Malley asked.

Meg wasn't sure how to answer. Rory seemed changed by what had happened, but she didn't know how to put it into words.

"Meg, are you all right?"

"Aye, Father. I just realized, I don't know where Rory is. I've been so busy helping my mam that I don't know what's become of him."

"You helped prepare the body? I thought you'd be inside sewing the shroud."

"No, Father. Kathleen did this. I'll tell them you've come."

201

Meg brought the shroud out back and announced Father O'Malley's arrival.

"We'll drape it over her for now until Father has finished," Deirdre said. "Meg, go bring him 'round."

The women widened the arc of their circle as the priest approached. He began the solemn intonation of the prayers for the dead. The women stood silently, hands folded, heads bowed. The slow steady drone of the prayers settled into Meg's soul with a calming peace. The husbands of the neighboring women returned, sweaty and dirt-smeared. They stopped, bunched together at a distance outside the ring of women. They too, clasped their hands and bowed their heads. Meg heard footsteps behind her. Her sisters had joined them.

Father O'Malley began, "Our Father, who art in heaven…" All the voices gathered behind the cottage immediately joined his in prayer. Then the priest moved out of the way and the circle of women closed once again to wind the shroud around the body. When they finished, Deirdre looked up and motioned towards Denis and Thomas who stood in the crowd of men with the coffin between them. At Deirdre's signal they carried it forward.

The two men placed the body into the coffin.

"We'll wake her with the coffin lid closed," Deirdre announced.

The men looked at her in surprise.

"We're all here. Take the coffin inside," Deirdre said. "So long as it stays closed, you'll have no worries about what the wee ones will see."

Thomas began to protest.

"If we don't, Thomas," Deirdre interrupted him, "your children won't be thanking you for it when they've grown and are remembering this day."

Thomas breathed a sigh. "I'm grateful to you for finding a way."

"Where is Rory?" Meg asked. He was not among the group of men who had returned from digging the grave.

"He went off with them." Dennis pointed to the group still milling about the yard. "I don't know where he is now."

The group of men carried the coffin into the cottage and placed it in the spot where the kitchen table used to stand. The others followed in a procession behind it. The tiny cottage was packed. The crowd, along with the peat fire, created a stifling heat so the door was left open for the air to circulate. Meg stood near the doorway, keeping a look out for Rory.

Father O'Malley came up beside her. "He probably just needed some time to be alone."

"He had such a fierce look about him after he saw his mam. I'm afraid he's gone off to do something that'll get him in trouble."

Before he could answer, they were jostled out of the doorway. One of the neighbor women was sending Brigid off to retrieve the Quinn children and the family members of those who were present. "And tell my Liam to bring his fiddle," the neighbor woman called after Brigid as she hurried away.

"If Rory doesn't return soon, I will go look for him," Father O'Malley offered when they reclaimed their spots.

"Thank you, Father. That would be a comfort to me."

He patted Meg's shoulder, then moved off to speak with the others in the room.

Deirdre and several of the women knelt beside the coffin to pray. Brigid returned with the Quinn children, who walked tentatively toward the coffin.

"Is my mam in that box?" one of them asked Kathleen.

"Aye, lass, she is."

"Why can't I see her?"

Kathleen knelt down, eye level with the little girl. "Listen to me, now. Your mother was a beautiful lady, wasn't she, Lizzy?"

Lizzy nodded, tears making tracks in her dirt-streaked face.

"Then that is how best to remember her."

The sound of the fiddle tuning up came from the far side of the room.

"Come now, dance a jig with Meg so your mam can look down on you from heaven and see how happy you are that she's with Jesus now."

Reluctantly, Meg came forward and took Lizzy's hands. She led the child to the center of the room. Meg began the familiar steps to the fiddler's tune, but breathing soon became difficult. She noticed the same slowness in the other dancers. Bodies that looked as though the slightest puff of air could push them around at will moved like they were weighted down with lead. Only the importance of the ritual gave them enough strength to finish.

As the first dance ended, Father O'Malley brushed past Meg, saying as he did, "I'm going to look for Rory."

The mourners took turns dancing. As each one tired, another came to take his place. The women kneeling by the coffin arose, mingling with the others. Meg and Kathleen gathered the children together in a corner of the room, keeping them occupied with simple games.

A gasp escaped Kathleen. Meg followed her sister's gaze. Kevin Dooley entered the cottage.

"I can't believe he came," Kathleen whispered. "He didn't even come to Aiden's."

Kevin was followed by his mother and sisters, all of whom appeared near death themselves.

"He's changed so much," Kathleen noted. "He used to be handsome."

Meg took in the emaciated form, the dirty ripped clothing and the scowl that replaced his former brilliant smile. "He looks awful," Meg agreed. "But probably no more so than any of the rest of us."

Kevin glanced in their direction, giving Kathleen the hint of a smile. She quickly busied herself with the Quinn children.

Thomas approached him. "You could see fit to come here, but you couldn't be bothered with the wake nor the funeral of your supposed best friend," he growled at him.

Kevin glared back.

"He'd of come if his da would have let him," Mrs. Dooley interjected.

"Have you heard from your da, Kevin?" Meg heard Mr. Welch ask.

Kevin's eyes narrowed. He shook his head ever so slightly, but remained silent.

"We just come to pay our respects," Mrs. Dooley continued. Turning to Thomas, she said, "We want you to know how sorry we are for your loss. For your wife and, of course, for Aiden, too."

Thomas nodded. "Thank you," was all he said before turning away.

She grabbed the arms of her girls to hurry them out the door. "Come, Kevin," she said.

"Noreen, wait," Deirdre called. "Stay a while and rest."

"Thank you, but I think we'd better go," she said as the family filed out the door. All but Kevin had their eyes focused on the floor. Kevin glanced at Meg and Kathleen. Meg met his gaze. The revulsion she usually felt for him suddenly turned to pity. He looked away quickly, following his mother and sisters out the door.

"That was odd," Kathleen stated, turning back to Meg. "I wonder where Kevin's da is?"

"Passed out drunk someplace, no doubt," Meg replied.

"Haven't you heard?" asked a man's voice.

Meg turned to see Mr. Kilroy next to her. "Colin Dooley up and left the family when they was evicted. While everyone was elsewise occupied in watching the cottage get torn down, he slipped away, never to be heard from again."

"We heard that, but didn't know if it was true," Kathleen told him.

"True enough. The rest are living in a *scalpeen*, but only God knows where old Colin's gone off to." Mr. Kilroy strode away to visit with the other men.

* * *

205

With the sound of the fiddle, the half-hearted whoops of the dancers and the chatter of the neighbors, Meg never heard Rory come up behind her.

"Look what I've brought for us," he said, reaching one arm around her so that he held a large chunk of cheese in front of her face.

"Rory! Where were you?"

"After digging my mam's grave, I went off to find us some supper."

He laid open a sack filled with fresh bread, more cheese, vegetables, a leg of mutton and two bottles of whiskey.

"Where in the name of all the saints—"

All the children in the room made for the sack and eagerly dug into it. The adults, too, crowded around, astonished. The women grabbed the food from the children and, breaking it up, fed it to them in tiny portions, admonishing them to eat slowly. One child was already vomiting.

"How ever did you come by this, lad?" asked one of the neighbor men.

"Since the Brits caused a wake, I decided they could damn well pay for it."

Meg remembered the last meal Rory had given her and forced herself to go slowly, letting each morsel settle in her stomach. As each bite entered her mouth her salivary glands overproduced forcing her to wipe the drool from her chin. An image of hands clawing up from the pit of her stomach desperately grabbing the food would not leave her. Soon the sounds of violent retching and the stench of vomit told her that others had lost the fight.

The two bottles of whiskey were passed around among the adults. Those who could keep it down quickly became drunk.

There was a lull in the wake while everyone tried to recuperate. Meg sat leaning against the wall. Her heart was pounding, sweat broke out on her body and her stomach churned while trying to decide whether to accept or reject the food. She had eaten only some bread and cheese, not daring anything else, but she felt as though she had consumed a huge meal.

She sat still, trying not to even turn her head for fear of making herself sick. The sun disappeared. Shadows fell across the room. The cottage had become close and fetid. When Meg decided it was safe to move, she crawled across the floor until she was outside in the night air. She breathed in deeply, feeling its coldness refresh her. She sat with her back against the side of the cottage. Slowly she felt a bit of strength return. Within minutes Rory joined her.

"A grand feast, was it not, Meg?" Did you have enough? There's plenty more where that came from."

"Where did it come from?"

"Our fine English landlord supplied the bounty."

Meg smelled whiskey on his breath. "You're drunk."

"Aye, that I am. I have no home, no clothes but the ones on my back, no belongings to my name, my mam is dead, and I am indeed quite drunk."

"You are also in danger."

"We're all in danger, Meg. In danger of starving to death, which is exactly what the Brits want. Either we help ourselves or we die."

"Rory, you stole that food. If anyone finds out it was you, you'll be sent to prison if they don't kill you."

"No one saw me, I'm sure of it. The landlord is in England, as always. Blackburn came by before dawn to serve the eviction notice. You should have seen the smug look on his face when he handed it to da.

"'Too bad that pig of yours ran off at the worst possible time'," Rory said, mimicking Blackburn's voice. "'You'll have plenty of time to search for it now since you'll be on the road from here on out.'" Returning to his natural voice he added, "Then he ordered us out and set the constable's men to pulling down the house."

"Oh, Rory!" Meg held him tight. "I'm so sorry."

He held her at arm's length, intent on telling her his story. "Ah, Meg, you would not believe how much food they've got stashed away up at the manor. That grand house is stuffed to the rafters with it. 'Tis like they be waiting for a famine." Rory fell over on his side, laughing.

"Rory, stop it!"

He pushed himself back up to a sitting position, but went on as if he hadn't heard her. "I loaded my sack up full and it barely made a dent. They'll never miss it. That is, if anyone ever shows up at the house to notice."

"There are always servants about. Blackburn will surely suspect you. Promise me you won't do it again."

"God damn Blackburn's rotten soul to hell!" Rory exclaimed. "Why should I let us starve? I fed us better today than I ever did before." He held his deformed hand before her face. "And this didn't hinder me a bit." There was a defiant look in his eyes that disturbed Meg.

"Don't even talk to me about it again until you're sober," she told him.

"I believe I will go back inside where the company is a wee bit more appreciative. Don't forget, Megeen, you are the one who insisted we survive at all costs." With that Rory returned to the cottage.

Tears stung Meg's eyes. In her mind was the image of Rory being dragged off in heavy chains to some dank prison.

Meg leaned her head back against the cottage wall. She drew her legs up, rested her arms on her knees. She listened as the women began to keen. Her ribcage convulsed. Frustration raked its claws across her like those of a caged wild animal trying to get free. Without realizing it, she found herself keening along with the others. It felt as though a host of evil spirits was being released out through her mouth. When nothing was left she lay on her side on the cold ground.

* * *

"Meg?"

She looked up to see Father O'Malley kneeling over her.

"Oh, Father. I must have fallen asleep." Still groggy, she pushed herself up to a sitting position.

"Out here? You'll freeze." He helped her to her feet.

"Rory came back."

"I know. He tried to give me some of the food he stole."

"What did you say to him?"

"Nothing. Tonight is not the time for it."

"But you will talk to him? He plans to keep doing it. They will catch him, I know it."

"I will try, but there is nothing to be done about it tonight."

He escorted her inside. The fiddle player had started again. Listless dancers began once more to force themselves through the motions. Meg and Father O'Malley entered the crowded room, then went in separate directions. Someone had cleaned up the vomit. She sat down by the fireplace.

"Will you have one dance with me in my mother's honor?"

Rory stood over Meg with an outstretched hand. Though she had no energy left, she could not refuse him this request. She took Rory's hand, letting him lead her to the center of the room. He spun her around and around. Her legs would have given out if he hadn't held her up. He was moving so fast that the other dancers had to make way until they were the only couple left. He stopped keeping time with the music and danced at his own pace. Sweat flew off his hair, spattering onto Meg. She wanted to scream for the fiddler to cease, but she knew Rory would never forgive her, so she danced on.

When the music ended, Rory came to a dead stop. He held her at arm's length. She tried to read the expression on his face but it was one she had never seen before.

"Thank you, my love," he said through deep, heavy breaths, then walked away.

Meg felt dizzy. After a few unsteady steps she was met by Kathleen and Deirdre who led her to a corner to rest. Father O'Malley sat next to her.

Meg watched Rory stagger around the room, boisterously bragging to each neighbor about how he had stolen their landlord's food right out from under his nose.

"Father, look at him. What can be holding him up?"

"Shock. Anger."

The fiddle had stopped. The women were no longer keening. The children slept.

Father O'Malley got to his feet. "The sun will be up soon. I must go prepare for the funeral Mass." He said a few words to each group of mourners before he left. Thomas was the last.

"Father, I wish to thank you for allowing a wake. I know there's many a priest who'd have forbidden it."

"It was decent and respectable. I see nothing wrong in the way you have sent off your beloved Anna."

"You're a blessed man, for sure."

"And may the good Lord bless you, Thomas, and all your family."

"I'm fearing we'll be needing all the blessings we can get now. We've no place to live. I'll have to put up a *scalpeen*."

"Let me know where you are so I can come to you."

"Thank you, Father."

The cottage door closed behind Father O'Malley. Deirdre drew a rosary from her pocket and knelt beside the coffin, the room now silent. The others gathered close, wrapping their own rosaries around their hands. Small crucifixes bobbed as they made the sign of the cross. Deirdre began reciting the first prayer of the sacred beads. A roomful of low, solemn voices joined hers. An Our Father, ten Hail Marys, a Glory Be, an Our Father, ten Hail Marys, a Glory Be. Over and over they repeated the words, the voices working together in perfect rhythm.

Meg let the low rumble her voice caused in her chest lull her into a hypnotic state. She was still except for the delicate motion of her hands as her fingers slipped from one smooth bead to the next. She closed her eyes, breathed deeply and felt peace enter her soul. When the last prayer finished, Meg raised the crucifix at the end of the string of beads to her forehead, then to her chest, then crossed over shoulder to shoulder, left to right. Bringing the crucifix to her lips, she kissed it reverently. When she opened her eyes the first rays of sunlight shone through the window. Dust motes danced in the patch of light resting across the middle of the coffin, making the wood in its path appear lighter than the rest. Meg stared at it, transfixed by its soft serenity.

The mourners pushed themselves off their knees. Six of the men picked up the coffin. Once outside, they hoisted it onto their shoulders. The rest fell into procession behind them. Feet shuffling over the earth, eyelids drooping with fatigue, they walked to the church. The pall bearers set the coffin down in the aisle just before the Communion rail and staggered to their pews.

The heavy smell of incense made Meg dizzy and sick to her stomach. She fought the urge to run outdoors where the cold air would clear her head. Keeping her eyes closed through most of the Mass, she tried to recapture the deep tranquility of the rosary but only its shadow remained.

When the funeral ended, another procession led them out to the burying ground. Meg stood next to Rory in the early morning air. She shivered uncontrollably. Her legs felt close to giving out. Rory's body shook, too, but he seemed not to notice. He stared down at the coffin resting in the earth. Meg reached for his hand. Icy fingers folded over hers but his gaze never wavered, his expression never changed. Others rubbed their arms and shifted their stance. A bitter wind picked up. Father O'Malley went through the graveside ritual at an even pace, neither rushing nor lingering.

Once their priest stepped aside, those who had dug the grave, except for Rory, began the work of filling it in while the rest of the mourners departed. Rory stayed just as he was, watching the clods of dirt fall heavily, bit by bit covering up his mother's coffin.

"Rory, come away, now," Meg whispered.

He didn't answer.

"Let's go home and warm up by the fire."

"I don't have a home."

211

Tears stung Meg's eyes. "I meant my home."

"Aye. I know what you meant." He turned and walked away with her.

"We will have a home of our own someday, Meg. A grand house with everything you could ever want."

Meg forced a smile. She had no heart to contradict him. Rory stopped walking. He put his hands on her shoulders and looked into her face. He had appeared so different since his mother's death. Meg felt she was looking at a stranger.

"You don't believe me, do you?" His grip on her shoulders tightened. "We will have everything they've got and more."

Chapter Twenty

Just as Father O'Malley tucked Meg's comb into his pocket, intending to return it to her when he checked on the O'Connor and Quinn families, the pounding of a small fist sounded at his door. Nathan Kilpatrick stood before him in tears saying his da needed him right away. Only last week they had buried the Kilpatrick's baby. Fearing the fever that took little Edwin had spread to others in the family, Father O'Malley packed anointing oils and hurried along.

Rose met him at the door, her face pinched. "Father, it is good of you to come on short notice."

"'Tis never a problem for me to be called upon. What can I do for you?"

"I wish to make confession, Father." It was Dacey who spoke.

Father O'Malley's head snapped in Dacey's direction. He couldn't remember him ever making a confession. He wondered if Dacey had the fever and feared he was dying.

They closeted themselves into a dark corner of the cottage while the rest of the family moved to the other side of the room.

"Are you sick, Dacey?" he asked.

"Aye, but not with fever. Sick with sin."

"I see. We'd best get on with it, then."

Dacey began his confession by delivering a shocking revelation to Father O'Malley.

"I am guilty of the sins of gluttony and pride, Father, and I have caused the famine upon this land."

Father O'Malley was stunned. Had the man lost his mind?

"How has this come to be?"

"It's as you and Rose have said, Father. I've kept all for my family. Never shared. Never helped another soul when I could have. That's why the famine that's upon us now is my fault."

"Dacey, I agree you should have been more generous, but you are in no way responsible for the famine."

"Oh, but I am, Father. God punished me by taking Edwin. Now I fear the rest of us will die along with all Ireland unless I confess."

This was not the first occasion Father O'Malley had heard the famine described as God's punishment, but it was the first time he'd heard someone take the entire blame upon himself.

"We've had famines before. You told me yourself you've always fared better than most. How do you see this as different?"

"That's just it, Father. I've been cursed with the most terrible good luck. But I've never given the Lord my thanks for it. Instead I acted like it was all my own doing. Puffed up with pride, I was. And in all the times of want, I never shared. Not even when Rose begged me to. If I'd fed the poor like Jesus taught, Edwin would still be with us. God took his life because of me."

"That's not true, Dacey. God would never take the life of a child to punish a parent. Edwin died from fever, not from God's anger at you."

"Begging your pardon, Father, but you've got it all wrong. It struck me like a thunderbolt on the day of Edwin's funeral. God has been blessing me with good enough crops in all the times of famine. It's been a test to see if I would show gratitude by sharing my blessings, but I didn't. I sneered at those who did. Then came this famine to see if I would finally do right by God and neighbor. At first, I fared well enough, if you recall. My crop failed like everyone's but I had enough put by to make it. God must have thought he'd given me enough chances. This was my final test." He hung his head. "I failed. And I am sorry. So sorry. More than I can ever say." Dacey covered his face with his hands and sobbed.

"Dacey, you love your family with all your heart. That's always been obvious."

"I do, Father. But I didn't love my neighbor as I should."

"Edwin's death has rattled your thinking. I will give you absolution, but I want you to think about what you've said."

"Oh, Father, I can do none else! You have to take it off of me. 'Tis a curse. Only you can get the Almighty to remove it. Otherwise, the rest of us..." he glanced in the direction of his wife and children. "We'll all be lost."

A lump rose in Father O'Malley's throat.

"And maybe," Dacey continued. "The Lord will remove the famine from the land once I've been forgiven?" The pleading look in his eye stabbed at Father O'Malley's heart.

"Dacey, I am happy that you have come to see the need for being compassionate towards others. God is pleased, too. But you must understand that ours is a just and merciful God. He would not lay this heavy a burden on you for any sin. No one person could bear the guilt of what is happening to this country. Why would He punish all of Ireland on account of one man? You must understand that the famine is not your fault."

"Aye, Father." His voice was flat. His dull eyes stared at the priest.

"Is there anything else you want to confess?"

"No, Father, that's the all of it."

"For your penance you are to pray the rosary daily until this famine ends, thanking God for the gift of compassion and asking Him to give you a better understanding of His love and mercy."

He thought of telling Dacey to ask God to cure him of believing the famine was his fault, but was afraid he would lose him if he pushed too much at once. Better to tread lightly and leave it in God's hands.

* * *

Rose followed Father O'Malley out of the cottage. "Father, I'm frightened. I've never seen Dacey like this." The look of a caged wild animal was in her eyes.

"Rose, I am so sorry. This famine is doing more damage than just starvation, as if that isn't enough. How are the rest of you faring? None are ill, I hope."

Rose shook her head. "Not yet. Every day I look for signs of fever in Nathan and Kate. I can't stand to lose another child." Her voice broke on the last words.

Father O'Malley took both her hands in his. "Rose, I will pray for all of you. You must pray, too."

Rose looked down, her words so soft he had to stoop to hear them. "I can't. I'm afraid."

"Afraid? To pray? Why?"

She glanced up at him, pain searing through her face. "You told me Dacey needed something to soften his heart so I prayed hard for it. I didn't say what because I thought God would know better than I."

Father O'Malley felt a tightening in his chest.

"Then Edwin got the fever. Dacey's heart has changed, but it took my baby dying to do it. Now I fear to pray. If I pray wrong again, who knows what might happen?"

Father O'Malley tipped his head back and closed his eyes. What had he done to this family? How could he make it right?

"Rose," he began, his voice gentle, soothing, though he wanted to cry. "God did not, would not, take the life of your child because you prayed for something to change Dacey. Edwin died because he got the fever. I promise you, God did not take Edwin's life. The fever did."

"But God sent the fever to Edwin," Rose insisted. "And it was because of my prayers."

"Rose, do you believe God would do anything evil?"

A look of shock blazed on her face. "I should hope I'd never believe such a thing!"

"Then you cannot believe that God gave the fever to Edwin because that would be evil. God does nothing evil. Ever. Do you see what I'm saying?"

She was quiet a moment. "Aye, Father, but look how it's all turned out. I prayed. Edwin died. Dacey changed." She let go of Father O'Malley's hands, holding her own palms upward in a gesture of incomprehension.

"That's all true, but God did not make Edwin die. God did, however, use a terrible tragedy to bring about something good. That is where God is in all this. God heard your prayers, Rose. When the tragedy came, not brought about by God, mind you," he emphasized, "God used it to answer your prayers."

Rose blinked several times. Her brow furrowed as she tried to find meaning in his words.

"The thing to do now," Father O'Malley continued, "is to keep praying. Pray that Dacey's newfound generosity continues to grow, but that he stops thinking he's responsible for the famine."

The cottage door swung open. Dacey ran out waving a loaf of bread. He shoved it into Father O'Malley's hands. "Take this, Father. Give it to whoever needs it." The urgency in Dacey's voice matched the wildness in his eyes.

Father O'Malley put a hand on Dacey's shoulder. "I know just the family who can use this. They will be most grateful."

"Good. God will be pleased, won't He?"

"I'm sure He will. God bless and keep you both and your children." Father O'Malley made the Sign of the Cross over them before taking his leave.

* * *

"It's only me, Father O'Malley. Is anyone about?" he called, nearing the entrance of the *scalpeen*.

Noreen stuck her head out. "Welcome, Father."

"This is for you," he said handing her the loaf of bread.

"Thank you, Father. Come in and have some with us."

Father O'Malley ducked into the low, three-sided structure, taking a seat on the leaf strewn dirt floor. Only Noreen and her two girls were there. She tore into the

217

bread, doling out a handful to each of her daughters. Her long, bony arm held out a lump of bread towards the priest.

"No, thank you," he said. "It's for you."

"It would be wrong not to share," Noreen argued.

Father O'Malley shook his head. "I have something at home. Save some for Kevin. By the way, where is he?"

"Town," Noreen said, her mouth full of bread.

"Begging?"

She shrugged as she continued chewing. Father O'Malley waited. Finally, she spoke. "Not sure what he's doing, Father. He won't talk about it. In fact, he hardly talks at all these days. Getting more and more like my lasses." She jerked a thumb at the two hollow-eyed girls, numbly chewing bread.

The girls, Addie and Liddy, were twins, about fifteen. They resembled each other so strongly he could barely tell them apart. Always huddled together, they seemed to be trying to disappear into each other. Dark haired and dark eyed, they never spoke. They barely seemed to notice when they were addressed, a small nod being the most one could get from them. Everyone knew of their existence, but most took no more notice of them than they would a pair of milking stools.

"Have they ever spoken?" he whispered to Noreen.

She nodded. "When they were quite young, they were normal lasses."

"What happened?"

"I went away for a day once a few years ago. Left them home with their da. When I got back they were different. Been silent ever since."

Father O'Malley was shocked. "What happened while you were gone?"

Again she shrugged. "They must have done something to anger Colin. Lord knows that was easy enough to do. They was covered in bruises and bleeding a little. I asked why he'd done it. All he said was they needed a beating so he gave 'em one. They've been bunched up in a corner, not saying a word ever since."

Realizing his mouth was hanging open, he quickly snapped it shut. Glancing at the girls he saw they'd melded even closer together, both staring into their laps, obviously upset by the conversation. He wanted to question Noreen further, but dared not speak any more in front of them.

"Has Kevin been able to bring anything from town?" he asked, changing the subject.

"Usually he gets something. Might be gone for a couple of days at a time, though. We never know when he'll show up."

"And you don't know what he's doing or where he's going?"

Her voice went quiet. "Last time I asked he said it was none of my business and if I asked again, he'd never come back. We can't risk losing the little food we can get so I let him do as he pleases and stay out of his way."

A look of sadness passed over Noreen's face. "He's getting more like his da in some ways," she said. Then she leaned in close and whispered to Father O'Malley, "Sometimes I smell whiskey on his breath."

"Where is he getting that?"

Noreen drew back. "You don't think I'd ask him, do you?" She shook her head. "Too much like his da."

"I'll speak to him about it next time I see him."

"No! Please don't, Father," Noreen pleaded.

A rustling caught his attention. It was the girls shifting, both of them now staring at him in horror.

"Don't worry. I won't let on that I've been here or that you've told me anything," he assured them.

Noreen looked uncertain. "I'd rather you said nothing at all. Even if he don't know about this talk we're having, he might still get mad and take it out on us. Better to leave well enough alone."

Father O'Malley nodded, not wanting to engender any more fear, but promised himself he would find out what was going on with Kevin.

"Finish that bread yourselves, then," he told them. "Otherwise, he'll wonder where you got it."

"We will, Father," Noreen said. "He's been gone two days already. There's no telling when he'll be back. I'd not let food go to waste waiting on him."

* * *

Father O'Malley's mind was reeling as he left the *scalpeen*. He was horrified at what he'd learned about the Dooley family. What they had endured over the years must have been truly awful. And what of their future? Two lasses mute from trauma were hardly marriageable. Heaven only knew where Kevin was going or what he was doing. Was he really in town begging or was he up to something dangerous, perhaps even sinister? He did not like the way Noreen talked about Kevin becoming like his da. The fact that he'd been drinking was especially concerning. Where was he getting it? If he had money to buy whiskey, it should instead be spent on food. Was he buying it at all or was he stealing?

"Damn this famine!" Father O'Malley said aloud as he walked towards the O'Connor cottage. He had made an inroad, or so he'd thought, with Kevin, but had become so consumed with the effects of the famine on all his parishioners that he'd had no time to follow through. He should have made the Dooleys a higher priority, especially after Colin abandoned the family, though he was now more sure than ever that they were better off without him. But if Kevin became too much like him, would they simply be replacing Colin with a younger version of the same nightmare? Why did I not spend more time with him? How could I let it come to this? And those lasses! Why had I never inquired before as to their condition? Had Colin done more than beat them? What will become of them? How can I help them? How can I change the course Kevin has set himself on? Why haven't I paid more attention to this family from the beginning?

Father O'Malley continued alternating between silently berating himself and trying to think of a way to help until he reached the O'Connors' cottage. His feet had kept pace with the rapidity of his thoughts. Now, as he knocked at the door, his breath smoked in the winter air. He had not realized until this moment how much of a toll the famine was taking on him. Somehow he'd felt himself set apart from it. He had little enough to eat, but still more than most of his parishioners. Since the Church paid for his cottage, he had no fear of eviction. The slight dizziness he felt, the emptiness of his cramping belly and the sudden, intense exhaustion impressed upon him the first inkling that he might be physically affected as well.

When the door opened he was hit with a wave of heat.

"Come in, Father," Deirdre said, ushering him into the crowded cottage.

The Quinn family had not built a *scalpeen* as expected. Instead, Denis, feeling guilty at removing his name from the letter sent to the landlord, insisted that the Quinns move in with them despite the risk. They could be evicted for it, but Denis was adamant that, at least for the winter, the Quinns would stay with them.

Father O'Malley squeezed inside. Between the peat fire and the bodies of twelve people and two piglets in one small room, the heat was almost unbearable. Sweat formed on his brow.

Father O'Malley sat on the floor with the others. "I just came to see how you were all faring."

"We're doing as best we can," Deirdre told him.

"Thomas, how are you holding up?" he asked.

The man looked a bit sheepish. "I still think we should be in a *scalpeen* rather than crowding out our neighbors, but this one won't hear of it," he said, pointing at Denis.

"Come spring, we can do something about that," Denis answered. "But for the winter, you're better off here. I can't see sending wee ones out to freeze."

"Are they well?" asked Father O'Malley.

In the corner the three youngest Quinn children, Lizzy, Seamus and Darien lay asleep on the floor. Their faces looked flushed but it was impossible to tell if it was fever or just the heat of the crowded cottage. The door could not be left open lest someone notice the Quinn family and report them to Blackburn.

"Fair enough," Thomas answered. "They sleep most of the time. The heat, I suppose."

"Rory doesn't, though." It was Loreena who spoke. She and Brigid sat together each with a piglet on their lap.

"Not sleeping, lad?" Father O'Malley asked.

"I'm fine." Rory said, but he had a restless look about him.

Father O'Malley glanced about the room. "Where is Meg?" he asked.

"Looking for mending work," Deirdre answered.

"I don't like that she goes alone," Denis said.

"I'm sorry, Da," Kathleen whispered.

"I'm not blaming you," Denis told her, patting her knee. "I know you can't make the walk. Wouldn't even want you to try."

"Your leg's no better, then?" Father O'Malley asked.

"It's a little better. Just not enough. I can't walk for long."

"She limps a lot," Brigid offered.

"Brigid!"

"Well, you do."

"Enough!" Deirdre admonished.

There was silence for a moment. Then Rory spoke. "I should have gone with her."

Loreena giggled. "To ask the town ladies for mending work?"

Rory shot a glare her way. "So Meg would not be alone. I would have, too, except she left before dawn and I didn't even know she'd gone."

"I thought you weren't sleeping?" Father O'Malley asked.

"That's what Loreena said, not me. As I told you, I'm fine."

"You're fidgety all the time. That's all I meant," Loreena corrected.

"And what's that to you?"

Loreena's eyes narrowed. "He goes outside in the middle of the night, too, and stays out a long time."

Father O'Malley looked sharply at Rory. Clearly the situation was getting to all of them. He especially worried about Rory. Ever since his mother's death there had been a change in him. Father O'Malley had hoped his stealing from the manor house had been a solitary escapade brought on by grief and anger. Now he wondered.

"I just need to clear my head sometimes," Rory said, staring into the fire.

"And just what are you doing awake that you know all of this, little lass?" Deirdre asked. How quickly she had taken over the role of mother to these children.

"It wakes me up when he leaves. Then I can't go back to sleep."

Father O'Malley felt as though he was dreaming. The banter in the cottage seemed incongruous with the gaunt eyes, bony limbs, and ragged clothes. So far, here at least, the strength of family was winning over the famine.

He chatted a bit longer, but soon became so sleepy from the heat he feared he would keel over. Once outside, the temperature, which had dipped as the sun began to set, roused him enough for the walk home. On the way, he saw Meg returning from town. Her gait had become a slow shuffle replacing her purposeful, confident step. Noticing how limp her once glossy dark hair had become, he remembered her comb.

"Meg! He called.

She looked up. Both hurried their steps to meet each other.

"Father, have you just been to see us?"

"I have. You've quite a crowd in there."

"Aye, that we do. Can't say we're not warm enough, though. Praise God for small favors."

"I'm glad to see you're in good spirits."

"I'm trying, Father, but Rory worries me. He fidgets a lot."

"That's what Loreena said."

"And he goes out at night."

223

"Where is he going?"

"I don't know. He won't tell me."

"Has he stolen more food?"

"No. He hasn't brought anything home since the wake. But I think he's planning to. He won't confide in me because he knows I'll be against it. I don't like us being on opposite sides, Father. It feels wrong. We're to be married. We should be together on everything."

"Meg, do your parents always agree on everything?"

Meg thought a moment. "Well, no. But somehow they work it out."

"As will you and Rory."

"Not if he won't talk to me."

"He tells you nothing?"

She shook her head. "I know he's still grieving for his mother. And Aiden. I know he hates the Brits. I think he blames his da a bit, but he won't come out and say it. He doesn't have to tell me those things. I can see them for myself. It's what he's thinking of doing that concerns me."

"So you think he'll go back to the manor to steal more food?"

"There or somewhere else. I think he's just waiting until he's got it all worked out in his head. But I fear he'll be caught."

"I wish I had all the answers, but lately I seem to have none." Defeat overwhelmed him. He hadn't meant to say this aloud. He must be more tired than he'd realized.

"I don't know that anyone has the answers right now, Father."

Meg shifted the garment bag so she could pull her shawl closer with her free hand.

"Did you get any work?" he asked, pointing to the limp bag.

"Only a mite. Hardly worth the walk." Meg shivered.

"You need to go inside," he said. "But before I forget, I came specifically to return this to you." He took the comb from his pocket. "I'm sorry I couldn't sell it before the eviction. It all happened so fast that I never had time to try."

"It's alright, Father. Blackburn planned it that way. Had you been able to sell it for a fortune, he'd have found some excuse to tear the cottage down. He was determined to get back at Rory's da no matter what."

"Sadly, I believe you're right. But at least you have your comb back. It's so lovely, Meg. Rory made it special for you. I'm glad you're able to keep it."

Meg took the comb from his hand. "For now," she said. "I may ask you again to sell it, Father. We may have no choice."

In the light of the rising moon, he saw her eyes glisten with tears.

"I hope you won't have to, but if you must, you know I'll try my best," he assured her.

"I know, Father. I just hope we don't have another disaster first."

"You mean Rory?"

"I don't know what I mean exactly. Just that something bad is bound to happen. Mam's feelings stopped after the eviction. But last night they came back on her." She stared into his eyes, a haunted look that startled him. "They came back fierce."

Chapter Twenty-One

"Are you going tonight, Rory?" Hope sounded in Brigid's voice.

It was early in the morning of a bright winter day. Both families huddled close to the cook fire to stay warm, gaunt bodies shivering in the cold. Meg saw Rory give a nod to Brigid.

"Do you think you will get much?"

"I'll do my best, lass."

Just as Meg feared, Rory was only waiting until he had a plan worked out before he resumed late night raids on the manor house of their landlord. Though Sir Alfred kept a skeleton staff, they were sometimes inebriated or simply lazy enough for Rory to make off with a chicken or two, but he had yet to equal the success he'd had on the night of his mother's wake. Rory felt it was his responsibility to continue raiding the manor as a way for his family to earn their keep in the O'Connor cottage.

"Perhaps Brendan will have some luck in town today," Meg suggested.

Brigid tilted her head. "Maybe, but Rory usually gets something. Brendan doesn't always."

"Rory will get something he doesn't want someday." Her words were barely audible but Rory caught them. Meg saw the look he shot her but pretended to busy herself by organizing her sewing box.

Since Kathleen's leg was still no better, she could not accompany Meg into town. Her parents grew more uncomfortable with her going alone, especially since Deirdre's feelings had suddenly increased. She argued she could come and go with Brendan, but as they would split into different directions once in town, it was forbidden. Instead, Meg accompanied her father, Thomas, Brigid, Aisling, and Loreena into the fields and woods near their cottage to scavenge. The weather was harsh this year, very unlike the mild winters to which they were accustomed. Often they had to push snow away to claw through frozen ground. The little they gathered was cooked and doled out by Deirdre and Kathleen.

Meg desperately wanted to go into town. She was confident that enough time had passed for her regular customers to start trusting her with higher paying work again. If not, she could beg as well as Brendan.

Rory stared absently into the fire. Was he more afraid than he would say? Rory's sister, Aisling, climbed into his lap, snuggling close. The firelight played eerily across Aisling's upturned face. There was a false sparkle in her big, blue eyes created by the dancing firelight. Her delicate face had grown skeletal. Bald patches amidst her wispy, blond hair gleamed in the light.

She shifted in his lap so that she was kneeling on his legs. The sticks of her fingers gripped his shoulders. She put her face close to his. "Will you get some food tonight, Rory, please?"

"I will, lass." He hugged her close.

I am going to town today, Meg decided.

"It's time we started," Denis announced.

"Perhaps you should stay in today, Aisling," Deirdre said. "I heard you coughing during the night."

"I wasn't coughing. It must have been someone else," she said, dragging herself up to join the group of foragers.

Meg pulled her shawl tightly around her shoulders. She turned back once before leaving. Rory was still sitting in front of the fire. He didn't go with them during the day, needing to conserve his energy for the night.

Meg's mother sat on the floor resting her arm on the stool and her head on her arm, looking wistfully up at the cauldron.

Rory's youngest siblings were huddled together in one corner making a shivering bundle beneath the blanket they shared.

Kathleen remained near the fireplace, her arms wrapped tightly around her drawn-up knees. Kathleen could not watch the others leave the cottage every morning. Saddened by her sister's downcast face, Meg walked into the breath-stealing air.

It had snowed the night before. Her feet were soon numb. She felt her muscles push her forward as she forced herself to walk. They approached a small ring of trees. Each piece of bark was peeled, then dropped into a sack. There wasn't much as most trees had been picked nearly clean. Meg scraped absently at the nearest tree, consumed with thoughts of how she could slip away unnoticed.

Cold and damp permeated the air. Meg peeked around her tree at the others. Then she looked away at the wide expanse of land. There was no way to leave without being noticed.

Meg stamped her feet trying to get some feeling back. She opened her sack, peering at the paltry amount of flaky bark. I know I can do better than this. She stamped her foot hard, this time in frustration.

"We've got all we can get here. Let's move on," Denis said.

Violent coughing made Meg turn in Aisling's direction. She had dropped her sack and was leaning the front of her body against the tree, arms thrown around it for support. Her body spasmed. Her face scraped the tree as she slid down but she hadn't the strength to push herself away. Meg hurried over. Aisling was on her knees, her whole body convulsing. Thomas reached them within seconds. He gathered his daughter to him, holding her until the coughing fit subsided.

"Are you alright now, lass?" Thomas asked.

Aisling's head bobbed, but her chin jutted back and forth as she gulped breaths of air.

"Look!" Brigid pointed at the ground near Aisling's feet. Bright red droplets lay like jewels in the sparkling snow.

"God in Heaven," Thomas moaned, staring at the blood. "I must take her back, Denis."

"I'll take her," Meg offered.

"Thank you, Meg, but I want to do it myself." Turning to Denis, he said, "I'll be back once I've got her comfortable."

"We'll be off that way." Denis pointed.

"I'll find you."

Thomas started down the hillside, carrying Aisling, her bluish legs dangled over the side his arm.

"I will come with you, then," Meg called. "In case you need any help."

She looked back at her father to see if he would object, but he made no comment. Brigid and Loreena knelt in the snow staring at the blood.

"Get up and go with Da," Meg admonished. "Quickly, before you freeze."

When Thomas entered with Aisling in his arms everyone turned.

"What happened?" Rory hurried to them.

Deirdre and Kathleen pushed themselves up from the floor to join them.

"She was coughing and couldn't stop," Thomas explained. "It came to where she could not stand up no more and so I have brung her home."

"Get her warmed up by the fire," Deirdre said.

"There's no more room under the blanket," Kathleen pointed out.

"Put her down on the floor directly before the fire," Deirdre instructed. "The dirt's fairly warm there. Kathleen and I will sit close by and keep watch that her clothes don't catch."

Deirdre made Aisling as comfortable as possible. She took the girl's blue-tinged hands and began rubbing them between her own, instructing Kathleen to do the same with her feet.

Aisling coughed again. Deirdre motioned to Meg who immediately knelt down at Aisling's head lifting her under her shoulders to a sitting position. She held her there until the coughing stopped, then gently lowered her. Thomas hovered over them, shifting his weight from foot to foot while passing his hat back and forth between his hands.

"Go on back, Thomas. We'll watch over her now," Deirdre told him.

He started toward the door, then turned. Crouching next to Deirdre he whispered, "She coughed up blood."

Deirdre patted his cheek. "We'll take care of her, Thomas."

Rory began pacing the corner of the room behind Meg. Thomas looked as though he might say something to Rory, but shook his head and left the cottage.

Meg spent the morning lifting Aisling whenever she was taken with a coughing fit. Each time seemed longer than the one before. Meg's back began to ache. Rory's incessant pacing itched her nerves. Meg's shoulders burned as she held Aisling during a violent fit. Laying her down, Meg noticed bright red specks dotted over the front of Aisling's dress. She jumped when Rory suddenly slammed the heel of his hand into the wall.

"Stop!" She screamed.

He stomped towards them, then, saying nothing, he left the cottage.

"Meg, what's got him in such a twist?" Kathleen asked.

"He's angry with me."

"Why?"

"For having the gall to worry about him. He thinks he's got to be the bloody savior of us all."

Deirdre glanced up at her daughter. "Maybe you ought not to fight him so on it, Meg."

"You think he should keep stealing?"

"I'd never ask him to risk himself. But you are going to be his wife. He's trying to prove his worth to you."

"And if they lock him up or kill him how much worth will he be to me then?" Meg's anger was rising.

"I'm only saying you should be more grateful that he's willing to take such risks for you and yours. It might be he sees your worry as nagging. Maybe a thank you now and then along with your worrying might not hurt." Deirdre moved off to check on the little ones under the blanket.

The cottage was silent for a moment until the door opened and Rory entered.

"What can I do to help?" He didn't look at any of them, just stared into the fire.

"There is nothing you can do, lad," Deirdre said.

"Aye, but there is," Meg announced. "You can take my place. Da expects me back."

Rory nodded, taking over her spot.

Once outside, Meg stood still getting her bearings in the icy air.

"I am going to do it," she announced to herself, heading off towards town.

Chapter Twenty-Two

Sitting by the roadside, Meg pulled part of her shawl over her head, curling into a tight ball trying for warmth. Crowds of people hurried about. Walking into town had taken most of Meg's strength. Well-dressed British ladies pulled their skirts away from her as they passed. Beggars cried out for food. An old woman dressed in rags that barely covered her scuttled along the curbside trying to avoid the bailiff. "Get out of here, you old hag," he shouted at the woman.

Meg peeked out from under her shawl. Across the street was a girl perhaps a year or two older than herself. She was tall and very thin. Though her long red hair was badly matted and her bones seemed almost to show through her skin, Meg thought she must have been pretty once.

The girl talked with three boisterous British soldiers. One of them pointed to a tavern. The girl nodded and the four of them headed towards it, the soldiers playfully shoving each other as they walked. The girl shuffled along with them, head down, rubbing her arms against the cold. They disappeared into the tavern.

It must be warm in there, Meg thought.

A carriage rumbled by, its wheels splashing icy slush onto her legs. Instinctively she scurried backwards, stopping short when her back hit a wall. The cold of the slush stung her skin. Using the side of the building for support, Meg inched herself up.

She knew the area well enough. Only a few streets away was the section of town where the grand houses stood. After a moment's rest she headed towards the cobblestone streets.

Meg walked to the servant entrance of one of her regular customers. A fat maid in a freshly starched black dress covered by a crisp white apron opened the door.

"What do you want?"

"I've come to ask if there is any mending work to be done."

The maid crinkled her nose.

"Please, may I see the mistress?"

A woman's voice came from inside the house. "Betty, why on earth are you holding that door open? It's causing a terrible draft."

"It's that urchin that does your mending work, Mum."

Hope nipped at Meg. "Please, tell her it's Meg O'Connor."

"Sally? Send her in. I've got some gowns and shirts for her."

"Not Sally, Mum. Meg O'Connor."

There was a muffled sound from inside the house. "Wait here," said the maid, closing the door in Meg's face.

Who's Sally? Meg wondered.

Within seconds the door opened again. "The mistress says to tell you we've a new girl now. She won't be needing you anymore."

Meg felt the world spin. She grabbed onto the side railing to steady herself.

"Please," she begged. "Even a few garments. Anything. I'll take anything at all."

"You heard me. Off with ya now."

Meg stepped forward preventing the maid from closing the door.

"It doesn't have to be sewing work. I'll clean. I'll do any job you like."

"And what do you think I do? Besides, the rags I dust with are a sight cleaner than the ones you're wearing. I wouldn't let one of you filthy urchins touch a thing in this house and neither will anyone else around here, so you'd best just go on home, if indeed you have one."

She slammed the door shut, forcing Meg to jump out of the way.

As she came away empty-handed from one house after another, Meg finally admitted it was useless. Weak and dizzy, she stumbled through the streets, dragging herself back to the market section of town. She thought of the long walk home. Worse was the thought of arriving with nothing to show for her running off against her parents' wishes.

The aroma of freshly baked bread engulfed her as the door of a building she passed opened and closed. She stood still, breathing it in, wishing she could eat its scent in the air.

The aroma dissipated, locked away behind the closed bakery door. She wanted to enter, but to smell that scent again only to be turned away, was an unbearable torture. Yet she couldn't make herself move.

When the door opened again a young woman in a maid's uniform emerged carrying a basket laden with bread and cakes. In the second the door was open, Meg's legs seemed to gain a mind of their own, carrying her inside. The smell of freshly baked breads, pies, cakes and tarts spun around her. Her eyes feasted on the delicacies lined up on the baker's counter.

She was alone in the shop except for the baker, a big man with long sideburns and deeply lined face. His large meaty hands, spotted with flour and dried bits of dough, rested on the counter. He watched Meg as she slowly ambled around his shop, open-mouthed. Wetness dripped from her chin and she realized she was drooling.

The baker shifted his position so that one elbow rested on the counter with his cheek in his hand, leaving a powdery smear across the side of his face.

"I don't suppose you have any money, Miss?" he asked.

Unable to meet his eyes, she looked down instead, noticing the large tears in the dress she'd been wearing day and night for months. Dirty ice particles clung to her skirt from where the carriage had splashed her. Her shoes were torn and rotted. For the first time she realized what she looked like. Just like the woman the bailiff chased and the girl who went into the tavern with the soldiers. She knew her face must be as thin as theirs and her bones must show just under her skin, too. She'd been glad enough to get her comb back, but it had been a long time since she'd even thought about her hair, much less had the will to put it up. Hidden under her shawl, she felt its dirtiness in the itching of her scalp.

She shook her head in response to the baker's question.

"Then why did you come in?" His tone was mildly curious.

Meg lifted her head and met his eyes. They were a pale blue set deeply into his beefy face.

"I was outside and the door opened. I smelled the bread and..." The memory of that first whiff of bread overcame her. How did she come to be in the bakery? "I didn't mean to come in. But I haven't eaten in so long. My family is terrible hungry. The smell... When the door opened again I just came in." Meg knew she was rambling, but seemed unable to stop.

"Come here. Over here to the counter. I don't bite." The baker motioned Meg towards him.

He handed her a large loaf of freshly baked bread.

"Can you hide that under your shawl?"

Meg thought that was an odd question, but she stuck the loaf into the crook of her arm, closing the shawl around it.

"Good," he said, eyeing her carefully. "I don't think it's noticeable. Now you keep it hidden like that until you get home. And whatever you do, do not tell a soul where you got it, understand?"

Puzzled, Meg nodded.

"I figured I could spare a little something. Certainly looks like you need it." He waved a finger at her. "But if word gets out that I'm giving away food I'll be beset by every ragamuffin in the streets and I won't have a business left. The government don't like anyone giving handouts, so not a word. If they all start coming in here, I'll know why. And if that happens you won't get any more from me."

His tone softened. "Otherwise, if business is doing well enough and no one is around, well...we'll see. Agreed?"

Meg nodded. "May God and his Saints bless you and all your family forever. May He keep you always in his heart. May the dear Lord…"

"Enough! Why is it you Irish can't just say 'thank you'?"

Meg hugged the bread so tightly she squashed it out of shape. A new idea sprang to her mind. "Do you think I might work for you?"

"Work for me?" He laughed.

"I'll bake, wash the crockery, anything. You can pay me in food or money, whatever you please." Meg bounced on her toes with excitement at the idea.

"Nah. I've got all the help I need. Take the bread and go home. And remember, don't tell anyone where you got it."

The walk home no longer seemed so bleak with the bread hiding under her shawl. *Maybe I can talk Rory into coming with me*, she thought. *It would be so much safer for him.*

The smell of bread emanating from under her shawl nearly drove her mad. She dared not eat any, fearing someone might see and grab it from her. She feared, too, that she would not be able to stop herself from devouring it all, leaving nothing to share when she got home.

Passing the workhouse, Meg caught sight of Brendan loitering just outside.

"Brendan, what are you doing here?"

"Never mind me. Why are you here?"

Meg pulled the shawl more tightly around herself. "I'll explain later. Come on, let's go." She tugged his arm. "'Tis an awful place. I don't want to be near it."

"Then go on back home. That's where you are supposed to be anyway."

"Aren't you supposed to be begging? How do you expect to get anything just standing here?"

"I was begging. Little I got for it, too." Brendan looked up at the imposing brick building. "I was just thinking we could all end up here."

Meg shuddered. "It won't come to that. It can't," she insisted. "I'd rather die than go in there."

"Do you think it's as bad as they say, Meg? At least we'd get fed, wouldn't we?"

"No one comes out of a workhouse alive. I've heard that too many times to take the chance."

"Die here or at home. What's the difference?"

"Brendan, please." She tugged on his sleeve. Something in his tone frightened her. Ever since the accident, he had changed. Now that Rory no longer had any carvings, there was nothing for Brendan to help him sell. A permanent darkness seemed to have settled over his once happy face. Meg suddenly realized that Brendan brooded as much as Rory, only he was quieter about it so no one took as much notice.

"If nothing else, I'll be one less mouth to feed," he said, storming to the workhouse door.

Meg stood frozen with fear as the door closed behind him. She could not let him do this, but found it impossible to move her legs toward the workhouse. Meg flashed back to the moment her Mam asked her to help wash the mangled body of Rory's mother.

You did it then. You can do it now, she told herself. She inched forward. The evil presence of the building hung in the air. Opening the door, she felt as though she was entering hell itself.

Meg gagged in the dark, fetid interior, waiting for her eyes to adjust. She spotted Brendan talking to a warden.

"Full up right now," the warden said. "There's plenty of others ahead of you."

Thanks be to God, she though. Now that her eyes could focus in the dim interior, she wanted more than ever to leave. Moaning came from just beyond a nearby doorway. Peering behind the warden she saw a large, long room. Row after row of beds were filled with the sick and dying. Women moved from one bed to another bending over the patients. Other women sat on benches with babies and young children on their laps. Everyone looked horribly ill. Some appeared to be dead. The smell of vomit, urine

237

and feces stung her eyes and throat. She moved closer to her brother.

"Brendan," she whispered. "Take a good look. I'll wager they didn't all come in this sick."

"Let's go," he hissed between gritted teeth.

Someone called from the other end of the hallway. "Come to pick them up."

"Go ahead, then," the warden called back.

The voice was familiar. Meg turned to look, but could see nothing in the dark hallway. Shuffling footsteps were all that signaled someone's approach.

"Pick up what?" Brendan asked.

"The dead," the warden answered. "Maybe you want to stay 'til he clears 'em out. Might be there's room for you after all." The warden laughed.

Meg grabbed her brother's arm, practically dragging him from the building in her hurry to leave.

Brendan walked with his head bowed, hands shoved deep into his empty pockets. The path narrowed as they moved up the hill. The rattle of a wagon coming from behind forced them to skitter into a ditch, their feet sliding from under them on the hardened snow pack. The driver from the workhouse rode past them, his cart piled with corpses.

"Did you see that?" Meg asked, disbelief in her voice.

"How could I miss it? He nearly ran us over."

"I meant the driver. Did you see him?"

"I was too busy trying to get out of his way without breaking my neck. Why?"

"It was Kevin Dooley."

"It can't be."

"It was," Meg insisted. "I knew the voice sounded familiar. Now I know why. He's the one picking up the dead."

They continued to lie on the ground, stunned and out of breath. The bread was now squashed flat beneath Meg's shawl. She could feel pieces of it sticking to her skin through the rips in her dress as she pulled herself up.

"I have something," Meg whispered.

"What?" Brendan hauled himself out of the ditch to sit next to her on the edge of the road.

"A loaf of bread."

"Where?"

"Under my shawl."

"Where did you get it?"

Remembering her promise, Meg replied, "I begged it."

"You begged it," he stated flatly.

She nodded. "It's mashed to pieces now."

"So what if it is? We'll still eat it." Brendan crossed his arms over his knees laying his head on his forearms.

"What's wrong?" she asked.

"I come to town every day and beg, get chased by bailiffs, almost put myself in the workhouse and what good does it do me? I go home with nothing. You come into town once and come away with a loaf of bread. I might as well not even exist for all the good I'm doing."

"Brendan, don't say such things. 'Twas luck for me and nothing more."

He opened his mouth to speak, but was stopped short by the sudden clip-clop of a horse's hooves. Not bothering to get up, Meg and Brendan half-crawled, half-dragged themselves back off of the pathway. Lying on her back, Meg had only to turn her head to see the white legs of the horse.

"Whoa," its rider called and the white legs stopped inches from her face. One black boot then the other dropped down as the rider dismounted and walked toward her.

"Well, who do we have here?"

The round, white face of Dr. Parker moved closer as he squatted beside her.

"Are you injured?"

Meg let her head flop from side to side.

"And you, young fellow?"

"Just tired," Brendan answered.

"Well," he said, "we cannot have you lying here on this frozen ground all day, tired or not. You will take ill."

He pulled Meg to her feet. She felt the bread start to slip and grabbed for it with her free hand.

"Settled?" he asked.

She nodded, grateful that he didn't question her further.

"I can walk," Meg protested as he started to lead her away.

"No need to. Lily will be honored to carry you home."

Meg felt herself higher in the air than she'd ever been in her life as he swung her onto Lily's back. She grabbed tightly to Lily's mane with both hands while squeezing the bread with her am. The horse's body swayed under Meg as the animal shuffled her feet.

"I want to get down," she demanded.

"Not to worry. She won't go anywhere until I give her the word," Dr. Parker assured.

Meg watched over the horse's head as the doctor helped Brendan to his feet. There was a mild commotion as he was deposited behind her. The mane of soft horse hair felt loose in her hands. No matter how hard she gripped, she could not feel secure.

"Hold on now," called Dr. Parker, walking around in front. He gave the reins a tug.

The saddle rubbed against the bones of Meg's backside. Her hips and back soon ached. She tried to move in unison with the horse's gait to hold her seat, but she dared not relax.

"Dr. Parker, I must get down. I am going to fall off."

"Nonsense. No one falls off of Lily." Nonetheless, he brought the horse to a halt. He looked Meg over thoughtfully. "The trouble is you are holding on too tightly. Hold the pommel, not her mane and let your legs dangle. Allow yourself to roll with her motion. We will go slowly."

Looking at Brendan, he asked, "How are you faring?"

"Grand." His voice was tired and flat.

Meg resigned herself to staying on the horse and did as Dr. Parker had instructed. Growing accustomed to the gentle gait, she began to trust the horse.

"How is the rest of your family?" the doctor asked as he continued to lead them along at an easy pace.

"Hungry," Brendan said.

"Did you meet with any success in town?"

Meg didn't answer. The doctor had been kind to them, but he was still British. She wasn't sure how far she could trust him.

"Meg managed a loaf of bread."

Meg felt her face flush at Brendan's words.

"Good," said Dr. Parker.

"I tried getting into the workhouse, but they were full up."

"Just as well."

Meg wished she could stop Brendan from talking, but he continued on.

"'Tis just that with fifteen of us in the family, I thought one less mouth to feed would help."

"Fifteen!" Dr. Parker interjected. "But there were only six of you at Gale Day."

"Rory's family has come to live with us now that they've been evicted and their house knocked down."

"Who is Rory?"

Meg groaned. She wanted to turn around, give Brendan a warning look, but she dared not make a move that could unseat her.

"Rory is going to marry Meg."

"Oh, I see."

"They pulled the house down with Rory's mam still in it and she was crushed to death."

Meg felt bristles of pain stab at her heart.

"Then they came to live with us."

"Is your landlord aware that they are living with you?"

"I...I don't think...," Brendan stammered.

Meg's heart pounded. Would the doctor turn them in?

"Better not let him find out. Taking in people who have been evicted is illegal. You could all be thrown out for it," Doctor Parker warned.

"You won't tell anyone, will you?" Brendan asked.

"You've nothing to fear from me. Just be cautious. Your family is taking a huge risk."

Fear ignited new strength in Meg. She twisted her body around enough to whisper "Brendan, keep quiet!" She prayed the doctor would be true to his word.

They crested the hill overlooking the bay.

"There's a profound insult to the gastrointestinal system, if ever I saw one."

His words were nonsense to Meg, but she followed the doctor's gaze toward the water. Several people milled about the shoreline, gathering the wrack washed up by the sea.

"Some of that seaweed is fine in small amounts, but too much of it is a poison to the system," Dr. Parker explained. "I've seen too many people die recently from thinking they could survive on it."

"They're hungry and they can't fish!" Meg burst out. Couldn't he understand? The once-skilled people were now too weak to manage the overturned *curraghs* that lay nearby.

"Yes, child, I know. But eating what poisons you will not help."

As he tugged the reins, Meg glanced backwards at the group huddled on the beach. They would probably be dead soon. *I wonder if it isn't better to be dead*, she thought. A shiver not caused by the icy weather ran through her.

The sun was inching its way out of the sky when Lily carried them up the incline to the door of their cottage.

"Meg!" Deirdre exclaimed. "Where have you been? You didn't go back to the others. Everyone is looking for you."

All but Kathleen and the children were missing from the cottage.

"I went into town. I knew I could do better there than I could picking bark off of trees and I have." Meg glanced toward Dr. Parker who had gone to check on the children.

"I got us a loaf of bread, Mam," she whispered.

"Where?"

"Here." Meg opened her shawl and peeled the flattened loaf away from her dress. Lint, dirt and sweat clung to the bread. "It got smashed because I had to keep it hidden, but it's a whole loaf."

Deirdre immediately began breaking it into pieces to pass around. Cold air hit Meg's back as the door opened behind her.

"We couldn't find...Meg!"

Hearing her father's voice, Meg whirled to face him. "I was in town, Da. I got us bread! And I think I can get more. Where's Rory?" she asked, noticing that he was not with Thomas and her da.

"He's out looking for you, lass, and God knows when he'll be back."

"I'm sorry, Da. I just knew I could get us something."

"And did you know you would scare us all to death? Did you know we'd think you'd dropped down dead somewhere? Did you know that?"

"I'm sorry, Da. But there's bread here now because of me."

"And Rory is not here because of you," Thomas interjected.

Meg fell to the floor in a heap, pain sparking a fire in the base of her spine as she hit the hard-packed dirt.

Dr. Parker scurried over to scoop her up. He placed her gently by the corner of the fire place. Turning to the two men, he said, "You have more important problems than being angry with her right now."

Deirdre handed the bread to Kathleen and said, "Finish" then moved quickly toward the doctor.

Kathleen continued doling out the bread. She slid herself across the floor in front of the fire and handed Meg a ripped fistful. Tears and too much saliva turned the bread to a pulpy mass. The feeling of real food filling her mouth only intensified the raw craving in her stomach. She groaned out loud as the first mouthful mashed against her teeth. Swallowing, she could feel every particle of it slide down her throat to drop like a stone into the empty cavern. Slumped against the wall, she left consciousness behind.

When Meg awoke Rory was sitting close, watching her.

"I got bread, Rory." She had meant to speak the words aloud, but they came out in a hoarse whisper.

"I know. I heard the whole of it from Brendan."

"When did you come back?"

"A bit ago."

"Are you angry?"

Rory shook his head. "I know you, Meg. You were bound to go eventually. I never could have talked you out of it any more than you can talk me out of what I'm doing."

Meg straightened up. "Rory, I was thinking that you could come into town with me from now on. Begging isn't as dangerous." After a pause she added, "Even though I do appreciate your risking your life for us."

Rory smiled but shook his head. "Meg, the town is full of beggars. You got lucky today, is all. My way is no guarantee, but it's a surer thing than begging."

"'Tis a surer way of getting arrested!"

"Let's not argue. You've got your way for tonight. After spending all day looking for you, I haven't the strength to go out. I don't think anyone could stand any more food just now anyway," he said, looking at all the bodies lying exhausted from keeping down the bread. "Besides, we have other problems."

Meg remembered the words Dr. Parker had spoken just before she had passed out.

"What is it?"

"Fever. That doctor said Aisling is in terrible fever and so are all the wee ones. 'Tis probably why most of them could not keep the bread in their stomachs."

"Did he do anything for them?"

"He left a bottle of medicine that we're supposed to keep giving them until the fever breaks. If it breaks."

"They'll be all right if we've medicine for them, won't they, Rory?"

"I pray so. Aisling's cough seemed to worry him, though. He said the medicine would make them sweat and puke. It's necessary to get what's making them sick out of

244

them. 'Tis awful to see. I think the medicine makes them worse."

Meg leaned into his arms. "It will work. It has to."

"But when they puke, nothing comes up. How can it work if nothing comes up?" He held her as tightly as his strength would allow. "Meg, I fear I'm going to lose my whole family."

Chapter Twenty-Three

Breaking the seal on the letter, Father O'Malley read by the afternoon sun streaming through his window.

Dear Father O'Malley,

It is with great sorrow that I must inform you of the death of Father Paul Gallagher of Clonmalloy. The town has been overcome by disease. Father Gallagher succumbed while tending to the suffering souls in his care. The town is now without a priest. Since you are the only priest within close enough proximity, I must charge you with the duty of administering the sacrament of Extreme Unction upon anyone still alive in the town. You are not expected to seek out individuals, but rather to walk to the top of a hill overlooking the town and from there deliver the sacrament. It is with distress I must inform you that you are not the first priest with whom I have been forced to charge such a duty. I urge you to go as soon upon receipt of this missive as you are able.

May God go with you. I assure you of my prayers and await your report upon your return.

Yours in Christ,

Bishop Ryan Kneeland

* * *

"Dear God." Father O'Malley clamped his hand over his mouth.

While preparing for his journey, he wondered how he could leave his own parish. He would be gone only a few days, but people were dying in Kelegeen every day. They, too, needed the Last Rights. Then there were the confessions which had increased lately. He thought of Cedric Dermott who had called on him for confession nearly every day, always because he had stolen food.

Father O'Malley worried on days when he didn't see Cedric. It meant he had nothing to feed his family. There was also the young Flynn lad who wondered if God would be less angry with him knowing that he was careful to go to another parish rather than stealing from anyone he actually knew.

He had his own sense of guilt to deal with, born of the fact that he was better off, if only marginally, than most of his parishioners. His salary, meager at best, came mainly from the few parishioners who could afford to pay a small offering. Beyond that, others who were still healthy enough brought the peat for his fire and provided some other necessities. The Church's pittance of a salary which had arrived with the Bishop's letter would be used to buy his bit of sustenance.

Father O'Malley always felt like a vulture when he handed over his money to fill his small sack with food. His conscience would ease somewhat when he gave away most of its contents on his way home, but he would always arrive back at his cottage with just enough to survive. He told himself that he had to. If he starved to death, who would minister to his people?

And how will I manage the walk to Clonmalloy? He wondered.

His only chance of surviving the journey would be to keep everything he bought at the market for nourishment along the way. But how could he pass those hungry shells and keep his sack closed against them? It was part of his sacred duty to administer the Last Rights and he was sworn to obey the bishop. He held these thoughts firmly in mind as he made his purchases, returning to his cottage, all contents of his sack intact.

His roiling mix of emotions drove him into the church where he lit the candles and knelt before the Blessed Sacrament. Alone in this sacred place he prayed for strength and guidance.

When he finished, Father O'Malley slowly rose from his knees. One by one, he blew out the candles. In darkness he moved down the nave to the door, letting himself out into the cold night air. Though he still had no answers, he did have a feeling of trust. It was time to prepare for his journey.

At the bottom of the church's stone steps he waited for a horse and rider to pass before stepping out into the lane.

"Father!" The horseman rounded back. He immediately recognized the rider as the British doctor he'd met at Gale Day. He stood mute as Dr. Parker brought his horse up beside him.

"Father, Providence that I bumped into you. I have just come from the home of your friends, the O'Connors. There is sickness there. I've done what I could, but I am sorry to say that your services may soon be required more than mine."

Father O'Malley's heart dropped to the pit of his stomach.

"Who is it?"

"All of the youngest Quinn children. Aisling in particular. They're failing rapidly. I left them with a purgative of mercurial chloride, but I don't have much hope. One never knows, though. I'll go back and check on them in the morning if I can."

Father O'Malley nodded. "And the others?"

"Tired, hungry, but not in fever yet. That girl, Meg, managed to obtain a loaf of bread in town today and that fed them a bit for this evening." He smiled. "She's a fighter, that one."

Father O'Malley nodded again. "I'll go to them," he said.

"Don't go tonight, if you please."

"Why not?"

"They are resting after a long ordeal of a day. Right now it is the best medicine for them. Go in the morning instead."

He was to begin his journey early in the morning. He could stop at the O'Connors' cottage, but it would take him well out of his way. He stood silently while he thought about what to do.

"I cannot go for at least two days, then," he finally said.

"I see. I stopped when I saw you because I understood you to be close to the family. Perhaps I was mistaken."

"I must travel to Clonmalloy." Father O'Malley was irritated at having to explain himself to this British doctor. "Your people have managed to let the entire town starve to death including their priest. Someone has to give the Last Rights and since I am the closest I've been ordered to go."

His calm of moments before was shattered as anger overtook him. He felt as if he had stepped outside of himself and was watching a madman rail at the doctor. "Would that I could be everywhere at once, everywhere that your people are making sure that my services are needed, but since there is only one of me, I can only be in one place at a time!"

"Forgive me for the misunderstanding, Father. Suppose I come by early in the morning and give you a ride to the O'Connors? I have patients to see that will take me in the general direction of Clonmalloy so I can get you started on at least part of your journey. Shall I see you in the morning, then?"

The man hadn't a note of anger in his voice. Father O'Malley stood, open-mouthed. He nodded his agreement, amazed and rather ashamed, as the doctor turned the horse down the path.

* * *

Father O'Malley awoke before dawn. Returning from morning Mass, he reluctantly picked up his food sack. It felt heavy. Taking out an egg and a few turnips, he fried them over his little peat fire. They sat heavily in his stomach, the hardiest meal he'd had in months. He tried to assuage his guilt by telling himself that without food he couldn't do the work the Lord had set before him.

"And am I fit to do it?" he asked himself aloud. All night he had struggled with his behavior towards Dr. Parker. So many years had passed since that terrible day, but the memory rose up again last night as if it had just happened and lingered still. He remembered Siobhan's brother, Quentin, filling the frame of his parents' door years ago...

"Have you seen Siobhan?" Quentin had asked.

"Not today. I've been working the potato bed with my da all afternoon. Why?"

"She went into town early this morning and she's not come back."

A boulder had dropped from Brian's heart to the pit of his stomach. The sun was close to setting. He took a torch and joined Quentin, Siobhan's da, and the rest of her brothers. They'd searched all night. It was early the next morning when Quentin called from the bottom of the hill. Brian followed Quentin's voice to a nearby riverbed...

Father O'Malley shut his eyes tightly against the memory. A knock at the door startled him. Sack of food in hand, he went out to meet Dr. Parker. A light wind billowed his coat, which now hung loosely from his shoulders.

"Brisk this morning," Dr. Parker observed. A plume issued from his mouth as he spoke. The frost glistened like a million tiny shards of glass on top of the snow.

The doctor mounted then extended his arm.

"I can do it, thank you." Father O'Malley swung himself up behind the doctor.

"You've experience riding?" Dr. Parker flicked the reins starting them forward.

"I learned a long time ago. It has been years since I've ridden, though."

"It'll come back to you quickly enough. Lily's a marvelous horse. She's as gentle as she is strong."

Father O'Malley had to admire the beautiful creature. Her strong muscles rippled under the smoothness of her immaculate white hair.

"Apparently she eats well." It was out of his mouth before he'd had time to check the words. He'd meant to apologize to Dr. Parker for his behavior the previous evening and belatedly thank him both for telling him about the O'Connors and for offering a ride.

"She'd better eat well or she cannot help me do my work. I'm not able to cover the territory I do on foot, so Lily is as much a part of my medical practice as any medicine or instrument I carry."

"And she carries me, as well," Father O'Malley admitted. He cleared his throat. "I wish to thank you for the ride. It was very kind of you to offer. And also for telling me about the O'Connors and Quinns." He wished the words came more easily, but he found himself having to force them out.

"My pleasure and not a spot of trouble in it. I wasn't sure you would accept since you refused my offer of a ride on Gale Day."

"I did not see that I had a choice this time." Father O'Malley wasn't paying much attention to the conversation. He knew he still needed to apologize. That was more difficult than offering thanks. He practiced it in his head, but couldn't find the right words. How could he explain why he'd had that outburst? He most assuredly was not going to tell this man anything about Siobhan.

The doctor gestured toward the O'Connor cottage just ahead of them. "I hope they're all still with us."

The stench of vomit and human waste assaulted their noses the moment they entered.

Deirdre ushered them into the room. "Doctor Parker, we didn't expect you back so soon."

"My friend must go to Clonmalloy. When I told him about the illness here he wanted to see you before starting his trip, so I offered a ride. How are my patients?"

"They're quiet now. It was so good of you to bring Father."

Friend. The word had not escaped Father O'Malley's notice.

"Why are you going to Clonmalloy, Father?" Denis asked as Father O'Malley approached the group by the fire.

251

"The bishop has ordered it. The priest there has died and they need a wee bit of help from me. I won't be gone long."

"That's good of you, Father," said Deirdre.

Father O'Malley knelt down beside Meg. "How is Aisling doing?" he whispered.

"I don't know. I just gave her some more medicine. It makes her horribly sick, but I think it has to do that to get the bad part out of her."

Father O'Malley looked at Aisling's bone-thin body. The dirt floor beneath her was soaked with sweat. A sour stench emanated from her. Suddenly, she jerked up and heaved violently. He thought her bones would snap from the force with which her body convulsed, but only a small amount of mucous was expelled onto the front of her dress. When it ended, Meg gently laid her down. Father O'Malley took one of the girl's hands in his own, praying while Meg pressed a rag soaked in cool water to Aisling's forehead.

"Oh, dear God in heaven!" Deirdre exclaimed.

"No, no, not my boy! They're going from me already," Thomas cried out.

Father O'Malley's eyes snapped open at the sound of a dull thud as Thomas dropped to his knees. They were all gathered around the children under the threadbare blanket. Dr. Parker was in the thick of the group, pulling a small boy from the pile. "Father," he called, "we need you here."

Father O'Malley crawled over to them. Dr. Parker cradled the tiny body on his lap. "Must have died within the last hour," he said quietly as he handed Darien's body to the priest. "The other children are too sick to have noticed."

Father O'Malley nodded, tears rolling down his face. He carried the child's body away to another corner of the room and laid it on the floor. Taking the vials from his pocket he anointed him. His voice choked often as he intoned the prayers. He felt the presence of others around him. When he began the Our Father he heard the voices of those still well enough to join with his, Dr. Parker's among them. When he finished, he looked up to see Deirdre, Denis, Brendan and Rory kneeling in a circle around the child. Meg was still beside Aisling, though her eyes were on the group around the body. Kathleen remained with Dr. Parker, helping with the other children. Thomas was still on his knees where he'd landed.

Father O'Malley crossed the floor towards him. As he did, he passed Brigid and Loreena who were sitting near the edge of the fireplace. They stared at the dead child with wide eyes. Something about Brigid particularly troubled Father O'Malley. Unlike Loreena, her eyes did not hold the look of fear and sadness. Instead they were vacant.

He squatted in front of her. "Brigid?"

She didn't answer.

He shook her shoulder lightly. "Lass?"

Her nod was barely perceptible. She continued staring at the dead child in that strange way. He left her and crawled to the agonized father.

"Thomas, there is no more pain and suffering for little Darien now. There is only perfect peace and joy for him. The Lord has taken him to Himself."

"Then I wish He would take me next!" He reared up as he bellowed.

"Thomas, I know this is hard on you."

"What do you know of it, Father? I saw my wife crushed to death. I am going to watch my children die one by one. You've no wife or children. How can you tell me you know what it is like for me?"

For a fleeting moment he considered telling Thomas about Siobhan, but this was neither the time nor place.

"Leave me alone, Father. This time there are none of us well enough for a wake. I'm going to bury my boy." Thomas went to the group encircling the body. He knelt down among them, pulled his own rosary from his pocket and joined in.

Father O'Malley sat listening to the sounds in the cottage. The mumble of voices praying together, the clink of metal as the doctor's instruments did their work, and the soft voices of Meg and Kathleen as they whispered words of encouragement to the patients swirled around him.

"Father?"

He looked up to see Dr. Parker beckoning to him. He crawled into the middle of the group of children where the physician was working.

"I think you had better proceed with the Last Rights for all of them. I've done what I can and will leave more medicine, but my hope for them has about run out. I cannot guarantee that they will still be alive when you return from Clonmalloy," he whispered.

Father O'Malley glanced toward the group praying the rosary. He could see that they were on the last decade. "I would like to wait until Thomas has left the cottage."

Dr. Parker nodded, then moved away to see Aisling.

Father O'Malley sat with the children. None of them seemed aware of his presence. He brushed wisps of straw-like hair from Lizzy's face. The fire in her skin burned his fingers. Kathleen's hand, holding a rag soaked in cool water, moved in to wet the girl's forehead.

"How are you faring through all this, Kathleen?"

"I will be fine, Father," she answered. Her half-smile disappeared before it was finished.

"How do you feel?" he asked.

"I'm not sick yet."

"And your leg?"

"Better. The camphor Dr. Parker put on it has helped. It only hurts now when I'm very cold. I can walk fairly well for a short time."

"I'm glad to hear some good news."

The rosary ended. Thomas gathered up his dead son and left the cottage with those who had encircled the body following behind.

"Are you not coming with us, Father?" Deirdre asked.

"I'll be along in a few moments." He turned to Meg and Kathleen. "Are you lasses going, too?"

"No," Meg answered. "We'll stay to help with the children."

Father O'Malley withdrew his vials from his pocket once more. One by one he anointed each child beneath the tattered blanket, then crawled over to Aisling and did the same for her. He began the Our Father, lifting his hands to signal the others to join him. The girls' voices accompanied his as did the lower, deeper tone of Dr. Parker. Father O'Malley glanced at the physician. Dr. Parker never looked up or stopped ministering to his patient.

He prays with us, Father O'Malley thought. He closed his eyes to pull his concentration back to the words of his prayer. When it ended, he gathered up his vials. As he returned them to his pocket, he noticed Brigid staring back at him with that same wide-eyed expression. He realized that he'd never heard her voice. Loreena spoke to her, but she didn't respond. He had the sensation that she was slipping into another world, though still able to see through some invisible veil, to the events of this one.

"I have to go to the burial site." Father O'Malley rose.

"I'm almost finished here," Dr. Parker said. "I'll ride out to meet you. Meg will tell me where."

Father O'Malley nodded toward the physician. He leaned down over Meg and said, "I'll keep your families in my prayers and I'll come see you as soon as I return from Clonmalloy. If any of them go to the Lord before I return," he indicated the group of sick children, "be sure someone tells their da I gave them the Last Rights. It will give him some measure of comfort to know they received the final sacrament."

"Of course, Father."

He had brought his food sack just inside the door, fearing it would be stolen if left outside. Before leaving the cottage, he took some eggs, cheese and bread from it and gave them to Meg. "This may help you out for a little while." Knowing he wouldn't have to make the trip entirely on foot, he felt safe to give some away.

"Thank you, Father," she said, gathering the bounty in her hands. She put the food on the floor next to her. Her tears made paths in the dirt on her cheeks.

"'Tis nothing," he said, feeling more powerless than ever.

Outside the freezing air cleared his head from the sickening stench of the cottage. A strong gust blew sharp particles of snow into his eyes. Once it died down, he started for the burying ground. The small group was digging through the frozen soil. Only Thomas and Denis had spades. Rory and Brendan clawed at the earth with rocks and their hands. Deirdre sat to one side with the body cradled in her arms. Bent protectively over the child, she rocked back and forth, keening.

"Deirdre?"

She looked up.

"Sit quietly. You'll tire yourself."

"'Tis a thing that must be done, Father, and none else but me is here to do it."

He left her to her ritual.

The digging stopped. Rory's and Brendan's hands bled into the dirt. The grave was shallow, barely deep enough to cover the body. Thomas took his son from Deirdre's arms. He gently kissed the cheek, then laid the boy into the grave beside his mother's.

Father O'Malley's voice broke as he began the graveside service. All waited in silence until he could continue. His throat closing up every few words made it feel like the longest service he'd ever performed. When it was finished, he could not bear to watch the dirt being shoveled over the body with no coffin or even a shroud to protect it.

In the distance he saw Dr. Parker approaching. Drawing close, the doctor jumped down from Lily, removed his hat and bowed his head, standing silently for a moment by the side of the new little grave. When he looked up, he said quietly, "My sincerest condolences to all of you." Then, "Are you ready, Father? I do not mean to hurry you at such a time, but I've many patients to see."

Father O'Malley looked at Thomas, who nodded to him.

"I will be back as soon as my business in Clonmalloy is finished. It shouldn't be more than a day, two at the most."

"We are grateful for your coming, Father," Deirdre said.

"I'll be praying for you all," he said as he mounted the horse behind Dr. Parker.

As they rode away he turned to look back at the line of mourners straggling towards the cottage and wondered how many times they would have to make that trip.

"You had better prepare yourself, Father. I do not expect any of those little ones to be left when you get back. And who knows who else will be sick by then."

Though spoken gently, the words pierced him.

Dr. Parker went on. "I am going straight to the Duffy cottage and work my way back. It shouldn't be too bothersome a walk for you from there. If you like, I will go back to the Duffy's in the morning. If you come while I'm there, I am quite willing to give you a ride home. Of course, you will have to spend the day making my rounds with me, but I suspect we see the same people anyway. I know you will want to go back to the O'Connors as soon as possible, though."

"'Tis a very kind offer." The time had come to swallow his pride. "I would like to humbly apologize to you. My behavior has been atrocious though you've done nothing but good for us all. I hope you will forgive me."

"No one's quite themselves these days, but if it makes you feel better, all is forgiven." He turned his head so that Father O'Malley could see a friendly nod in his profile.

"How long have you been visiting patients out here?" Father O'Malley asked, curious that he had not bumped into the doctor while on his own rounds. "No one, other than the O'Connors, have mentioned your coming."

"I began the day I brought the O'Connors home from Gale Day. As I was heading home, I encountered many others returning from the Fair. None looked well so I decided to start checking in on folks. My practice in town limits my visits to twice a week, though if I'm having a particularly light day, I'll make a run out to check on the worst patients."

"Hmmm…" Father O'Malley, wondered why no one had mentioned it to him.

257

As though the doctor could read his thoughts, he said, "Several have asked me to tell no one that I visit them?"

"Why is that?"

"Some of them live in those strange structures of three makeshift walls. What is it you call them?"

"A *scalpeen*."

"That's it. They seem terribly anxious that no one knows where they are. Then there are those like the Quinns who've been evicted, but are living with another family. An illegal arrangement, as you know. I've found it best not to mention my business out here to anyone and apparently your parishioners have decided keeping quiet about it is the best course of action for them as well."

"I suppose they have." The words fell heavily from his lips. He was hurt that his own parishioners didn't trust him enough to mention the doctor's visits. He was quiet for a time until his curiosity got the best of him.

"How did you know about the *scalpeens*?"

"I didn't at first. Just stumbled upon one. They're well hidden, I'll say that."

"They're meant to be. They, too, are illegal. It's as if once a family has been evicted their feet are not to so much as touch the landlord's ground. They have to leave, but where are they to go?"

"Yes, I've come to understand that system as I've gotten to know some of the people. It makes no sense. Are they expected to disappear into thin air?"

"There's some who wish all the Irish would do just that," Father O'Malley grumbled.

"I suspect there are plenty of Irish who wish the British would do the same." Dr. Parker laughed.

"Can you blame us, Doctor?" Father O'Malley bristled. "I am truly grateful for your kindness to my people and to me, but I suspect you are unique. Just look at the number of people dying slow, agonizing deaths of starvation and disease. Then go into town and see the stores of food readily available to any who can pay for it. But if you've no money, you get no food. It's pay or starve. All would pay willingly, but few have money or a way to earn any."

"You needn't preach to me, Father. I'm in complete agreement. Have you heard about the corn meal that's coming in from America?"

"Corn meal?"

"As I understand it, it's a food commonly eaten by the Indians of that country. They are sending it here to help feed the poor. But the government has put a catch or two on that as well. Their ships have to dock at British ports first and pay a tax. Even once the corn meal gets here, the poor are expected to pay for it. It's a small fee, but for those who have no money at all any fee is impossible. So I ask, what is the point?"

"I believe the point is that your government wants to make money off the generosity of the American Indians and still manage to starve out the Irish in the process. They've taken more than enough of our land as it is, but they continue to covet the rest of it. They'd like us all dead so the space we take up could be used to graze their cattle, which in turn, will further line their pockets. And you wonder why we wish you British would disappear?" Father O'Malley heard his voice rising, but could not control it.

The doctor sighed. "I don't wonder at all, Father. I only wish the world was a much different place than it is."

Father O'Malley stared at the doctor's back. A tall man, but not nearly as broad as himself. White hair under his hat. His straight back shifting slightly with the easy gait of his horse. *This is a man I could like.* The thought surprised him. Liking, not just tolerating, but actually liking a Brit was not something he ever expected could happen. Especially not after Siobhan died.

"Well, that makes two of us," he agreed.

* * *

When they reached the Duffy cottage, Father O'Malley stopped in, blessed the family, made a short visit, thanked the doctor for the ride, then stepped out into the biting cold.

259

He was very near the border of Clonmalloy. The only cottage he would pass from this point on before reaching Clonmalloy was that of the Hoolihans. As he approached, he found Adam hustling his children out the cottage door.

"Over there. Go! Quick!" Hearing these instructions, Father O'Malley looked to where Adam pointed. A small fire had been built some distance from the cottage. The children ran towards it.

"Adam? What's going on?" he asked.

"Father," he said, looking up. "Don't come any closer."

Father O'Malley stopped. He looked towards the children, barely covered by the rags that passed for clothing, trying to get as close to the fire as possible. Adam came to him.

"It's Corinne," Adam explained. "She's taken the fever. I had to get the children away from her as quick as possible else they'd have it too. It may be too late, but I have to try."

Fever was rampant, but no one he knew was sending the other inhabitants out into the cold because of it. "Is it just fever, Adam?"

"She's making no sense when she talks. Covered in a rash, too. Horrible to see."

"Is that why you got the wee ones out? So they wouldn't have to see her? It's awfully cold out. They won't stay warm enough out here even with the fire. They may take sick from the cold."

Adam, put up his hands, palms out, shaking his head while Father O'Malley spoke.

"It's not as simple as that, Father. This same kind of fever came upon my cousin's wife but a few months ago. Before long the whole family had it." He stopped, swallowed. "They're all gone now."

"This was your cousin in Clonmalloy?"

"Aye, Father. My cousin, Rodney."

Father O'Malley's thoughts returned to the day he'd come to the Hoolihan cottage to find Corrine dancing a jig

260

from the joy of Rodney sharing food they'd found in the cottages of some who'd died of fever.

"I'm told if you stay near a person who has this fever, you'll get it too. I've got to keep my bairns safe. Try, at least," Adam continued. "I'm not sure what I'll do for shelter. I can't very well knock down the house to build a scalpeen. It's certain I won't be moving Corinne out here to die in the cold so it's us that have to come out. It's bad enough I have to leave her alone inside. I'd die alongside her if I had a child old enough to take over the care of the others, but they're all still too young."

"Is Corinne conscious?"

"Aye. She's still enough in her own head to know what's happening. Some of the time, anyway. It was she who insisted we leave the cottage."

"Has the doctor seen her?"

"What doctor?"

"Doctor Parker."

"I don't know a Doctor Parker." Adam rubbed his chin, a puzzled look on his face. Apparently, Doctor Parker's rounds had not taken him this far out into the country yet.

"There is a doctor who's been coming out to see patients. He'll see Corinne. Can you leave the children long enough to fetch him?"

Adam nodded. "Where is he?"

"Last I saw him he was at the Duffys' cottage. He may be gone by now, but they might know where he went next."

"He's a Brit?"

"Aye, but a good man." Father O'Malley said, surprised by his own words.

"I can't pay him."

"I doubt he'd take it if you could. Hurry to the Duffys now. I'll give Corinne the Last Rights before I go on. I'm headed to Clonmalloy."

Father O'Malley noticed Adam twitch at the mention of the neighboring town.

"I'll go look for this doctor, Father, but if I were you I'd not go to Clonmalloy."

261

"Why is that?"

"They're all dead. There's nothing there now but haunts." Adam's eyes grew big with fright like that of a child hearing a ghost story.

"Adam. There's no such thing," Father O'Malley reasoned.

"Oh, but there is, Father. I've seen them myself. Not from Clonmalloy, but another place. Long ago. And now every soul in one town dead. It must be filled with them. I'll never step foot in Clonmalloy again." He crossed himself as he spoke.

"Just go look for the doctor," Father O'Malley urged him.

He stepped inside the cottage as Adam hurried off. Upon opening the door he was hit in the face with the stench of rotting flesh.

"Corinne?" he called. It took a moment for his eyes to adjust to the dim interior.

There on the floor in front of the fire was a small heap that appeared to be no more than a bunched up blanket. He knelt next to it. Corinne's eyes seemed made of glass. Was she gone already?

"Adam?" The word came so softly he could barely hear it.

"It's Father O'Malley. I've sent Adam for a doctor."

She stared at him with a vacant look. Even if Adam did find Doctor Parker, it was undoubtedly too late for Corinne, but perhaps he could prevent the children from taking ill.

"Corinne, I'm going to anoint you," he said. He thought he saw a barely perceptible nod. He pulled the vial of Holy Oil from his pocket.

* * *

It should have taken less than an hour to reach the village, but he stopped often to turn his back on the wind that swept crystals of snow from the ground and whipped them into his face. His legs felt like frozen lead. An occasional tingling in his feet was the only feeling he had. *I*

262

will never make it, he thought, his heart racing in panic. He calmed himself by silently calling on God for strength. It was God's work he was doing. God would sustain him.

Once in Clonmalloy, he headed for the first cottage he saw, expecting to rest there and perhaps eat a bite of food. Upon opening the door he was assaulted by a stench far worse than that of the Hoolihan cottage. It made his breakfast threaten to leave his stomach. He slammed the door shut leaning against it for support, thankful that the cold air held the smell at bay. He doubted anyone in the cottage could possibly be alive, yet he knew his conscience would never rest if he did not make certain. Steeling himself, he opened the door again. Holding his breath as long as he could, he quickly scanned the room. He counted ten bodies on the floor. Tentatively, he walked around, peering at each one. All were dead and in various states of decomposition. Three were adults, the rest children. Most were naked. Bits of cloth lay strewn near the bodies as though the pitiful rags had rotted off their wearers. Satisfied that no living souls were among them, he said a prayer over them, then left the cottage.

He decided to search out a high-looking hilltop as quickly as possible. Along the way he noticed what appeared to be shells of cottages, some torn down, others burned out, the evidence of mass eviction. He forced himself to enter the few cottages still intact to be sure they held no living soul. None did.

He came to a hill. Whether it was the highest or not, he'd no idea, but it was high enough to suit his purposes so he began his ascent. He got partway up the rugged slope when a terrible wrenching in his stomach doubled him over. He stayed there, curled in a ball, fearing to move while he watched the land whirl around him. He closed his eyes, but even the blackness behind his lids spun. The sensation of falling enveloped him. He dug his hands and feet into the ground. It seemed forever that he lay on the hillside, holding onto the earth, waiting for the world to stop reeling. *Surely Bishop Kneeland is trying to do me in,* he thought. When he finally opened his eyes and sat up, a pain shot from the back of his head, crashing relentlessly against the front of his skull.

He had lost the desire to eat after leaving the first cottage, but now hunger and lack of strength conquered him. He reached into his bag and pulled out a turnip. Grains of dirt crunched in his teeth as he chewed. When he finished he lay still, praying it would stay down. Slowly, he rolled to a kneeling position.

"Lord, help me do this," he pleaded.

Staying close to the ground, he climbed like a sheep, using his feet and hands to help him. Upon reaching the summit, he rose and looked over the landscape.

Spread below, the black gaping holes of burned-out cottages formed ugly wounds on the snow's white glitter. The wind whipped harder at the hilltop. His stiff hands made the sign of the cross, then pulled the vials of holy oil from his pocket. He sent their contents flying into the air. The wind threw some of it back in his face. He raised his arms over Clonmalloy and prayed. The words blew away on the wind. No voices joined his for the Our Father. He could barely hear his own. When he finished he sat down hard on the ground.

"Why, Lord? Why is this happening?"

Shivering in the wind, he realized he would die if he did not find shelter. It was too late in the day to walk back to Kelegeen. He would have to find a place in this desolate town to spend the night. The only parts of most cottages still standing were the outer walls. They afforded no shelter. The few still intact housed occupants as grisly as those in the first cottage. As much as he was repulsed, he was even more saddened at his inability to give them all a proper burial.

He continued to stagger through the snow. *Maybe I have completed the mission for which God has sent me and it is time to go*, he thought. His muscles screamed with every step, making him almost welcome the idea of death.

He walked with his head bowed to keep the wind from throwing snow in his face, but his neck grew stiff. As he lifted his head, he caught sight of wood sticking out of the snow. Under the wood was a snow-covered mound, a *scalpeen*. Brushing away the snow at the entrance, he crawled inside. Above his head was a load of thatch taken from one of the demolished cottages. Chunks of plaster and stone from smashed walls, a wheel, and boards from a cart supported the tiny structure. Whoever had converted the remnants of their shattered home into this cave-like dwelling had gone. He curled himself into a ball, placing his nearly empty food sack under his head. He prayed for whatever had become of the *scalpeen's* former occupants. Then he thought of Corinne. He wondered if Adam had found Doctor Parker. If Corinne was still alive. He wondered if the sickness that had taken most of the inhabitants of Clonmalloy was already on its grim march toward Kelegeen. It was with these thoughts in his head that he fell asleep.

Chapter Twenty-Four

Images of decomposing corpses haunted Father O'Malley's dreams. There were hundreds of them lined up on the floor of a cottage, waiting to be anointed. Whenever he looked up to count how many were left, he found himself back at the start of the line. The other end of the cottage was impossibly far away. Each corpse was rotted more than the last. His stomach grew queasy at the feel of moldering skin beneath his fingertips.

As he was making the sign of the cross on the exposed skull of a young woman, her eyes suddenly snapped open. Startled, he jumped back. She couldn't be alive. Most of the skin of her face was gone. Her ribcage stuck out like the carcass of a devoured chicken. The flesh fell away from her arm as she lifted it. The clicking bones of her fingers closed around his wrist. Her jaw moved, at first only scraping its hinges. Her throat, slowly turning to dust, rasped out *"tá ocras orainn." We are hungry!*

She let go of his wrist and wrapped her clicking finger bones around his small sack of food. With surprising strength she tugged at the bag.

"No," he said, trying to pull the bag away from her.

"Tá ocras orainn!"

"No!" He pulled the bag free of her grasp, hugging it to his chest.

She sat up. He heard rustling noises. Glancing around, he saw other dead eyes opening. Grating neck bones turning their owners' heads in his direction made his skin crawl. He backed away.

"Tá ocras orainn. Tá ocras orainn." They chanted in unison.

"No! None of you need it. You're all dead."

He wanted to race from the cottage, but it felt like running under water. Bony fingers grasped at his trousers, trying to pull him back. Suddenly he was outside.

Exhausted, he leaned his back against the cottage door. A woman's voice came from inside. She spoke as if in conversation with her neighbor.

"We can't go now, can we? No one has waked us."

A loud bang hit the door behind him.

He awoke with a jolt.

His heart pounded, sending blood coursing through his body, pulsing in his ears. He sat up, pressed his hands to his forehead and tried to shake the nightmare from his mind. Mercifully, light shone into the *scalpeen*. It was morning. He would not have to go back to sleep. He thought of eating something before beginning his journey, but when he looked at his food sack the vividness of the dream returned.

The wind had stopped. The air, though still cold, was milder. He moved past the same burned and broken cottages he had seen the day before. He shifted his gaze skyward. It was a soft rose. He searched for the connection with the earth he always felt when walking in the countryside. Nothing. There was some vital element missing, but he couldn't name it.

Blue slowly replaced rose in the sky. A sense of desolation wrapped itself around him; intangible, smothering. Unlike his walks in Kelegeen, this one was a burden. Even when he had just buried a parishioner or had been to house after house of sick and dying friends, he could always find solace in the walk back to his cottage. He was comforted by the wind, winter birds, the sea crashing in the distance, the branches of trees nudging each other to whisper their secrets high overhead. That's what Siobhan had always said they were doing when branches scraped against each other. He'd believed her, too. He could almost believe she understood their language.

He stopped and closed his eyes, concentrating hard on picking up one of nature's sounds. He stood very still, listening. There were no sounds. That was the missing element! An icy current ran through him. Not a thing lived in this town. Complete silence was a torture he had never before experienced. He tried now to pray, but no words came to him. Not even God seemed to be in Clonmalloy. He had to dig down to the very depths of his faith to believe that God was present here.

Lord, Jesus Christ, have mercy on me. He repeated over and over, focusing intently on an image in his mind of Christ walking beside him, guiding him from this barren land.

His legs started moving again.

"I must get out of here," he said aloud. At least his voice was a sound. He thought of singing. *Panis Angelicus* came to mind, but he had neither the strength nor the heart for it. So he walked as fast as he could. He listened to the sound of his quickened breathing, his feet crunching snow and frozen grass, anything that made a sound.

By the time he reached Kelegeen his body dripped with sweat, making him shiver uncontrollably. The muscles in his shoulders and the back of his neck quivered. He prayed that Dr. Parker would be at the Duffys cottage when he arrived.

In the distance he could barely make out the dot that was the Duffy home. He squinted, looking for any sign of a white horse.

The little cottage was a beacon. Now that he could see it, he knew he could make it. The blood rushed in his ears, but he couldn't slow himself. He had to get there. He had to be where there was still life.

The cottage grew larger. No horse was in the yard, but at least he could go in and rest. He could talk to people and listen to their voices. His knuckles grazed the door but his arm dropped limply down at his side. He waited. The door opened. Mrs. Duffy's sunken eyes widened when she saw him.

"Father? What has happened to you?" A feeble hand tugged his arm. He staggered into the cottage, sliding down to the floor. It smelled of sickness and human waste, but everyone in it was still alive, though some just barely.

"Nearer the fire, Father," she urged him.

He shook his head, unable to move. His words came slowly with many pauses for breath between them.

"Has Dr. Parker been yet?"

"Aye, earlier this morning. He waited a bit for you, but said he must go. He had other patients to see."

Father O'Malley nodded. "May I stay a bit?"

"Of course, Father."

He closed his eyes, his head against the wall. In a moment, he felt something warm touch his lips. He opened his eyes to see Mrs. Duffy leaning over him with a large spoon that she seemed intent on pushing into his mouth.

"'Tis water, Father. Warm from being near the fire. 'Tis all we've got."

The water released the bond that stuck his throat shut.

"Bless you," he whispered.

"Ah, 'tis nothing, Father," she said, going back towards the fire.

He raised a hand as she approached with another spoonful.

"Don't worry any, Father," she reassured him. "We melt the snow and we've all the water we might ever want."

"You are very generous."

"Generosity comes easy when there's plenty."

He stayed the rest of the morning leaning against the wall. He knew he was facing a long walk back to his cottage. He was torn between wanting to go straight home and stopping to check on the O'Connors. If Dr. Parker's prediction had been correct, could he face the scene there? Not after what he had just come through. Yet he had promised. "I must leave," he said, rising slowly.

Mrs. Duffy came to the door to show him out. The food sack dangled from his hand. It was nearly empty, but felt heavy to him. He looked past Mrs. Duffy to the group of huge eyes staring at him from near the fire. He pulled a dirt-smeared turnip from his sack and thrust it into his pocket.

"Please, take the rest." He placed the sack in her hands.

"Oh, Father!" She hugged the sack to her concave chest, never bothering to look at its contents. "May all the saints in heaven be praying for you forever."

The sight of the food sack had begun to make him sick. "Eat slowly. I only wish it could be more. May God bless you and your family." He made the sign of the cross over them, then left the cottage.

As he walked, he kept a constant watch for Dr. Parker. His heart tugged at him as he passed by cottages he knew he should visit.

The whinnying caught his attention, turning him toward a cottage in the distance. A white horse stood just outside the door of the Flaherty home.

"Lord, bless that horse and make her stay right where she is until I reach her!" He tried to run, but only stumbled and tripped his way to the yard.

Reaching the mare, he threw his arms around her neck, letting the animal support him. Dr. Parker' voice called out.

"I see you've developed an appreciation for my Lily!" He gave the horse a brisk pat on her flank.

"An appreciation for a ride is more the truth."

The doctor's smile left his face. He grabbed Father O'Malley by both shoulders and held him upright.

"You've taken ill. Up you go." He boosted Father O'Malley into the saddle. He submitted, having no strength left to refuse.

Dr. Parker swung himself up and urged the horse forward. "Lily will take you right to your cottage."

"We must stop at the O'Connors. I promised I would see them on my way back."

"You'll be stopping nowhere."

"But they need me."

"Not now," he said quietly.

"All those wee ones died?"

"Brigid's little friend is still alive. She doesn't seem to have the fever yet. But the two wee ones, Lizzy and Seamus..." he shook his head.

"Aisling?" asked Father O'Malley

"Still with us. And that, I tell you, I do not understand. She was the first to take ill and the sickest of all, or so I thought. Her condition is still no better, mind you, but she

270

clings to life with such tenacity. It sounds callous, but I hope she will let go soon. She hasn't a chance."

"I must go then."

"Why? You've already given her the Last Rights."

"I could pray for her."

"You can pray from your bed."

"I could comfort the families."

"They are beyond comforting. No words will do any good."

Father O'Malley bowed his head. He didn't speak for the rest of the ride. When they arrived at his cottage, Dr. Parker dismounted and brought him inside. He turned down the blanket, helped him off with his shoes and tucked him in like a child.

"Father," he began, drawing up a chair beside the bed. "I didn't mean to imply that you have no purpose amongst your people. They beg for you constantly. Their faith is strong. Any who live through this will do so because of it. But you must regain your own strength if you want to be of help to them."

Father O'Malley said nothing. He had his own ideas about how much good he could do.

"Well, what have you for food?" Dr. Parker asked.

Father O'Malley reached under the bed cover to pull the turnip from his pocket.

"That's all?"

"Aye."

"What happened to that sack of food you started out with yesterday morning?"

"I gave some to Meg yesterday, some to Mrs. Duffy this morning. I ate the rest."

"When was the last time you ate?"

"Yesterday."

"What did you have?"

"An egg and a few turnips."

"Keep it down?"

The scene of the first cottage in Clonmalloy returned fresh to his mind. "Barely."

"Hmm. I'll be back. In the meantime go ahead and eat that," Dr. Parker said, indicating the turnip. Then he left the cottage.

Father O'Malley closed his eyes and prayed. "Thank you, Lord. With your help, I have completed the duty Bishop Kneeland sent me to do and returned home safe. I felt so alone in Clonmalloy, but the very fact that I am still alive proves that you indeed walked with me. Thank you also for the help of this doctor, though he be British, and for his horse. Bless them both. For Aisling, I pray your healing power as I do for all our suffering, starving people. Be with us here, oh Lord, and help us. Amen."

Father O'Malley fell asleep with the turnip still in his hand. He awoke to sounds of hushed bustling. He rolled over to see Dr. Parker building up the fire. The one window let in the waning afternoon light. The doctor's shadow jumped up and down the wall as the flames flared and retreated. He bent over a cauldron. Chunks of something he was cutting splashed into the liquid. He picked up a large spoon and stirred. Father O'Malley's cottage was submerged in the aroma of stew. It pulled him to an upright position.

"What are you doing?"

"You're awake." Setting the spoon on the table, Dr. Parker turned towards him. Father O'Malley's gaze followed the spoon's path. He saw his table set for two.

He got to his feet. The room spun and he sat down hard. Suddenly, the doctor was in front of him.

"Sit still until you regain your equilibrium. When you're ready come and have a seat at the table."

He is inviting me to a meal in my own home. The idea seemed absurd.

"I think it's about done." Dr. Parker picked up a bowl from the table and ladled some stew into it. Father O'Malley watched the steam rise off the thick, dark liquid. Large chunks of white, orange and brown slid off the ladle along a waterfall of broth into the waiting bowl. The doctor picked up the other bowl.

Father O'Malley stood over the table staring in amazement. The bowls were filled with carrots, onions, and mutton. "Where did you get this?"

"You know as well as I do that with enough money one can get nearly any food one wants. Sit down. Mind, go slowly or it won't stay with you. And don't burn your mouth. It's hot. Have some bread as well. It soaks up the broth quite nicely."

Father O'Malley continued to stand and stare. How could he eat this? He would feel like a villain dining on what his own parishioners had to watch being purchased by the wealthy or shipped out of their country while they died from starvation.

His stomach ached and his mouth watered. He felt disoriented. He gripped the edges of the table for support.

"Oh bother! I will seat you myself." The doctor got up, took the priest by his arms and pushed him gently into his chair. "I would rather not have to spoon feed you, but if you do not start filling that gaping mouth of yours, I swear I will do it myself."

Father O'Malley abruptly shut his mouth as the doctor returned to his seat. He stared at the stew, wanting it and hating it.

"How can you expect me to eat this?" He thundered, both fists slamming down on the table making the bowl jump, precious bits of liquid spilling over the side to leave a splatter of brown dots. A tiny bit splashed onto his fist, burning it. He wanted to lick it, but fought the urge.

"I don't say I'm a culinary expert, but it's not all that bad if you'd give it a try."

"This is not humorous! Thousands of people, my people," he jabbed a finger at his chest, "are dying of starvation! Do you expect me to gorge myself and then go out and watch them die?" He glared at Dr. Parker, who had just swallowed a large mouthful of stew.

The doctor put down his spoon and leaned over his bowl, matching Father O'Malley's stare. "I will tell you what is not at all humorous. A priest upon whom everyone is depending refusing to take care of himself so that he can do for them what he has been sent to do."

"What would you know about what I've been sent to do?"

"Why did you become a priest?"

Father O'Malley drew back as though he'd been struck. "How dare you ask me that?"

"Because I want to know."

"Well, I am not going to tell you."

"Fair enough. That is your own business. However, it is my business to heal every sick person I can. I take that obligation seriously. If that means I have to eat well enough to continue to do that, then I will. God has seen fit to give me the means to eat so that I can carry out this service. He has also provided you the means to survive to do the same. Are you going to accept it and respect your obligation or are you going to throw it back in His face?"

Father O'Malley swallowed hard. He knew after the experience of the last two days that he would shortly be in no better condition than any of his parishioners. He looked down at the stew. The steam no longer poured from it. Soon it would be cold. The words he'd "heard" spoken by Siobhan's spirit suddenly returned to him. *God sends gifts in many forms. Have the grace to accept the one you will be given.*

Almost to himself he said, "How will my people feel when they see me well while they are so sick?"

"How will they feel if they see you dead?" Dr. Parker picked up Father O'Malley's spoon and held it out to him. Reluctantly, he dipped it into the bowl. Raising it halfway to his mouth, he stopped and replaced it. "I almost forgot," he whispered.

He made the sign of the cross. "Bless us, O Lord,"

Us. This Englishman and me.

"And these, Thy gifts"

Gifts. There was more of a gift here than just food.

"Which we are about to receive from thy bounty"

Bounty. Aye, a real bounty set before him like a miracle.

274

"Through Christ, our Lord. Amen."

He retrieved the spoon and filled his mouth with the succulent mingling of meat and vegetables. He wanted to shout. He started to rise from his chair, got half-way up and sat back down. He chewed, unaware of the mechanics of eating, while reveling in the exuberant celebration dancing on his tongue.

Then he swallowed. His stomach revolted and tried to send the celebrants back to where they came.

No! Stay down! He reprimanded them. He held the sides of the table again, feeling as though he could break the wood with his grip.

"Fight." He heard the word as though through a foggy distance. "Do it for them," the doctor urged him.

His stomach held the food. He tried another spoonful. The constant exchange of extremes between his mouth and his stomach continued until the last bite. It was dark when he finished eating. He felt as though lead weights had been placed in his stomach. He sat still while the doctor cleaned the dishes. He felt hands reach beneath his armpits tugging him upwards. Pushing against the floor with his feet, he found strength in his legs.

"Off to sleep now." Dr. Parker led him back to his bed. "I will be here early in the morning with more food to start your day as it should, though I won't promise such a feast as you've had tonight. We will have a long day of it tomorrow, so rest well. Mind you, I'm taking time away from my practice in town so please don't dawdle. I suppose you will want to begin with the O'Connors."

Does he mean he will carry me with him on his rounds? Father O'Malley wondered. He wanted to question him, but as soon as he lay down, the lead weights in his stomach distributed themselves throughout his body, falling most heavily on his eyelids. Before sleep claimed him entirely he had a moment for a silent word with God. *Father, I don't know why you've seen fit to send an Englishman to me for assistance, but I will try to accept it. Thank you for this man and please do bless his soul. Amen.*

Chapter Twenty-Five

"Rory, why aren't you going with them today?" Meg asked, indicating Thomas and her brother and father who were leaving the cottage. "Are you sick?" She held her hand against his forehead. "You don't feel feverish." Another thought struck her. "They've not found you out, have they?"

"I'm not sick and they've not found me out. I'm just not going."

"Why not?"

"Because it's nothing but a grand joke. The government has us walking miles to do a job that doesn't need doing."

"They pay you. We need the money."

"You don't understand, Meg. We're building a useless road that goes nowhere and what they pay us to do it won't even buy enough to feed one person, never mind the whole lot of us."

"All four of you are working. At least that's a wee bit of money."

Denis, Brendan, Thomas and Rory had all found employment on the Public Works. The pay was a pittance, but their combined incomes bought just enough to keep the family from total starvation.

"We cannot live on it. And now that it's been snowing every day, we can't even see the cursed road we're supposed to be building. So they give us half pay and tell us to go home. Yesterday they said if it snowed again today they'd turn everybody to breaking rocks. For what?"

"It may be useless, but that's the fault of the government, not the workers. At least there's no shame in doing it. Not like what Kevin Dooley is doing." Meg shuddered at the memory of Kevin driving the cartload of corpses to the burial pits. She thought her estimation of

Kevin Dooley couldn't get any lower until she'd seen that. No wakes, no funerals, no prayers. Simply dumped into a mass grave. His own people. It was revolting.

"I heard some of the supervisors saying that in Glownmearith they've got them building a bridge in the middle of a pasture," Rory went on as if she'd said nothing. "The Brits think it's all a grand joke. A few days ago they just stood there watching as a man died trying to swing an axe he was too weak to lift. Then they laughed about him being such a lazy Paddie that the thought of work was what killed him."

"Why didn't you tell me?"

"It happens too often to bother mentioning. People die on the Works all the time. My da's going to die from it." His emotionless voice frightened Meg.

"No. Your da's a strong man."

"He doesn't care about living anymore. All it takes is giving up. The supervisors call him a shiftless slacker and he acts like he don't hear them. There was a day he'd of whipped the lot of 'em. Not anymore."

"He goes on as best he can. You can't expect him to fight them, Rory."

"He thinks he's got no reason to live."

"What of you and your sisters?"

"That's the very thing of it. He doesn't want to be around to watch us go. I don't think he can bury another child, Meg."

"You're not sick and Aisling's holding on. She may live yet." Meg looked at the supine form of Aisling before the fire. Deirdre was bathing her forehead with a wet cloth. Meg wished she could believe her own words. It was not just that Aisling was so sick, but that Deirdre's nightmares had become worse than ever. Sometimes, even during the day she would shake violently. At first, Meg thought her mother had contracted the fever, too, but it was fear that made her quiver. Deirdre had confided in her that she was consumed with a "powerful feeling" stronger than any of the feelings she'd ever had. Meg was becoming anxious, too. The list of things Deirdre's feeling might foreshadow

277

was growing ever longer. Meg tried not to think too much about them because whenever they slipped into her mind they threatened to engulf her in a paralyzing panic from which she feared she could never escape.

"If you're not going to the Works, will you come begging with me?" she asked.

"What good would it do?" Rory sounded exasperated. "Everyone's begging. I'll get nothing that way."

Meg had to admit he was right. Since there were so many beggars in town, Meg's best hope was still the baker. Most days she waited near the bakery until it was empty and tried to slip in unnoticed. On occasion Mr. Breckett would give her some bread or buns. He warned her, though, not to come too often. He was afraid someone would notice a pattern, he said, and he'd be beset by beggars. He told her he'd taken a liking to her because of her determination, but that didn't mean he'd risk his business for her.

Meg had been so relieved when Brendan had found out where the Public Works project was operating. Rory had agreed to join and leave off stealing. The men started off before sunup and came back long after it went down. They'd return to the cottage only to drop sound asleep on the floor. The first time it happened Meg was terrified all four of them had dropped dead, but it soon became an expected occurrence. For Meg, the biggest relief was that Rory was no longer risking prison. Now his flat out refusal to accompany her coupled with his absence from the Public Works could mean only one thing.

"Rory, don't do it."

"You wish to eat, don't you?"

"It can't keep snowing forever," Meg told him. "So what if you break rocks? You still get paid. If you skip a day they may not take you back. There are too many others waiting to take your place."

"They can have it. Kill themselves for eight pence a day when corn meal costs three shillings a stone. Good luck to 'em, I say. I've passed men lying dead in the snow on my way home. They drop from exhaustion with the pitiful pence in their hands. What good did it do them? I doubt

278

their families even got their last pay. There's those that would steal it right out of their hands."

"Have you ever?"

"Ever what?"

"Stolen money out of a dead man's hand?"

"How could you ask me such a thing?"

"You steal, Rory."

"Not from any of us!" He shot her an angry glance that did nothing to cow her.

"But you're going back to stealing, aren't you?"

"I am. I'm going tonight and I don't wish to hear another thing about it."

Worry nestled itself into a ball in Meg's chest. She wrapped her arms around her drawn up legs. Turning her head away from Rory, she rested it on her knees staring at the wall. She felt his arm over her rounded back. He leaned his body against hers and whispered in her ear.

"Don't worry. I know what I'm doing." His breath brushed her ear as he spoke. Meg pulled away, crawled across the room to sit with Kathleen.

"I wish Brigid would speak," Kathleen whispered to her.

Meg avoided looking at her youngest sister. She couldn't stand those staring eyes. Brigid never spoke, just stared. Loreena tried in vain to elicit some response from her. Finally, she gave up, dividing her attention between Aisling and the piglets.

When Meg didn't answer, Kathleen changed the subject. "Do you think we'll end up in the Workhouse?"

Meg noted a look of wild fear in Kathleen's eyes. "We'll never go there. Why would you ask such a thing?"

"Brendan told me what it's like inside. Meg, I'm terrified of the Workhouse."

"Well, stop thinking about it. We're not going."

"Others are."

"We're not others."

"But Mam's feelings. Something awful is going to happen. With the Quinns living here, Aisling with the fever, Brigid not speaking, Rory stealing, everyone coming back from the Works looking like they're about to drop dead. Something's bound to happen. And I just can't get it out of my head that we'll be evicted and end up in the Workhouse. You're as good as dead in there, you know." Though Kathleen's voice never grew above a whisper, it was tinged with rising hysteria.

Meg clasped her hands over her ears. "Stop!" She whispered harshly between clenched teeth. Kathleen was listing all the fears that Meg was trying desperately to keep at bay.

Grunting noises caught their attention. Tucked into the opposite corner with Deirdre was Brigid whose outstretched arm was pointing directly at Aisling. Brigid's mouth opened and closed, her throat trying to make words, but emitting only guttural sounds.

Meg couldn't stand to watch and turned her head. She heard Kathleen's dress drag along the floor as she moved away. Then she heard her sister's voice ask, "What is it, Brigid?"

Kathleen huddled over Brigid, partially obscuring the younger girl from Meg's view. Her struggle intensified as if fighting to remember how to talk. Suddenly, the dam burst and words ripped from Brigid's mouth. "Blood! She got blood on the white. You can't get blood on the white. It won't come out." Tormented screams filled the cottage. Kathleen took her sister in her arms trying to comfort her. Deirdre wrapped her arms around both of them. Embedded between her mother and sister, Brigid slowly wound down until she was still. When they released her she crumpled on the dirt floor.

Rory crawled to Meg. "What is she talking about?"

Meg's mind went back to how transfixed Brigid had been by the droplets of Aisling's blood in the snow.

"Brigid pricked her finger when we were sewing once and got blood on the cuff of a white shirt I was mending. We lost customers because of it. When Aisling coughed up blood onto the snow, Brigid couldn't stop staring at it. Somehow she's connected the two. It's all I can figure."

The cottage was quiet for a long time. Side by side, Meg and Rory fell asleep. She awakened late in the afternoon when the opening of the door sent the colder air bursting into the room. Meg heard the dragging sounds as the newcomers crossed the floor. One thud, then another, sounded as they fell before the fireplace. She waited a moment for the third. It never came. Meg heard her mother's voice whispering words she couldn't understand. No other voice responded. She lifted herself up onto her elbows looking at the row of bodies lined up before the fireplace. Her mother was sitting bent over her father, whispering in his ear. Her father lay on his face, both arms stretched above his head, not moving, already asleep. Deirdre stopped whispering. She sat for a moment, perplexed, before lying down beside him. Brendan was there, asleep next to Denis. Thomas was missing.

Meg became aware of Rory's body. His head rested on his forearms. His back moved in a barely discernible up and down motion. He hadn't looked up, Meg was sure of it, but somehow he knew. She lay her chest on top of his back, wrapping her arms around his shoulders. "Rory, I'm sorry. I'm so sorry."

"I told you, Meg."

They said nothing else, but waited for Denis and Brendan to awaken.

When sunlight sent a sliver of itself into the cottage, its inhabitants began to stir. The fire had gone out during the night. No one had rekindled it. Only the heat produced by so many bodies pressed closely together for warmth prevented them all from freezing. Meg was torn between a desire to get the fire going and an unwillingness to leave the niche between Rory and Kathleen for the frigid air of the room. At the sound of rustling, she lifted her head to see her da move in the shadows. He shivered violently, rubbing his arms and blowing on his hands as he made his way towards the pile of peat. He threw a load into the fire making it blaze again. Meg felt heat on her face. Denis held his frozen hands dangerously close to the flames.

Slowly, the long line of bodies came to life. Kathleen, Loreena and Deirdre raised only their heads and shoulders a few inches from the dirt floor, dragging themselves towards the heat. Instinctively, they laid their hands down near the edge of the fireplace until they thawed enough for their fingers to uncurl. Deirdre pulled Brigid closer to the fire.

Kathleen leaned over Aisling. "She breathes still."

"Good," said Deirdre.

"Rory, are you awake?" Meg whispered.

"Aye."

"Let's move up."

It was Sunday. The Public Works were not in operation so the day would be spent with all of them shut in the cottage, Deirdre lamenting over the family's absence from Mass.

"Not fit to be seen," she would say every Sunday. Deirdre's clothing had been mended and re-mended so many times there was almost nothing left of it. She was ashamed to step foot inside the church.

Meg had grown to hate Sundays. Every day passed slowly, but Sundays crawled by as they waited them through to the next day when work would resume and she could take the tidbit of money the men had earned into town for food.

"Where's my da?" Rory's question hung frigid in the air.

Meg curled herself into a ball, trying to wrap her shawl around as much of her body as it would cover. She watched from her sideways position. Brendan looked down when Rory spoke. No one answered.

"I know he's dead. What did they do with him?"

Denis sighed. "Took him off somewhere in a cart."

"What happened to him, Denis?" Deirdre asked.

"The snow was too much to work on the road, so they set us to breaking rocks. 'Twas the first swing of the axe that did him. He had it up in the air, never did get it above his head, and was bringing it down, though it was more like

282

it was bringing him down. When the axe hit the ground, he fell right over it. He was dead when we got to him."

Rory stared into the fire. "How long did they leave him there?"

Denis shook his head. "Why torture yourself with this, lad?"

"Because I hate them."

"Hating them more won't bring your da back."

"I didn't go yesterday."

"You couldn't have done anything. I think you da would have been glad you weren't there to see it."

"How long did they leave him there?" The intensity of Rory's voice increased a notch.

"A while."

"How long?" Red spots stained his pallid cheeks. Meg untucked herself and crawled to him, but he took no notice of her.

"Until they had enough bodies to fill the damn cart and then they took it away."

Deirdre gasped. "God in heaven! How many others died?"

"Six or seven, I suppose. I didn't count 'em."

"Eighteen." All eyes turned to Brendan. He didn't look up from the floor as he spoke.

Deirdre encircled her son in her arms. "Denis, don't go back." Her eyes pleaded with her husband.

"We must. There's no other way to keep us fed."

"Aye, there is," Rory whispered.

Meg was the only one who heard him. She rested her head against his shoulder.

"Leave Brendan home then. He's only a lad." Deirdre broke down in a flood of tears. "I can't be losing both my husband and my son."

"He's not a child any more. 'Tis up to him," Denis answered.

Brendan looked at his da. "I'll go."

"No. I won't allow it," Deirdre insisted.

"He can make up his own mind."

"He's only fifteen."

"I'll go." Brendan shrugged off Deirdre's arm.

Deirdre's face crumpled. "I can't be losing you both."

"Will they give us his body to bury?" Kathleen asked.

Denis shook his head almost imperceptibly.

"But we must have a funeral."

"They've likely already done away with him."

"What does that mean?" Loreena asked.

Denis went silent.

Staring straight ahead at the fire, Rory explained. "They take them to mass graves and dump them in. The pits is what they call 'em. The graves, I mean."

Loreena screamed. "My da? In a pit!" She broke down in tears.

"Rory!" Meg admonished.

"I'm sorry, Loreena," he said, looking contrite. "I just..." He pounded his good fist on the dirt floor. "I just hate them so much!" The words hissed through gritted teeth.

"They've left us not even a decent Christian burial to give our dead." Deirdre's eyes narrowed to slits and she spit into the fire.

The rest of the day passed quietly. No food in the cottage meant that energy had to be conserved. By mid-afternoon the snow stopped. When the cottage was dark they resumed their sleeping places in front of the fire.

"Meg, here's the money from yesterday." Denis dropped a few coins into her hand before joining his wife at the far end of the line. "But don't go out if the weather's bad. We can wait another day or two if we must."

Meg looked at the coins. Two salaries less than usual. It wouldn't get much. She'd try the baker again. She couldn't remember how long it had been since she'd gone to his shop, but she hoped it was long enough. As she rolled over, she felt the comb dig into her thigh, reminding her of its presence, of its power to help. Is now the time? She wondered.

Chapter Twenty-Six

At least it's not snowing today, Father O'Malley thought as he huddled into his worn woolen coat. The sun shone brilliantly, but it was still cold. The soft sounds of a melting world only increased the feeling of dampness.

"Perhaps the weather has taken a turn for the better," Dr. Parker called over his shoulder.

"It's still February. I wouldn't count on it just yet." Father O'Malley rocked with the horse's steady gait. He'd accepted that riding with Dr. Parker was in his parishioners' best interests. He could see more of them on the days the doctor came out to the countryside than he did the rest of the week together. It also allowed him to carry a few more supplies to ease a bit of their suffering. He tried hard to keep his angry feelings towards the British from spilling over onto the doctor.

"You shouldn't be such a pessimist." Dr. Parker admonished.

"Why not?"

"It isn't healthy."

"What is healthy here?"

"You are. I am. Lily certainly is and aren't you glad of that, else we'd both be trudging along on foot."

"Don't you ever feel guilty that we're not?"

"You are thick-headed."

"Stubborn."

"If that's the word you prefer."

"'Tis."

The doctor chuckled.

The O'Connor cottage was always their first stop.

The scene inside changed little from day to day. Deirdre's and Kathleen's words of welcome. Denis and Brendan gone. Aisling lying in front of the fire, a breathing skeleton, baffling everyone by clinging to life. Brigid staring into space, going deeper every day into another world. Loreena holding the piglet in her lap, timidly glancing from her sister to her friend. Rory asleep near the fire, saving his energy for the night. Meg was the only one not a constant. Sometimes she would be in the cottage, other times she would have already left for town. Occasionally, she would be on her way out just as they were coming in. If they came on a day following one of Meg's trips into town, they would find her asleep.

With the weather so mild they expected her to be gone, but she was still in the cottage when they arrived.

"Meg, I was sure you'd be in town today."

"I'm off soon, Father, but I didn't want to miss you. I've something important to talk to you about." She beckoned him to a corner of the room as she spoke.

"I think Rory's in trouble."

"What makes you thinks so?"

"When he came back last night he acted nervous. He kept looking out the window. He said nothing was wrong, but when we asked too many times, he got mad. Would you talk to him, please, Father? He can't lie to you. 'Twould be a sin."

"I'll see what I can do. I don't care to wake him, though." Father O'Malley looked at the sleeping lad feeling both pity and fear for him.

"I will then." Meg shook Rory's shoulder until he rolled groggily onto his side.

"Time to go?" Rory muttered, struggling to sit up.

"For me. Not you." Before leaving, she looked at Father O'Malley and nodded towards Rory.

Aye, Meg, Father O'Malley thought, catching the commanding gesture, a glimmer of the old Meg. It made him smile.

"What in the world?" Rory asked, still trying to shake the sleep out of his head.

"She's worried about you, lad, and so am I," the priest told him.

"Why, Father?" His face turned slightly sideways as he spoke, an undercurrent of suspicion in his voice.

286

Father O'Malley motioned to the far corner of the cottage away from the others. They spoke privately, in low tones.

"Something has gone wrong for you. What is it?"

"I don't know what you mean."

"You most certainly do. So out with it, and don't try to bluff me any."

Rory sighed. "They might be on to me."

"What makes you think so?"

"Someone from the house may have caught a glimpse of me last night, followed me for a bit, but I think I lost him. Must have, as I'm here and not in gaol."

"Anything to show for the risk you took?"

"A chicken."

"So you ate last night, then?"

"We did. 'Twas scrawny, but better than nothing. MacAllister's not got much in the way of good chickens."

"MacAllister? So you've moved on from your own landlord to stealing from others now?"

"Aye, Father. I'll be caught for sure unless I keep moving around."

"Becoming quite adept?" Father O'Malley crossed his arms over his chest.

"You mean good at it?"

The priest nodded.

"I suppose I am. 'Tis not what I want, Father, truly. I'm not a thief. I just don't see another way."

"You gave up the Public Works?"

"It killed my da and it doesn't do us any good. It will kill Meg's da and Brendan too before long. If I'd stayed on it would have killed me."

Father O'Malley didn't speak right away. Enough of his parishioners were on the Public Works that he made it his business to investigate for himself. His conclusion was that it was a ploy to kill them all the faster. The British claim was that the Irish must pay for their food, otherwise they would become too dependent on charity so they provided them with employment, paid them a pittance to do backbreaking, yet wholly unproductive work and clamored to be seen as great benefactors. To Father O'Malley it was nothing more than legalized murder. Still, he couldn't condone theft.

"I wish I knew what to tell you, lad."

"There's no good answer. I'm going to keep doing it and take my chances."

"It's killing Meg."

Rory hung his head. "Aye, but if I don't do it she will die anyway."

Dr. Parker stood up from the midst of the group by the fire. "Father, we need to be moving on."

"I'm ready."

As he was about to step outside, Father O'Malley felt a hand close over his arm.

"Father," Rory whispered, "do you think God understands why I'm doing it?"

"God knows. Pray to Him, Rory. Maybe He will give you a better answer than I can."

"I will, Father," Rory consented then went back to his sleeping spot by the fire.

"I don't envy your position," Dr. Parker said as they got back on the horse. "I wouldn't know what to tell that lad, either."

"Well, it's my problem, not yours," he muttered, still lost in thought.

"So it is, but it might help to talk it over."

"Not now, thank you. I prefer to think it through on my own." Undoubtedly, this English doctor wouldn't like to hear what really troubled him. As it was, he had to bite his tongue to hold back a barrage of invective against the British.

"Suit yourself."

* * *

The scenes inside each cottage varied little from one to the next. Skeletal forms sat motionless, staring ahead. Stringy hair drooped over bony shoulders and sunken eyes.

Lips puckered inward over spaces where rotted teeth had fallen out.

One of those mouths struggled to form words. Father O'Malley held the stick-like hand while leaning in close trying to catch the words seemingly so urgent to their speaker. *"Tá ocras orainn,"* she said in a hoarse whisper. He felt instantly swept back to his Clonmalloy nightmare. Though the blood pounded through his body, he forced himself not to pull away. "Aye, Moira, I know you're hungry."

Worse still were those succumbing to illness. Typhus had begun to spread among the starving. Others had Black Leg Disease. Living bodies were swelling, their limbs turning dark, rotting before his eyes. Dysentery, fever, scurvy, all manner of sickness surrounded them. Starved bodies totally depleted of nutrients lacked the strength to fight; indeed, they became a haven for all manner of horrid contagion. Worst of all were the children whose bodies changed in the most bizarre ways. They lost most of the hair on their heads, but grew it instead, boys and girls alike, on their faces.

They entered the yard of yet another cottage, the eighth one that day. Father O'Malley eyed the group clustered by the fire.

"Friend Martin, it is so good to see you." The smooth feminine voice surprised the Father O'Malley.

"Friend Sarah!" Dr. Parker took the plump, white hand. "I didn't know you were in Kelegeen."

Dr. Parker turned to the priest. "This is Friend Sarah Hay." Turning back to the woman, he said, "and this is my friend, Father O'Malley."

"Father, I am happy to meet thee." She enfolded his right hand between both of her own.

"The pleasure is mine, Ma'am." The words came out of him automatically, but felt like niceties that belonged to another time and place.

"Friend Sarah belongs to the Society of Friends," Dr. Parker explained.

"I understand." Father O'Malley knew the connotation of the word "friend" before a name. His bewilderment came from the image of this plump, rosy woman with creamy, glowing skin. Where had she come from?

As he and the doctor did their work Sarah hovered close by, cooing over the cottage's inhabitants. Listening to her soft, calming sounds, Father O'Malley felt himself begin to relax for the first time in many months.

He was soon on his knees, leaning over a parishioner. Holding her wasted hand in his, he closed his eyes and quietly prayed.

"Friend Sarah, hand me that fleam, would you, please?" the doctor requested.

She bustled away behind Father O'Malley.

"Here 'tis," her heard her say.

"Fine, now if you'd be so good as to give me a hand here."

Father O'Malley finished his prayer. As if pulled by an irresistible force, he turned to watch. Capable hands moved knowingly among the physician's instruments. They placed a wet cloth upon the sick woman's forehead and gently patted her cheek before returning to their work with the doctor. For the first time since the famine started, Father O'Malley did not want to leave a cottage. He wanted to stay in this woman's motherly presence. A light seemed to play about her. It was only the reflection of the firelight, but it gave her a glow of holiness.

"We are finished here," Dr. Parker announced. "Are you ready to move on?"

"In a moment." Father O'Malley suddenly realized that he'd spent more time watching Sarah than he had doing his own work. He felt the blush of shame flare up in his cheeks. He turned away from the two healers, moving among the sick, speaking softly to them and praying for them.

When they were once again mounted upon Lily, Father O'Malley was compelled to ask his companion about her.

"How do you know that woman? She cannot be from Kelegeen. I've never seen her before."

"I don't know where she's from originally. I've met her and other of the Friends in town, but it's the first time I've seen her out here. They've been helping with the sick. We may see more of them, though probably not too many. Their numbers are few and there is so much territory to cover. They do what they can, though. Good people. Very good people."

"Well, for once I agree with you about something. I have heard of the work they do."

Dr. Parker turned to look over his shoulder. "I thought you agreed with me about everything."

"Hmph!"

Dr. Parker chuckled. As they crested an embankment, Father O'Malley sensed a tightening of the doctor's back. His own throat seemed to close up, almost choking him. The Hoolihan cottage was in sight. Adam had located the doctor on the day of Father O'Malley's trip to Clonmalloy. Typhus coupled with Black Leg Disease was the diagnosis. A contagious and deadly combination.

Once dismounted, they approached Adam who was lying prostrate on the ground just outside the cottage door.

"Any response?" Dr. Parker asked, squatting down beside him.

"Not yet. Seems to take longer every day." Adam held the end of a long pole which disappeared through the cracked door into the dark interior of the cottage.

Father O'Malley began to invoke the help of the Lord in low, soft tones.

"Corrine, are ye with us still?" Adam called through the narrow opening. He waited, but there was no response.

"I believe I will take a look at the youngsters." Dr. Parker headed off toward the group of ragged children huddled around the fire some distance from the cottage. "Call if you need me for anything."

"Ah, there she is," Adam said, as his pole jerked slightly. He withdrew it and removed the can that hung from the other end. "She lives yet," he whispered. "'Twas your praying just now that made her still alive, Father. I thought she was gone this time."

291

"No, Adam, it was not my praying, but the Lord's will. He alone decides when we go to Him. I asked for His strength to help you."

Adam sat up, pulling the ends of his tattered swallow-tailed frieze coat around him, as if they could give his legs any warmth.

"Father, there is something I must confess," he said, his eyes on the ground, unable to look at the priest.

Father O'Malley placed a hand on his shoulder. "What is it, my son?"

"'Tis about Corrine. I'm afraid I've been praying wrong about her. I fear God may be pissed as hell at…I mean angry with me. Sorry about that, Father."

Father O'Malley shook his head. "No need. Go on."

"The thing is I know she won't get better. When we left the cottage she was in terrible high fever. Not long after, her legs started swelling and turning black. I had to get the bairns out else I knew they'd have it, too."

"And you were right to do so."

"Not that any of us is doing so well out here in the damned cold, excepting that we've got a fire to sit about and a few bits of board I've found from pulled down cottages for shelter. But, Corrine, she just suffers. I kept asking God to make her better, seeing as that's what you're supposed to pray for. But yesterday, when it took so long for her to tug on the pole to let me know she'd taken the mush, I thought she was dead. I called and called, but she never answered. I was about to pull the pole back, thinking it was over when the tug finally came. The worst thing of all happened then." He stopped talking and settled his gaze on the half-empty can sitting between his knees.

"What was that, Adam?" Father O'Malley coaxed.

Without looking up, he answered, "I was angry, Father. I was terrible angry that my wife was still alive. I prayed to God she would hurry up and die." Tears landed in the slush.

Father O'Malley took Adam by both shoulders. The skin under Adam's coat slid over his bones feeling ghastly to the touch. His sunken eyes had dark rings beneath them.

He was sure he knew the answer, but needed to ask. "Why did you want her to die?"

"I can't stand for her to go on suffering like this, knowing there's no hope of recovery." After wiping his nose on his sleeve, he looked Father O'Malley in the eye. "Do you remember how she used to laugh and dance? My Corrine mixed her legs the best of all in a jig, everyone said so."

"I remember." Father O'Malley nodded.

"Oh, Father, how could I pray for her to die? What the Almighty must think of me now I don't want to imagine."

"Adam, God knows what misery we're all going through. You don't suppose He hasn't looked down here lately, do you?"

"I do wonder at it sometimes."

"The Lord knows how much you love Corinne. He understands that you didn't really pray for her to die so much as you prayed for her to be out of pain. And the only way out is for her to go to Him; surely a much better place than this. So your prayer was a good one. You felt love in your heart for Corinne when you prayed it. That's more important than the words you used. You can say whatever words you like and let the Lord figure out from your heart what you mean."

"Then He won't be after sending me to hell for it, Father?"

"I'd be very surprised."

"From now on, how would it be if I just ask Him to get Corrine out of her pain in whatever way He knows is best?"

"I think that's the best prayer you could say. It shows you put all your trust in Him."

"Thank you, Father. 'Tis what I'll do. I'd still feel better in my mind, though, if you'd treat this as a confession."

"You want absolution, then?"

"Aye, and a penance, too."

Father O'Malley said the prayer of Absolution over him while Adam recited an Act of Contrition.

"For your penance I will have you say an Our Father, a Hail Mary, and a Glory Be once for your wife and once for each of your children."

"Thank you, Father. It was weighing heavy on my mind. I do feel much better now."

Relief flickered for a moment in the man's tortured face. Father O'Malley smile. "I'll leave you to your praying now and go see your bairns."

"Adam was smart to get them out when he did," Dr. Parker commented, after they were back astride the horse. "Most stay in the cottage alongside the infected patient, then contract the disease themselves. I've only seen a few families impose a quarantine on themselves like that."

"Adam was concerned about his children, but he would never have left if he'd had none to think of. If it were me, I would not leave. As it is, there isn't much greater chance of survival out here in the cold, now is there?"

"Bad as it is, it's a better chance than inside with a typhus patient. In there is certain death."

"Those children didn't look as though they have much hope."

"They don't, but they also don't have typhus yet."

"Do you know the Dooley family?" asked Father O'Malley as Lily carried them towards home.

"Name's not familiar."

"There's a lad a bit younger than Rory, named Kevin. There's also the mother, Noreen, and twin girls."

"No father?"

Father O'Malley snorted. "There was, if you want to call him that. He abandoned the family when they were evicted. The four of them live in a *scalpeen* now."

The doctor shook his head. "They must be well-hidden. I'm sure I'd remember twins."

"You'd certainly remember those two."

"Oh? Spitfires are they? Seen more than a few of those in your Irish women." The doctor laughed.

Father O'Malley chuckled. "You mean like Meg O'Connor?"

"Indeed! That one for sure."

"Sadly, the twins are not made from the same mold."

"Oh?"

"No. I've never heard either of them utter a word. They stay huddled so close to each other it's near impossible to tell where one lass leaves off and the other begins."

"Well, twins are known to be unusually close. Identical, I suppose?"

"I certainly can't tell one from the other."

"And they don't speak, you say? Can't or won't?"

"At this point I'm not sure. According to their mother, they were normal children when they were young. Then she left them alone for a day with their da. When she got home she found he'd beaten them. I suspect he may have done more than that, but that's my own conjecture."

Doctor Parker swiveled in the saddle to look at the priest. "They've not spoken since then?"

"So their mother claims. Won't let go of each other, either."

Dr. Parker turned forward again. His voice became rough. "Seems their father did the family a favor by leaving."

"I won't argue with that. He was drunk most of the time anyway. Had a nasty temper."

"Well, they are free of that now, at least."

"Perhaps."

"What do you mean?" asked the doctor.

"The lad, Kevin. He's filled with anger and bitterness. He lost his best friend, Rory's brother Aiden, in an accident with the *curragh*. His father blamed him for the loss of the boat, which also meant loss of fish to eat and sell. Beat him something terrible and wouldn't even let him attend his friend's funeral."

"Has the lad inherited his father's temper?"

"I fear he has. And, from what I gathered the last time I spoke with his Mam, his father's penchant for the drink as well."

"A dangerous combination," Doctor Parker acknowledged. "How are they managing?"

"Noreen said that Kevin goes into town. She assumes he begs because he brings them food, but when she asks how he got it he gets angry and won't tell."

"So at least they are eating?"

"When he comes home. Apparently, he stays away for days at a time. Noreen and the twins have nothing until he returns. They never know how long it will be." Father O'Malley noted the sun sliding down the western sky. "I know it's getting late, but if you wouldn't mind, it's been a bit since I checked on them. Would you mind stopping by? The *scalpeen's* nearby."

"Just tell me where to lead Lily."

When they reached the *scalpeen,* they found it empty. A knot formed in the pit of Father O'Malley's stomach as he scanned the area. "Something's not right," he said.

Doctor Parker was busy admiring the *scalpeen.* "I must say, this is the best made one I've seen yet. It's no wonder I've not come across them. I would never have noticed it, it blends in so well."

"Aye, Larry did a magnificent job." Father O'Malley's voice was flat, so distracted was he that he barely thought about his words.

"Larry? I thought you said the lad's name was Kevin."

Father O'Malley looked at the doctor. "Sorry. It is. But Kevin didn't make this *scalpeen*. A man by the name of Larry Donnelly built it. He and his boys lived here until they all died of fever. I told Kevin about it. Told him to keep it secret and only bring his mother and sisters here if he needed to escape his father."

"Things turned out a bit differently, though," said Doctor Parker.

"They did and now I wonder what other turn they've taken."

"Couldn't they all have gone into town to beg?"

"Possible, I suppose, but not likely. It's a rare thing when the mother and girls leave. They wait here until Kevin returns with some food."

"Perhaps they got tired of waiting," suggested the doctor. "The sun will be down soon. Since they're not here, I think we must move on."

Father O'Malley conceded, but his mind kept returning to the empty *scalpeen* and the feeling that something was terribly wrong. They were half way between the O'Connor cottage and Father O'Malley's home when they came upon Denis and Brendan returning from the Public Works.

"I wish I had my phaeton," said Doctor Parker. "They look as though they'll fall down before they get home."

"Why don't I get off and walk the rest of the way," suggested Father O'Malley.

"Excellent plan. They can ride and I'll lead Lily."

Father O'Malley dismounted once they came even with the two staggering figures. Just before Doctor Parker led them off towards home mounted on Lily's back, Father O'Malley thought to ask, "Do either of you have any idea where the Dooleys might be?"

"They're living in a *scalpeen,*" Denis said. "Couldn't tell you where it is, though."

"We just came from there. It's empty."

"Don't know then," Denis said, his head drooping with exhaustion.

"If you want to find Kevin, try the Workhouse," Brendan offered.

"He's gone into the Workhouse?" Father O'Malley was stunned.

"Not to stay," Brendan explained. "He drives the cart that takes away the dead. They might know when he'll come next."

Father O'Malley stared after them as the horse and riders moved on. Kevin had become a cart driver for the Workhouse. No wonder he didn't want to tell his family. Only a paid informant would be considered more heinous. It had to be pure desperation that had pushed him to it.

The poor lad, he thought. A more soul crushing job could not possibly exist.

Chapter Twenty-Seven

Meg awoke to the soft scuffing noises Rory made as he slowly pulled himself up from the floor. He went to the fire, poking about the few utensils lying near the empty cauldron. He selected a large, sharp knife, the only one they had. Intrigued, Meg continued to watch in silence. Turning, he crouched over Aisling. Meg's heart hammered in her chest. He'd been acting so strange and secretive lately. Meg now wondered if he'd lost his mind, suddenly intent on murdering his own sister, thinking to put her out of her misery. Her fear subsided as he merely stroked Aisling's cheek. She remained motionless as he walked out the door.

She could not let go of the image of Rory with the knife; pictures of what he might do with it chased each other across her mind. His hatred of the British permeated every bit of flesh and bone left clinging to him.

He will get himself killed, sure as he breathes. Consumed with worry, she decided to follow. Out in the cold air, she pulled what remained of her shawl around her arms. He hadn't much distance on her, but she knew she could not propel herself fast enough to catch up with him. With strength enough for only one chance at getting his attention, she gathered up all the breath inside her.

"Rory!" Once his name was out on the air, she waited.

He turned, paused, as if weighing his decision. Motionless but for the shivering, she waited. Relief flooded her as he started back.

He was nearly out of breath when he reached her. "What's wrong? Aisling?"

She shook her head. "Why did you take the knife?"

"Because I've need of it."

She grabbed his arm. "Rory, please don't kill anyone!"

"I'm not after killing anyone, Meg. Let go now and let me be off."

He started away. Meg walked with him.

"If you don't tell me, I'll come with you and see for myself."

"You haven't the strength for it."

"Then I'll drop down dead halfway, and that'll be on your head, Rory Quinn, so you might as well tell me what you're doing."

Rory stopped. "May the saints give me the patience to be married to you. I'm going up to the cave beside Blaine's pasture. Since the thaw, he's been grazing sheep up there. There's a few of us decided to wait until dark to get a sheep."

"Who is Blaine?"

"A Brit farmer. What he don't eat gets shipped to England so's they can eat. Time we got a bit to eat from him, too."

"You're bound to get caught."

"The lads I'm to meet up with have done it before. We wait until it gets dark, then go quick. Kill the sheep, then get out with it as fast as we can."

"You'll be seen running away with the dead sheep. You don't suppose that might look a wee bit suspicious to anyone?"

"The lads know how to do it. Take the sheep to a graveyard to skin it on a flat stone. Cut it up. Then hide the pieces along the way. We keep coming back to where we hid them and we can eat good for a time. I do this once and I don't have to steal again for a while."

The idea of meat made her mouth water. Tormenting hunger and fear for Rory competed in her mind. Perhaps it was worth the risk.

"I'll go with you," she announced. "I can help."

"You've been in town just the other day. You're too tired for another long walk this soon."

She knew Rory was right. If she failed to make it, it could ruin their best chance yet for survival. Meg was not ready to give up, however.

"What graveyard will you take it to?"

"Wherever the other lads go. I'll follow them."

"But you'll not hide many of the pieces too far from here, will you?"

"I haven't thought yet where to hide them."

"Well, you'd best think it all through first. I could help with the hiding. I'll meet you closer to home and we'll work together."

Rory sighed. "Meet me in our own burying ground after dark."

"I'll be there." For the first time in months wings of hope fluttered within her, making her giddy at the thought of real food.

Meg walked back to the cottage on wobbly legs. She hit the floor hard, falling asleep immediately. It was dark when she awoke.

Mist surrounded the moon as she made her way to the graveyard. She crouched among the graves of Rory's family, believing that would be the most likely place to meet him. A recent thaw had melted much of the snow, leaving the ground soggy. Her feet sank in the thick, cold mud. Fog swirled eerily around her, the dampness permeating her skin. Meg prayed that she was not too late.

She kept as still as she could, sitting on her haunches, her feet like blocks of ice. The mud had sucked off her shoes as she walked. There was no sign of Rory. Then came the terrifying thought. What if he had been caught? What if right now he was being dragged off to some dank prison cell or lying dead from the farmer's bullet?

Meg huddled into a shivering ball. Every so often she would lift her head but she only saw the dark, white-misted landscape. She tried not to think about dying, not to think about Rory, not to think at all.

The sucking sounds of feet pulling their way through the mud broke through.

"Rory!" she called while trying to stand. Her legs threw her forward, sprawling her onto the ground.

"Shhh…," he admonished, coming up to her with two bloody cuts of meat, one perhaps from the shoulder, the other part of a leg, under each arm.

Meg pulled her feet free of the mud. Cold slime clung to them in clumps.

"You did it!"

"Aye, and I'm nearly ready to keel. Help me with this, Meg. I can't go much longer." Barely able to speak, Rory fell to his knees in front of her.

Meg grabbed the leg, slippery from the blood. She hugged it tightly to her chest to prevent it from sliding away.

"Where are we going to bury these?" she asked while Rory rested.

"We'll only bury the leg and half the shoulder. The other we can eat tonight."

Meg's mouth watered at the thought. "Let's hurry with the burying, then. Should we do it here?"

"No. Too many people come looking among the graves for nettles. Let's get closer to home."

When the O'Connor cottage came in view, Meg said, "The ground is soft out in the old potato bed. It's mostly mud now. Let's put it there."

Rory nodded.

They rested in the potato bed before beginning their last work of the night. Cupping their hands, they dug a shallow grave for the leg and half the shoulder, dropped them in and covered it over with cold mud. Meg scooped up some snow that hadn't yet melted with the thaw and patted it down over the mound. Rory dug a few rocks out of the earth, placing them on top to mark the exact location.

They stumbled through the doorway, dropped the meat near the fire and collapsed in their sleeping spots.

No one stirred.

Meg's words came out in a single rush of air. "There is food." Then she fell silent, completely spent.

The rustling of rags and shifting of limbs filtered through the cloud of exhaustion in Meg's mind. Words began to prick their way into her brain.

"There's food! Blessed be God, we've food!" It was her mother's voice.

Meg's eyes blinked open long enough to see her father crawling toward the spot where they had left the portion of lamb shoulder. She listened to the voices exclaim over the miracle.

"Kathleen, help me with this. Get it over the fire now."

"No. The smell of roasting will bring others. We'll be killed for it," Denis warned.

"What are we to do, then?" asked Deirdre.

"Da, we must have it. Please, I am so hungry." Kathleen gave way to tears.

"We will eat it lass, don't you worry. It just can't be cooked here. The smell would bring 'em all down on us. Let me take care of it."

Meg heard scuffling noises. The cottage door opened and closed. Only the voices of her mother and Kathleen could be heard as they marveled at the event. Meg listened until her mind went black.

The smell of roasted meat pulled her from her slumber right up to a sitting position. Blindly, she fell forward onto her hands and knees crawling in its direction. She sensed the nearness of others but paid no attention. She grabbed at the meat trying to pull some free, but her hand was pushed aside. She saw a knife plunge into the roasted lamb, haphazardly cutting out chunk after chunk. She grabbed the first piece that fell free and thrust it into her mouth. Other hands reached for their own pieces.

"Go slow." The whispered advice from her mother was not necessary. Meg had long since trained herself to eat any morsel that came her way with deliberate patience. The quiet room was filled with the sounds of chewing and swallowing. Deirdre's knees shuffled along the floor as she brought a handful of the succulent meat to Brigid, who had not stirred from her place by the fire.

Deirdre tried to entice the child. "Eat, lass, eat."

Meg could picture Brigid staring vacantly ahead, not even comprehending her mother's presence, let alone the fact that there was food.

"That's it. Now chew it slowly. You're doing fine, lass. Oh, aye, you're doing fine, Brigid."

The joy in Deirdre's voice compelled Meg to look. The sight she beheld almost took her breath away. Brigid had been quiet and still so long they'd assumed she'd lost the ability of speech and movement. Whenever anyone managed to come by some crust of food, Deirdre would have to forcibly thrust Brigid's allotment into her mouth and pray she didn't choke.

Now they all turned to look at Brigid. Even Rory stared at her as he held his own sister upright while placing the tiniest pieces of meat in her mouth.

Brigid was methodically taking piece after piece from Deirdre's hands, depositing them in her own mouth and slowly chewing. She still stared straight ahead, all but her shaking arm remained rigid, but she was completing the task of eating all on her own.

"Saints be praised," Denis mumbled and crossed himself.

Meg's earlier feeling of elation returned with renewed strength. *We will make it.*

* * *

The last days of February and early March were the best for Meg since the starving time began. The lamb restored a bit of her old strength, giving her the ability to trek into town more often. On good days she could supplement the few handfuls of meat each family member received with some bread from the bakery or a few morsels purchased with the wages her da and Brendan brought home from the Public Works.

She still worried whenever Rory went out at night to unearth another section of the lamb in the still-frozen ground. She worried, too, for her da, who continued to roast the meat in a spot he would not disclose. Still, it was nothing compared to the fear she had felt at Rory's night time raids. Even Brigid seemed more animated. Though she still stared into space, she ate on her own, occasionally making sounds as though trying to speak.

"She'll talk again one day." Deirdre had said after Brigid made a humming noise while pointing to a piece of bread.

Loreena tried again to attempt conversation with Brigid. Though her friend was still silent, Loreena was occasionally rewarded with a brief look of comprehension.

Aisling was still a puzzle. She hadn't been able to partake in much of their new-found bounty. Deirdre made Denis take a pan and some water with him when he went to roast the meat for a broth. Though it wasn't much more than greasy hot water, Deirdre would pour as much of it as she could into Aisling. Aisling gagged and sputtered, though some did get down along with the tiniest bits of meat. Mostly she just lay still in front of the fire. Hardly moving, seldom awake, in and out of fever, there was little left of her. Dr. Parker had ended the purgatives as they convulsed the tiny body to the point he worried her bones would snap.

On the doctor's last visit Rory and Meg had asked him what was happening to Aisling. Dr. Parker had shrugged. "I have no medical explanation. Perhaps you should ask your priest."

Meg turned to Father O'Malley. "Father?"

"I don't know either, lass. The good Lord has seen fit to keep her among us. We don't always understand the reason for things, but often, in time, He shows us."

Late one afternoon, Rory leaned in close to whisper in Meg's ear. "I must go again. This time it will be to MacGurdy's. We've planned it for tonight. Will you be at the burying ground as before?"

"Aye, but it seems so soon." Meg hated the idea of another raid.

"There is but one piece left."

"Go then and I'll meet you," Meg told him.

There had been some change in Aisling in the past few days. Whether for good or ill no one was sure. She had surprised them by thrashing from side to side one day for a few seconds, then lying still again, only to repeat the odd behavior at intervals.

They had questioned the doctor about it. All he could say was that Aisling was indeed at a turning point, but in what direction he was not sure. They hoped the bit of broth was giving her strength to fight for her life. Meg had no heart to try to deny Rory the only available means of keeping his sister alive so she stifled her fears and acquiesced.

"I'll sleep now. The other lads won't wait for me so I'll be off before the sun goes down. You should sleep now, too, Meg. You'll need your strength if you want to help me again with the hiding of it."

Meg glanced at Brigid, still sitting in her corner, then, looking away, she glimpsed the top of Aisling's head. A pink bald patch glimmered in the firelight between limp strands of golden hair. The hope she held out for them was only a shadow. But to let it slip away was to lose everything.

Meg was awakened by a gentle shaking of her shoulder.

"I'm leaving now," Rory whispered. "Hold off until it's been dark a while." His breath tickled her ear. "Don't come if you can't do it, Meg."

Rory let the cottage door bang shut behind him. Meg started to drift back to sleep. The sound of the cottage door closing again entered her awareness, puzzling her, but almost instantly she was overtaken by sleep. She had no idea how long Rory had been gone when she awoke. The cottage was quiet which meant he had not yet returned. Meg pushed herself to her knees.

Stepping away from the fire was the hardest part. Before she had even opened the door her body was wracked with shivering. Pulling the remains of her shawl around her was now only habit that served no real purpose.

Once outside, Meg moved as quickly as she could. She slipped often. Most of the snow had melted, but the air had turned bitterly cold again after a week of mild weather, making the mud hard with a slimy film over the top. A patch of snow stung the ball of her bare foot. Once at the burying ground, she crouched among the graves.

305

Hurried, uneven footsteps approached. Meg lifted her head from under the shawl. A form slid towards her.

"Rory, what it is? What happened?"

"They've seen us! They're coming! We've no time to talk. Run!" He grabbed her arm pulling her along.

How close are they? Did they know it was him? Had any of the others been caught? She had no breath to voice the questions racing through her mind as she ran behind Rory. When they reached the cottage, he shoved her inside and slammed the door behind them.

"Get to the fire, Meg. Lie down. I don't believe they've seen my face. If they come in here they will only find us sleeping."

"Jesus, Mary, and Joseph! May the saints preserve us!" Deirdre cried out.

"Hush!" It was Denis. "Don't make a sound, any of you."

How could she fake sleep in this state? Meg closed her eyes willing her body to relax, but her chest ached with each involuntary gasp for air. Time wore on. No one barreled through the door looking for a thief. Finally, she fell asleep.

The screaming woke her just before dawn. Deirdre's voice. "Don't take him! Don't take him! Don't go! Please don't go!"

Meg's heart squeezed so hard bright lights burst in the darkness before her eyes. Had someone come after all? Was Rory being dragged out? But there was no sound other than her mother's screams. Lying face down, Meg's pounding heart seemed to strike the dirt floor beneath her.

Then her father's voice, soft and soothing. "Calm down, *mo grá*. No one's taking anyone anywhere."

Meg heard rustling, felt a rush of heat as someone threw more peat in the fireplace, making the flames flare up. She raised herself onto her elbows. Her father cradled her mother in his arms, rocking her back and forth, stroking her hair. Slowly, she came fully awake. Her screaming stopped. She tilted her head to look in her husband's face.

"Someone will go from us, Denis, sure as I'm sitting here. The feeling is strong."

Meg turned towards Rory, caught his eye. Quickly, he looked away.

Dawn's first rays threw a dim streak through the cottage window making a pale patch on the floor.

"Time to go," she heard her father say. "Where is Brendan?"

"He's not here?" Deirdre asked. The fear that had only begun to abate now threatened to escalate into hysteria.

"Don't worry, now, Deirdre," Denis said. "He must have left early for the Works." His voice shook just enough that Meg knew he didn't believe his own words.

She remembered the sound of the door closing for the second time after Rory had left the cottage. "God save us!" she said. "I think he followed Rory."

Chapter Twenty-Eight

"Saints in Heaven!" Deirdre clutched one hand to her heart.

Denis dropped his hand from the door latch. "Rory, did you see him?"

"No. What makes you think he followed me, Meg?"

"After you left I heard the door open and close again."

"How long after I left?"

"I don't know. It woke me up, but I went right back to sleep."

"For sure, I'd have seen him." Rory spoke as though trying to convince himself.

"Maybe he didn't follow Rory. Maybe he went somewhere else," Kathleen offered.

"But where?" Denis kicked the door. "Ah, damn it all! I'll not be going to the Works now. I've got to look for the lad. Rory, where did you go last night?"

"To MacGurdy's place."

"That's where I'll start then."

"I'll come with you. I can show you where I went." Rory started to push himself up, but instantly collapsed, grabbing his calf muscle in agony.

"Don't try to get up, Rory." Meg told him. "I can't move, either. You won't get far."

Rory's face clenched in pain. Through gritted teeth he said, "You've no argument from me this time."

Denis headed toward the door. "I'll be back when I know something."

"What's happened to my lad?" Deirdre sobbed.

"Mam, don't cry." Kathleen tried to console her. "Da will find him."

Meg had learned that sheer will could accomplish many things, but that practicality was just as important. She would sleep all day. Tonight she and Rory would unearth the last piece of lamb. If Brendan still had not returned, then she could join in the search for him when she had more strength.

* * *

Darkness had engulfed the cottage again when Meg awoke. The door opened bringing a blast of cold air. Two shadows approached the fire.

"Who's there?" Deirdre's voice quavered.

"Myself and Father."

As they approached, Meg could just make out the shadowy outlines of her da's face and that of her priest. Deirdre moved closer as the two men crouched near the fire.

"Father? Oh, please no!"

Denis' arm reached toward Deirdre. "Calm yourself, now. The lad's not dead."

"Thank you, Jesus," she whispered, crossing herself. "Where is he?" she asked.

The two men glanced at each other.

"Deirdre, prepare yourself," Father O'Malley began.

Deirdre grabbed the sleeves of Denis' coat, her eyes wild in the firelight.

"He's in gaol," said Denis.

"No," she said, her voice still a whisper, softer than before, filled with disbelief.

"So he did follow me?" Rory forced himself to sit up. "I never saw him."

"He probably knew you'd send him back, so kept his distance." This time it was Father O'Malley's voice, disembodied in the darkness.

"Aye, and I would have, too, only how did he get caught?"

"He lagged behind, out of sight. He ran when the rest of you did, after MacGurdy started shooting."

"Shooting! " Deirdre gripped her husband's arm. "Is he hurt?"

"No, Deirdre, he's not been shot."

Meg felt sick to her stomach.

"One of MacGurdy's men caught hold of him" Father O'Malley explained. "They took him into town and put him in prison."

"What will happen to him now, Father?" Deirdre asked.

"He will stay there until his case comes to trial."

"How long?"

"I've no idea. I will go into town tomorrow and see what I can find out."

"Bless you, Father."

Kathleen sat, leaning her head against the wall. "Father, will they let him go, do you think? He's only a boy."

"He's fifteen. That's not so much a boy in the eyes of the court. I don't know what they will do with him. Stealing is a serious offense."

"Father, they wouldn't hang him, would they?" There was a catch in Deirdre's voice.

"I don't think so, Deirdre. Though he may spend a while in prison."

Deirdre put her head in her hands.

"There is one favorable aspect in all this."

"What could that possibly be?" Denis asked.

"The prison has food. If nothing else, Brendan will get at least one decent meal a day. I know some who've gotten themselves arrested on purpose just to get into gaol to eat better for a while."

"'Tis something, I suppose." Denis nodded.

"Before I go home for the night, I think we should pray together."

Meg made the sign of the cross and folded her hands over her chest. She wished she had the strength to push herself onto her knees, but knew it would take too long. Father had already begun to pray.

"Heavenly Father, please keep young Brendan safe. Keep all the O'Connor and Quinn families safe and in your holy care. Grant that when this calamity has ended these families are found unbroken in your love. Amen."

"Father, is it far into the night yet?" Meg asked.

"Not much. It's still a bit this side of midnight. Good night." He let himself out.

"Rory, should we try to uncover the last bit of lamb, do you think?" she whispered to him.

"Do you feel up to it?

"I won't know until I try to stand. Should we try?"

"I will if you want to."

Slowly, Meg and Rory brought themselves to standing positions.

"What are you two doing?" Deirdre's voice came from across the room.

"We are going to fetch the last piece of lamb. Pray it's still good, Mam."

"No. Don't go."

"Don't worry. We can make it. If we don't, there will be no food at all."

"I've already lost Brendan. I'll not be losing you, too."

"Deirdre, let them go." Denis' voice was resigned.

"How can you say that? You've lost a son today. You want to lose a daughter as well?"

"I didn't show up at the Works today. If you don't appear they assume you're dead or damn close and you get replaced. That last piece of meat is all that's left to us."

"Then Rory can go alone. I'll not risk my daughter."

"Mam, it needs the two of us."

"Your Mam is right, Meg. You'd best stay here," Rory said.

"But there's no danger in it, Mam. We're not stealing. Just digging up what's been stole already. No one will see us."

"You're not to go, Meg. Denis, you tell her."

"Rory, I'd go in her place, but after being out all day looking for Brendan—"

"I understand."

"There's no need to go in my place. I will go myself."

"Meg, you're not going!" Meg realized the energy it cost her mother to put that much force behind her words.

311

She also knew the energy it would cost Rory to do all the digging and carrying on his own.

"Fine, Mam." She lay down, pretending to go back to sleep. Shortly after Rory lft, she rose and crept toward the door.

"Where do you think you're going?" Deirdre's voice was sharp.

"Just to pee."

"Be quick about it, then." The worry and distrust in Deirdre's voice pricked Meg's conscience.

Looking in the direction she knew Rory was headed, she expected to see him up ahead, but there was only empty, barren land in front of her.

"Get back inside, Meg." Rory's whisper startled her.

"Why haven't you gone after the lamb?"

"I knew you would follow. Now go back in."

"I'm going with you."

"It's not safe, even with the field being so close. They could be watching for us."

Ignoring him, Meg started off in the direction of the field, trying not to think about the cold. Rory soon caught up with her. Upon reaching the field, they stopped to catch their breath.

"Your Mam'll be bloody pissed." Rory leaned forward with his hands on his knees, sucking big gulps of air.

"Are you afraid of her?"

"What do you think? She's where you came from."

"What do you mean by that?"

"I mean I can't do a thing with you. You've got a will that may well drive me to an early grave."

"Have you just discovered it, then?" Her words, like his, came out between gasps for breath.

"No. But I thought I could tame you."

"Does my Mam seem tame to you?"

"No, and that's the reason I dread walking back into that cottage..." he took a few breaths. "Even if I had a ten course meal in tow." Rory moved to a large rock barely discernible in the moonlight. One side extended outward to end in a sharp point as if forever gesturing west.

He took out the large kitchen knife. Laying it down so that its handle touched an indent in the base of the rock, he used it to measure five lengths, the proper distance away. When he was sure he had the right spot, he stabbed the knife into the frozen mud. Rory chopped at the mud until he had enough turned up so that they could start digging.

Forming her nearly numb hands into scoops, Meg pulled up one fistful of mud after another. Rory employed the knife several times to loosen the hardened earth. It seemed to take forever. Meg's arms burned with the effort.

"I feel it." Rory darted the knife around, jabbing at a mass in the mud. "I've just got to get it free."

He dug with the knife all around the slab of meat until it was worked loose, finally pulling up the slimy chunk. He scraped away the mud with the blade of his knife. They took turns carrying the slippery meat back to the cottage.

Meg was momentarily grateful to step through the door into the relative warmth.

"Meg? Is that you?" Deirdre's voice sound so haunted that guilt suddenly consumed her.

"Aye, Mam." She expected a scolding, but Deirdre remained silent. "Rory's got the meat."

A little before sun-up, Denis awoke. He held the meat close to the light to inspect it.

"Give me the knife, lad. I'll need to cut out some before I roast it."

"It's gone bad, then?" Deirdre asked.

"Some has. I think there's still enough to give us each a bite or two, though."

Denis left the cottage. Meg stretched and turned over, exhausted. All she wanted was to sleep until her father returned with the roasted meat. She didn't care if it was rancid. She'd eat it anyway. She'd heard enough stories of folks eating rats and dead dogs to figure she could live through a bad piece of meat.

Dawn was just creeping into the sky when Denis returned. A mix of foul and succulent odors swirled in the air. Meg's mouth watered despite the unpleasant layer of aroma.

"I kept as much as I could." They gathered around while he cut it up.

Meg held hot pieces in her hand. Grease smeared across her palms. She bit into a chunk. She forced her mind to focus only on the mechanics of chewing and swallowing.

"This famine is going to destroy us." Deirdre's voice was flat.

"We've made it so far." Denis tried to sound encouraging.

Meg looked at her parents.

"We may live, aye, but what about our souls, Denis?"

"What do you mean?"

"This famine has caused our children to break the commandments. It makes me ashamed."

Meg wanted to soothe her mother's pain. "Brendan didn't steal, Mam. He only followed Rory. And Rory only steals what he has to because there's no other way. He'll stop when it's over and we can grow potatoes again."

"I was speaking of you as well, Megeen. And a commandment that goes, 'honor thy mother and father'? You'd best make a good confession the next time Father is here."

"Aye, Mam." Meg's voice cracked on the words. She lay on her side holding the last bit of meat, cooling it in her hand. She cried as she clung to it, wanting to eat, but knowing nothing would stay down now. Instead she passed it to Kathleen.

Chapter Twenty-Nine

Father O'Malley's eyes slowly adjusted to the lack of light as he was led through the prison's dim interior. Fetid air carried the stench of long unwashed bodies, many dying of illness. The guard stopped in front of a group of dejected forms sitting in silence on the cell floor.

"The new ones from last night was all tossed in here." The guard gestured toward the cell ahead of them.

"Brendan? Brendan O'Connor?"

A head lifted. "Aye, Father."

The guard unlocked the cell door. "Ten minutes."

Hearing the lock clink as the door shut behind him, Father O'Malley wondered what it must feel like to have no hope of it opening again for a very long time. His heart went out to the group on the floor.

"Brendan, are you alright, lad?"

"Just scared. What will they do to me? Will I be here forever?"

"No, Brendan."

"Will they hang me, then?"

"No, lad."

"Do you know what they will do, Father? The not knowing is killing me."

"You'll have to wait for your trial to find out."

"When will that be?"

"I don't know, but I doubt it will be long."

"That's good. When I tell my story, they will let me go."

"What makes you sure of that?"

"I did nothing wrong. I only followed Rory. I wasn't going to steal. I just wanted to watch how he did it, preparing myself, if ever I needed to help. But I only would have done it if I had to. So I needed to know how. If anything should happen to Rory I wanted to be able to take over. Without him we'd all be dead."

"Didn't you fear getting caught?"

Brendan shrugged. "Rory makes it through every time. I thought if I did just as he does I'd be fine." Brendan paused for a moment. "There was shooting. Rory made it back, didn't he?" His youthful voice pitched high on the last word.

Father O'Malley put a hand on his shoulder. "Rory made it home safely."

Brendan relaxed. "Good."

"Brendan, we are all quite concerned about what will happen to you. Your poor mother—"

"You'll please tell her I'm fine? I've eaten since I've been here. Stirabout, I think. The other lads say food comes round once every day!"

"That is one blessing. Brendan, would you like to make a confession while I'm here?"

Brendan thought a moment. "I suppose I should, Father.

"Let's move off a little ways for privacy."

They inched over to a spot near the damp wall. "And try to remember, Brendan, that contemplating theft is a sin as well, though I know you meant well."

"Aye, Father."

In softly whispered tones, Brendan made his confession. Afterwards, keeping his confessional tone, Father O'Malley asked, "How do you expect to present your case to the judge without mentioning Rory?"

Brendan's eyes widened. "I hadn't thought of that." He pondered for a moment then said, "Suppose I just say I heard of some lads who were going off to steal a sheep and I followed them?"

Father O'Malley shook his head. "They'll want to know who they are and how you knew of it. I suppose you could say you saw a group of lads going off, thought they might know the whereabouts of some work and followed along. It might save you."

"From hanging?"

"Brendan, stop worrying about hanging. It's not the penalty for minor theft anymore."

"What will they do to me? I can't stand wondering after it!" His voice rose in frustration.

"It's to Van Diemen's Land we'll be going," offered one man from the center of the cell. "That's what they do with thieves now and it's glad I am to go. At least they've no famine in Australia."

"Is that true, Father?"

"There's no telling for sure. A first offense, a lad so young as yourself and as you've said, you actually stole nothing."

Father O'Malley realized he was engaging in wishful thinking as much as trying to calm the lad. There was a very good chance he'd be deported. The British seemed intent on ridding Ireland of the Irish.

The guard's footsteps echoed down the hallway.

"Our time must be up. I will tell your family I've seen you—that you're being fed and are well enough."

As Father O'Malley rose to leave he felt Brendan's hand grasp his coat.

"Father, tell them I love them, please." His voice broke. "Especially my mam."

"I will." He clapped Brendan's hand in his own. "You will be in my prayers, Brendan. Pray for God's mercy." He patted the boy's shoulder.

The guard unlocked the door. "Time's up."

As he stepped outside the sunlight blinded him. He squinted his eyes against it, shading them with his hands, stumbling as pain seared his forehead. He sat down on the steps leading up from the prison doorway, waiting for his vision to adjust and his head to tolerate the light of day.

"Oh, Brendan," he muttered to himself. "How is it a good lad gets himself into such a muddle?"

Trudging into the street, he watched as hordes of the starving begged for the slightest scrap, while fancy carriages passed them by. On occasion a kind soul would hand a walking skeleton a pence or two.

The rumble of wheels caught his attention. A black horse's head bobbed along as the animal hauled an empty wagon. Their driver cracked the whip, urging them on through the throngs of people. The driver was Kevin. *It's time I had a word with that lad*, thought Father O'Malley as he made a grab for the wagon.

"Back off, ye bloody bastard!" Kevin's whip was about to descend.

"Kevin Dooley, just to whom do you think you are speaking!"

Recognition dawned in Kevin's eyes. "Oh, Father. Sorry. I didn't realize it was you." He brought the horse to a halt.

"That's apparent. It's also appalling that you should speak so to anyone. Now, if you'd be so kind as to make room, I've some things to discuss with you." Father O'Malley didn't wait for a response, but climbed into the driver's seat next to the lad.

"I can't stop in the middle of the road, Father," Kevin protested.

"Drive on, then. You're headed towards the workhouse, I presume, since your cart is empty."

Kevin feigned ignorance. "Workhouse? Why would I be going there?"

"Oh, stop your nonsense. I well know what you've been doing to feed your family."

Kevin bristled. "'Tis an honest job." He flicked the reigns moving the horses forward.

"Not a very pleasant one, though, I'll wager."

"I do my job and try not to think about it." Kevin kept his eyes focused straight ahead.

"I'm not judging you, Kevin. I'm concerned about you. What you're doing could steal the heart right out of you."

Silence followed for a moment. Then Kevin said quietly, "Doesn't feel as though I have a heart anymore so I guess it don't matter."

Father O'Malley looked at the lad's profile. Thin, gaunt, skeletal. The same words could apply to most Irish faces these days. Another word bothered him more. Hard.

Kevin's face had taken on a stone-like quality. Father O'Malley feared it was a reflection of the lad's soul.

"When was the last time you were at the *scalpeen*?" he asked.

"Don't know. It's been a bit."

"Why is that?"

"Busy."

"Doing what? You can't make that many daily trips to the workhouse and the pits."

"A man's got to relax a bit, don't he? As you say, it's not a pleasant job."

"In what way have you chosen to do that, if you don't mind my asking?"

Kevin's body stiffened. "Meaning no disrespect, Father, but as it happens, I do mind."

"I see. Well, a man looks after his family, Mr. Dooley. When you don't show up, they don't eat."

"They're eating alright now." Kevin's voice had lost the blusterous tone he'd adopted a moment ago.

"How is that?" asked Father O'Malley, fear creeping over him. "And, by the way, where are they? I stopped by the *scalpeen* recently and found it empty."

"Oh?" Kevin's voice sounded small, almost frightened.

"Aye. It seems unlike them to leave. I thought they stayed put waiting for you. Perhaps you kept them waiting too long?"

Kevin remained silent.

"You do understand that if you don't show up with food, they will starve? If you're gone for days—"

"I know what's what, Father! You don't have to lecture me." Kevin's sudden explosion took Father O'Malley by surprise. He hadn't realized how raw and unbalanced the lad's emotions had become. He tried a gentler tact.

"I'm sorry, lad. I know you've a terrible heavy burden on you now. I'm simply concerned for you and for your family."

Kevin nodded, looking away.

"Do you know where they went?" Father O'Malley asked.

"They're around, to be sure," he said, quickly. "Father, I've work to do and carrying passengers, live ones anyway, isn't allowed. We're getting near the workhouse. If I'm seen with you, it might not go well for me so I'll have to ask you to step down."

He brought the horses to a stop. They were not that close to the workhouse and Father O'Malley had the feeling Kevin sorely wanted to be rid of him.

"I will leave, Kevin. But please tell me just one thing. How is your family surviving?"

He had leaned over, putting himself so much in Kevin's way that it was not possible for the lad to avoid his eyes.

"I believe Mam's doing laundry. I assume the lasses are, too." The words were spoken so quietly, Father O'Malley barely caught them despite their close proximity.

"Where?" he asked. It was not possible to wash clothes in the *scalpeen*.

"They've found jobs. Now could you please go, Father?"

The lone tear that rolled down Kevin's face right before his jaw tightened returning Kevin's face to stone confirmed what Father O'Malley most feared. Noreen and the twins were in the workhouse.

"Kevin, why?" he whispered.

"Because I couldn't keep them fed well enough. They get food there, you know." His voice was desperate. "Please go now, Father. Please!"

The boy struggled to keep from breaking down. A great sadness washed over the priest. He wanted to do something for them, but what? Before descending from the wagon, he said, "Kevin, my child, when you get to craving the *poteen*, come see me instead. We'll talk. No judging, I promise."

"Aye, Father," he whispered without looking at the priest.

Father O'Malley jumped from the cart. As he watched it roll away, he saw the sagging back of its driver and wondered if he'd have the strength to forego the lure of the whiskey's numbing effects. It was clear now that Kevin's earnings bought more *poteen* than food for his family, driving his mother and sisters into the workhouse. The lad rationalized it with the thought that they'd be fed. Probably convinced himself they were better off this way, then drowned his guilt in *poteen*.

As he watched the cart disappear, he remembered a very dark time in his own life. Estranged from his family, hungry and alone he'd wandered the countryside, a young man lost in a world of misery because Siobhan was gone from his life. All he'd wanted then was to forget, so he'd lived on *poteen* to numb his mind. The powerful homemade whiskey had twisted his emotions from black rage to an ugly melancholy, until he became convinced that life meant nothing without Siobhan.

One day, sitting alone at the top of a cliff, he'd thought of throwing himself into the sea to be bashed to bits on the jagged rocks below.

"One more drink and I'll do it, I swear I will!" he had threatened to the crashing waves before downing another mouthful.

"Waiting for me? Well, I'm coming!" he'd shouted to the white foam.

His taunts to the sea continued as he'd teetered about the edge of the cliff in his drunken dance with death.

Not for the first time, he was flooded with gratitude that the last drop of *poteen* had knocked him over backwards, saving his life. He prayed that as God had saved him, so would He save Kevin.

* * *

He was roused just before daylight by a loud banging on his door. Hurrying from bed he opened it to find Dr. Parker standing outside in the chill air.

321

"What's all this?" he asked, pointing to the doctor's phaeton.

"The judge arrived in town last night, earlier than expected. I brought the phaeton so we can gather up the O'Connors and see to that boy's trial."

Having slept in his clothes, Father O'Malley needed only to throw his coat over his shoulders. Bolting past the doctor, he leaped onto the driver's box alongside the doctor. They rode quickly for the O'Connors, Father O'Malley praying his Office as they traveled. The mud and snow lay in shallow pools of muck smeared across the land. Dr. Parker urged his horse as fast as he dared through the slickness. They reached the O'Connor cottage as dawn was spreading a deep pink stain across the sky.

* * *

"Father, Doctor, come! Come!" Deirdre was moving toward them, her hands outstretched. She clutched their sleeves feebly, trying to pull them toward the group huddled in a circle by the fireplace.

They were grouped around the spot where Aisling had lain for so long, obscuring her from view. Father O'Malley steeled himself for the sight of yet another dead child.

He heard the doctor's gentle voice. "What has happened?"

"Only, a miracle, is all!"

As the priest and the doctor approached, the circle of family members melted away bringing Aisling into full view. Father O'Malley dropped to his knees in front of her. The child was sitting up! True, Rory was holding her. But her eyes were open and focused. She was aware of her surroundings.

"Aisling, can you hear me?" the doctor asked.

She made no sound, but her gaze shifted in his direction.

"'Tis a miracle, isn't it, Father?" Kathleen asked.

Father O'Malley could not drag his eyes away from Aisling. "Can you explain it?" he asked the doctor.

"I would like to examine her before making any judgment. Rory, lay her back down."

They all moved away while the doctor made his examination.

"What do you make of it, Father?" Denis asked.

"I'll leave the medical answers to the good doctor. Have you given thanks to the Lord for this new hope?"

"Ehm, no, Father. We've all been so amazed."

"Then it's time we did." He led them in a prayer of thanksgiving, then waited for the doctor to finish his work.

"Well, what do you think, Doctor?" Rory asked.

"She's much improved. I am very glad to say that the fever has left her and she is recovering, though I've no idea why."

"Oh, 'tis a miracle!" Deirdre's voice rose with joy. "Now if only Brendan was back with us, I know we would all make it through just grand!"

"Brendan!" In his astonishment over Aisling, Father O'Malley had forgotten the lad. "He is the very reason we're here with the phaeton. The judge is in town and will hear his case today."

"Today?" Deirdre's voice trembled.

"What is the worst that might happen, Father?" Denis asked.

Wishing he did not have to say the words, he answered, "Deportation to Australia."

Denis blanched. "But that's a world away!"

"The waves," Deirdre whispered, turning away from the group.

"Waves?" Father O'Malley asked Denis.

"The feeling has been on her something terrible of late," Denis explained. "Last night she dreamed of waves in an endless sea."

"I've brought the phaeton so that as many of you as would like to can come with us to the courthouse." Dr. Parker interrupted. "It may be your last chance to see him."

"I am going," Meg announced.

"I as well," Rory added.

"Denis and I will go." Deirdre turned to the others by the fire. "Kathleen, you'll have to stay with the lasses." She crossed the room to stroke Kathleen's hair. "I'm sorry, child."

"I can stay," Loreena said. "I'll watch over the others so Kathleen can go."

"Bless you, child," Deirdre said. "You're a love and that's for sure, but you are too young to be left alone with two as sick as these."

"Brigid's not sick," she protested. "Just…different. And Aisling is better now. We'll be alright."

"No, lass. I'm sorry. If anything should happen, I can't have that on my conscience."

Deirdre turned back to Kathleen, wrapping her in her arms. "If we're allowed to speak to Brendan I will tell him why you aren't there and give him your love."

When Deirdre rose, Father O'Malley saw Kathleen lean her head against the wall, one hand covering her face. Once all were settled in the phaeton, Dr. Parker jumped into the box and took the reins.

Father O'Malley called to him, "I need to go back inside. Only a moment."

He found Kathleen huddled into a tight ball, her arms wrapped tightly around her head resting face-down on drawn-up knees.

"Kathleen." He gently drew her arms downward, tilting her chin to look her in the eye.

"Talk to me, lass." He felt the tugging of time as the others waited.

"They will see him one last time, but I will not!"

"You must go. I will take your place here." He knew it a rash thing to do. He should be with the family. When the verdict came, they would need him for support, but Kathleen needed to be with them even more. He had never wished he could be in two places at once more than he did at this moment. At least they would have one another and Dr. Parker. This poor lass would have no one, her only companion tormenting grief that might last a lifetime.

"You go, Kathleen." He helped her to her feet. Her legs wobbled from lack of use. Scooping her up, he carried her out to the phaeton, feeling her boney frame in his arms. Gently, he placed her on the seat between her parents.

"I am going to stay in her place. She needs to see her brother as much as the rest of you." He went back inside to help Loreena keep vigil by the fire.

Chapter Thirty

On the ride home, Brendan's image hung in the blackness behind Meg's closed eyes. He'd smiled when he'd seen his family, his spirits better than expected. Perhaps Father O'Malley was right about him being fed. He had studied their faces, seeming to tuck away in his memory the features of each, only glancing away to face the judge when necessary.

"My boy. My lad." Deirdre's weak voice cried softly above the rumble of the phaeton.

The words disturbed Meg's thoughts making Brendan's face slip away.

"They only gave him but ten years transportation." Denis patted Deirdre's hand. "That's not forever."

"It might as well be."

"It feels like it now. But when they're spent and the lad walks through the door, won't all the joy of heaven break loose?"

"And if he dies 'tween now and then? There's no one will tell us. I can't go those ten years, waiting, hoping and then…" Deirdre's breath caught in her throat. "I can't do it."

"Australia's a different world, Deirdre. Perhaps he'll make a life for himself there. Might be the lad does well. Might be his going away from Ireland saves his very life. Hold onto that thought. Hold on to thinking that his life's being saved."

"Did you see his face when they took him away, Denis?" Deirdre asked.

"He's a strong lad. He'll make his way. We've just got to have faith that the good Lord has set him on a better path."

"Aye, but what a terrible burden for a mother's heart to bear."

They were quiet again. Meg wished her father would keep talking. His voice was soothing, his words brought comfort. Meg thought of Brendan as he was led from the courtroom. He kept twisting around, trying for one last glimpse of his family. Then the door closed. Meg tried to imagine what he must have felt as the door between them shut, but the pain was too great.

Rory glanced at her, misery in his face.

"It should have been me." He hung his head. "I'm sorry."

"No one blames you, lad," Denis tried to reassure him.

A painful silence permeated the vehicle.

As the phaeton pulled up to the cottage, Father O'Malley opened the door for them.

"How did it go?" he asked.

The doctor explained all that happened.

Father O'Malley nodded. "I am so sorry."

"Thank you, Father." Deirdre barely got the words out before silent sobs robbed her of any remaining strength.

Denis caught her, guiding her towards the fire. The others sank into their usual spots.

"All's been well here, while we were gone, I take it, Father?" Denis asked.

"Aye. Quiet. Loreena and I prayed much for Brendan and for all of you. And for the lasses, too, of course." He indicated Aisling and Brigid.

"We thank you for that."

"Perhaps we should all pray together now," Father O'Malley offered.

Meg felt as though she hadn't the strength even for prayer, but she closed her eyes and followed along in her mind. Her priest's words seeking healing and guidance from God comforted her, gave her something to hold onto.

"If it's not too much trouble, would you mind using your phaeton for one more mission of mercy?" Father O'Malley asked the doctor as they showed themselves out.

Meg wondered for only a moment what Father O'Malley meant before her thoughts were immersed in concern for her family. Having missed another day of work, her father might not have a place at the Works tomorrow. He was lucky not to have lost his place the day he went looking for Brendan. It wasn't likely he'd be as fortunate a second time. The small amount Brendan had brought in was gone. Rory would continue to steal, but it was now more dangerous than ever. She would have to go into town more often though things were getting tougher there. More and more beggars and petty thieves swarmed the town now that spring had brought better weather.

* * *

Meg slept much of the next day. Her father had a pittance from his last pay, but sure enough he no longer had a job. Rory took the money into town to buy what food he could.

Accepting that begging was the only recourse left to him, Denis decided to accompany Meg into town. The next day they walked together into the cold morning air.

"I've come to believe that with you, me and Rory all out, we'll manage. God forgive me for saying it, but there's one less mouth to feed." His voice broke and he wiped his hand across his face.

"Da, I've been thinking about what you said to Mam on the way home from the courthouse. Brendan could be starting a whole new life for himself. He might even be the only one of us who survives in the end."

Denis stopped walking. He took hold of her shoulders, looking her in the eye.

"Your brother will survive. I've decided to believe that. Now you better be believing that you'll survive, too. I'm telling you right now, lass, sure as I'm standing here, if you don't survive no one will. Now's no time to change your mind."

"But –"

"Don't argue, lass. You've got the strongest will of all. If we lose you we'll lose all hope, every one of us. If you lose your belief in yourself, you'll die." He held her chin between his thumb and forefinger, pinching it slightly in his

328

determination. Her head tilted so that she had no choice but to look directly into his tear-glazed eyes.

"You are going to live, Margaret Mary O'Connor. Do you understand me?"

A lump welled up in Meg's throat making it painful to swallow. "Aye."

He let go of her, walking on. Meg followed in silence.

Once in town they were quickly swallowed up in the crowd. They separated, feeling they would have a better chance going in different directions. Meg headed toward the wharf. Fishermen were gutting and cleaning their catches. A girl, much younger than Meg, stood behind them, staring intently at the ground. Meg approached the fishermen.

"Sir," she asked one of them, "Could ye spare a fish, please? Though I can't pay, sure enough the good Lord would bless you a thousand fold. 'Tis for certain ye'd be forever in my prayers."

He glanced up for a brief second, his eyes steely grey like the roiling of a stormy ocean.

His gaze returned to the belly of the fish he was gutting even as he spoke to her. "I've lost count of how many have said the same to me today. If I gave a fish to everyone who asked I wouldn't have one to sell. Go on your way."

"May your fish be filled with maggots," she muttered.

Meg's attention was once again captured by the girl behind him. Something flew through the air from the direction of the man landing with a splat in front of her. The girl, who looked to be about twelve, was rummaging through the offal with her bare feet. Deftly she curled her toes around the innards. She bent her knee, reaching behind her to grab the offal from her hand and drop it into her pocket.

Meg had never imagined eating from a pile of waste.

"What are you doing?" she asked.

The startled girl didn't answer, just cringed. Her whole being seemed haunted. Meg left her and wandered to the end of the wharf where she sat down at the water's edge.

She held her head in her hands and thought, *It gets worse. I could be doing that.*

Rather than revolting her, it was a thought she tucked away in her mind as a possible option for the future.

Meg looked out over the cold ocean. She thought of walking into it, letting it take her under. It seemed so easy, she ached to do it. Then her father's words returned.

Meg got up. She headed toward the bakery. Perhaps Mr. Breckett would take pity on her.

* * *

"Meg O'Connor, have you heard the news?"

Meg turned around on the busy street to see who had spoken. It was one of the neighboring women, Mrs. Flaherty.

"News?"

"My nephew, Alan is going, he is. On the next ship out."

Meg thought of Brendan.

"I'm so sorry. I'm sure he'll make it safely though, and have a better life there. My brother Brendan is going, too. Perhaps they'll be on the same ship."

"Brendan, too? I hadn't heard. 'Tis a grand thing, isn't it? Of course we will miss him terrible, but he'll send us money once he's settled. Things will be better for everyone. His mother's near inconsolable, but even she sees it's for the best."

"He will send money? Can convicts do that? I didn't know they'd be paid for their work. Or do you mean when his term is up?"

"My nephew's no convict. He's going to America. He'll find a job there and send us money when he can. Whatever are you thinking?"

"Oh!" Meg realized her mistake and suddenly felt as though she had betrayed her brother.

"Aye and sure 'tis he'll make a grand life for himself there," Mrs. Flaherty continued. "Where is Brendan off to?"

Meg swallowed the lump in her throat. "Australia. But he'll have a better life there, as well."

Mrs. Flaherty's face softened. "I'm sure he will. Give my best to your family, Megeen, and may the good Lord bless ye."

"Thank you, Mrs. Flaherty."

As the woman turned to go, a sudden inspiration took hold of Meg.

"Mrs. Flaherty?" she called.

"Aye?" she turned back.

"What it the price of passage to America?"

"Four pounds for passage in steerage."

Meg's heart fell. Where would she ever get four pounds?

* * *

The bakery was filled with people, a few there to shop, most to beg.

"Off with you now and don't come back here again until you've money to spend. This is a place of business, don't you know that?" Mr. Breckett ushered an elderly woman out the door. Meg watched as the baker slipped a biscuit into the old woman's hand.

"Awful! Been putting them out all morning," he said coming back into the shop. "Yes, Miss Fitch? How may I be of service to you?" He turned his attention to the woman in a crisp, clean maid's uniform.

He'd looked right at Meg as he came in but pretended not to know her. Meg lingered in the bakery, hoping that her turn to be put out and perhaps have a little morsel slipped into her hand would come soon. While she waited, her thoughts turned to Mrs. Flaherty's nephew. How grand to be going to America. A place with no famine. A place with a future. A place with life!

Looking out the bakery window, Meg caught sight of her father across the street. He was speaking with a well-dressed gentleman. The man shook his head and walked away. Her father grabbed the man's arm and fell to his knees. The man jerked away from her father's grip. He shoved his hand into his pocket then tossed some coins in Denis' direction before striding away. Tears welled up in Meg's eyes as she watched her father, still on his knees, scramble for the coins. Others nearby dove for them as well.

Watching this made her decision. "I am going to America." Meg hadn't realized she'd said the words aloud until Mr. Breckett's voice announced in her ear, "Fine, but don't be awaiting your ship in my bakery."

She felt strong but gentle arms rush her out of the shop. Once outside Mr. Breckett said to her, "Are you really going?"

Meg stiffened her back. "I am."

"You've got the money, have you?"

Meg felt despair overwhelm her at the mention of passage money. Still, she was determined to find a way. "I will get it."

"How much do you have so far?"

Meg looked at the ground. It was impossible to say the words.

"None, is it?"

She shook her head.

"I've only a bit on me. It's not much, but it's a start for you. Take it and don't tell a soul where you got it. I'll not be handing out money to everyone who comes looking for passage. You're the only beggar I give a thing to."

Meg remembered the old woman and wondered how many people he fed, telling them the same.

"Now be off with you and don't come back here again!" Meg felt cold metal pressed into one hand and hard crust in the other.

"Best of luck in the new world," he whispered, turning his back on her.

Meg deposited the coins into her pocket. The biscuit she kept in her hand, hidden beneath her shawl. Her legs felt stronger than when she'd walked into town this morning. She had a start now. There was hope. One day her family would be telling the news that Meg was going to

America. She had to think hard. How could she get the rest of the money?

Meg walked on, continually turning the problem over in her mind. Certainly the few coins Mr. Breckett handed her couldn't total even two pounds. It was possible he might give her more money, but she dared not ask right away. She thought briefly of begging again for sewing work, but realized it would likely be a waste of time. Then she remembered the comb. She suddenly felt sure that God had not let her sell it before because she was meant to use it for passage money.

Meg took the comb from her pocket. Lifting it to her face, she inhaled the pungent scent of the wood. She ran her fingers over the delicate hearts and roses as she walked, paying little attention to where she was going. Would it sell for enough money to pay her passage to America? How would she even know if she was getting a good price for it? Who would buy it from her? Should she ask again for Father O'Malley's help? Meg continued walking as she mused until one thought stopped her. Leaving Ireland means never seeing Rory again, never seeing my family again.

Tears stung Meg's eyes. She leaned her back against the brick wall of a building, looked up at the heavens and let the tears stream down her face. God, what does it profit me to go away from all whom I love? Mightn't I as well be dead if I'm never to see them again? She thought of Mrs. Flaherty's words about her nephew finding work and sending money back to the family. She could do that. Perhaps she could send enough for Rory's passage. They could marry in America, work together, sending twice as much home. They could bring over Kathleen or Loreena. The more who came, the more money they could send until they got both families with them. From what little she'd heard about America, she gleaned it was a place where anything was possible. They could all start a new, better life. The memory of her da begging on his knees, chasing after tossed coins like a dog after its master's scraps, decided her. She would do as her da had said this very morning. She would survive. And her survival would ensure that of them all.

Meg's plans fed strength and hope into her, but it was getting late in the day. Across the road was the Harp and Sword Tavern. Meg observed a young blond lass stride toward the entrance. She was quickly joined by a man. They spoke for a moment. He took something from his pocket and showed it to her. It flashed silver in the sunlight. The girl nodded. Replacing it in his pocket, he took her arm. Together they disappeared inside. Meg remembered another lass she'd seen months ago who had gone into the tavern with the soldiers. She remembered on that cold, wet day, she'd thought how warm it must be inside and had longed to be there.

She held tightly to the money Mr. Brecket had given her, feeling the cold round metal press into her palm. In her other hand, the biscuit felt light. She squished it with only the slightest pressure. She'd rarely held money in one hand and food in the other. For the first time, she liked the money better.

Meg knew well what sort of deal the lass had struck with the young man. She had no intention of making a similar arrangement. But the men entering and exiting the tavern had money. Perhaps one who had a sweetheart would buy her comb. With luck, it might even be a lad who'd had a bit too much of the drink, causing him to pay more than he would sober. Memories of the lads at the fairgrounds on last Gale Day sent a shiver up her spine.

Don't be a coward, she told herself.

At first it felt like walking towards the mangled body of Rory's mother. Slow, tentative steps brought her closer to the tavern entrance. She lingered by the corner of the building, her heart pounding each time the door opened. Patrons came and went, none taking any notice of her. A trio of young British soldiers hasten toward the tavern. Taking a deep breath, she stepped before the door, blocking their way. Bemused, they looked at her and one another. Meg held out her comb.

"Tá mé é seo a dhíol. An bhfuil aon cheann de tú a bheith ar leannán? Tá mé cinnte go mbeadh aon londubh grá é."

They shrugged and snickered. "Stand aside!" one ordered.

At the sound of the soldier's voice, Meg suddenly realized she'd addressed them in Irish. The language forbidden by law. Why had she done that? She fought for the words in English. Stammering, she tried again.

"I have this to sell. Do any of you have a sweetheart? I'm sure any lass would love it."

The soldier in the center, the biggest one who had told her to stand aside, moved toward her. Just as he laid hands on her, the tavern door opened behind her, knocking her into his arms. Out spilled a young man about the same age as Rory.

"Pardon, ma'am." She could smell whiskey on his breath, but at least he seemed polite. "I didn't mean to hit you with the door."

"Lucky for her old Bruce was here to catch her," said one of the soldiers making the rest laugh.

"Are you together then?" asked the polite young man.

"Naw," said Bruce. "We're just trying to get in and this Irish slut was blocking our way, trying to sell some stupid comb. I was about to move her when you opened the door."

Meg, now free of the soldier's hands, looked at the young man. He reminded her of Rory with his tall, slender frame, his curly mane of auburn hair and sparkling blue eyes. But Rory's hair was falling out in clumps, his eyes dull and listless. His body was becoming bent, like an old man's. His face, no longer full and laughing, was hollow and haunted. Meg felt as though she was looking at the ghost of what Rory had left behind.

"You've got lovely eyes. I've never seen eyes as blue as yours before." He sounded kind, though his speech was a bit slurred.

"Thank you." Meg suddenly felt exhausted. She wanted nothing more than to go home. As she turned to leave, he caught her around the waist.

"Don't go. You're a pretty lass."

Meg thought of how she must look. Bone thin, haggard, and wearing smelly ragged clothes.

"Why don't you come in and have a drink with me?"

"I don't think I should." The memory of the drunken youths at the fair returned.

"Why not?" He didn't let go, but his hold was gentle.

Meg easily broke his grasp. He smiled congenially, easing her discomfort a bit. He seemed nice enough. Perhaps he would pity her and buy her comb. She started to speak, but realized her words were again coming to mind in Irish. Why was this suddenly happening? She felt too weak to focus. *I'll have to speak English in America*, she reminded herself.

"Come on. Let me buy you a drink to make up for almost knocking you over."

"I didn't come here to drink," she said, the English words flowing back now. "I just hoped to sell my comb." She held it out for him to see.

"It's lovely," he said. "But wouldn't a lady be more likely to buy it?"

"Aye. But men seem to have more money. And if one has a *leannán*...I mean a sweetheart—"

"Oh, I see," he interrupted her. "And if she ever found out he was coming here, he might need a nice gift to make it up to her." He laughed. "You're smart."

Meg had not thought of that, but she didn't disabuse him of the idea.

"Good business sense like that should not go to waste. Let's find you a buyer." He wrapped his arm around her shoulders, ushering her toward the door. As she walked into the tavern, filled with smoke and the smell of stale beer, bile rose in her throat.

The young man escorted her to a table. "What'll you have? And I won't take 'nothing' for an answer so speak up."

336

"Ale, please." It was all she could think of.

"One ale for the lady. The usual for me."

Meg took in the sights of the tavern. Men in various states of intoxication sat at tables, singing, laughing, talking loudly, bragging and swearing. There were only a few women in the room one of whom was sitting on a man's lap. Meg looked for the blond lass she had seen earlier, but couldn't find her.

"Looking for someone?" her new companion asked.

"No. Just looking around. I've never been here before."

"Thought you might be looking for someone you know. Like maybe you don't want to be with me." He sounded hurt.

"I know no one who comes here."

"So your da does his drinking at home, then?" He laughed.

"My da don't drink much." Meg cringed at the thought of her parents. They would be horrified if they knew she was here.

"Enjoy." He smiled as her ale was set before her.

She took a sip. She hadn't realized until that moment how thirsty she was. A long draught made her head spin.

"What's your name?"

"Meg."

"Mine's William."

Meg said nothing, but took another gulp of ale.

"You look tired."

"I am."

"After you finish your drink, maybe you should have a rest upstairs."

Meg stared into her ale. "I thought we came in so I could find a buyer for my comb." Fear crept over her. Perhaps this William was not as much a gentleman as he seemed. "I think I should go home," she stammered. "My mam and da are probably worrying after me."

"But you can't go, yet," William said. "You haven't sold your comb."

"I'm too tired. I should go."

337

"Nonsense! I'll help you." William took the comb from her hand, stood on his chair and shouted above the din. "A beautiful, hand carved wooden comb I have here. The lass has come to sell it. Which of you scoundrels needs to make up with your lady?" He held the comb high in the air, turning in all directions.

"What's the asking price?" A voice called out.

William looked down at Meg. The room seemed to spin and she couldn't think straight to answer.

"What's your best offer?" William called.

"How about a roll upstairs with me?" came another voice, followed by laughter.

"The lass is trying to sell it my good man, not pay to be rid of it," William retorted.

More laughter followed that felt like thunder in Meg's head.

"Let me see it," said one man, striding up to William's chair. He looked it over, then called to his companion. "Bess, will you take this in lieu of cash. I'm a bit short tonight."

"I've heard you're a bit short every night," a voice called from the back of the room. The boisterous laughter felt like waves buffeting Meg from all sides. Engulfed in a billowing fog of cigar smoke, she could no longer concentrate. Her throat ached. She drained her mug of ale. She heard the voice of a woman. "I like it well enough. I suppose it will do this one time. But don't think you're going to make a habit of not paying me cash in full."

"You can pay for the comb, but not for Bess's favors?" William asked, now off the chair ready to haggle with a sincere customer.

"Comb will cost less."

"Perhaps, but not much. It's a fine piece of workmanship. She'll want a good price for it."

"By the looks of her, she'll be happy to take whatever she gets."

"But I am her representative. I'll see to a fair price."

"And what's your cut?" Another voice shouted from across the room.

338

What was happening? Meg wondered behind the wall of fog forming in her brain. How had she let William take over? Would he take some of her money? Or would he expect another kind of payment?

"My cut is the satisfaction of doing a good deed. A thing I suspect few here would understand."

"Here," said the prospective customer. "How's this?" Meg assumed he was offering money, but her head felt so heavy she could not look up.

"Hmmm…Not as much as we'd like." He got back on his chair. "Perhaps there is another who can appreciate fine craftsmanship when he sees it?"

"Alright! Alright!" said the first man. "I'll give you this, but not a bit more. It's almost as much as I'd pay Bess tonight."

"Sold!"

The word cut through the haze of Meg's mind, like a hot brand dropped through her head searing its way to her heart. The comb was lost to her forever. Gone to some whore to pay for a night of sin. Meg put her head on the table and cried.

"What's wrong, love?" asked William, pushing the coins across the table to her. "I got a decent price, don't you think?"

With great effort, Meg lifted her head. She swept the coins from the table into her pocket. She counted four, but had no idea how much they were worth.

"Tá mé cinnte go bhfuil sé seo an praghas iontach," she whispered. *"Gabhaim buíochas leat as é agus don beoir. I mo thuairimse, caithfidh mé dul, anois."*

"I'm sorry. What did you say?"

Meg struggled for the words in English. "I'm sure you got an excellent price. I thank you for it and for the ale." The words felt heavy, like bricks falling from her mouth. "I think I must go now."

William reached across the table, taking her hand in his. "You're crying. You were serious about selling the comb, weren't you?"

She nodded.

"It really is unique. Where did you get it?"

"Rory," was all she could mutter.

"Rory? Is he your beau?"

She nodded again.

"And he gave it to you?"

"He carved it. Gave it to me when he asked me to marry him."

"He does magnificent work. Can he not make you another?"

She shook her head. Sobs now racked her body.

"I'm sorry. Is he...gone?"

"No. His hand was ruined in an accident."

"Too bad. He had talent." William moved closer to Meg. "Do you mind if I ask, if it means so much to you why did you sell it?"

Astonished, she stared at him open-mouthed. "I'm starving."

He cast his eyes downward in embarrassment. "I know. It's a terrible shame." Then he looked back at her. "But that comb obviously means a lot to you. You'll not eat long or well enough on any amount you could have gotten for it." His voice was gentle. "I hope you didn't take my little performance as making fun in any way. I truly was trying to help you sell it for a good price. I had no idea how much it meant to you."

"I know. You have been very kind. Again, I thank you." Meg's whole body felt heavy. She had no idea how she would make it home, but she knew she couldn't stay any longer. It was probably already dark out. "I really do have to leave," she said.

"Alright. May I see you home?"

Meg thought of Rory and the others seeing her escorted home by this rather handsome young man. Again the hot dagger stabbed her heart. "Thank you. No. I can manage." As soon as she stood, the whole room spun violently. She grasped for the edge of the table, but missed and crashed to the floor. Voices, shoes and table legs whirled together around her, then everything went black.

Chapter Thirty-One

Meg awoke just as the sun was coming up. The second she opened her eyes pain stabbed her forehead, making her squeeze them shut. She slept again. When she awoke the second time the sun was high in the sky. She looked around, confused. She was in a small room with one window directly across from the bed, out of which she could only see patches of blue sky. The room was furnished simply with a small washstand by the bed and a chair near the window. She sat up. Her head ached fiercely. Slowly, the events of the previous evening came back to her. She realized she must be upstairs in the Harp and Sword.

Meg had never been in a bed before. She almost fell getting out of it. Once on her feet, she held onto the edge of the washstand as the room whirled. Grateful for the cold water in the basin, she splashed some on her face. She remembered the biscuit Mr. Breckett had given her, pulled it from her pocket and bit into it. Her stomach churned. Fearing she'd vomit, she returned the biscuit to her pocket, feeling for the coins at the same time. The four from the sale of her comb were there along with what the baker had given her. Why hadn't she asked William how much money it came to? William! *Oh God!* she thought. He must have brought her to this room. *Think! What happened last night?* All she could remember was sitting at the table, loud voices, suds slipping over the side of a mug. A stale taste pasted her mouth. The ale. She'd drunk a whole mug on an empty stomach. Her head swam just thinking of it. She splashed more water on her face. Then there was her comb. William, standing on a chair, announcing it for sale. Coins being slid across the table towards her. She remembered crying. Remembered telling William about Rory making the comb for her, giving it to her the day he proposed. Everything after that was a blank. She must have fainted.

William must have brought her to this room. But where was he? Did he stay with her? Had anything happened? He'd seemed a gentleman, but he was a man and somewhat drunk and she, just a peasant girl. Would he have been above taking advantage of her?

Once steady, she moved away from the washstand. She had to know. She lifted her gown. There was no blood. Gingerly, she probed with her fingers. No soreness. "Thank you, God!" she whispered.

Her shawl was folded at the foot of the bed. As she picked it up, something fell with a clinking noise and a soft thud at her feet. When she looked to see what she'd dropped she did not trust her eyes. There on the floor amid a handful of coins lay her comb. Meg knelt. Picking it up, she held it to her face. She really had her comb back. But how? Tears flowed as she realized that William must have bought it back for her. And left her with more money besides. "Bless him, Lord," she prayed.

Wobbling her way down the stairs, she hoped she wouldn't be asked payment for the room. The tavern keeper said nothing as she walked past him and out the door.

The roads were muddy, the air cool and damp. Breathing it in restored a little of her strength. As she walked, gnawing on the biscuit, she wondered what spring would be like in America. Would it be as beautiful as in Ireland? Would there be rainbows and lush green pastures? She was missing home already.

* * *

The sun was low in the sky when she reached the cottage. She opened the door and dragged herself to her sleeping spot.

"Meg!"

"Where have you been?"

"We've been so worried?"

"What befell you, lass?"

She heard all the questions, but hadn't the strength to respond. She hadn't even considered how she would explain her long absence and didn't want to think about it now. She simply dropped down and went to sleep.

It was dawn of the next morning when she awoke.

"...now and at the hour of our death. Amen." The soft tones of Deirdre's prayer were the first sounds Meg heard upon awakening. She opened her eyes to see her mother on her knees, hands clasped before her.

Kathleen crouched beside Meg. "Where have you been? Da and Rory are still out looking for you."

"They are?" Meg was coming fully awake now despite the remnants of a headache pricking her skull.

"Aye. You've scared us nearly to death. Mam heard the banshee last night. She thought it was for you. She's been thanking God ever since you came through the door."

Meg peeked over Kathleen's shoulder to see her mother make the sign of the cross with a shaking hand.

"Meg, you're awake. Where have you been, lass?"

"Just in town, Mam." Meg's mind raced to concoct a believable tale. "I was too tired to walk all the way home. I wore out on the way and fell asleep in an empty *scalpeen*." Her voice shook. She hoped she wasn't giving herself away.

"Poor lass. Lucky it is you didn't take sick in the night air." Deirdre was at her side now, gently feeling her forehead.

"Only a bit of a headache. Mam, how long have Da and Rory been gone?"

"Since early yesterday morn."

"Father O'Malley and Dr. Parker are looking for you, too," Kathleen told her.

"They are?"

Deirdre shook her head as she spoke. "You should have seen the look on poor Father's face when we told him you'd gone into town and never come back."

Kathleen continued explaining. "I think Father's terrible worried, Meg. He grabbed Dr. Parker's arm and near dragged him out to the horse, so fast did he want to get started looking for you. Mam and I watched them from the doorway. 'Twas a sight they made flying down the hillside."

Meg pulled herself up to sit. Before she'd come into the cottage, Meg had made sure her coins were well concealed in her pocket. She was careful not to jingle them as she moved. Meg's mind searched for a way out of the cottage to find her da and Rory.

"Meg, I was terrible worried. I almost..."

A piercing scream cut off Deirdre's words. Both turned toward Brigid who was wild-eyed, slapping at Loreean and pulling her hair.

"Help me, please!" Loreena cried. "She's taken a fit again."

"Oh, good Lord!" Deirdre exclaimed as she and Kathleen moved off to help settle Brigid.

Brigid now had outbursts that lasted a while, taking some effort to subdue. Meg pushed herself to her feet.

"I'm going to find Da and Rory," she called over the din as she slipped out the door.

Tired and weak, she made her way back to town. Once there, her eyes darted everywhere through the bustle. The streets seemed more crowded than ever.

The bakery. They know I go there. She headed off for Mr. Breckett's.

Entering the bakery, she weaved through the line of maids at the counter. A middle-aged woman in a starched uniform recoiled from her.

"Mr. Breckett, I say, throw this urchin out, would you?"

He handed his customer her bundle and came out from behind the counter. Meg nearly collided with him in her earnestness to reach him.

"Mr. Breckett, I'm looking for my da. Have you seen him?"

"How would I know your da?" He took her gently about the shoulders, guiding her towards the door. "Pardon me, ladies. Be with you in a moment." He nodded at the maids as he passed them.

344

"Please, Mr. Breckett. I must find him. He's a bit short, very thin, most of his hair and teeth are gone and his clothes are all torn. Have you seen him?"

"You've just described most of the population of this town." He opened the door, nudging her out. "Come back at the end of the day. If I've got anything left you can have it," he whispered before slamming the door in her face.

Meg stood on the sidewalk searching the throngs when a glimpse of auburn hair caught her attention.

"Rory!" she yelled. He turned in her direction.

He embraced her for only a second before holding her at arm's length. "Meg, where have you been? We've been searching day and night for you."

"I was in town, got tired and slept in a *scalpeen*." The lie was getting easier to tell. "When I got home, they told me you and Da were out looking for me. Where's Da?"

"We split up, but he's in town. I saw him a while ago. Father O'Malley and Dr. Parker are looking for you, too."

"Let's find Da first."

Wearily they walked the streets together, each looking in different directions. The crowd suddenly parted at the sound of horses' hooves and wagon wheels.

"Meg! Meg!"

"Da!" Meg called. She started towards her father, who was calling from across the street.

"Wait!" Rory caught her arm, pulling her back. A supply wagon headed for the wharf had just rounded the corner.

"Da! Wait!" The scream ripped from her throat as she watched her father step blindly into its path.

The horses reared. Heavy hooves came down atop him, knocking him to the ground. Wrenching free of Rory's grasp, Meg ran towards him. The driver snapped his reins, spurring his horses forward. Meg watched, horrified as first the horses' feet and then the wagon's wheels crushed her father beneath them.

Once the wagon had passed she ran through the dust, fighting her way through the crowd that had closed around them.

She screamed, clawing at everyone in her way.

She heard a voice call, "He's the lass's da. Let her through." The crowd backed away.

"Da." Meg dropped to her knees by his side, leaning in close, hugging his shoulders, then straightening up to touch his face, then leaning over to hug him again, all the while crying hysterically, "Da, please! Da, please!"

Blood gushed from a wound on his head, pooled around his broken body, trickled from his mouth. For a moment his eyes focused on his daughter. He lifted his one unmaimed arm toward her face.

Lightly he traced a finger down the side of his cheek. "Meg. You're all right." As his words came, his lips tried to form a reassuring smile. His eyes lost their focus, his arm dropping over his chest.

"Da, no. No, Da, no." Meg fell atop him, her body giving out completely in her agony.

"Let him go, lass. He's in a better place now," an old man's voice whispered in her ear. He and Rory had hold of her, one on each side.

Meg fell into Rory's arms, her strength gone. She didn't know how long they sat in the road. Feet shuffled in and out of her view. Voices spoke above her head. Many hands dragged her father's body to the side of the road. Meg felt as though a mist surrounded her that only lifted now and then, bringing with it a fresh wave of agony.

Father O'Malley's face appeared before her. His lips formed words, but she didn't hear them. More feet came and went. The white legs of a horse pranced at the perimeter of her sight. Strong arms grasped her shoulders, pulling her upward and into Dr. Parker's phaeton.

When the vehicle stopped, she made no effort to move, but leaned against Rory's chest. The realization that they were sitting outside her family's cottage entered her awareness, but just barely. Her mother's scream pierced her consciousness, making her sit up straight.

The phaeton jolted and bumped a bit. Meg wondered only slightly at the jostling. Then her eye caught sight of

Father O'Malley and Dr. Parker carrying her father's body into the cottage. A moment later they returned.

"Come on, Meg. You'll have to go in now." Father O'Malley gently slid her towards the edge of the seat to lift her down.

"Can you stand on your own?"

Meg nodded, but when she took a step forward her legs buckled. Father O'Malley carried her into the cottage. She stared into the fire. She knew her father's body was here but she couldn't stand the thought of looking at it. Numbness was beginning to wear off. The realization that if she hadn't had the thought of selling her comb in the tavern, her da would be alive now haunted her.

"'Tis all my fault." The words cascaded out on a waterfall of tears. Prayers and words of comfort uttered in hushed tones melted away from Meg's awareness. She crumpled before the fire, feeling as though her whole being was dissolving into the floor.

"Meg, move, lass. I must get in here." Deirdre's voice was in her ear, her hands gently nudging her.

"What?" Meg lifted her head.

"Move, please." Deirdre was more forceful this time, pushing herself between Meg and the stones in the fireplace wall.

Meg watched in disbelief as her mother worked a stone loose. Reaching into the hole, Deirdre pulled out a small handful of coins, then replaced the stone.

"This should buy one, Father?"

Father O'Malley took the coins. "Aye. A very plain one."

"'Tis all we need. Just for decency's sake. You'll see to it, then?"

"I will."

"Thank you, Father."

The door opened and closed.

Meg sat dumbfounded at the mysterious appearance of money in the cottage.

"Mam? You've had money here?" It was Kathleen's voice.

347

"Aye. Most folks have a wee bit hidden away."

"But why didn't we ever buy food with it?"

"Because that's not what it was for. 'Twas kept to bury us."

"Mam, we could have eaten with that money." Kathleen's voice was indignant.

"How much, lass? A decent Christian burial is more important. Too many aren't having them these days. Your da will have one. He deserves it, don't he?"

Meg stared into the fire. She wanted neither to think nor feel. She tried to keep her mind blank but images of the horse knocking down her father and the wagon wheels rolling over him, twisting and crushing him beneath them, kept returning.

"Kathleen, over here, lass. You'll have to help. Meg's of no use." Meg heard her mother speak, felt the slight swish of air as Kathleen brushed by her. It occurred to her that they were preparing her father's body for burial, but she quickly banished the image.

Hours passed, she didn't know how many, before Father O'Malley and Dr. Parker returned carrying a coffin.

"Mrs. O'Connor, with your permission, Rory and I will go prepare the grave." The doctor's voice spoke somewhere behind her.

"Meg?" Father O'Malley seated himself on the floor beside her. She couldn't look at him. "Meg, we were all very worried about you."

"I was just in town. I got tired and..." The lie she'd told so easily to others choked in her throat. As she sputtered, the firelight became a dancing prism in her tear-blinded eyes.

"Meg, I hope you realize everything that happened was an accident. You went into town to help your family. You couldn't make it home. That's not your fault. Your family and friends love you dearly so of course we went to look for you. But that's not your fault either. And your da. In his relief at seeing you, it was natural for him to rush towards you. That too, is not your fault. I don't want you blaming yourself, Meg. No one here blames you."

With every word Father O'Malley spoke, guilt plunged its poison sword further into Meg's heart. She felt sin after sin piling up on her soul, turning it black and rotten.

Deirdre sat down on the other side of Meg. "Supposing your da died never having found you? Ah, the anguish it would have been, him not knowing what had become of you. But the good Lord saw fit to let him see you for one last moment, to know that you were safe. I'm sure your da counted it a blessing."

"See, Meg," Kathleen added, coming to join them. "You were Da's last blessing."

"No! No, no, no!" Meg dropped forward in a heap, her head on the floor.

"Poor lass," her mother's arms went round her.

"Meg, don't do this to yourself," Father O'Malley cajoled.

"Meg, it wasn't your fault," Kathleen insisted. "Da would never blame you."

Meg pressed her hands over her ears and screamed. Helpless to fight, she felt herself being pulled up and cradled in her mother's arms. Gently, Deirdre rocked her back and forth, cooing as if she was a baby.

Late at night when the mourners, a handful of neighbors, straggled in, it was more a sad vigil than a real wake. If a fiddle played, Meg did not hear it. If the women keened, Meg's screaming heart drowned them out. The only thing she remembered was kneeling before her father's casket, rosary in hand, silently begging God and her father to forgive her as she mechanically followed the prayers down the beads. Meg's only other memory of that night would be Father O'Malley draping his cloak around Deirdre's shoulders just before he left the cottage.

"Such a good man," one of the neighbor women had whispered. "She'll be covered decent enough to enter the church tomorrow."

The following morning too was as blur. There was the walk to the church, the funeral Meg knew she attended, but of which she would retain almost no memory. Then another walk to the burying ground. She did remember standing over the open grave, the coffin resting at the bottom, waiting to be covered forever. The weather was beginning to warm. Shards of sunlight pierced a lingering early morning mist. It was the sort of day her father had loved. She looked up to see a shaft of sunlight streaming down through an opening in the clouds. Her father's voice spoke in her mind, a thing he'd often said on days like this. *Ah, look, Meg, 'tis the very light of heaven shining down on us. But 'tis only a mere shred of it. Just imagine what it must be like to be standing up there with all the angels and saints, and God Himself. Glory be!*

Tears spilled down Meg's cheeks. She imagined her father standing with the Lord, surrounded by the full power of the dazzling rays. *I'm sorry, Da. So sorry. Please forgive me.*

Chapter Thirty-Two

"Father, could I ask you a favor?" Father O'Malley had just said good day to the last of his parishioners after Mass, when he heard the woman's voice.

"Mary, I didn't see you there," he said as the woman, Mary O'Dell, peeked out from around the corner of the church. "What can I do for you?"

"I was wondering if you would pray for my brother, Jack." She kept her eyes on the ground, her hands fidgeting with the ends of her shawl.

"Of course I will," said Father O'Malley puzzled by the woman's discomfort. "For what intention?"

"He's doing a thing he ought not to do." Her voice was barely above a whisper. "I fear it will damage his soul."

"What is it he's doing?" Father O'Malley bent close to the small woman, keeping his tone gentle.

Mary looked around furtively. Father O'Malley glanced about as well. "Everyone's gone," he said. "But if you'd be more comfortable we can go inside," he said, making ready to open the church door.

"No, thank you, Father. This will do. I'd as soon not even speak of it in a place so holy as the church." She drew a deep breath, closed her eyes, then blurted out, "Jack's become a cart driver for the workhouse."

Father O'Malley sighed heavily. "He's not the first nor will he be the last. It's an awful job, but perhaps it's the only way he can keep from starving."

"It's an evil place." Her agonized face pleaded for understanding. "Any food he brings home comes from the pay he gets from doing evil. I'd almost rather starve than eat it." She bowed her head, seemed almost to crumple into herself. "But I do eat it," she whispered. "And then I feel as though I've eaten the devil's own food." She leaned against the side of the church, crying.

"Mary, you must eat. Someone has to take the bodies to be buried. What would happen if no one did it?" The words seemed pathetic even to his own ears, but it was all he could think to say.

"'Tis not a decent Christian burial, Father."

"I know. But most in the workhouse have none to give them one. If it helps, I do visit the pits on occasion and pray the prayers for the dead over them. It's not the same as a funeral, I know, but 'tis something I can offer the poor souls." Father O'Malley's conscience tweaked him a bit. He had indeed prayed at the pits, but not recently, as he found being there revolting. It reminded him too much of Clonmalloy, giving him nightmares upon his return. Now he made it a priority to go again. A great many bodies had been dumped in the pits since his last visit. He silently vowed he would not allow his own frailty to render him remiss in tending to their holy souls.

"It's not just the job itself, Father. It's what the job is doing to Jack," Mary continued, interrupting his thoughts.

He nodded, indicating for her to go on.

"Jack's a hard man to begin with. I fear this work will push his soul completely into the darkness."

"I will pray for him, Mary."

"I'd thank you if you would, Father. I couldn't live thinking my own brother had turned into a monster like that Kevin Dooley."

"Kevin? What of him?"

"Didn't you hear, Father?" Suddenly animated, Mary regaled him with a horrifying tale. "He was carting away a load of corpses when one of them spoke right up and said, 'I ain't dead yet.' Well, that Kevin, half-way to the pits, was in no mood to turn back just for him so he told him, 'If you ain't dead by the time I get you to the pits, you will be soon enough after.' He's done turned his own soul black. He'll rot in hell for it. I don't want Jack going that way, too."

* * *

Father O'Malley's thoughts were in disarray after their conversation. Mary's story might only be that, a story. The hard-heartedness of the cart men was becoming legendary. It was getting difficult to distinguish reality from this new form of folklore. He worried, though. Those who carted away the dead soon damaged their souls. So much death numbed them to compassion. Given Kevin's current state, he could believe it was possible.

His legs felt heavier than ever as he walked. Intent on finding Kevin he headed straight for the workhouse.

"You've a cart man by the name of Kevin Dooley," he asked the official on duty. "Has he been by yet today?"

"I don't keep track of who's who. There's many come and go. But one went out with a load over an hour ago. Just a lad, he was."

Father O'Malley headed straight for the pits. If he didn't find Kevin he would at least keep his promise to pray for the dead there. The site, an expanse of land, covered over with the regrowth of grass in some places and newly dug earth in others, held an aura of unearthly quiet. It reminded him so much of the silence that engulfed him on his walk out of Clonmalloy that Father O'Malley had to steel himself to pass through the opening in the low stone wall surrounding the pits. Standing at the edge of the newly dug section, one part just covered over with fresh dirt, another open, waiting for occupants, he made the sign of the cross, then held his hands in blessing over the upturned earth.

"Eternal rest grant unto them, O Lord, and let perpetual light shine upon them. May the souls of the faithful departed, through the mercy of God, rest in peace. Amen." His hand traced a cross in the air over the site. Then, pushing his own revulsion aside, he stood in silent prayer, allowing all the sorrow of the place to sweep over him. Falling to his knees, he picked up a clump of dirt mixed with lime. "My people," he whispered, his words choked with tears. "How many more? How much longer?" He wept, his tears falling atop the newly dug graves.

The whinny of a mule pierced the still air. Father O'Malley lifted his head searching for a sign of life. Beyond the stone wall surrounding the pits, his eye caught movement. The flicking ears of an impatient mule. It had to be a cart man. He rose, hurried across the field to the waist-high wall. There on the other side stood the animal, harnessed to an empty driverless cart. Scrambling over the wall, Father O'Malley patted the beast's neck.

"Where is your driver, my friend?" he asked, hoping his voice would attract whoever had left the mule and cart. A snort was the only answer. He was standing in a hilly pasture, large rocks jutting up here and there, some actual boulders. Perhaps the cart man stopped to relieve himself, but he could see no sign of human existence. Giving the mule another pat, he started towards the open field.

"Is anyone here? Who belongs to this animal?" He called out as he walked. About midway across the field he came upon a stone like a giant globe large enough to hide behind. As he rounded it, he nearly tripped over Kevin Dooley, coiled up and laying on his side.

"My lad!" he exclaimed, kneeling next to him. "What are you doing here?"

Receiving no answer, Father O'Malley feared the worst. He shook Kevin's shoulder, gently at first, then more forcefully.

"You don't need to convulse me out of my skin, Father." Kevin said without looking up.

"Thank God! I thought you were…what's wrong?"

Kevin rolled to a balled up sitting position. "Thought I was dead? Is that what you were going to say? Well, I wish I was."

"I'm glad you're not. What has happened?"

Kevin's face crumpled. The once defiant look replaced by wretched misery. "I took them out today." Great sobs broke up his words. "I buried them. Where you were praying. I saw you pray over them. God granted me that bit of comfort, but I don't know why He would after all I've done. I don't deserve the slightest mercy."

Kevin's words were such a tangle, Father O'Malley feared for the boy's mind. This job could do the worst to grown men. It was no work for a mere lad.

"Kevin, please. Begin again. You took a load of bodies for burial today. That much I comprehend. But you do that regularly. How was today different?" In the back of his mind, he thought he knew the answer, but hoped he was wrong. Perhaps the job had finally gotten to the lad, that's all. He prayed it was so.

"I was putting them in the ground. I didn't even notice before. Not on the way out here. Not until I took them from the cart to lay them in. And then…" His mouth gaped open, tears and saliva dripping. His eyes had gone wild, as if seeing again what he had witnessed a short time ago.

"Go easy, lad," Father O'Malley coaxed. "Take your time." He held Kevin by his shoulders wishing to transmit a bit of his own waning strength into the boy.

"I took up a woman. Hardly a thing left to clothe her. It was…it was…" He shook his head, unable to go on.

"Was it someone you knew?" Father O'Malley was now certain his worst fear was Kevin's reality.

"It was my Mam!" Kevin's cry echoed across the empty field. He fell into Father O'Malley's arms. The priest held him close, one hand on the back of his head. He squeezed his own eyes shut, wishing he could blot out what that moment of recognition must have been like for the lad.

"I'm sorry, Kevin. I am so very, very sorry."

Kevin pulled away from him. "I buried her, Father. I took extra care. I…I prayed."

"Good. That was the right thing to do."

"And then I went back to the cart. And the next one…" he stopped, overcome with convulsive weeping.

Father O'Malley continued to hold onto Kevin's shoulders, now holding him upright for all the strength seemed to have left the lad's body. It took some time, but finally Kevin continued. "And the next one was Addie."

"Dear God!" Mother and sister.

"I'm sorry, Father. I've done such wrong. But I didn't mean it. I swear I didn't mean it. I never wanted for them to

355

die. I couldn't get back to the *scalpeen* often enough to bring food. I knew the workhouse is a bad place, but some seemed to fare well enough. They were given food. I thought they might make it. I thought I might be giving them a fighting chance when I took them there, but I was wrong. I was so wrong." His eyes held Father O'Malley's gaze, but the light had gone out of them replaced by deep pain and shame. "Instead, I have killed them," he said. His head dropped forward as though his neck had suddenly snapped. "I have killed my mam and my sister."

"No! Kevin, you must not think that. Your intentions were good. You meant to help, to give them the only chance they might have had. If God was ready to take them home, there's none could have stopped it. They have no more suffering, only light and peace with our Lord. Think only of that."

Kevin shook his head. "I can't. I can't, Father. I've done too much wrong. I'm just what my da always said, a lazy, no-good, wretch not fit to have been born."

Anger arose in Father O'Malley like a lidded steaming pot about to explode. "That's what your da said of you, is it? A fine one to talk! A drunk who abandoned his family when they needed him most." He gave Kevin's shoulders a shake. "Don't you be listening to the likes of one such as him. Banish his unworthy voice from your head!"

Kevin's eyes widened in disbelief. "Father?"

"I mean it. I know he's your da, but he doesn't deserve the title. He is a vile man, may God have mercy on him before it's too late. But for you, there's still time. You are loved by God who in His great mercy will forgive you everything. It is not too late for you to turn your life around, Kevin."

"I don't know how." The words were heavy with despair, yet Father O'Malley though he heard the tiniest hint of hope at their fringes.

"But I do!" he declared.

Kevin looked at him with both skepticism and doubtful expectation.

"Come," he ordered, tugging Kevin to his feet.

"Where are we going?"

"We are returning the mule and cart to the workhouse. Then you are coming home with me. Where have you been living anyway?"

"Out and about," he answered. "Nowhere really. I sleep where I can find a decent spot."

"So you've not been back to *the scalpeen*?"

"Not since I moved them out."

"I thought as much." That, in one respect was a relief to Father O'Malley. Upon leaving the O'Connor cottage the day of Brendan's hearing he had asked Dr. Parker to pick up the Hoolihan family and drive them to the empty *scalpeen*. He knew Adam would continue to return to the cottage as long as Corrine lived, but at least the children would be sheltered. Corrine had left this life within days and Adam had joined his bairns in the *scalpeen*.

"For now, you'll stay with me," he told the startled lad.

"You can't want me to stay with you," Kevin insisted.

"Oh, and why not?"

"You're a priest. You're holy. I'm wicked and evil."

"You are neither. You are a young, confused, hurting lad who needs much guidance and compassion. I was like that once myself. It was a priest who saved me. I believe it is time for me to pass on the favor."

"You don't mean to try and make me into a priest, do you?"

Father O'Malley almost laughed at the astonished look on the lad's face as he helped him up to the driver's box. "That is for the Lord to determine, not me. My only goal is to help you straighten out your life and show you your worth in the eyes of God."

As they rode towards the workhouse, Father O'Malley driving the cart as Kevin was in no condition, a thought arose in the priest's mind. "Kevin? He asked. "You mentioned your Mam and Addie. What of your other sister?"

"Liddy? I did not see her."

"Then she is still alive?"

"I don't know. She might be. Or she might have been taken out by one of the other cart men if she went at a different time."

"But there is a chance. We shall ask at the workhouse."

"Father, if she's there, can we get her out? I'm afraid if she stays she'll die. I don't know how she'd ever go on without Addie as it is."

"Of course we'll get her out. Have no worry about that."

After returning the cart and mule, Kevin resigned his job. Yet they could find out nothing about Liddy. The workhouse was holding three times its allotted capacity and record keeping was shoddy. No one seemed to know or care if a lass named Liddy Dooley lived on in the workhouse or lay in the pits.

Distraught, Kevin pleaded to be allowed to search for her, but was strictly informed that he could not enter the women's section. "You're no longer employed here, so you've no more business with us. You'll need to be off now," he was told.

Father O'Malley ushered the protesting lad out the door. "This isn't the end of it, Kevin, I promise. Somehow we will find a way to learn of Liddy's whereabouts. For now, let's get you home."

The lad stared at him, uncomprehendingly. "I have no home."

"You do now. You're coming with me."

Chapter Thirty-Three

It was late in the afternoon when they reached Father O'Malley's cottage. Exhausted, Kevin dropped in a heap before the fireplace. It was not long before he was asleep, never stirring even when a knock sounded at the door.

Dr. Parker had come to give Father O'Malley the names of those who had died that day so he could record them and go to their families. They spoke softly so as not to wake Kevin. Father O'Malley explained the lad's presence and circumstances.

"Ah, the one who's family you expected to find at the *scalpeen*," the doctor said.

"Indeed. Before you leave, I've a favor to ask of you in regards to his sister. The one who may still survive."

"You'd like me to check for her at the workhouse?" The doctor guessed.

"If you'd be so kind. We are not allowed access to the women's sections and no one could be bothered to check for us. But as a doctor…"

"As I doctor, I can enter the women's section. I'll be happy to do so, but how will I know her? I've never even seen the girl. All I know is her name. Depending on her condition, she may not answer to it. Besides, you've told me she does not talk."

Father O'Malley pondered this wrinkle. "Before you go, we'll wake Kevin and ask him how to identify her."

"Fair enough. We should get onto our grim business of the day, I suppose," said Dr. Parker. Taking a seat at the table, he opened his ledger book.

"How many today?" Father O'Malley asked, opening his own register to record the names of the dead.

"Too many."

"It's always too many."

"Jonah Burke, for one."

"I suspected it wouldn't be long for him."

"I wish you would explain something to me, Father."

"If I can."

"How is it they've managed to purchase yet another coffin? I was surprised enough at the first one, though it was a plain, cobbled together affair. The next time I returned there was another one in the cottage. I know death in that family is almost a foregone conclusion, but to have it sitting there waiting seems morbid. And if they can get the money for all these coffins, why in God's name don't they spend it on food?"

Father O'Malley sighed. "It's the same coffin."

Dr. Parker looked perplexed.

"Then next time you go take a good look at it. You'll notice a hinge. The bottom opens up. Once they've reached the grave they release the trap door and drop the body in. Then they carry the empty coffin home for the next one."

Dr. Parker's eyes widened.

Father O'Malley leaned back in his chair. "Don't judge them too harshly. Many families are doing it. It's the closest anyone can come to giving a shred of dignity to the departed. Even if it does only last until they've reached the graveyard."

The doctor shook his head. "Well, I'll be."

"Who else went today?"

When the doctor finished with the list of names he asked, "Do you remember the woman we met, Friend Sarah?"

"Sarah Hay." Father O'Malley nodded, recalling fondly the motherly woman who worked so hard.

"She contracted the fever and has succumbed. I've heard she was buried this morning."

"I am so sorry to hear it. She was a good woman. May the Lord rest her soul in peace."

"Indeed. Did I ever tell you my mother was of the Society of Friends?"

"No. I was under the impression you were Anglican."

"I am. My father was Anglican as was my mother, at first. She converted shortly before I was born. My father was never pleased about it, but apparently he couldn't stop her. He saw to it, though, that we children were brought up in the Anglican faith. However, I got to know the Friends and their religion well."

"You are rare."

"What do you mean?"

"You are of one religion and yet you condone other religions. Most people believe theirs to be the one true faith."

"Do you believe Catholicism to be the one true faith?"

"Aye."

"Then do you think Friend Sarah is not in heaven? You think that God would not save her even though you've said yourself she was a good woman?"

"I think there are some who will attain heaven, through the grace of a merciful God, despite their being of another faith, like Friend Sarah. And you, perhaps." A smile played about his lips.

"I'm honored." The doctor replied, trying not to laugh.

"How did your mother come to convert?"

"I've never learned much about it. My father didn't want her to talk about it. But I believe having parents of different faiths is what has prevented me from bigotry against any one in particular."

"Your father didn't feel this way, though?"

"My father adored my mother. He would never deny her anything. I'm sure my mother must have had times when she was not in good spirits, but she didn't show it. She seemed always to be happy. I think it was mostly genuine."

"It appears to have rubbed off on you."

"My mother taught me to love without condition. She is the one who taught me about mercy and respect for all others. My father taught me many valuable things, too, but my mother gave me her faith."

"I thought you said you were of your father's faith."

"I don't mean the doctrine of her faith, necessarily. I mean her devotion, her dedication, if you will, the depth with which she lived it out. Oh, I don't profess to be the

Christian my mother was, though I do my best. But I have learned from her what it means to live a Christian life. Luckily, I have also inherited something of her disposition."

"Lucky for me, as well, since I must work with you." Father O'Malley said.

"And you, Father? Do you mind if I ask again? What did make you decide to become a priest?"

Father O'Malley put his elbow on the table, resting his head on the palm of his hand. The sun was sinking low in the sky. Shadows had begun to creep along the cottage walls.

"That is a bit of a story. Are you sure you want to hear it?" He lit the two candles on the table. It would be painful to relive all that had led him to the priesthood. A part of him, though, ached to tell it.

"I would truly like to know." The conviviality in the doctor's voice erased Father O'Malley's last doubts.

"I became a priest because of a woman."

Dr. Parker raised his eyebrows, but remained silent.

"Her name was Siobhan O'Toole. She was the loveliest, cleverest, most gracious woman I have ever known. We planned to marry, but that never happened."

"Why not?"

He stared into the candle's flame. "Because she died before we could wed."

"I'm so sorry. What did she die of?"

"You are thinking of disease?"

"I had supposed—"

"Siobhan was like a faery, delicate and beautiful, but at the same time mischievous and seemingly indestructible." Father O'Malley smiled at the picture of Siobhan floating in his head.

"She made you very happy."

"Oh, aye, she did. She was no bigger than a waif, but she had me wrapped about her little finger. 'Twas those eyes that did it. They were a green I've not seen the likes of before or since. I can't describe them except to say they were like the grass of the field when the sun comes out

362

after a rain and the droplets sparkle like emeralds upon the blades."

"That says quite a lot, indeed."

"And her laugh. It was like music, like the plucking of harp strings. It was magical. Teased me mercilessly, she did, and I loved every moment of it. Oh, she could regale you with stories made up out of her own head that would make you believe she was one of the wee folk."

"A born story-teller."

"Indeed. We would go walking through the glen behind our cottages or climb the hill overlooking the bay. We had a game we played when we walked. We would look for the wonders. I saw things I would never have otherwise noticed had I passed by them a thousand times.

"You've no idea how terrified I was the day I asked her to marry me. If she had said 'no' I don't think I could have born the pain. But she said 'aye' and my world felt perfect."

Father O'Malley closed his eyes, allowing himself the splendid joy of reliving the memory of Siobhan smiling and laughing. Her red hair spilling all around her in a tumble of curls, her eyes filled with exuberance.

"Then one day, one beautiful summer day, she took it into her head to go into town for something. I'll never know the full story of what happened, but I know enough." Father O'Malley shut his eyes tightly, rubbing at their closed lids as much to blot out the images that were rising to the surface as to acquire the courage to go on with his story.

"She didn't come home that night. Her brother, Quentin, came to ask me if I knew of her whereabouts. We searched all night but found nothing.

"The next morning I was halfway up a hill when I heard Quentin's voice calling from below. He'd been searching near the riverbed. I ran down the hill and..." Father O'Malley's voice broke off. A lump tightened in his throat. He swallowed hard several times, inhaled a deep breath of air and expelled the next words along with it. "And there she was lying dead."

"I am truly sorry." Dr. Parker whispered.

"Quentin had pulled her out from beneath a bramble bush. Her dress was ripped clean off. Her body bruised all over. There was blood everywhere. Her throat had been slit. Worst of all for me were her eyes. Those beautiful eyes." He felt the muscles of his face tighten. "Open and staring. They'd become a flat, dull green. It seemed the worst of the horrible things that British soldier did to her. He took the life out of her eyes."

Father O'Malley stared into the dark corner of his cottage. He almost couldn't bear the nearness of another human being at this moment, yet he was grateful not to be alone.

"How do you know it was a soldier who killed her?"

"She had a gold button from his uniform gripped in her hand. Fought for her life, she did. He probably killed her for ripping it from his bloody precious uniform. I don't know how he got her from town to that spot. But I do know that Siobhan did not give up her body willingly and she paid with her life."

Dr. Parker shifted in his chair. His voice was tentative when he spoke. "It is enough to make you hate the British."

"I did for a long time."

"I'd say we're still not your favorite people."

"Forgive me, but your people have been anything but kind to my people for a very long time."

"England did not acquire her empire through the virtue of kindness. Neither, I believe, has any other empire."

"True enough." Father O'Malley could feel anger rising within him. He didn't want it. He wanted to go on with his story and let it all leave him.

Dr. Parker continued. "It is never the way decent human beings should treat one another."

"You have a different perspective than many."

The doctor offered his friend a weak smile. "My mother to thank," he said. "But this led you to the priesthood?"

"I went through a very dark time in my life after Siobhan's death that could have ended in disaster. It was a man, much like you now that I think of it, who literally saved my life."

"Who was he?"

"A priest named Father Francis Coogan. He found me one day when I was lying drunk by the roadside. I was far from home and in desperate condition. I had no money and had had nothing to eat in days. I was bent on obliterating any feelings I had because they were too painful. I had murderous fancies of finding Siobhan's killer and cutting his throat as he'd done to her. Terrible fits of anger would overcome me. I left home one day and went up the hillside. I bought some *poteen* from an old farmer and got roaring drunk. Spent most of my time wandering about aimlessly. I begged what food I could get, but mostly I wanted to drink. It numbed me. It was the only way I could forget.

"After a while my rages died down. I was still filled with hatred, but I moved from that overpowering anger to a dark, ugly melancholy. I wanted to die. I thought often of taking my own life.

"I wandered into the town of Glenmoorey. 'Twas there that I passed out drunk by the roadside. All I remember of that day was the feeling of strong hands lifting me off the ground and the image of my own feet stumbling beneath me as someone tried to walk, or more honestly, drag me away."

"That was Father Coogan?"

Father O'Malley nodded. "If Father Coogan had been the sort of priest that Bishop Kneeland wants me to be I would probably be dead now!" Father O'Malley darted his finger against the table top for emphasis. Kevin shifted in his sleep. "But that is another story," he whispered, silently reminding himself to speak quietly.

"What did Father Coogan do for you?"

"What didn't he do? He allowed me to stay at his cottage. He fed me. When the pain was too great and I wanted to drink again he prayed with me, all night sometimes. Held me in his very arms, he did, praying for me while I cried and raved. It could not have been easy for him, but he was a man of powerful faith. The best thing he

365

did was to take me with him to visit his parish families. He left me outside to talk with family members while he was inside hearing a confession. I was forced to speak with people. I learned of their cares, their joys and sorrows. Slowly, I came out of myself and began to think of others again.

"It was a little lass by the name of Alison Kittle who helped me break free. The poor child's Mam had died in childbirth only a month before and the wee lass was having a terrible time adjusting to such a severe loss. I was sitting outside with her one morning while Father Coogan was inside with her da. She was crying. She told me she missed her mam so much she thought she would never be happy again. My heart went out to her. I wanted more than anything to comfort her. I tried to think of what Father Coogan might say. 'Alison,' I said, 'I know it hurts terrible when you lose someone you love, but when you think of your mam now picture her in the arms of Jesus, looking so very happy being with him and the Blessed Mother. Go on', I said, 'give it a try right now. See your mam's face all smiling, looking as happy as you've ever seen her sitting right up in heaven with all the angels flying about.'

"Well, the little darling closed her eyes and tried. Don't you know there was a just the wee bit of a smile coming right through her tears. It was like a rainbow growing in my own heart to look upon it. When she opened her eyes again she said, 'Thank you, Father.'

"She thought you were a priest?" the doctor asked.

"In those days it was hard to tell a priest from anyone else. That was during the Penal Laws. Priests had to operate secretly and so dressed like everyone else, in order not to be caught.

"I told her I was not a priest, just a friend of Father's. I almost laughed aloud at the thought of myself as a priest. She said to me, 'But you will be a priest one day, won't you? That's why you're with Father. He's teaching you how.' Her words stunned me. I don't remember answering, but the thought stayed with me."

"That is what made you realize you should become a priest?"

"It wasn't all at once. But little by little I paid more attention to what Father Coogan did and said to me and to others. To my surprise I was starting to be far more interested in the Mass than I ever had been before. It became something beautiful to me, not a mere obligation. It held a healing power.

"We had no church building, of course, as they had all, by law, been closed. Mass was held in secret locations. Ours was in a lovely glen. I grew rather enamored of the place. One day I felt compelled to go there alone to pray. It was the first time I prayed for Siobhan's soul. I was overcome with shame that it had taken me so long to pray for her. I'd spent so much time wrapped up in my own pain that I hadn't even thought of it. I know Father Coogan had prayed for her, he'd even prayed with me, but I was not really praying then, I was just hurting. Now I was truly praying. After a time I began to feel peace.

"I stayed with Father Coogan for two years. He had long before found my parents, told them I was safe and staying with him so they wouldn't worry. I eventually went back home and worked my family's potato bed again. My mother was quite relieved at the change in me. The memories there were too strong, though. I knew I had to leave for good. I wanted to go back to Father Coogan. I wanted to live the life he lived, to reach out to other hurting people and help them as I had been helped. After losing Siobhan a celibate life did not seem like a hardship for me. I prayed about this decision all the time, asking God if this was His will for me. Little Alison's words kept coming back to me. I came to understand that the Lord had been speaking to me through that child.

"When I told my parents that I had decided to become a priest, they were amazed but pleased. I went back to Father Coogan to tell him of my desire to enter the priesthood. He was happy with my decision, but did not approve of my lack of education."

"Why is that? I've heard that many priests are nearly illiterate. An education doesn't seem to be a prerequisite."

"It isn't, more's the pity. Father Coogan had a strong respect for the value of education. He did not believe that ignorant priests were fit to lead the people. So that good man spent countless hours tutoring me. I took to it well. After five years of working his potato bed, doing his cooking, cleaning and laundering to earn my keep while studying every evening, he pronounced me ready for the seminary.

"I was educated in France, studying for the priesthood being illegal in Ireland then, and returned home after my ordination. He paid my way, God knows how. My first assignment was as a curate in a parish in Cork. Later, I was transferred here to Kelegeen where I hope to end my days."

It was the first time Father O'Malley had shared this story with anyone. The irony of it being with an Englishman was not lost on him. *Your sense of humor never fails to astound me, Lord!* He thought.

"I thank you for sharing your story. I am honored and humbled by your confidence in me." The doctor's compassionate eyes glimmered with a fine sheen of moisture in the candlelight.

"I am grateful that I was able to." Father O'Malley realized for the first time how deep a bond of friendship had been forged between them. Despite, or perhaps because of, all the misery that was Ireland right now, his heart was near to bursting with gratitude for it.

"I am curious about something, though," Dr. Parker said. "I hope you don't think me presumptuous for asking, but have you ever forgiven Siobhan's murderer?"

Something like a heavy stone dropped from Father O'Malley's heart to the pit of his stomach. "Why do you ask?"

"Because I wonder if I could. As a priest, it's your business to forgive no matter the circumstances. Yet as a man, it seems nearly impossible."

"Forgiveness is not only the business of a priest but of every Christian." He was buying time. His struggle with this very matter often led him to question his fitness for the priesthood. It was difficult to answer with honesty, but he felt his friend deserved his trust.

"You are right. As a man, it took me a very long time to even want to forgive. It's hard even now for me not to become angry when I think of it. However, Father Coogan emphasized most vigorously to me that I had no business becoming a priest if I did not learn to forgive this man."

"So you were able to. How?"

Father O'Malley sighed. "Many times I've believed I have. Then something will happen that seems to undo it all and I feel as though I'm starting again." He considered a moment before continuing. "Forgiveness is a tricky thing. For a long time I confused forgiving someone with condoning their wrong actions. Then I thought it meant that I would actually have to like the man, which I could never do. But through time, prayer, and the help of people like Father Coogan, I came to realize that forgiveness doesn't mean any of that at all. It's more of a release; a letting go of the pain and anger. It's not harboring resentment. You release yourself, but you release the other person as well. Sometimes you have to do it over and over again. But with God, nothing is impossible."

"But have you achieved it? You said yourself just thinking about it makes you angry."

Father O'Malley looked at him, silent.

"I'm sorry," the doctor said, dropping his gaze. "I don't mean to interrogate you. It is just that I can't imagine being able to forgive such a thing. I am in awe of your ability to do so."

"Don't be. At least, not in awe of me. It is with God's help alone that I have achieved anything. Tell me how I would ever forget that this happened? That is not humanly possible. Nonetheless, I have prayed that God help me to forgive. I have also prayed that God forgive the man who killed Siobhan. The miracle is that I actually came to mean it. I do want God to forgive and heal that man. When I think about the hatred and violence that must consume his life I realize what a horrible existence it must be. To be so

369

far removed from feeling God's love is the most horrible thing I can think of. It helps me to be able to pray for him. I also believe Siobhan prays for him from heaven. Still, to be at peace with it, to be totally released from it is something I must pray for every day. It is an ongoing battle, but to give up waging it is to lose."

Dr. Parker sat back in his chair. "Father O'Malley, I consider myself honored to count you as my friend," he stated.

"And I you," Father O'Malley concurred.

"You are a fine priest. Your people are fortunate to have you."

"I thank you for that." He chuckled. "Now if only my bishop would agree."

The banging at the door made both men jump and snapped Kevin from sleep so fast, he sprang to his feet.

"What now?" Father O'Malley grumbled, crossing the cottage floor. "I'm coming!" he called, alarmed at the incessant pounding.

Opening the door, he found a tear-streaked, nearly incoherent Dacey Kilpatrick.

"Dacey, my man, what is it?" he asked.

"My bairns! They've gone! Oh, Father, it's too much to bear." The man collapsed on the doorstep, wailing his misery.

Dr. Parker joined Father O'Malley at the door, helping him raise Dacey and pull him into the cottage.

"Gone where?" asked Father O'Malley, once he had Dacey seated inside.

"To heaven, I should hope, Father. They was good children." He broke down again, his head on the table, his back heaving with sobs.

The priest and doctor stared at each other, open-mouthed. Dacey's two surviving children had succumbed to the same fever that had claimed the baby, but were holding on with the help of medicine left for them by Dr. Parker.

"They were sick, but not mortally so when I saw them this morning," Dr. Parker told Father O'Malley.

370

"Aye. I thought they would make it," came the muffled words from their father, his head face down in his folded arms. "But just then, they turned. At the same time almost," he said, lifting his head. He looked into the faces of the other men with a searching, desperate expression. "And now they're gone. Just like that." He snapped his fingers. "How can it be? How can it be?" he repeated, dropping his head once again.

"What of your wife, Dacey?" asked Father O'Malley.

"Preparing them. Sent me to fetch you."

Father O'Malley turned to the doctor. "I must go at once."

"Of course," the doctor agreed. "I will speak with your young friend about how to recognize his sister while you're gone."

Father O'Malley glanced at Kevin. For a moment, he'd almost forgotten the lad was there. Kevin was standing, his back against the wall, taking in the scene before him.

"Kevin," he called to him. "I've to go to the Kilpatrick's. This is my friend, Doctor Parker. He may be able to help us find what's become of Liddy." Grabbing Dacey by the arm, he helped him from his chair. "Let's go," he said and hurried him out the door.

Chapter Thirty-Four

Father O'Malley breathed deeply of the late spring air as he and Kevin left the church. He hoped the scent of loamy earth held the promise of a good crop. Some still had the strength to work the fields. By the grace of God they would bring Ireland back to life. He glanced at Kevin by his side. Kevin accompanied him to daily Mass. Father O'Malley had him working around the church, keeping the building and its sacred objects tidy. They prayed together every morning, recited the rosary together at night. In between they talked. Kevin would begin to open up about his life, but it always seemed that when he reached some crucial point, he would stop.

The lad had yet to make a confession. This bothered the priest, feeling that doing so would unburden his soul and open to him the graces of the sacrament, allowing him to move beyond this point where he seemed to be stuck. All in the Lord's time, Father O'Malley reminded himself.

Kevin had been with him almost a month now, and, though not strong yet, he did feel as though a nascent bond was beginning to form between them. Father O'Malley tried to remember how long it had taken for him to truly trust Father Coogan, but his memory did not serve. He resolved not to compare the two situations. Each soul's journey is unique. He should not expect Kevin's to follow the same progression as his own.

"I have a surprise for you today," he told Kevin as they headed up the lane.

"What's that?"

"A trip to the Kilpatrick cottage."

Kevin's eyes widened. "I can see Liddy?"

"The good doctor believes it to be safe, so, aye, you may!"

A genuine smile appeared briefly on Kevin's face, then vanished. "I won't know what to say," he whispered. "Does she know about Mam and Addie?"

"She's been told that they died," he answered, softly.

"But does she know about me taking them to the pits?" His voice quivered.

"Only Dr. Parker and myself know of that."

"What of the Kilpatricks? Do they know?"

"Not to my knowledge." He watched Kevin walk with his head down. "Don't take on about it, Kevin. God has spared your sister and returned her to you. Give thanks for such a miraculous blessing."

Whenever Father O'Malley mulled over the events since Dacey Kilpatrick arrived at his cottage, he could not help but believe he had witnessed a genuine miracle. While he'd been at the Kilpatricks' Dr. Parker had learned from Kevin that Liddy had a jagged scar on her right forearm. Her da had cut her with a broken *poteen* bottle to punish her for accidently dropping it. The deep wound, a long snaking line from crook of the arm to wrist, had left a ridge of hardened skin. Equipped with this information, Dr. Parker searched the women's section of the workhouse. Astoundingly, he found Liddy scrubbing clothes in a washroom, the long hard scar shining an angry red under the water dripping from her arms.

Even more astonishing than the fact that Liddy was alive, was that she had not contracted the fever that killed her mother and twin. Dr. Parker surmised it was because they had been separated the moment they entered the workhouse.

"How they disentangled those two lasses is beyond me," Father O'Malley had mused when the doctor told him.

"The workhouse doesn't care much about family ties. In fact, the whole idea is to make life miserable so it does not become viewed as a way to get free room and board. They want it to be as brutal as possible in the misguided idea that it will encourage people to work for a living rather than accept a handout," the doctor explained. "I'm sure when they saw the two girls clinging together, their first thought was to separate them for their own good." Dr. Parker's voice dripped with sarcasm on the last words. "As it happens, it undoubtedly was to Liddy's good. Had they been left together, she'd have succumbed to the fever as well."

The next in the extraordinary string of events was the Kilpatricks' decision to take in Liddy. Father O'Malley had expected the loss of Dacey's remaining children to completely destroy him. Though devastated, he seemed to have a breakthrough instead. Just days after burying the two Kilpatrick children Father O'Malley brought Kevin along when he visited Dacey and Rose. Rose, with her usual thoughtfulness, inquired after Kevin's family, thinking they were still in the *scalpeen*. Kevin informed them that they'd gone to the workhouse, but gave no details other than to say that his Mam and Addie had perished and that Dr. Parker was to find out if Liddy still lived.

"If she lives yet, will you take her back to the *scalpeen*?" Rose had asked. "The workhouse is a dreadful place I wouldn't wish on the devil himself."

"The *scalpeen's* not mine anymore," Kevin had told her. "After we left another family took it. I'm staying with Father O'Malley now."

"Then she'll have to remain." The defeat in Rose's voice gave Father O'Malley a jolt. He had promised Kevin they would get Liddy out of the workhouse, but where would she go? Propriety, even in these times, would not allow a lass of her age to live with him, despite her brother's presence. He wondered if Adam would consent to take her into the *scalpeen* along with his bairns. They seemed to be faring well enough, but as Liddy had been exposed to the workhouse she could well be carrying contagion. No one was likely to risk that.

It was with enormous shock that Father O'Malley found Dacey and Rose at his door two days later announcing that if the girl were found alive, they would take her to live with them. Dr. Parker, who was present at the time, asked "You do know she could be carrying dread disease even if she herself appears well enough?"

374

"We do," Rose said. "We'll take the chance."

"But why?" Father O'Malley could not help but ask.

"The cottage is empty without our bairns. The loneliness is too much for us."

"Are you sure, Rose? Dacey?" asked Dr. Parker.

"Father, may I speak with you alone?" Dacey had asked.

In that short conversation, Dacey explained his belief that the Lord had completed his punishment of Dacey by taking all his children. "Now he has given me a way to make amends by offering a home and kindness to one in dire need. I've made a vow to God to spend the rest of my life doing good so that the Lord may see fit to allow me to spend my eternity with my family in heaven. I can't stand the thought of being separated from them forever."

Father O'Malley inwardly shook his head at Dacey's faulty theology. But if the thought eased the man's pain, so be it. "God will indeed bless you, Dacey. Of that I am certain," he'd told him. And so the hunt for Liddy was quickly and successfully undertaken. She was removed from the workhouse at once and brought to the Kilpatrick cottage. But the doctor had imposed a quarantine until he was certain she was not carrying anything communicable.

Enough time had now passed for the ban on visiting to be lifted with relative surety. As soon as he got the word, Father O'Malley made ready to reunite Kevin with his sister.

Rose welcomed them warmly when they reached the cottage.

Liddy was sitting on the floor near the fireplace, dipping a dress in and out of a washtub. She took no notice as they entered.

"Liddy?" Kevin squatted next to her. "Liddy. It's me, Kevin."

She continued scrubbing the same garment, never speaking, never looking at him. Tentatively reaching out, he took hold of her arm. A scream pierced the room as if she'd been scalded. Kevin jumped away. The others hurried to her. Rose caressed her shoulders. "It's alright, Liddy. Go back to your washing," she soothed.

While Rose worked at calming the girl, Dacey drew Kevin and Father O'Malley into the yard.

"She's still getting used to being here," he said, by way of apology.

"But I'm her brother." Kevin looked as though he might cry.

"Lad, you know she's not right." Dacey tapped his head. "She probably doesn't even recognize you."

"Why do you make her do the washing?" he asked, indignant.

"We don't make her. She wants to. It's what she got used to at the workhouse, so it seems to comfort her, being something familiar."

"How do you know?" Father O'Malley asked. "She can't speak."

Dacey looked puzzled. "What do you mean she can't speak?"

"Kevin?" Father O'Malley looked at him. "Your Mam told me your sisters hadn't spoken since the day she left them alone with your da. Isn't it true?"

"They've spoken to no one but each other in years. And that in a language no one else could understand. Though they seemed to know what the other was saying."

"Well, that explains one thing," said Dacey. "She prattles on now and then since she got here, but for the lives of us neither Rose nor I can make out a word she's saying. Didn't seem as though she was talking to us anyway. It always seems as though she's conversing with a person who isn't there. A bit eerie, it is, but Rose says perhaps she's saying her own kind of prayers, speaking the language of angels."

"She's talking to Addie," Kevin said. "Or at least thinks she is."

"She was told that Addie and your Mam are gone to God," Dacey said.

"She may not remember or simply doesn't understand," Father O'Malley offered. He thought of his own conversations with Siobhan and wondered if Liddy understood more than any of the rest of them.

Dacey gently pushed open the cottage door. "Seems quiet in there now."

Father O'Malley started forward, but Kevin hesitated. "Kevin? You coming?" he asked.

"She seems afraid of me. I don't think I should."

"It's just that she hasn't seen you in a while," Dacey offered. "If you stay a bit and come back often, it might be she gets used to you again."

"Please," Father O'Malley urged.

Kevin entered the cottage, but kept his distance. His eyes ever on his sister, he listened as the others talked. Her back to them, she immersed herself in washing the same garment over and over again, taking no notice of anyone's presence. Just as Father O'Malley completed a prayer of blessing over the home and its occupants a torrent of babble erupted from Liddy.

"That's the language I meant," Kevin whispered.

"Aye," said Dacey. "She does that every so often. Goes on like that for a while then falls silent."

They watched as Liddy turned her head, nodding as though to someone next to her. She uttered more gibberish, waited then laughed lightly, shaking her head.

"Well, that's new," said Rose. "I've never heard her laugh before."

"Nor have I." Kevin stared at his sister in amazement.

"I take it as a good sign that your loving care is doing her good, then," Father O'Malley told Rose and Dacey. "Come, Kevin, we must take our leave." He wanted Kevin's last impression of this visit to be of his sister happy so ushered him out before anything could happen to change her mood.

They walked much of the way in silence, both lost in thought. Finally, Kevin asked, "Do you think she'll ever be right in the head?"

"Probably not completely," Father O'Malley admitted. "But she could improve. She's in a loving home now. That's got to help."

Again there was a long silence.

"It's mostly my fault." Kevin's matter-of-fact tone took Father O'Malley by surprise.

"How so?" he asked. "From all I've seen and heard, your da's the one who shoulders most of the responsibility."

"Oh, he's to blame for starting it all. There's no doubt of that. But I never stopped him. I should have protected them."

"But you were just a lad. There's not much you could have done against your da."

"True, Father, but I should have at least tried. I saw him beat my Mam and sisters all the time, but did nothing. I was too afraid. He always called me a coward. Maybe if I had stood up to him he would have had more respect for me. Maybe I could have stopped him."

"Or maybe you could have gotten yourself killed."

"At least I would have died doing right, instead of hiding and skulking in fear." Balling his hands into fists, Kevin slammed them into his own chest. "I've been and always will be useless."

Father O'Malley stopped walking. He grabbed Kevin's shoulder, turning the lad to face him. "Your da set you up from the start to be just like himself. I'd be surprised to find that his da didn't do the same to him. It probably goes back many generations. But you have the power to change all of that right now!"

Kevin stared at him. "How?"

"By deciding not to be like your father."

Kevin looked away. "I don't want to be like him. But I don't how else to be."

"Then learn," he said. "Whatever he did that hurt and angered you, the minute you catch yourself doing the same, stop. He drank. Don't drink. He lied. Be honest. He was cruel. Be kind. He was thoughtless. Think more of others than yourself. Most of all, he was faithless. Put your faith in God. Pray for guidance, for help, for forgiveness." He gave Kevin's shoulder a shake. "God wants to save you, lad. Let Him!"

"I know what not to do, Father. I just don't know what to do." His words were drenched in anguish.

Father O'Malley thought for a moment. "What does a person do if they wish to learn a trade?"

Kevin looked confused.

"You'll see where I'm going with this, just answer," Father O'Malley told him.

"Well, if he can, he finds someone who knows the trade and asks to be taught."

"Exactly! He apprentices himself to a master."

"So?"

"So, you should do the same. But instead of learning a trade, you'll learn a way of life."

"I don't know what you mean, Father."

Father O'Malley sighed. "If you apprentice yourself to a man bad at his trade, you will only learn the most slipshod methods and never make anything of yourself. You'd want to be apprenticed to someone highly skilled, who did his work with diligence and integrity so you'd learn the best way, would you not?"

"Aye."

"Then find the best men, the best husbands, the best fathers you see around you. Watch how they behave. Listen to what they say. See how they interact with others—men, women, children, creatures. Learn from how they handle the most difficult situations. Most especially see how their faith sustains them. Apprentice yourself to them, lad. There are plenty around if you'll open your eyes. Let them be what your da should have been to you and put an end to his legacy."

"But, Father, everyone knows my da. They all think I'm just like him. They'll never give me a chance." Kevin's eyes narrowed.

"And is that entirely their fault?"

Kevin rolled his eyes.

"Own up, lad. You've got to admit your own mistakes in order to correct them. What do you want for your future? Your da's way or a different way?"

Kevin nodded. "I suppose..." he began slowly.

Father O'Malley gave him an encouraging look.

Kevin blew out a long breath. "They are not entirely wrong," he finally said. "I have done things I knew were sins. But Father, how could I convince anyone now that I want to change? Who would believe me?"

"You'll come with me on my rounds. You'll help Dr. Parker with whatever you can. The more you continue to be of service to others, the more they will observe the change. It will take time, but you can make a whole new identity for yourself amongst your neighbors. I warn you, though, it must be genuine. This is not a scheme to make people like you. The desire for change must come from deep inside you."

Kevin stood quietly staring over the hilly fields. "It does, Father," he whispered.

Thank you, Jesus. May it continue, Father O'Malley prayed.

* * *

"Good afternoon, Father O'Malley." A sharp voice in the dim interior startled them as they entered the priest's cottage.

"Your Excellency! I was not expecting you." Father O'Malley moved quickly as Bishop Kneeland rose from the table, dropped to his knees and kissed the bishop's ring.

"I see you have a young friend with you," said the Bishop, eying Kevin.

"Aye, Your Excellency. Kevin Dooley, one of my parishioners." He pushed a stunned Kevin forward as the bishop held out his hand. "Kneel and kiss his ring," he hissed in Kevin's ear.

"We have just returned from visiting Kevin's sister," Father O'Malley explained as Kevin rose from his knees. "She's all the family the poor lad has left in the world."

"I'm sorry to hear it," said the bishop. "I hope you found her well enough." His eyes bored into Kevin's. The trembling lad merely nodded.

"What brings you here, Your Excellency?" asked Father O'Malley.

"You did not receive my missive then?"

"I received nothing."

"Ah, the post these days is intolerably slow. It will probably arrive after I'm gone if it gets here at all." The bishop resumed his seat at the table, indicating for Father O'Malley to join him. He glanced at Kevin, who had not moved.

"Is the lad staying?" Bishop Kneeland nodded his head towards Kevin.

How to explain this? The last time he was here, Bishop Kneeland had thundered on about not becoming too friendly with parishioners, but leading them like a general leads an army. What would he think of Father O'Malley having taken him in? Would he go so far as to order him out?

"As it happens, the lad has nowhere to go," he began.

"He cannot stay with his sister?"

"She is not well. She's staying with a parish family."

"And where does this young man reside, then, Father?"

"Well, at the moment, Your Excellency, he is, for lack of another place—" A knock at the door interrupted his stammering. "Excuse me." Jumping up, he hurried to the door.

"Meg," he said, finding her on the other side.

"Father, I've come to you for confession—oh!" Meg's eyes quickly roved the cottage's interior taking in Bishop Kneeland and Kevin Dooley. "I'm sorry, Father. I'll come back another time."

"No need," called Bishop Kneeland. Father O'Malley turned toward him.

"The lass has asked for the sacrament, Father. You've a duty to hear her confession. Go on, go on." He waved a hand at them. "This lad and I will take the opportunity of your absence to get to know one another."

Father O'Malley's mouth gaped open.

"Have a seat, my lad," said Bishop Kneeland. Kevin glanced at Father O'Malley who nodded to him. "I'll be back shortly," he said overwhelmed by the sensation that he was dreaming.

Chapter Thirty-Five

"I'm sorry, Father. I didn't know the bishop was here," Meg said. There was so much on her mind, so much she needed to talk over with him, but here he was busy with a visit from the bishop. And he, Bishop Kneeland, sitting at table with Kevin Dooley. An odd combination to say the least. Meg had heard rumors that Father O'Malley had taken Kevin in, but she paid them no mind. There was nothing regarding Kevin that interested her in the least. He was a beast who didn't deserve the kindness one would show a mangy dog, but she supposed that as a priest, Father O'Malley must make all sorts of concessions due to his state of great holiness.

"No need to apologize, Meg. The bishop took me by surprise as well. I didn't know he was coming."

"Oh." Meg's mind was so full of all she needed to say that she could not focus on anything else. "Rory is waiting for us in the church, Father."

"Has he come for confession, too?"

"No. We've something extremely important to talk to you about. Will you have time? Must you get back to the bishop quickly?" Meg's heart hammered. This was so urgent and her priest so necessary to her plan.

"Don't worry about that. You may have my attention for as long as needed," he assured her.

The last rays of sunlight came through the church windows, throwing bars of colored light across the pews. Rory stood as they entered.

"I understand you've something important to discuss with me."

Rory nodded.

"Father, if you don't mind, I'd like to make my confession first," Meg interrupted. "I need to do it and the rest of what we want to say will make more sense afterwards." Meg's whole body trembled. The walk to the church had tired her, but more than that, she was on the brink of a monumental decision, the most important one of her young life. If she could find the courage to go through with it, everything she'd always expected for her future would change.

"Very well," Father O'Malley agreed, leading the way towards the confessional.

"Bless me, Father, for I have sinned. It has been one month since my last confession."

She stopped.

He waited patiently, but she didn't speak. "Go ahead, Meg. I'm listening."

She was never slow about her confessions. Her little sins usually rolled off her tongue glad as she was to be rid of them. Now she knelt, biting her lip, not knowing where to begin.

"Meg, it's alright to tell me. You'll feel better after you do."

She nodded resolutely, then dissolved into tears.

"Meg, have you stolen something? Food? Money?"

She knew he was trying to help, but he would never guess what she must confess. "No, Father, I'd tell that well enough. 'Tis much worse."

"Whatever it is, God will forgive you. Obviously, you're sorry for it."

"I know God will forgive me. I'm afraid of what you will think."

"Me? I could never think ill of you. Remember, all repentant sinners are beautiful in the eyes of God. How could I think less?"

Meg felt somewhat reassured, but getting the words out was still an effort. The lump, like a knot in her throat, seemed to hold her speech captive.

Meg squeezed her eyes shut and forced out the words. "I caused my da to die."

"No, Meg, no. Nothing you did caused your da to die. It was an accident." His voice, coming from the other side of the confessional screen was soothing

384

"Him getting run over was an accident, but it was my own fault he didn't see the wagon because he was looking for me."

"You mustn't blame yourself. You were right not to try to walk home once you realized you were too weak to make it. We all understand that."

"'Twas a lie." There. It was said. The knot loosened a bit.

"What do you mean?"

"About sleeping the night in a *scalpeen*. I made it up."

"Why?"

"Because I didn't want anyone to know what I'd really done."

"What had you done?"

Meg clenched her folded hands tightly. "I spent the night in the Harp and Sword."

The knot in her throat tightened again.

"How did you come to be there?"

"I heard of someone going to America. I had some money, a little, I don't know how much. It was just what Mr. Breckett gave me."

"The baker?"

"Aye. Oh, I wasn't supposed to tell anyone. Please don't let on you know."

"This is a confession, Meg. Not another soul will ever know what's said here."

"Well, then I suppose I can tell you. Mr. Breckett gives me food sometimes when I go into his shop. He says he doesn't want every beggar coming there, so I'm not to tell."

"Don't worry, Meg. I think Mr. Breckett himself is the only one who thinks no one knows."

Meg thought of all the people she'd seen the man help and realized it was only a small portion of his generosity. It was surprising he had a business left, but surely he was being blessed far and wide by those he aided.

"He has always been generous to me, but I was sure what he gave me could not be nearly enough for passage. So I thought I would sell my comb. You remember my comb, Father?"

385

"I do."

"Well, I found myself across from the tavern and thought I could sell it there. I never meant to go inside. There were so many people coming and going I just thought if I kept trying someone would buy it, but then there were some who were like to get rough until another lad, a lad named William, came out and rescued me. " Now that she'd started, she felt as though her mouth was moving on its own, spilling out the whole story, the words tumbling over each other as they battled their way off her tongue. "He insisted I come inside with him, bought me an ale. I drank though I shouldn't have. I was so thirsty."

"Didn't you realize it could be dangerous?" She heard concern, not condemnation in his voice. It gave her the courage to continue.

"Of course I did, Father. But my da told me that very morning that I had to live no matter what because if I didn't surely no one else would. When I heard from Mrs. Flaherty that her nephew was going to America, I knew it was the only way. I must go. Then I can send back money to help my family. But I had to get passage money first and I had to do it quickly. I was only going to sell the comb, Father, nothing more, I promise it."

"And did you sell it?"

"Aye. Well, that is, William did. He sold it for me. Gave me the money. But when I got up to leave, I felt dizzy and fainted. When I awoke the next morning I was upstairs in the tavern."

"So this William? He took you upstairs?"

"I suppose he must have."

"Was he there when you woke up?"

She could tell he was trying to keep his voice calm. She hated that her actions caused so much anguish to those around her. But this, at least, was not as bad as when she had told Rory. He had shifted between anger, confusion, frustration, and betrayal. Though she knew he believed her intentions completely innocent, he'd been terribly hurt that she had taken such a drastic step without so much as consulting him. He'd also been aghast at the thought of

386

what could have happened to her. It took hours of talking to make him understand that William was not a villain. When she'd finally convinced him that she left the Harp and Sword with her virtue intact, the comb he had given her, and extra money besides, Rory had had to concede. Still, she could see that it pained him for another man to have played the hero to her when he could not.

"No, Father. I never saw him again," she answered. "And I am absolutely certain he did me no wrong. I...I checked." Meg's cheeks burned at the words. Quickly, she continued, "Before I left I found that all my money was still there. He must have bought back my comb because I found that, too, and a little extra money besides. I suppose he took pity on me."

"Thanks be to God in His great mercy!" Father O'Malley's voice came through the screen as a sigh of relief. "Is there anything else you want to tell me?"

"Only that I couldn't tell them at home where I'd been so I made up the lie. Meanwhile, my da and the rest of you were looking for me. If only I hadn't been in that tavern my da would be alive right now, but he's not and it's all my fault." The relief she'd felt from telling her story evaporated and Meg crumpled into a shivering ball.

"Meg?" His voice called softly through the screen.

"Aye, Father?" She lifted herself to kneel while tears coursed down her face.

"Meg, it was a rash decision to even go near that tavern, but I understand why you did. Our Lord understands, too. Thankfully, He kept you safe through it all. It was not so much a sin as a grave lapse of judgment."

"Aye, Father. But my da..."

"It was an accident that he was run over by the cart. Your da knew how to cross a street whether he was looking for someone or not. If he stepped out at the wrong moment, it was a horrible mistake, but only a mistake. The real fault belongs to the driver. Not stopping once his horse had knocked him down was inexcusable."

"But I feel so guilty, Father. I feel as though I killed my da."

"It pains me terribly to say this, Meg, but you did have some small part to play in it. You did go where you knew you shouldn't have and then lied about it. But remember, exhausted as you were, you also went out to look for your da, so you did your best to right the wrong the only way you could. Our Lord knows all this and that you are very sorry. Certainly He forgives you. But can you forgive yourself?"

"No, Father, I don't think I ever can."

"That's what worries me."

"Whenever I think of my da now, I picture him in heaven looking down on me. He knows everything I did. It makes my heart ache."

There was silence for a moment. Then he asked, "Meg, do you believe that in heaven everything is made perfect?"

"Of course, Father."

"Then you believe that your da, now that he's in heaven, understands everything about why you went to the tavern? That you lied to save your family from any possible shame? That you tried to find him and that you are sorry for all of it?"

Meg thought over his words. "I suppose he must," she said slowly.

"Then don't you think your da forgives you? He loved you with all his heart. I know you were precious to him."

"I hope so, Father, but it still doesn't make the ache go away."

"I know that, Meg. We make choices in our lives and then, like it or not, we have to live with the consequences. But with time and the grace of God the hurt will lessen. You must pray for God's help. Trust Him that He will not abandon you."

"I will, Father." Meg wiped her palms across her face, feeling the muddied streaks of caked dirt her tears had made.

"Make a good Act of Contrition now, Meg and I will give you absolution."

* * *

388

By the time they left the confessional, the church had grown almost completely dark. Father O'Malley lit several candles before joining Meg and Rory in one of the pews. "What is it you two wanted to discuss with me?" he asked.

Meg nodded to Rory. She'd decided to let him do most of the talking since she'd already unmanned him enough.

"Father, Meg and I have talked it over and we feel it's best if she goes to America."

"Why her and not you?" asked Father O'Malley.

Meg felt Rory's body stiffen beside her. His bones, weakened from starvation, had caused a slight hump in his back, but he drew himself us as straight as he could.

"I am the only man left to provide for two families. I cannot leave them." His words, though softly spoken hung heavily in the air.

"Do you think this voyage safe for Meg to undertake alone?"

"At first, I was opposed. But the more we've thought on it, the more it seems to be our best hope. Meg is smart and resourceful. Of all of us, she is the most likely to survive such a journey. I would rather go in her place, Father. I am no coward. But if I go, I will only be abandoning the others. I fear that by the time I reached America, found work and started sending money back it would be too late. So Meg must go while I continue to provide as best I can."

"And that would be by continuing to steal?"

"If I can find another way that's not likely to kill me, I'll take it. Otherwise..." Rory held out his hands in a helpless gesture. "I know it's a sin, Father. I'll come to confession and never steal again once this famine is over. But for now, I must do what allows us to survive."

"And if you're caught? How will that help the families?"

"I know it's a risk, but I've become quite good at it, Father. I don't think I'll be caught."

It had grown too dark to see faces, but Meg could hear the exasperation in Father O'Malley's sigh. "We'll leave that subject for now," he said. "Meg, how does your mam feel about you leaving for America?"

"We've not told her yet, Father. That's the other thing we wanted to talk to you about. I'm afraid she won't want me to go. We were hoping you'd convince her when the time comes."

"Your mam just lost Brendan. She can't take losing you, too."

"It might be the only chance for all of us. Other than Rory, I can do the most. I can't find mending work here anymore because of the Hoffreys. But I'll find work in America and send back money. Mrs. Flaherty's nephew is going to do the same. He's leaving on the next ship."

"I know. I've spoken with him about it."

"You knew he was going?" Meg asked, surprised.

"Aye. His landlord is paying for his passage. Yours won't."

"His landlord? He must have the kindest landlord in the world."

"Kindness, maybe. Another way to rid Ireland of the Irish, more likely," said Father O'Mally, dryly.

"Tell Blackburn that and perhaps he'll pay for all of us to go," Rory suggested sarcastically.

"Would he?" Meg wondered aloud. The thought had never occurred to her.

"No." The two men responded at once, sinking her momentary hopes.

"How far in the future are you two thinking?" Father O'Malley asked. "You've been planning to marry for some time. Would have by now, too, if not for this famine. Is that all over with, then?"

Meg felt a catch in her throat. She nudged Rory in the darkness, urging him to speak as she couldn't.

"We would like you to marry us before she goes," Rory said. "We want to be bound together for life one way or another."

"Yet you would be living an ocean apart. That's not much of a marriage. Do you realize that if Meg leaves

Ireland there is a very good chance you two may never see each other again?"

Meg fought back tears. She knew in her heart this would be the most likely outcome, but continually forced the thought from her mind. "Father, that is one reason we want to be married first," she said. "Our plan is for Rory and the others to come over when they are able. If we are married when I go we will have an unbreakable bond. It will keep us both working towards being together again no matter how much we have to struggle."

"Meg, how much money do you think you are going to make in America? You will need to send money back here, have money for a place to live and to feed yourself as well as save for passage for Rory and the rest of your family. How do you think that is possible?"

"Oh, but America is a land of riches! Everyone says so."

"For some, perhaps, but they have their poor, too, and more likely than not you'll join their ranks."

"But I'm a hard worker, Father. I will do whatever I must. I can live in the worst hovel if need be while I save. With just a bit more food than I've got now, I can survive. I can do this, Father, I know I can." Meg's throat strained with the urgency behind her words. "Please, Father. We need your help. It may be our only hope."

"What would you have me do?"

"Marry us before Meg goes," said Rory.

"And, if you would, please try again to sell my comb." She pulled it from her pocket, her thumb caressing the carved rose petals nestled in the smooth wood.

"Meg. I don't want to take that comb from you."

Confused, Meg didn't know how to respond.

"Why not, Father?" Rory asked. "It should fetch a good price. It would be a considerable help with passage money. I'd prefer Meg had some extra beyond the passage sum to help her get started once she's there. It's the only thing we've got worth selling."

"How much money do you have at present?" Father O'Malley asked.

"I think it's almost three pounds," Meg said. "I recognize some coins from my mending pay, but there are a few I've never seen before, so I'm not certain. Here, Father, look for yourself." Meg dropped the coins into the priest's hand. He held them near the candlelight, sorting them in his palm.

"You are correct, Meg. That's just under three pounds."

"So that's not much more she needs for passage and then if she could get just a bit beyond, I'll feel safer about her going," Rory said.

"You seem awfully calm about this, lad," Father O'Malley noted. "It doesn't bother you to lose Meg?"

"It bothers me a great deal, Father. More than I can tell. 'Tis a terrible sacrifice for us both, but it seems the only way. That's why we want so much to be married before she goes. We will have that bond before God. We've both prayed on it. We believe God will bless our marriage by reuniting us, though we understand it may be a long wait." Then he added, "We think, too, that it might be safer for Meg to go as a married woman."

Father O'Malley handed the coins back to Meg. "If you are determined to go and you can raise the fare, there's not much I can do to stop you," he said. "However, I will do nothing without your mother's approval, Meg."

"Do you truly think my going would be a mistake, Father?" Meg asked. She had made so many mistakes recently, she was beginning to doubt herself.

"Honestly, Meg, I don't know. It may be as you say, your best hope. I would not want you to lose that. But I also know that it may be the cause of great heartbreak. Both your families have already lost so much. For your family to lose you—for you to lose each other—it's...well it's a dreadful decision to make. Have you thought what it will be like to be alone in a foreign land? You know no one there. What will you do upon arrival? All these things must be thought through."

"That's why we want your help, Father," Rory explained. "You can think of things we can't."

"Do you know others going?" Meg asked, certain that he must. "Can I not go with someone?"

"Let me think on this," he said. "I cannot give you an answer right now. And you must tell your mother. I will not attempt to overrule her if she objects. Is that understood?"

They agreed.

"Good. Now I'd better return home. I've kept the bishop waiting long enough."

As they left the church together, Meg asked, "Father, why will you not sell my comb for me? Even if I were to stay, the money from it would still help us."

"Meg, how many times have you tried to sell that comb?"

She thought of Gale Day, the time she had given it to the priest to sell, and William's sale of it in the tavern. "Three," she answered.

"Yet there it is in your hand. And that despite it actually having been sold once."

"So?"

"That comb is trying to tell you something. It doesn't want to leave you."

Such strange words, she thought. "I don't understand. It's not magic."

"Magic?" he laughed a little. "If only you knew. Just hang on to it, Meg. It's meant to be with you."

Chapter Thirty-Six

"You've come alone? Where is Father O'Malley?" Deirdre asked, opening the door to admit Dr. Parker.

"Father O'Malley has been detained by an unexpected visit from his bishop. I'm on my own today. How are our patients faring?"

"Still holding on," Deirdre answered.

Aisling continued with a plodding improvement while Brigid had more frequent moments of lucidity. Meg took both as signs that it was safe to leave them. They would continue to improve while she worked in America. By the time she could arrange their passage, they would be well. Someday they would all be together in a much better place.

"Good day to you all," said Dr. Parker as he exited the cottage having finished his examinations.

Meg had been turning over an idea in her mind ever since Father O'Malley had refused to sell her comb. She could not understand his reluctance and his final words to her made no sense. But if he would not sell it for her, she would find another way. A visit from the doctor without Father O'Malley was a rare occurrence. It was her one chance.

"Dr. Parker," she called, catching up to him a few steps from the cottage.

"Yes?"

"I was wondering if you would do a favor for me."

"If I can."

Meg wondered how his eyes always seemed to twinkle even in the most horrible conditions. It was a pleasure to look upon them. The eyes of most were now lifeless, haunted, barely more than glassy orbs stuck into sunken faces. The doctor was British, he obviously had enough to eat, as did his horse, which rankled Meg. But he had proven himself most helpful and tender-hearted. Father O'Malley had grown to trust and like him. She would have to take the chance that she could trust him, too.

"Would you please sell this for me?" She held out her comb.

"My, but that is exquisite!" he said, taking it from her to study.

"Rory made it for me. Before the accident. There's not another like it and never will be."

"Why would you sell it then? It must be very precious to you."

"It is. He gave it to me when he asked me to marry him. But it is the only thing I have worth selling. I think it could fetch a good price, but you would be better than I at getting it."

The doctor looked reluctant. "I could bring you some extra food next time I come. Does Rory know you're selling it? Does he mind?"

"He knows. We have agreed it is the best way." Seeing the doctor's unwillingness, she decided to risk the full reason. "Rory and I have agreed that I will leave Ireland for America. He will stay behind to care for the others while I work and send money back. When it's possible, we'll bring them all over. But for now, it's just me. I need money for the passage. Four pounds, but I only have three. The comb is all I have to make the rest of the fee. Please, won't you help me? It may be the only way our families survive." Every nerve in her body seemed to twitch, so desperate was she to make him understand.

"Going all alone to a strange land is a dangerous undertaking. Many are doing it now though, as they think it's the only way. But, I can tell you that the ships are overcrowded and unsanitary. Disease is rampant. Many don't survive the voyage."

"But some must."

"Say you do. What will you do when you arrive in America? There are many waiting to take advantage of people alone and unfamiliar with their new surroundings. I must urge you to think carefully about this."

"I have. Rory and I have talked to Father O'Malley about it."

"And he agrees?" The doctor looked surprised.

Meg started to feel disheartened. "Not entirely. I think he understands, but he said much the same as you have. Rory and I've decided to see Mrs. Flaherty. Her nephew is going to America. We'll ask her how he plans to manage. I won't go unprepared, I promise."

"Does your mother agree to your going?"

"Mam doesn't know yet. She's going to be the hardest to convince. I want to have the passage fare in hand before I tell her so she sees that I'm well prepared."

"Simply having passage money is in no way enough preparation."

"I know that now. That's why we'll see Mrs. Flaherty. But I must have the money and my Mam must not know yet. Please, will you help me?"

The doctor sighed. "I will sell your comb for you, but you must make me a promise first."

"Anything."

"Promise me that you will not buy passage until after you have spoken with your mother, Father O'Malley, and me. If you are truly determined on this course, at least let us help you construct a plan for your safety."

Meg felt a smile spread across her face of its own free will. "I promise," she agreed, relieved at the thought that she would not be walking blindly into a new life.

As the doctor turned away, Meg thought of one more thing. "Dr. Parker," she said, reaching for his arm to turn him back. "Please don't tell Father O'Malley that I gave you the comb to sell."

"Why not? You did say that he knows of your plan to emigrate." The doctor's face looked stern. She could not lose his trust so suddenly, but she could not tell him the real reason. It was odd enough to her. Imagine how it would sound to the doctor.

"You know my family is close to Father O'Malley. I'm afraid his feelings might be hurt if he knew I gave it to you instead of asking him. It's just that, I think you know more rich people. You could probably get a better price than he could." Meg bit her lip. She hated to lie, especially to those trying to help her.

Dr. Parker smiled and nodded. "I understand. I'll not let on. It wouldn't do to have the good Father's feelings hurt."

* * *

"I'm not sure. I suppose he'll look for a job right away," Mrs. Flaherty said, when Meg and Rory arrived at her cottage to ask about her nephew's plans. "If they were giving him a wake, you could go to it and ask him yourself, but I doubt they'll be able to."

"A wake?" Meg asked, confused.

"An American wake. That's what they call the grand send off when one leaves Ireland. Just like a real wake, only the deceased isn't dead."

"Why have one, then?" asked Rory.

"Don't you know? The person who's going's not likely to be seen again in this lifetime, so they might as well be dead. Give them the wake now to send them off in fine fashion. Alan, poor dear, could barely scrape together the money for passage. Then there's only a few family members left alive and them not in condition for such festivities. But I've heard of others who've had them."

"What others? How many are leaving Ireland?"

"How many?" the woman looked incredulous. "I don't know the number, but you can bet they're boarding them ships in droves. By the dozens. Nay, thousands! And some's got enough for the grand send off." She sniffed. "Seems to me if they can do so, they could just as easily skip and share some passage money with others who'd like to go."

"Would you go if you could?" Meg asked.

"I'd jump on that ship faster than my own heart can beat, lass. But I've no way to pay for it."

"I've heard the ships are dangerous. Full of disease," Meg said.

397

"Tell me how that's different from the whole of Ireland. Full of disease and starvation, this entire country is. I'd take my chances with a ship sailing me away from it if I could. I'll pray for Alan and hope he gets there alive. It's all I can do."

"I wonder what it will be like in America," Meg mused.

"Oh, I don't doubt it will be grand indeed," said Mrs. Flaherty. "Jobs everywhere is what I've heard. Why, you've just to ask for one and it's given you. Food and plenty of it. A place to live with all four walls, too! No worries about that. Though I'll tell you," she leaned in close to Meg and Rory. "It's glad I am he didn't listen to his mate, John Barnsby. John told Alan to take the ship for Canada. Three pounds instead of four. He almost did it, too, but that ship sailed before he got that last of the money."

"Only three pounds?" Rory asked. "It's cheaper. Why not go to Canada?"

"Oh, laddie, don't even think on it. 'Tis not Canada that's the problem. 'Tis the ship that takes you there. Coffin ships, they're calling 'em. You think the ones going to America have sickness. They're nothing compared to those bound for Canada. I'd sooner move straight into the workhouse than step foot on one of those."

* * *

"Do you believe everything she said?" Meg asked Rory as they walked home.

"I don't know. Some of it's probably true, some not. But which is which?"

"What about the ships going to Canada? They're cheaper?"

Rory stopped. "Absolutely not! Don't even consider it."

"We should ask Dr. Parker what he knows of them. Maybe they're not as bad as she says."

"Let's not take the chance."

"What about the jobs? Do you think they're as plentiful in America as she says?"

Rory shrugged. "There's none I know who've gone and come back to tell us one way or the other. Still, it might be easier for Alan to find work. Being a man, he could work on the docks as soon as he gets there. If he's well enough, that is. What will you do?"

"Are you having second thoughts, Rory?"

"Maybe." He shrugged. "What if it happens that we never see each other again?"

"That won't happen. The whole reason I'm going is to get everyone else over."

"But suppose it doesn't work out that way. I'm feeling that it's more than likely this could part us forever." He traced the side of her face with his finger, pushing a strand of her thinning hair behind her ear. "I would miss you so much, Megeen, I think I'd die from it."

Tears clouded Meg's vision. "I would miss you, too." They stood alone in the lane, their arms wrapped around each other, both crying. Weak, they sat down by the roadside to rest.

"Should I go or not?" Meg asked.

Rory stared at the ground. "Dr. Parker promised to help prepare you before buying passage. Let's not decide now. Let's wait until we know more.

Hoof beats thundering up the path signaled to them to scuttle out of the way. As if the mention of his name had conjured him up, Dr. Parker atop Lily suddenly rounded the lane. They watched as the horse skiddered to a stop in a cloud of dust a few feet ahead of them.

"Oh, good. I thought that was you." He said, jumping from the saddle. "I haven't much time. An emergency." His words came out in gasps. "Here. This is for you." He held out a pouch towards Meg.

"What is it?" she asked.

"The money from the sale of your comb." He said heading back towards Lily.

"How much?"

"Five pounds."

Meg and Rory stared wide-eyed at him. Meg pushed herself from the ground. "Thank you so much, Dr. Parker!" she said, trying to catch him.

"You're welcome. And remember your promise," he called as he remounted Lily.

"I will."

Meg sat down next to Rory. They opened the pouch and looked at the coins.

"I can't believe it!" Rory exclaimed. "There's no way that comb was worth this much. He must have added to it."

"Aye, but I'll not complain." Meg dropped the money she kept in her pocket into the pouch. It felt heavy in her hand. "We have the money. Now comes the hard part."

"Your mam?"

Meg nodded, starting to get up. Rory held her back. "Before we speak to her, I just want to say that you don't have to do this." His dark eyes, bigger than ever in his bone-thin face, shone with both pain and love. "I mean it, Meg. If you don't want to go, don't. We can take the money and buy food. If we ration it well that will keep us a good while." He pointed to the bag in Meg's hands.

"Do you want me to stay, Rory?"

"I want you to do what's safest. Only I can't see the future so I don't know what that is."

"None of us can."

"I just don't want you to feel as though I forced you into this."

"How could I feel that? It was my idea."

"I know, but ever since you convinced me of it, I've been helping to bring it about. Now I'm worried you may not want to go after all, but will because you think I want it. Just know, Meg, that you can change your mind any time. Even right up until the ship sails. I'd not make you go. I don't want you to go. Oh God, Meg, what if we never see each other again?" For a second time, they dissolved in tears, entwined in each other's arms.

"I hate this famine," Meg whispered in his ear. "'Tis the cruelest thing in all creation." Meg had never felt such hurt in her life. As she rested her head on Rory's shoulder, she thought of sailing for weeks on a ship, leaving everyone she knew and loved behind. She was weak from starvation, probably closer to death than she wanted to believe. She could easily sicken and die, her body thrown overboard, her family never to know. Or, she could get to America and find it held no hope after all. Homeless, friendless, she'd only starve to death alone in a strange place instead of at home with loved ones. Was that possibility worth the risk? Even if she did find work, a place to live, a way to make a new life, could she stand the awful loneliness? The longing for home and family would be a constant aching she was sure would never leave her. She suddenly realized how daunting would be the task of bringing the rest of her family to America. Was the slight chance going to America offered worth the gamble?

She looked up at Rory. "I know you would never make me go. I know you'd rather be the one going, if you could. I don't know any better than you what to do."

"Aisling and Brigid are getting better," he said, hope in his voice. "The planting we just put in might take. Why don't we wait and see?"

Meg nodded. "What of this?" She asked, holding up the money pouch. "If we use it for food instead, we'll never be able to raise the money again."

"Hold onto it for now. We'll know soon enough if the crop fails."

"Let's ask God to make that our sign. If it fails, I go. If not, I stay. That way we leave it in God's hands."

Chapter Thirty-Seven

Father O'Malley sat at his table, a pile of newspapers in front of him. When he'd returned home after meeting with Meg and Rory, he'd found Bishop Kneeland gone. Kevin told him the bishop had returned to town for the night, but that he would be back the next day. Today, after morning Mass, Father O'Malley lined up enough chores in the church to keep Kevin busy all morning and accompanied the bishop back to his cottage. Still unclear as to the purpose of his visit, Father O'Malley was surprised when the bishop plopped the stack of newspapers before him.

"What is this?" he asked.

Bishop Kneeland picked a paper from the top of the pile, opened to the editorial page and placed it before Father O'Malley. "Read this, please." He pointed to a specific column.

As Father O'Malley read, he moved from astonishment to near giddiness. The newspaper article recounted the horrors of the famine in authentic detail. It also related how little England was doing to offer relief, how she'd even endeavored to make money from the calamity by forcing ships carrying donated food to dock in London first and pay duty before entering Irish ports. Father O'Malley was elated that the plight of his people was finally being conveyed to the world, but what did it have to do with him and why would it bring the bishop to his doorstep?

"This is amazing!" he said, folding the paper when he'd finished. "Do these all contain similar sentiments?" he asked, indicating the pile of newspapers.

"Indeed they do. That top paper is a bit older as you can see by the date. As you may know, the ships no longer dock in London first. But that's only because of stories like that which have outraged the wider world. More recent editions feature articles that address the new soup kitchens, supposed relief from the British."

"Soup that wouldn't keep a family of mice alive," Father O'Malley muttered.

"Here. Read this one." Bishop Kneeland pulled a paper from further down in the pile. "It details how people walk for miles to reach the soup kitchens, exhausted by the time they arrive. Then they're given a bowl with little more than boiled water and a few herbs, forced to eat in shifts, then sent on their long journey back to wherever they came from. Whatever good, if any, the soup has done them is long gone by the time they get home. All the while the wealthy British sit in viewing boxes watching the wretched masses guzzle their soup, and puff themselves up with self-righteousness at viewing the wonderful good deeds they're doing."

Father O'Malley was astonished by the sarcastic tone the bishop had adopted. What happened to his deference to his British overlords?

"And these papers are the reason why I am here." Bishop Kneeland continued, jabbing a stout finger at the pile.

"I don't understand."

"Many of the bishops have decided it is time to speak out. We've had to be careful up to this point. Frankly, we still do. Being forced to work directly with British politicians, I understand how they think." He began to pace. "I have to walk a fine line, standing up for my people without bringing the slightest offense to Her Majesty's government. Not an easy task."

"I would think not."

"So it is imperative that I have help in the fight to protect our people and to let the world know what is happening."

The bishop stopped pacing, stared at Father O'Malley. "Why that look, Father?"

"Look?"

"You stare at me as if I'm some sort of specter. Are you so amazed?"

"Forgive me, but I had thought that you followed the British to the letter. I am sorry to say it, but I have wondered how much you cared about our people." Father O'Malley could not believe he was speaking these words, but they seemed to pour forth of their own volition.

"You question my concern for the welfare of my own people, Father? Am I not an Irishman, too?"

"Begging your forgiveness, Your Excellency, but you seemed to want no vestiges left of our culture. No moondances, no wakes, no speaking of the Irish language, even. It appeared you wanted us all to be British. With the exception of the faith, of course. After your past visits here, it has been difficult for me to believe otherwise."

"I see." As Bishop Kneeland drew himself up to his full, towering height, Father O'Malley waited for the hammer to come down upon his head for his unchecked speech.

"You do me a grave injustice, Father."

"My apologies, Your Excellency," he whispered.

"However," continued the bishop, "I suppose I can understand how you would see it that way. Please remember Father O'Malley that I am responsible for an entire diocese full of souls. It is true that I would prefer the old, superstitious ways to die out in favor of pure faith—the Catholic faith. But not for reasons of dismissing our culture. Rather for reasons of survival. Like it or not, and to be clear, I do not, the British are in control. The Catholic clergy is lucky to be allowed to exist in Ireland. 'Twas not so long ago we were hunted down and killed. At the very least, driven out."

"I know all that, but the Penal Laws were repealed over a decade ago. What has that to do with us now?"

"Would you like to have them back? We must tread carefully. Anything we do to aggravate the British only causes more troubles and setbacks. They are beginning to help us now, granted a bit late. Which brings me back to my reason for being here. They are feeling the pressure of the world's dismay. We cannot allow this opportunity to pass us by."

"I agree, Your Excellency. But what has it to do with me?"

"You, Father O'Malley, are one of the few priests with an excellent education. You are directly involved in the day-to-day lives of those suffering beyond belief. You are also well lettered. You can write. You can contribute articles to these papers from your own experience with reason and clarity. You are in a unique position to make a real difference. I've come to ask you to do so."

Father O'Malley was surprised to find himself quaking with both excitement and anxiety. "I will do whatever I can to help. I must ask, though. The people who write these articles? Are they then persecuted? I will accept whatever fate awaits me, but I would like to be prepared."

"As you'll notice, the authors don't always sign their names. You could use a pseudonym or sign your articles 'a Parish Priest'. When writing for a paper in a Catholic country, one identity may be safer than when writing for a Protestant paper. Use your best judgment."

"It seems dishonest, even cowardly to assert my views without signing my own name."

"It might seem so, but you will need to continue unhindered if you are going to be effective. It may simply be a necessity."

"How would my word alone make any difference?"

"Your word alone?" The bishop raised an eyebrow. "Are you lacking humility, Father, or just intelligence?"

Father O'Malley felt his face redden.

"Yours will be one voice among many. But that is the point. One alone can do little. But many voices together forcing the truth that no one wants to hear into the conscience of the world—that, Father, is how peaceful change is made."

"Of course, Your Excellency. Forgive my hubris. I am just amazed at this turn of events. I never expected to be asked to do anything of this sort."

"I've a few other priests in mind whom I will also recruit, as my fellow bishops are doing in their own dioceses."

"And will you be writing to the papers as well?" He wondered just how far the bishop was willing to put himself at the same possible risk he was asking of his priests.

"As a group, we bishops have already begun. We will decide soon whether or not to make individual contributions. I will accept the responsibility upon which all the bishops agree."

Father O'Malley nodded. It was true the bishop was in a very different position than he. What more could he ask of the man? "I am honored that you have thought of me. I will do my best."

"I know you will. Despite how you may think of me, Father O'Malley, I am no lackey to the British. If it seems so, it is solely for the purposes of protecting my people. I will humble myself to save them whenever I must."

Father O'Malley swallowed hard. "You Excellency, I have indeed misjudged you. I am sorry. Please forgive me."

"It seems we are both in the same boat on that score."

Father O'Malley realized his face must show his confusion.

"I, too, have misjudged you."

"How so?"

"I knew you were well-educated. However, I also thought that meant you'd been coddled and become soft. Then I had no choice but to do something utterly repugnant, though I tried all I could think of to escape it. Something you had already done with immediate obedience."

"What is that?" Mystified, Father O'Malley's mind searched for meaning in the bishop's words, but found none.

"You remember my sending you to Clonmalloy?"

He nodded. He would never forget.

"I've had the misfortune to send the same instructions to other priests, all of whom did as I bid them. Then came the time when the town in question had no priest in a parish close enough or well enough to go. Reluctantly, I went myself." Bishop Kneeland, now sitting across from Father

O'Malley, put his head in his hands. "The things I saw, Father O'Malley. I would say you can't imagine them, but I know all too well you can. When I returned I found your letter upon my desk informing me that you had completed your assignment. I had sent you on that mission knowing it would be unpleasant, but never dreaming the degree of horror to which you would be exposed. Upon my return, I knew. The experience nearly broke me."

"I am so sorry, Your Excellency." Pity engulfed him. "It was something I will carry with me all my life as I'm sure you will. But it was the work of God. We can both take comfort in that."

"When I arrived here yesterday, I expected to find you much diminished by the experience. Instead, I found you going on stronger than ever. That young lad you have living here. A troubled lad if ever I saw one. Yet you've taken him in. You've become his mentor. He thinks highly of you. Wants to be just like you."

"He told you that?" Father O'Malley was astonished.

"He told me a good many things. I cannot share most of them as they were part of his confession, but—"

"His confession!" Father O'Malley was so shocked he could not help cutting off the bishop in mid-sentence.

"Why are you so surprised?"

"I've been praying long and hard for that lad to desire the sacrament, but as yet he has never confessed to me."

"It seems, Father, that your prayers have been answered." He leaned toward the priest. "Do not be offended. For some, it is easier to confess to someone who does not know them well and whom they are not likely to see often. He is one of those."

Father O'Malley nodded. It made sense that Kevin would be more comfortable with someone who would take his confession out of Kelegeen within days, probably never giving it another thought. He was grateful that the lad had unburdened his soul. Perhaps now the path forward for him would be a bit easier.

"After hearing the lad's story, including the role you've played and continue to, I see now that your people are very fortunate to have you as their priest. I don't worry as much anymore. I know they are in good hands."

The praise of Bishop Kneeland meant more to Father O'Malley than he would have expected. He would never have believed that such a conversation between them was possible. Feelings of being enmeshed in a string of miracles continued to set off within him a fluctuation between near ecstasy and unreality. They only persisted when it turned out to be the bishop who gave him the answer to his dilemma about whether or not to marry Meg and Rory.

"If indeed she goes to America, marry them right before she leaves," the bishop advised after Father O'Malley explained the situation. "They should have the benefit of the sacrament. Besides, she may be safer going as a married woman."

"But if they never see each other again? They will be bound to each other in marriage, but never be together and yet never free to find another if it becomes apparent that they will never reunite. It seems cruel to bring them into an indissoluble bond when they could be separated for life."

"Exactly my point, Father. Marry them right before she leaves. That way if he does manage to join her, they can move right in together as they'll already be married. However, they'll not have time—nor, I daresay, are they in any condition at present—to consummate the marriage. If it becomes apparent that they will never reunite, the marriage can be annulled on the grounds that it was never consummated."

Father O'Malley thought over the bishop's proposal. It made sense. "I will explain that to them beforehand," he stated.

"I would expect so, Father. I'm not suggesting trickery!"

"Of course not, Your Excellency. Thank you. That would resolve the matter. I still worry about Meg going to America, though. 'Tis such a dangerous voyage for anyone, but a young lass alone..." he shook his head. "She's a bright lass and courageous, but still, it can't be other than a harrowing journey. And what will she do once she gets there?"

"You must know of others going. Heaven knows half the country seems to be pouring onto the ships. Find someone to take her with them," the bishop suggested.

Father O'Malley nodded. Once he was sure Meg would go, he would search out a suitable chaperone for her. He wished he had the power to send one of God's own angels to go with her.

"Siobhan!"

"Who?" asked the bishop.

Father O'Malley felt his face flush. He hadn't meant to say her name aloud. But a vision of Siobhan had arisen in his mind the moment he'd had the thought of an angel.

"Just a possibility of someone to go with Meg," he mumbled.

He would find a flesh and blood chaperone for Meg, but he would send Siobhan as well.

"See there," said the bishop. "All will be well."

* * *

One evening soon after the bishop's visit, Father O'Malley found himself alone in his cottage. In an attempt to reconnect with Liddy, Kevin was spending more time at the Kilpatricks', even staying the night on occasion.

Father O'Malley drew his chair up before the fire. "Siobhan" he whispered, staring into the flames. "My heart aches to lose you again, but in this case I make the sacrifice willingly. If Meg goes to America, I want you to go with her. Watch over her from heaven. Pray for her protection before the throne of God and, if the Lord allows, never leave her side. Will you do this, Siobhan? Is it possible?"

Eyes closed, he waited and prayed. His communication with Siobhan he believed to be a manifestation of the Communion of Saints, and, therefore, not at odds with his faith. God would allow Siobhan to accompany Meg or God would not. It was the will of the Lord for which he prayed. Yet he felt that if Siobhan's spirit went with Meg, it would

409

leave him. He prayed for the strength to accept the loss, to let her go.

Father O'Malley had no notion of how long he sat in the chair, eyes closed, deep in prayer. He only knew it was far into the night when his eyes finally opened. Behind their closed lids a lovely scene had played out. Siobhan, her long red curls flowing, emerald eyes glittering, had spoken in her golden tones. "Aye, Brian. I will go with Meg. I will remain by her side as I was to remain by yours in life. But I am spirit now, with the will of God to do." Then she'd held out her hand. In it was the comb Rory had carved for Meg. Siobhan's eyes twinkled like the stars, the joyful mischief she'd loved in life glimmering in them. "The wood for this was blown upon the shore by the West Wind. I could not allow the owner of her comb to come to harm, now could I?"

Eyes open, he stared into the fire, peace filling his soul. "All will be well," he whispered.

Chapter Thirty-Eight

Summer was taking its time coming as all waited to see what this year's crop would bring. Meg and Rory explained to Father O'Malley their plan to let God and the crop decide Meg's fate.

"Have you raised the full amount of passage?" Father O'Malley asked when they met him outside their cottage. It was a Sunday afternoon and as Dr. Parker took Sunday as his day of rest, Father O'Malley was on his own.

"Aye, Father. I sold the comb." The look on his face puzzled her. "I know you told me not to, Father, but I saw no other way. I don't understand why you didn't want me to."

"'Tis nothing, Meg. The ramblings of an old fool." A wistful look passed over his face. "How much did you get for it?"

"Five pounds."

"Five pounds!" Father O'Malley's eyes widened in astonishment. "That's more than the price of your passage! To whom did you sell it?"

Father O'Malley was eyeing her suspiciously. "I don't know who bought it, Father. I gave it to Dr. Parker to sell."

"And he found a buyer at five pounds, did he?"

"So he said. He gave me the money, though Rory and I suspect he may have added a bit of his own."

"Aye, a bit! Bless him."

"We still have to tell Meg's mam," Rory interrupted.

"You said you would help us convince her," Meg reminded him.

"How has she been of late?" Father O'Malley asked.

Meg knew what he was asking, but wasn't sure how to answer. Her mother had been quieter than usual. It seemed that something was on her mind, but if so, she did not share

411

it with Meg. "Fine, Father," she answered, not knowing what else to say.

"None of her feelings, then?"

"Not that she's spoken of. But she's been uncommon quiet. She doesn't speak of it, so that's the best I can describe it."

"It seems the right time to tell her," Rory added. "May we do so now?"

Father O'Malley entered the O'Connor cottage with Meg and Rory. He gathered them along with Deirdre in a circle at one side of the fireplace. Kathleen moved between Aisling and Brigid on the other side, but kept an inquisitive eye on the little group. Loreena attempted to interest Brigid in the piglet by placing it on her lap. Brigid stroked the little body, smiling shyly.

"Making progress," Deirdre said, indicating the two girls. "Loreena works so hard with her. Brigid is blessed to have such a friend. True *anamchairde* they are."

"I am glad of it," Father O'Malley told her. Then, clearing his throat, he began. "Deirdre, there is something of great importance we have to discuss with you."

Meg watched her mother's face pinch. "I don't like the sound of that."

"Meg and Rory have made a difficult decision. They have talked it over with me and Dr. Parker at length." Meg held her breath as Father O'Malley plunged ahead. "If the crop fails again this year, Meg will leave Ireland for America."

"No!" The word burst from Deirdre's mouth.

"Mam, please hear us out," Meg pleaded. "I've got the passage money and a little extra besides. I will find work in America and send money back here. I'll save, too, and bring you all over."

"We could go to America?" Kathleen's hopeful voice interrupted as she scooted towards them.

Deirdre's head snapped towards Kathleen. "This does not concern you, lass."

"It concerns me if Meg is leaving us," Kathleen answered.

Seeing the fear rise in her mother's face, Meg shook her head at Kathleen who sighed heavily before retreating to her corner.

"And what of you?" Deirdre asked, looking pointedly at Rory.

"I'll stay for now. I'm the only man left to the family. I'll care for you all as best I can until we're all able to...what was that word again, Father?"

"Emigrate."

"Aye. Emigrate."

Deirdre looked puzzled.

"It means to move to another country," Father O'Malley explained.

"And what of your marriage?" Deirdre asked. "Aren't you still planning to wed?"

"We have asked Father O'Malley to marry us before Meg leaves," Rory answered. "If she has to leave, that is," he added. "And if she doesn't we will marry anyway. I've changed my mind about waiting until the famine is over."

"You have?" Meg was astonished.

"Aye. I've thought about it and only just reached this conclusion." He gave Meg a sheepish look. "But I think it's best we marry before the next Gale Day. Aisling, Loreena and I are living here illegally. Blackburn hasn't taken any notice, but only because he doesn't care what's become of us. I'm sure he assumes we're all in a *scalpeen* somewhere. That or dead. But if he catches word that we're here, we'll all be thrown out. You as well." He indicated Meg and her family. "If you and I are married, then we'll be of the same family. We'll have the right to live in the same place. It seems the safest thing to do."

"Father, what do you say to all this?" Deirdre asked, her face registering a jumble of emotions.

"What Rory said makes sense. I spoke with the bishop on the matter when he was here last. He believes I should marry them just before Meg goes. If she goes," he stressed, with a nod towards Rory. "Remember, Deirdre, it is only if the crop fails again. Pray God, it doesn't." Then he added,

"Nonetheless, I agree that the two should wed before the next Gale Day as the safest course for all."

"I see." Deirdre drew a sharp intake of breath. "So a mother's heart is not to be considered." Her hands twisted the worn fabric of her dress she held bunched in her lap.

"Don't you want us to marry, Mam?" Meg asked.

"'Tis not to your marrying that I object. That I'd have you do today, if it were possible. It's of your leaving us that I'm thinking."

Meg took her mother's hands in her own. "Mam, we'll take very seriously what you have to say on it."

Father O'Malley drew Deirdre's attention. "Meg's brave," he said. "She has a strong will. She could make a life for herself away from here. It's quite possible she could find work and send money back to help you. It might be the best thing she could do for herself and for all of you."

"America is a long way from here," Deirdre's voice shook. "How will she survive the voyage?"

Father O'Malley dropped his voice low. "She'll go with our prayers. If God wills it she will make it safely to America. But, I cannot lie to you, Deirdre. It is possible she will not. That is always a risk."

Seeing Deirdre's look of alarm, Meg quickly added, "Father says that only because we want to be completely honest with you. There is a risk in taking such a voyage, but there is as much risk in staying here to starve if the crop fails again."

"One thing is certain, she would not be the only Irish to arrive in America. I'm sure I can find a good family making the journey who will allow her to join them, keeping her in their care. God knows, our people are leaving Ireland by the thousands. It should not be a difficult task."

He patted Deirdre's shoulder. "No one but God knows what is truly the best thing to do right now."

Meg squeezed her mother's hands, bringing Deirdre's attention back to her. Holding her mother's gaze, she said, "Rory and I have prayed about this. We've decided to leave it in God's hands. If the crop fails it will be a sign that I should go. Otherwise, I stay and we need never think on it again."

Deirdre's body sagged as what little strength she had seemed to drain from it. "This does explain something, then," she said.

"Mam?"

"My feelings."

"Have you been having the feeling? You've not said a word."

"That's because it has been so different. Not like the feelings I'm used to at all. I've been dreaming of waves, ocean waves, but not like the wild ones before the accident or before Brendan left us. They are quiet, peaceful waves." She shook her head slowly. "But they are sad."

"How are they sad, Mam?" Meg held her mother in her arms as she spoke.

"They are made of tears," she whispered. "A whole ocean of tears." Deirdre closed her eyes, letting her own tears roll quietly down her face.

* * *

On a Sunday late in August, the family sent Loreena to bring Father O'Malley to the cottage. All but Aisling and Brigid assembled outside to await his arrival.

"Come 'round to the potato bed with us," Deirdre said, when Loreena returned with the priest in tow. 'Tis time to see if Meg stays or goes."

Meg shook as Rory made ready to plunge his spade into the ground. She felt her mother's hand grip her own and knew that she trembled, too.

"Before you start, perhaps we should have a word with the Lord," Father O'Malley suggested.

"Aye, for good potatoes, Father," Deirdre pleaded.

"Heavenly Father, please grant us the blessing of a good harvest so that this and all other families have food to survive and not have to be separated one from another. As in all things, Lord, may your holy will be done. Amen."

Rory's spade struck, slicing easily into the dark, rich soil quickly reaching the spot where he'd planted. They were all on their knees, leaning in close, breath coming in short gasps, fear and anticipation palpable.

Rory reached into the ground and brought up a pile of black mush. "Rotten!" He shook the slime from his hand as if it was covered in something as foul as the guts of a dead rat. He dug a few others, but all were the same.

"Why?" Deirdre asked. "Why? Why? Why? Why?" She had wrapped her arms around Meg, crushing her against herself. "I can't lose my baby."

Father O'Malley looked at Rory who was kneeling across from him. Rory stared at the ground, Loreena close by his side. His body was rigid, his hands clenched into fists in the dirt. Kathleen sat on Meg's other side. Her forehead wrinkled up with the pain of tears she barely had the strength to shed.

Meg looked from one person to another. Father O'Malley stretched out his arms as though he could take the whole family into them, gathering them as close together as he could. They huddled in each other's embrace, smeared with dirt and potato slime.

"We must pray again," he told them.

"Why? Don't do a bit 'o good." Rory's voice was hollow.

"Now is the most important time to pray. If we don't rely on God now we are lost."

"We are already lost. 'Tis over for us." Rory slammed a handful of muck to the ground.

"It is not over for you," Father O'Malley urged. "You've come this far. You can make it."

"We still have Meg to go to America for us. God has given us that." Kathleen had said the words no one wanted to. But they seemed to inspire the tiniest shred of hope in the family.

"Meg will live," Deirdre announced, her head nodding. "And the rest of us will live, too, because of her."

They all stared at Deirdre, shocked at this sudden change.

416

Deirdre took Meg's face in her hands. "You will live, Margaret Mary O'Connor. Do you hear me? I won't lose you. You will live." Her voice was strong. Her eyes burned into Meg's as if willing her spirit for the life of her family into her daughter.

"Aye, Mam. I will. And I'll send money back. We'll all live. I promise."

"Thank you, God", Father O'Malley whispered. "Now then, let's pray together."

They huddled in their tight circle, arms entwined around each other.

"Dear Heavenly Father, we know not for what reason we've been struck with the blight to our crops again, but we trust that your holy will is right despite our inability to understand it. Give us strength, hope and faith. Bless this and all the families of Ireland. Please keep Meg safe in her journey. Thank you for the gift of hope her going ahead of us provides. Amen."

Father O'Malley took Meg's hand in his. She looked into his eyes. Suddenly, the enormity of what was coming struck her. How could this be real? How could any of it be real?

Though close enough to feel his breath on her face, she heard Father O'Malley's voice as if coming from a long way. "Give me the passage money before I leave today. I will buy your ticket in the morning."

Chapter Thirty-Nine

"Father, you're coming tomorrow?" Meg asked as Father O'Malley opened his cottage door to let her in.

"Indeed I am."

"Aye. And you'll see that Dr. Parker comes, too?"

"He'll be there."

Tomorrow was to be Meg's last full day in Ireland. Though Meg had balked at the idea, Deirdre insisted on giving her an American wake. They'd had such a row over it, Father O'Malley had been called in to settle the matter. Knowing it was done because the family left behind expected never to see the person again, Meg insisted there was no need. "'Tis like saying she's made up her mind I won't manage to bring them all over," Meg had lamented to Father O'Malley. But Deirdre's argument that she needed it to keep Meg's memory alive should she never see her again won out. "Give this to your Mam," Father O'Malley had counseled Meg. "It will be your parting gift to her."

"And you'll bring my passage ticket with you, too, Father, don't forget," Meg said, pacing the floor of his little cottage.

"Aye, Meg. You may take it with you now, if you like." He picked up the ticket from his desk.

"What does the writing say?"

"It says that your passage is paid and that you are entitled to ten cubic feet of space in steerage. Water and provisions are provided as well as a hearth for cooking. Bedding and utensils are up to you. Have you got anything to take with you?"

"My mam and I sewed a few rags together to make a pouch. I've a cup, a plate, a knife and a spoon for eating."

"What about bedding? The only blanket I've seen is the one Aisling and Brigid share." Father O'Malley quickly inventoried his own supply, thinking what he could give her.

"I'll have to do without. I can't take the only blanket we've got."

"Here's a blanket I hardly use," he said, picking up his only one folded at the foot of his bed. "And a sheet. I think there is…let's see…aye, there's a spare one here." He took his one extra sheet from the cupboard.

"Are you sure, Father? I've been going without bedding for so long I'll hardly notice not having any on the ship. Don't you believe you'll be wanting them?"

"I've plenty. Don't worry about me."

"Thank you, Father. I'd better go before it gets dark."

"Before you leave, there's something I must tell you." Father O'Malley pulled a chair from the table, motioning her to sit.

"Please take this with you." He handed her a sealed envelope. "When you get settled you are to seek out a Catholic church as soon as possible. Give this letter to the priest. It explains your situation and tells him how to contact me. I've asked him to write me so I can tell your family that you are safe and well. I also ask him to keep a correspondence between you and your family through me."

Meg flew from her chair throwing her arms around him.

"Thank you, Father! Thank you so much!"

He hugged her for a moment, then gently set her away, all the while beaming at her.

"I'm sorry, Father. I forgot myself."

He waved a hand. "No harm done."

He hesitated a moment. He was glad Kevin was not here so he could have this conversation with Meg. Kevin had been spending more and more time at the Kilpatrick's cottage. It was a blessing to see how gentle and patient he was with Liddy. She was even beginning to respond to him. Dacey and Rose had asked if he might move in with them. Their landlord's permission would have to be sought, but

419

he was kinder than most and Father O'Malley prayed he would allow it, as the Kilpatricks provided Kevin with a stable family environment. Already, they loved both Kevin and Liddy as though they were their own. Kevin seemed to have taken Father O'Malley's advice of apprenticing himself to a good male role model to heart. With Dacey's conversion having taken deep root, he was becoming the sort of man Kevin could emulate. Father O'Malley never ceased to marvel at how God could take the most tragic situations and turn them into something wonderous.

"I'm sorry you had to sell your comb, Meg," he began.

"I am, too, Father. But if it turns out to be the thing that saves us, it will have been worth it." He watched her blink back tears as she spoke.

"Meg," he began, not sure how to explain. "There's a reason I didn't want you to sell the comb. More than just the fact that Rory made it for you."

She cocked her head. "What is that, Father?"

"Well, you see," he laughed a little, feeling slightly embarrassed by what he was about to say. "That comb reminded me of someone. It brought back a very precious memory. I guess I didn't want you to give it up as much for me as for you."

My looked mystified.

"Long ago before I was a priest, I was in love with a beautiful woman named Siobhan O'Toole. We planned to marry."

"You, Father? You were in love? Going to get married?" Her voice rose with each question, eyes nearly popping out of her head.

"Why so surprised, Meg? I wasn't born a priest, you know!"

She covered her mouth with her hand. "I'm sorry, Father. I just never thought of you being anything other than a priest."

"Well, once I was a simple young man very much in love. A lot like Rory, I suspect."

"What happened? Why didn't you marry her?"

He dropped his gaze to the table top, not wanting to dwell on the details with Meg. "She died before we could wed," he said. "But," he quickly went on, "Siobhan was a grand storyteller. She once told me about the West Wind who had long, dark hair. Just like yours, I should think." He smiled at Meg. "And she had a magical comb that she kept on a cloud. It would come whenever she called it."

It was the first time he'd seen her smile in months. "When you gave me your comb to sell, that memory returned as I sat here one evening. I had the strangest feeling that your comb looked exactly like the one the West Wind owned.

Meg laughed outright. "Rory would surely be surprised to hear that!"

"I suppose he would," Father O'Malley agreed.

"I'm sorry Siobhan died, Father," Meg said, her smile gone. "I think I would have liked her."

"You would have, Meg. It was almost impossible not to."

"Do you miss her terribly?" She asked.

Father O'Malley closed his eyes for a moment. "I do miss her, Meg. I suppose I always will. But she is with God now. I believe I will see her again in heaven."

"I'm certain of that," she agreed.

"Meg, do you understand what is meant by the Communion of Saints?"

"I believe so, Father," she answered. "We ask the saints to pray for us. They bring our requests to the Lord."

"That's part of it. Do you also realize that everyone who is in heaven is a saint, even if they have not been canonized?"

"Canonized?"

"Officially declared to be a saint by the Church."

"Oh." Realization dawned in her eyes. "You mean my da is a saint?"

"Most likely."

Meg's eyes grew almost as wide as they had when he'd told her he'd once been in love.

"They are very close to us, Meg. Though we can't see them, sometimes we can feel them with us."

"Like ghosts?"

"No. Not in a frightening way. More like a comforting presence."

Meg looked thoughtful. "I suppose I do feel Da with me." She dropped her voice to a near whisper. "Sometimes I talk to him."

"Does he answer?"

Meg blushed. "No, Father. If he did, I'd be terrified."

"Not out loud. I mean do you ever get a feeling that he hears you? And you somehow know in your heart what he would say?"

Meg nodded. "In that way, aye."

"Good. Then I hope you will understand what I'm going to tell you." He took a deep breath. "I often talk to Siobhan. And, in a way, she often talks to me. Sometimes it's almost as though she's right by my side. It's been a great comfort to me over the years."

"That's lovely, Father. She must pray for you very much."

"I'm sure she does. But now she's going to pray for you."

"Me?"

"Aye. You see, once I knew for sure that you'd be going to America, my greatest concern was for your safety. So, I asked Siobhan to go with you."

"And did she say she would?"

"Aye."

"But won't you miss her?"

"She's always in my heart. That will never change. But I am glad to send her with you. I wanted you to know that you have a very special guardian going with you. Talk to her often, Meg. She'll be a delightful companion."

"What did she look like, Father? I want to picture her in my mind."

"A tiny, slender creature. Strong, she was, too, though you wouldn't know it to look at her. She had long red hair—a mass of curls that bounced as she moved. And deep green eyes. She'd make you think of a faery. I half believed she was one."

"She sounds beautiful," Meg said.

"Oh, she was! But more than that she was kind, loving, thoughtful, generous—all the best things you can think of."

"I will be glad to have such a one with me."

Meg got up to leave. "Thank you for everything, Father. I'm so relieved that you found the O'Sullivans for me. I feel better traveling with another family."

"They're good people. You'll like them, I'm sure."

"Father, I want you to keep this until it's time to go. I'm afraid I'll lose it." She handed her ticket back to him. "I don't want it around me. 'Tis a thing I'm grateful for but also a thing that will separate me from everyone I love. Not forever," she insisted. "But for a long while, I suspect."

"I understand, Meg. Good night. Try to sleep at least a little."

* * *

Once Meg had left, Father O'Malley took out his writing implements and began work on his latest letter to the newspaper. He'd written to several, even seen a few published. Meg's imminent emigration fired his passion for letting the world know the truth of Ireland's plight. He'd thought to turn in early tonight, but now he was compelled to put pen to paper, all thoughts of sleep dispelled. The words poured out of him as if of their own volition. He wrote of mothers carrying dead children on their backs to the burying grounds. And of the child who dropped dead at his feet when he gave her a bite of bread because her body could no longer accept food. And he wrote of the multitudes who were leaving family and friends for a dangerous journey and uncertain future. He wrote of the American wake trying hard to convey the feelings of a family so certain they will never see their departing loved one again that they mourn them as though they had died. How could hearts not be moved, aid not come, England not be shamed at such circumstances? He knew that most

423

would shake their heads, feel sorry for them, then move on with their lives, giving the Irish no more thought than they would an annoying gnat. But there would always be some who would act. The Lord would prompt them, knock at their conscience, compel them to obey His command to help those in need. He prayed over each letter, imploring God that his words would reach at least a few such people—people who could attract others, sway them to their convictions, enlist their help.

Finished, he put down his pen. It was the most strident and, he hoped, heart stirring he'd written yet. He may never know if his efforts made a difference, but he decided he did not need to know. The fact that he was doing something was what mattered. God would take care of the rest.

His thoughts turned to Siobhan once he'd crawled into bed. Meg had asked if he would miss her. Strange, now that he thought of it. Did his sending Siobhan to accompany Meg mean he'd lose his connection with her? She was no longer of this world, but of the next. It seemed that she could easily be with them both. How else did the saints manage to intercede for so many at once? But something did seem different about this, as though he was giving her up to Meg. *Oh, but you're an odd old man*, he told himself. "Well, you haven't boarded that ship yet," he said aloud to Siobhan. "So, be with me in my dreams tonight. Just in case I need to give you an American wake, as well." Laughter like a tiny waterfall in a hidden glen delighted his ears as he drifted off to sleep.

Chapter Forty

Relief flooded Meg when Father O'Malley and Dr. Parker entered the cottage. It was as though everything would be all right so long as their priest was with them. Liam Devlin had brought his fiddle. Rory had gone begging the day before. There was a paltry amount of cheese and bread set out, a pathetic attempt at hospitality. Still it was more than they would otherwise have had if Rory hadn't explained the situation to Mr. Breckett.

"I don't really understand this notion you people have about wakes, but if it will ease your burden at losing Meg, I suppose I can spare a few extra loaves," the baker had told him.

Meg's gaze swept the room. A tight knot of neighbor men gathered in one corner fondly reminiscing about her da. Brigid and Aisling huddled together in another corner. Aisling looked weak, but alert. Brigid still wore her strange, haunted look. She appeared mildly interested in the goings-on, but at the same time seemed not to grasp the reason for them. "She's fey now," Deirdre would say whenever anyone inquired about Brigid's state of mind.

A small group of women, including Deirdre and Kathleen clustered about Meg. Deirdre hovered close, constantly touching her.

"Father O'Malley! Dr. Parker!" Catching sight of them, Rory pulled himself away from the other men to welcome them.

Deirdre tore her gaze away from Meg long enough to take notice of the newcomers.

"Father, you'll say a blessing for us, won't you?" Deirdre called.

The room fell silent as Father O'Malley stood in the center of the little cottage and made the Sign of the Cross.

"Heavenly Father, in your mercy you send us strength and help during our times of trouble. You have graciously sent the O'Connor family a way to give two of its members a new chance at life. Brendan O'Connor has left us for Australia where we pray he will eventually prosper. When his sentence is complete may he return safely to his family. You have given Margaret O'Connor a chance at a new life in another new land. May she and all who journey with her be granted a safe passage, find prosperity and good health in their new home. May your hand guide Meg, keeping her devoted to her faith all the days of her life. Please comfort her family and friends whom she leaves behind with the knowledge that she is safe in your holy care and the hope that they will one day be reunited. And may the beloved souls of Denis O'Connor, Anna, Aiden, Lizzy, Seamus, and Darien Quinn rest in peace in heaven with you forever. We ask this in the name of Jesus Christ, our Lord. Amen."

"Amen." The word echoed throughout the room.

Across the room Rory signaled Liam who began to warm up his fiddle, then held out his hand to Meg.

"I want to dance with you once like we used to before the starvin'. I want it to remember you by."

"The moon's full tonight," Meg answered. "Let's go outside."

He motioned for Liam to follow. Leaning against the open doorframe, Liam began to play the jolliest tune he could wrestle from the fiddle. He did his best to keep up the pace, though his bone-thin arms shook causing him to falter occasionally.

Rory and Meg began slowly, having grown unused to dancing. They circled each other with leaden steps, their faces masks of concentration in the moonlight. As the music increased in tempo, they held hands and helped each other spin. For a brief moment they managed to lift their knees high, spinning quickly. Their feet began to remember the old, intricate steps. The magic of the music, the moonlight and the determination for one last dance, made that brief moment the dance of their lives. Their bodies forgot their starvation. They danced like their old selves, whirling and jigging. Smiles spread across their faces as joy returned to their limbs feeding them the memory of the dance.

They couldn't sustain it, but they had had it and would keep it in their hearts forever. They dropped to the ground, gasping for breath. Liam's fiddle smacked the dirt by his feet, his arms having grown too shaky to hold it.

A noise came from inside the cottage. Starting low, it steadily rose in pitch. The keening had begun. Deirdre was the loudest, the other women keening in sympathy with her. If Meg had died the lament could not have been more heart rending. Meg and Rory sat on the ground, their arms around each other, their foreheads touching, tears mingling in each other's faces in a soft keening of their own meant only for each other. Eventually, it slowed until all was quiet. Meg and Rory dragged themselves back to join the others in exhausted sleep until the earliest hours of the morning.

"Father," Meg heard her mother's voice whisper. "Could we have a rosary for Meg before it's time to leave?"

"Of course, Deirdre."

All over the room hands pulled rosaries from pockets. Meg took her own from the patched together bag she was taking on her journey. The bag bulged now with Father O'Malley's gifts. She shifted herself onto her knees holding her rosary before her. An eerie feeling overcame her as she thought about this being her own wake. Within hours her ship would sail, taking her far from the only home she'd ever known.

Meg prayed her rosary, clutching it against her breast, her tears spilling over the beads. She knew it was being prayed for her, but in her heart she prayed for her family and for Rory. She prayed with all her soul that the Blessed Mother, who had known so much sorrow of her own, would watch over them and ease the pain of their coming separation, but most especially that, however long, it would not be forever.

After the final Amen, she felt hands on either of her arms, gently lifting her to her feet. It was Rory on one side and Father O'Malley on the other. Dr. Parker had graciously offered to take them to the docks so they could stay with her until the very last moment. But first they had one very important stop to make.

Meg went to the fireplace and hugged Brigid tightly. "I love you, lass. Try to come back to us if you can, unless it be better where you are. If it is better, stay there until it's better here. But come back for Mam when you can. She will need you." She kissed her on the check and leaned her gently against the wall, like putting away a doll. Then she kissed Aisling and Loreena goodbye.

Neighbors who had come to Meg's wake offered to stay so that Kathleen could go to see her sister off. The family climbed into the waiting phaeton. Meg turned to look back at the home she had known all her life. Her father's face floated before her. She wondered what he would have said at this moment. Her eyes filled with tears distorting her vision, making it swirl as though the cottage was melting. She ran back to it moving her hands over the walls, trying to soak up through her skin the feeling of the smooth plaster. She lay her hot cheek against it and cried. A sound echoed in the ear she pressed against the wall. Then Rory's voice spoke in her other ear, "Take this."

He placed a broken chip of plaster in her hands.

"You'll always have a bit of your home with you."

"Thank you." Meg smiled through her tears. "Take good care of them, Rory."

"I will." He took her hand in his. Together they walked to the waiting phaeton.

Meg clutched the bit of plaster throughout the ride. Her fingers stroked its smooth surface.

The sun had not been up long when they reached the church. Dacey and Rose Kilpatrick who had agreed to act as witnesses to the marriage waited at the door. All but Meg and Deirdre entered, giving the others time to take their places.

"It should be your da doing this," Deirdre said, a catch in her voice.

"It's alright, Mam. Da would want you to do it in his place. Besides, I feel him here. He'll be walking down the aisle with us, sure enough."

Deirdre gave Meg an inquisitive look. "You feel him lingering about, too?" she asked.

"Aye. I do. I hope I'll still feel him with me when I'm in America."

"Ah, lass, he'd go to the moon with you, he would." The two laughed even as tears slid down their cheeks. Deirdre cracked the door and peeked into the church. "They're ready," she said.

Taking Meg by the arm, she walked her down the aisle, handing her over to Rory who waited to take her hand. Throughout the ceremony, Meg and Rory could not keep from looking deeply into each other's eyes. Meg saw a hunger and longing in Rory's and knew he saw the same in hers. She had dreamed of this day for so long. A day meant to be the beginning of a new life. And indeed it would be, but not in the way they could ever have imagined. They proclaimed their vows with more intensity than they realized they could muster. Though Father O'Malley had explained to them the possibility of annulment should it become obvious that they would never be reunited, Rory had declared to Meg that he would never consent to it. Even should he never see her again, she would always be his wife. He could never love another. She had told him the same. For them, this marriage was as everlasting as it would have been had she been going nowhere but home with him afterward.

* * *

All too soon, it came to an end. For Meg, the trip to the dock was both the longest and shortest of her life. She never saw the land over which she traveled. Her eyes looked only at the others and at the plaster in her hands. Tears blurred everything. Rory's arms wrapped around her, never letting go throughout the journey, while Deirdre and Kathleen kept reaching out, unable to stop themselves from touching her as though they could absorb the memory of her through their skin.

When they came to a halt at the docks, the sounds of the crowd and the lapping water entered her awareness. She felt anxiety rise within her. This was it then. An end to her life with all she knew and loved. Dr. Parker helped her down from the phaeton. The others walked with her as far as they could go. She stood with them at the dock while Father O'Malley searched out the O'Sullivans.

Mrs. O'Sullivan grasped both of Deirdre's hands in her own. "Now don't you be worrying about your darlin'. I promise to take care of her like she was my own."

"Thank you. We are very grateful to you." Meg knew her mother meant the words with all her heart, but there was a strange look on her face. She thought she understood. She threw her arms around her mother, whispering in her ear, "Don't worry, Mam. There's none can replace you."

Deirdre smiled through a fresh outpouring of tears.

"Here's your ticket, Meg, and don't forget about the letter," Father O'Malley reminded her.

"I won't."

The call came to board the ship. Meg burst forth in tears that made her feel as though all the water in the world was spilling out of her eyes. Her family gathered around her, arms clinging to her, wails of anguish renting the air.

The last call to board. Slowly, the arms unwound. The cluster of bodies reluctantly pulled away. Father O'Malley made the Sign of the Cross over her, blessing her one last time.

"Good-bye. I love you all." She could barely get the words out through her sobs. She turned towards the ship walking up the gangplank along with the O'Sullivans, Rory at her side until the last moment.

"Meg!"

Hearing her name, she turned to find the doctor. He handed her something wrapped in paper. "Take this with you."

430

"What is it?

"You'll see. Have a safe trip, Meg."

"I'm sorry, lad. This is as far as you can go," Mrs. O'Sullivan informed Rory as they reached the gangplank. Rory took Meg in his arms. Caring nothing about all the eyes on him, he kissed her passionately. Her knees weakened and she held tightly to him. Then he pressed his forehead to hers, speaking softly so only she could hear. "That's the beginning. We'll take up where we've left off as soon as we're together again." He kissed her gently once more, slowly slid his hands down her arms, loathe to release her, then walked backward from the gangplank, never taking his eyes from her.

Mrs. O'Sullivan's arm went around Meg's shoulders as she guided her forward. Meg handed over her ticket and stepped onto the ship. She was jostled by the crowd on board. Determined, she forced her way to the rail, searching the throng on shore until she caught sight of Rory and her family. She looked at each face, trying to trace every feature with her eyes and lock it into her memory forever, just as Brendan had done.

Little by little they became harder to see as the ship pulled away from shore. Finally, they were gone for good, only the rocky coastline remaining. Meg stayed above deck, watching the land recede into the distance. When finally, it too had vanished from sight, she felt overwhelmed by sadness and a terrible fear of what might lay ahead.

"Dear Lord," she prayed. "I'm so lonely for them already. Please take care of them. Don't let me give up hope that I'll see them again someday."

Feeling a stab she realized she was clutching the package Dr. Parker had given her tightly against her chest. With shaking hands she unwrapped the brown paper he had meticulously wound around the object. There in her hands lay the comb Rory had made for her.

"He never sold it!" she whispered aloud. "'Twas all his own money he gave!" Meg couldn't get over her

431

astonishment. "Oh, Lord, bless him! Please do bless him!" She nearly shouted it.

Meg hugged the comb tightly. Gazing at it again, she stroked every detail lovingly with her fingers. "Are you here, Siobhan?" she whispered. She felt the slightest nudge against her shoulder though no one aboard was close enough to have touched her. Perhaps it was only a slight breeze, but tears of relief pricked her eyes.

'Tis a sign, she decided. *I shall see them again. Rory will come as will the others.* Meg's spirits lifted as she focused her mind solely on that one hope. She knew now that she would handle whatever her new life brought her. Hope gave her strength. She would survive.

The End

PLEASE LEAVE A REVIEW
THIS AUTHOR IS
COUNTING ON YOU

About the Author

Eileen O'Finlan lives in central Massachusetts. She holds a BA in history and MA in Pastoral Ministry and facilitates online theology courses for the University of Dayton's Virtual Learning Community for Faith Formation. Eileen is a great lover of history, books, cats, and classic rock.

e

Made in the USA
Middletown, DE
25 August 2018